Bo<

Tracy

Murder at the Mill
The Legacy

www.trevorbelshaw.com

For Colette

Best Wishes

T A Belshaw

Edited by Maureen Vincent-Northam

Cover design by: J. D. Smith Design

http://www.jdsmith-design.com

ISBN: 978-1-8383202-4-9

The Reckoning

By
T. A. Belshaw

For Janice Rosser.

Online magazine editor. Quiz Meister supreme and my
fab Beta reader.

Thank you.

The Reckoning

Chapter 1

'Happy Christmas, Aunty Marjorie.'

Jessica Griffiths smiled as her elderly aunt opened the front door.

'We aren't having Christmas.' Marjorie looked back into the house, then beckoned Jessica to come closer. 'But I've got a tree up in my room,' she whispered.

'Good for you,' said Jess as she stepped into the wide hallway.

'Martha's in there.' Marjorie pointed to the door of the lounge.

Jess pushed the door open and stepped into the spacious, beautifully furnished room. She looked around as she spoke.

'Happy Christmas, Grandma. It doesn't look right without the decorations.' She glanced to her left where a small pile of letters that appeared to contain greetings cards, sat on a highly polished dining table. 'You haven't even opened your cards.'

Martha got up from the comfortable armchair and turned to face her granddaughter. There was no grunt, no sign of stiffness in the eighty-year-old's body as she stood. Her steel-grey hair highlighted a pair of piercing ice blue eyes. She was a plain-looking woman, unlike her mother, Alice, who had been classed as a beauty, even into old age, but she did have an air of youthfulness about her. The thin crow's feet that formed on the edges of her eyes were also known as laughter lines. Jessica wondered how she got them; Martha never laughed. Her lips formed a thin line as she looked her granddaughter up and down.

'I see no reason for celebration, Jessica. Especially after the events of the last few weeks.'

Jessica nodded. 'I understand that, Grandma, but, well, it is Christmas. We have to allow a bit of light to penetrate the gloom that has descended upon us.'

Martha narrowed her eyes.

'Have you been to see your mother?'

'Not today, they won't allow me to visit. There aren't enough staff to keep an eye on us on Christmas Day. I'm going in again on Friday. She looked a lot better when I saw her yesterday, most of the bruises have come out now and the swelling has begun to go down.'

'Have the police charged her yet?'

'Charged her? With what, Grandma?'

'Oh, I don't know, I'm not the Crown Prosecution Service.' She held up a hand and began to count on her fingers. 'Murder... Manslaughter... The killing of a dumb animal...'

'Grandma!'

Martha shrugged. 'I'm just saying, I—'

'She killed Dad whilst defending herself from a brutal attack. She had no choice but to fight back.'

'There's always a choice, dear.' Martha turned away and motioned to the armchair facing hers. 'Sit down and we can discuss the matter in a civilised manner.' She looked across to her cowering sister. 'Marjorie, don't stand there, gawping, make yourself useful for once. Put the kettle on.'

Jessica sat down in the cream-coloured chair and put her shoulder bag on the floor at the side. She waited until Marjorie had left the room before she spoke.

'Grandma. Imagine if you had been in that situation. Are you really telling me you'd have just let him beat you black and blue and throttle you to death without putting up a fight?'

'I'd never have allowed myself to be put in that position to begin with.'

'But she was put in that position, Grandma. She did what she had to do to survive.'

'Drink put her in that position, it was her own fault, no one else's.'

Jessica curled up her lip.

'You weren't there, you don't know how it was.'

Martha sighed but said nothing.

'She's your daughter, Grandma. Don't you have any feelings for her at all?'

'Of course I do,' Martha snapped. 'But she made her bed, she has to lie in it.'

Jessica shook her head. 'You are unbelievable. Surely you want to help her get over this?'

'She's a big girl, she can stand on her own two feet. I managed to do it when I had my problems. I had precious little help.'

'Nana would have helped you, Grandma. You were too stubborn to ask for it.'

Martha scowled. 'The one time I did ask for help she refused to even consider it.'

'There was more to it than that, Grandma and you know it.'

'There you go, Jessica. You always take her side, even when you know nothing about it.'

'I'm reading her memoirs. I know more than you think I do.'

'As I said, you always take her side.'

'I'll show you her memoirs one day, Grandma. You might be surprised by how much she loved you.'

'Piffle.'

There was silence for a full minute, then Jessica spoke again.

'So, are you going to see her?'

'No. I can't see how any good would come of it.'

'Please, Grandma. She only ever gets to see me, the nurses and her Police Support Officer. I'm sure she'd love you to call in.'

When her plea was answered with silence, she continued.

'She's lost that dullness in her eyes, she's sober. You'd be surprised at how lucid she is. It's been a long time since I saw her like that.'

'She'll be back on the sauce as soon as they let her out. If they ever do let her out.' Martha wasn't to be convinced.

As Jessica was about to respond, the door to the kitchen opened and Marjorie came in carrying a rattling tea tray. She placed it down on the coffee table at Martha's side, then turned to Jess. She smiled weakly, took a quick glance at Martha and motioned towards the hall door.

'Would you like to see my room, Jessica?'

'Of course she wouldn't like to see your room! For pity's sake, Marjorie, you're not five years old.'

Jess got to her feet. 'I'd love to see your room, Aunt Marjorie,' she said with a smile.

Without glancing back at her older sister, Marjorie led Jessica across the lounge, chattering excitedly as she hurried up the stairs.

'I used the tree we normally have in the hall. I dressed it myself. Martha usually helps me do it.'

At the top of the stairs, she turned right and ushered Jessica through her open bedroom door.

The room was sparsely furnished, just a single bed with an ottoman at its foot, a double, walnut wardrobe and a set of matching drawers that sat in the bay window. On top of the chest of drawers was a three-foot, silver-leafed Christmas tree, bedecked with blue, gold and silver baubles. Marjorie giggled like a child as she bent down and pressed a switch on the wall socket causing a single string of fairy lights to begin to flicker. She looked over her shoulder guiltily.

'Martha says we have to be careful with the electricity,' she said.

'It looks beautiful,' said Jess, giving her great aunt a big hug.

'I miss Christmas,' Marjorie confided. 'I miss Nicola. She usually comes over for Christmas lunch.'

Jess patted her hand. 'I know. I miss her too.'

'Martha says she got what she deserved but I don't think so. I'd like to go to see her, but she won't take me and I get nervous when I'm out on my own.'

'Would you like to come with me on Friday?' Jess said with a smile.

'I'd love to, but Martha...'

'Leave Grandma to me,' said Jess firmly. 'I'm sure we can talk her round.'

They returned to the lounge to find Martha sipping at a cup of tea.

'I've poured one for you, sit down,' she said curtly.

Jess sat down in the armchair while Marjorie pulled out a soft topped stool from under the dining table. She carried it carefully across the room and set it down at the side of Jessica's chair. She looked nervously at the two full cups on the tray. When Martha pointed to the one on the left, she picked it up and took a big mouthful before placing the cup back on the saucer.

'I've been thinking,' she began.

'I wondered what the rattling noise was,' replied Martha.

'Grandma, don't be so mean.'

'Oh, I'm only joking. You know that, don't you, Marjorie?'

Marjorie nodded. 'Martha's always joking,' she said.

'Well, out with it. What have you been thinking about that is suddenly so important?' Martha put her own cup down and looked across at her sister.

'I was thinking that I'd like to see our Nicola this Christmas and Jessica said she'd take me.' Marjorie shot a quick glance at her older sister, then looked down at her lap.

Martha pursed her lips and said nothing.

'I'd really like to see her, Martha. Christmas isn't the same.'

'Of course it's not the same, Marjorie. My son-in-law, loath as I am to give him that title, is dead and my

9

daughter, your niece, is lying in hospital awaiting a place in a prison cell. How could Christmas possibly be normal?'

'She won't be charged with anything,' said Jess confidently. 'Women have more rights than they had in your day, Grandma. Men can't just beat us and get away with it anymore.'

Martha tilted her head to one side. A look of pain flashed across her face.

'Not before time, either.'

'Hang on a minute.' Jess looked confused. 'You were just saying she deserved what she got.'

'I was talking metaphorically,' said Martha. She bit her bottom lip. 'Back to the subject in hand. You won't be going to see Nicola with Jessica on Friday, Marjorie.'

Marjorie looked crushed. Jess was about to argue when Martha held up a hand to silence her.

'You won't be going with Jessica, because I'm going to take you to see her myself.' She looked inquiringly at Jess. 'What time do they let visitors in?'

Jess grinned. 'Between six-thirty and eight.'

Marjorie whooped.

'I'll give you a lift over, save the taxi fare,' Jess offered.

'We are quite capable of making our own way there, thank you, Jessica. We don't want Nicola thinking we only turned up because you were going anyway.'

Jess nodded, trying her best not to smile.

'I've, erm, got you a Christmas present... Now, I know you aren't celebrating it this year, but I don't care.' She reached down, picked up her bag and pulled two envelopes from it. 'This is for you,' she handed one to Martha... 'and this is for you, Aunt Marjorie.'

Martha nodded curtly as she took the envelope from her granddaughter. She turned it over in her hands as if looking for a clue to its contents. Marjorie, meanwhile had torn hers open and had pulled out a card with the picture of a huge cruise ship on the front.

'The Paradise Pearl,' she whispered.

'Look inside,' Jess encouraged her.

By this time, Martha had ripped open her envelope and had opened up the card inside to reveal a ticket inviting her to embark on the Paradise Pearl Cruise Liner on the 20th January 2020 at Yokohama harbour in Japan for a three-week cruise around the South China Sea, including stops in Hong Kong, Vietnam, Thailand and Singapore.

'Hong Kong.' Marjorie's mouth dropped open. 'Singapore,' she added.

If Martha was as excited as her sister, she hid it well.

'Japan... How are we supposed to get to Japan? Do we swim?'

Marjorie laughed like a demented hyena and threw her arms around Jess's neck.

'You fly to Tokyo, from London, Grandma. I've booked the flights and the transfers on the bullet train from there to Yokohama.' She eased Marjorie from her neck. 'You can see Mount Fuji from Yokohama,' she said.

'Mount Fuji,' whispered Marjorie. 'Oh, Martha, Mount Fuji.'

Martha read the itinerary again.

'I'm not sure about Vietnam, Jessica.'

Jess laughed. 'The war finished in the mid nineteen-seventies, Grandma, don't worry, you won't be taken prisoner. They don't shoot westerners anymore. It's a lovely place. I went there with my Uni mates on our gap year, remember? And Thailand is beautiful too. You'll love it.'

'I'm sure we will, Jessica, and don't think I'm ungrateful, but this doesn't mean I've given up on getting what I'm owed out of the farm.'

'Can we forget about that for now, Grandma. Just be happy that you'll be gallivanting around the South China Sea while we are freezing at home in February.'

Martha sniffed and looked across at Marjorie.

'It appears we are to share a cabin. I do hope we're not below the Plimsol Line. It would be nice to have a bit of a view.'

Jess tutted. 'Grandma, please! You have a very nice cabin on deck six. You have room service thrown in too. I was lucky to get it at such short notice, there had been a cancellation.'

Martha was appeased. She turned over the ticket in her hands and re-read the information it contained.

'We'd better start making plans, Marjorie. We've only got a few weeks before we go.'

Jess reached into her bag and pulled out two glossy brochures. She handed one to each of the elderly ladies.

'This will tell you what you're getting. All meals and drinks are included as well as the use of equipment, computers, or anything else you might like to try. It has pictures of the places you're going to stop at and a guide to what you'll find there. The only things you'll have to buy are your souvenirs at the port stops.'

Marjorie held her brochure to her chest as though it was the most valuable thing on earth while Martha flicked through the pages, nodding to herself as each location was revealed. Without looking up she addressed her excited sister.

'Marjorie, get the present we bought for Jessica, please.'

'Oh, I'd forgotten all about that. I didn't think we were doing presents this year.' Marjorie got to her feet and rushed out of the room, returning a few moments later with a neatly wrapped parcel.

'You were going to get this for your birthday,' Martha announced. 'But, as you've been so generous, I think you should have it now.'

Jess took the parcel from her aunt and tried to guess what was beneath the wrapping paper. *Clothing of some sort?*

'Don't get excited,' said Martha. 'It's only a pair of fleece pyjamas. Those things you wear verge on the indecent. At least these will keep your backside hidden from view first thing in the morning.'

Jess bit her cheeks to try to hold back the laughter that was welling up inside her. Instead of thanking her grandmother she nodded and turned her face away.

'I expect you to make use of them too,' Martha said with a stern look.

'I will, Grandma, thank you. Thank you, Aunt Marjorie. It's a very kind thought. My pyjama shorts aren't really made for winter.'

'Or any other time of year,' replied Martha.

Jess checked her watch and got to her feet.

'Well, it's been lovely to see you both, I'm so glad you're going to see Mum on Friday. Are you sure I can't give you a lift? I'm going anyway.'

'We'll make our own way, thank you all the same,' replied Martha. 'Besides, I'm sure it's only two visitors to a bed these days.'

Jess gave Marjorie a big hug. As she pulled away, she found Martha offering a cheek. She pecked it and turned towards the door.

'One last thing,' said Martha. 'I've dropped the inquiry into your lawyer boyfriend's behaviour, though I still think the relationship between you is wrong.'

'There is no relationship now, Grandma,' Jess replied. 'I'm all on my own again.'

'It's probably for the best, dear,' said Martha. 'You could do with a break. Get a few weeks proper sleep. Men can be so demanding.'

Chapter 2

When Jess got home, she found a Christmas card stuck in the draught excluder brushes in her letterbox.

She carried it into the kitchen and dropped it on the table before putting the kettle on. She recognised the writing on the envelope. Calvin's good wishes could wait.

Jess opened the American style fridge and looked forlornly at its contents. She had recently converted to vegetarianism but was still finding it a struggle, her love of a bacon sandwich had got the better of her on a few occasions.

Closing the fridge door, she opened the freezer and dug about under the bags of frozen vegetables. To her delight, she found a small turkey crown that she had bought prior to her plant conversion, the week she had moved in. She pulled it out and sat it on a baking tray on the big table. *Quorn fillets for Christmas dinner, turkey for Boxing Day.*

Pulling a face at the thought of a meat free Christmas lunch, she decided to have her main meal in the evening, and make do with a cheese and tomato sandwich for now.

Ten minutes later, she was back at the table with the sandwich and a steaming mug of coffee. She was just about to tuck in when her phone announced that she had received a text message. It was from her best friend, Sam.

Jamie just proposed. He did the one knee and everything. Even bought a ring.

Jess replied typing one of the few abbreviations she allowed herself to use.

OMG! I'm so pleased for you!

Can I call? I no its Xmas day, Sam replied.

Of course. Ring now. I'm so excited.

Thirty seconds later her phone rang.

'Oh, Sam, I'm so pleased for you. That is so romantic how—'

'I turned him down, Jess.'

'What the... Why? I thought you two were together forever.'

'I've told you many a time, I'm not the marrying kind. At least not yet. I've got a lot of life to live before I settle down. I thought Jamie understood that too.'

'Oh, no, the poor man must be devastated. How did he take it?'

'He was crushed. I felt so bad I almost changed my mind and said yes but I couldn't. It wouldn't have been fair on him or me.'

'Oh, Sam.' Jess's voice cracked with emotion.

'The silly man. We only talked about it a couple of months ago. I really thought he had accepted the fact that I wasn't interested in getting married.'

'How is he now? Your refusal must have felt like a right kick in the guts... Not that I'm saying you were out of order, it's your future too, but it must have hit him hard. Men's egos are fragile things at the best of times. They are used to having them massaged, not punched.'

'I don't know how he is now. He stormed off... well, he stormed off for a full five minutes, then he came back for his coat and car keys, it's freezing out. Oh, he took a bottle of scotch from the sideboard too so I can guess what he's doing right now.'

'Poor Jamie,' Jess said, softly.

'He'll come back when he's sorted it all out in his head but I'm not sure things will ever be the same again after this.' Sam sighed deeply. 'The daft bugger.'

'I hope you can work it out. You're so good together.'

'To be honest, Jess. I've been feeling a bit uncomfortable for a while now. He's been very clingy recently.'

'I suppose men want a secure relationship too. Some men, that is.'

'He was starting to get a bit jealous when I talked to other blokes. You know me, Jess, I can flirt for England, but I never mean anything by it.'

'Not all men see it as just flirting though, Sam. Look at Calvin.'

'That creep. He thought every woman on the planet fancied him.'

'I know. What I don't understand is why it took me so long to see him for what he was.' Jess paused and looked at the envelope on the table. 'He pushed a Christmas card through my letterbox. There's no stamp on it.'

'What does he have to say? Not that I care anyway.'

'I don't know, I haven't opened it.'

'Just burn it, love.'

When Jess didn't reply, Sam's voice became harder.

'I mean it, Jess. Set fire to it. Don't let his weasel words get to you.'

'Oh, I won't, Sam. It's over. He should have realised by now.'

'People like that never learn because it's never their fault... in their own minds anyway. For pity's sake, the man virtually controlled every aspect of your life. You even needed his permission to wear perfume.'

'I know, I know. I let him get away with too much. It seemed easier somehow.'

Jess thought back to the awful day that Calvin had viciously attacked Sam in their flat. She quickly pushed the thought away and brought the subject back to Jamie's proposal.

'So, are you going to phone him? Jamie, that is.'

'No, I'll let him come around to the reality of the situation in his own good time. I don't want to get his hopes up. If I call him, he might think I've reconsidered.'

'Poor Jamie.'

'Poor me you mean. I've got to spend Christmas Day on my own.' Sam tried to make light of the situation.

'I'm on my own too. Do you want to come round?' Jess offered.

Sam went silent for a moment. 'No, I'd better wait here in case he comes back.'

'I won't come to yours for the same reason,' Jess replied. 'I wouldn't want to be in the way when you start to sort the mess out.'

'It's probably best you don't. Right, I'm off to raid the fridge. I've got a nice bottle of red with my name on it. Catch you later, hun.'

Jess put the phone on the table and sighed. *Why were relationships always so difficult?* It wasn't just her ex, Calvin, that Jess had problems with. She had become too close to her lawyer and Family Trust partner, Bradley, a man she had thought was single, but was in fact still married to his scheming Italian wife, Leonora.

'Bloody men,' she said under her breath.

Jess suddenly realised how much the phone call had dampened her mood. She had been on such a high when she had given Martha and Marjorie their cruise tickets but now she felt completely flat. Opening a drawer in one of the units, she pulled out a packet of cigarettes and a disposable lighter. Sticking them in the pocket of her cardigan, she picked up her coffee, opened the back door and sat on the top step willing herself to resist the temptation of lighting up.

Jess had given up smoking when Calvin insisted, but it had been such a difficult thing to do. She enjoyed a smoke. She found it calmed her in times of stress. She was sure she wouldn't have picked up the excellent grades she had managed at Uni without them.

She took a sip of the cooling coffee and looked across the yard towards the old barn, the only structure left apart from the house itself. In her mind's eye she saw Alice, her beloved great grandmother, the woman who had run a working farm on her own for all those years before selling off the land, parcel by parcel and investing the money in property and shares. When she had died, just short of her hundredth birthday she had left everything tied up in a trust fund with Jess the only

17

beneficiary, much to the chagrin of the rest of her family. She felt the ownership hanging like a lead weight from her shoulders at times.

Absentmindedly, Jess pulled the packet of cigarettes from her pocket, slipped one into her mouth and lit it. Drawing deeply, she took the smoke into her lungs and held it there for some seconds before exhaling. She closed her eyes, sighed contentedly, then took another long draw.

Three cigarettes later, with freezing cold hands, Jess picked up her empty cup and carried it into the house. She put the cup in the sink and the pack of cigarettes and the lighter, back into the kitchen drawer before picking up the plate containing her uneaten sandwich. She walked through to the lounge, sat on Alice's lumpy old sofa and switched on the big screen TV.

At six o'clock in the evening, Jess was woken from her Christmas Day doze by someone hammering at the door. She shook her head to clear it, then pulled aside the curtain and looked outside. Leaning on the front door with an almost empty bottle of whisky in his hand, was Jamie.

'Jamie, what on earth are you doing here?' As Jess opened the front door, Jamie practically fell inside. He steadied himself and waved the bottle at her.

'Fancy a drink?'

Jess shook her head. 'I don't touch that stuff, Jamie.'

'Nor do I, usually,' he slurred. 'Can I come in? It's cold out here.'

Jess stepped aside to allow Jamie to enter, then closed the door and followed him as he walked unsteadily into the lounge. He stood, swaying slightly as Jess caught up. She took the bottle from him and carried it through to the kitchen where she emptied the small amount that was left down the sink. When she returned to the lounge, Jamie was slumped on the sofa with his head in his hands.

'She turned me down, Jess. Sam turned me down.'

'I know, Jamie, I'm so sorry.'

Jamie began to sob.

'I'm not good enough for her. She turned me down.'

Jess hurried across to the sofa and sat next to the sniffling man.

'It's not that, Jamie, Sam isn't ready to settle down yet. It's not you, it's the timing.'

Jamie flopped over, his head landing on Jess's lap. 'I feel such a fool.'

Jess resisted the temptation to stroke his hair, instead she eased herself to the side, leaving his head on the sofa.

'Sam said you had a conversation about marriage a few weeks ago. She thought you understood that she wasn't ready to settle down just yet.'

Jamie struggled to a sitting position before leaning back on the sofa. 'I thought she'd come round when I actually presented her with a ring.' He shook his head slowly. 'How could I have got it so wrong?'

'It happens, Jamie. Look, should I give her a quick call to let her know you're here? She must be worried about you.'

Jamie shook his head again. 'No, she doesn't care what happens to me.'

'That's not true, Jamie and you know it. Just because she doesn't want to get married yet, it doesn't mean she doesn't care for you.'

'You care, don't you, Jess?'

'Of course, I care.'

Jamie forced a smile. 'I knew you did. I can tell.' He edged towards her.

Jess eased herself to the side but suddenly found herself wedged against the arm of the sofa. Suddenly, Jamie was on her, one hand squeezing roughly on her breast, the other around the back of her neck.

She tried to push him away but he was too strong, even in his drunken state. Before she could warn him off, his lips were on hers and his hand had found its way up her jumper. She managed to turn her head away from him as his fingers began to pull at the button on the waist of her jeans.

'Jamie, no... Get off!'

'Come on, Jess, you know you want to. I've seen the way you look at me.' He turned her half around and forced her down onto the sofa, still trying to open up her jeans. Pulling up her jumper he pushed his face into her breasts. 'Oh, Jess...'

Jess began to rain blows onto the back of his head. 'GET OFF ME!' she yelled. When his head lifted from her chest, she hit him as hard as she could on his temple. The blow seemed to bring him to his senses and he rolled off, onto the floor.

'Jess... Jess, I'm so sorry... I'm drunk and miserable, forgive me, please.' Jamie burst into tears again.

Jess got to her feet and rearranged her clothing. 'I think you'd better go, Jamie,' she said.

'Please, Jess, I'm sorry... don't tell Sam, I beg you. I didn't... I wasn't...'

Jess took in the pathetic man as he looked up at her beseechingly.

'Get on the sofa, sleep it off,' she commanded.

Jamie nodded meekly and crawled onto the settee.

'I'm sorry,' he slurred turning away from her.

Jess sighed and walked through to the kitchen to make coffee. When she stuck her head through the doorframe five minutes later, he was fast asleep.

As Jess sipped her coffee, she pondered on how to handle the situation. She had to let Sam know where her boyfriend was, that was for sure. She decided not to tell her about his drunken attack, that would only make things worse for all of them. After fifteen minutes thinking about the best way to approach it, she picked up her phone and rang her best friend.

'Sam?'

'Hi, hun,' Sam seemed to be almost as drunk as Jamie.

'You've been on the red, haven't you?' Jess laughed.

'Guilty as charged,' replied Sam. 'I'm only surprised you haven't hit the vino yet. Have you run out?'

'No, I've got a couple of bottles in the fridge. I'm just not in the mood.'

'Oh dear, come on, Jess, it's Christmas.'

'Jamie's here,' Jess blurted out.

'Jamie... what's he doing there? I assumed he'd gone back to his parents' house.'

'Nope, he's here, drunk as a skunk. He's sleeping it off on my sofa. He's had a whole bottle of scotch, pretty much.'

'Why... I don't get why he came to you?'

'Nor do I, Sam, he turned up about an hour or so, ago.'

'And you only just decided to let me know?'

'He was in a state, rambling on about you. I thought it best to let him get it out.'

'Did you now?' Sam laughed harshly.

'Sam, come on, this is me, you know I wouldn't do anything like that.'

'I thought I knew, but then maybe I don't know you as well as I should.'

'Sam!' Jess felt the tears welling up.

'Why you, Jess?'

'I don't know, Sam. I honestly don't know. I had to let him in. God knows where his car is, it's not on the lane. He could have driven it into a hedge for all I know.'

'Is he injured?' Sam seemed suddenly concerned.

'No, at least I don't think so. He's just totally out of it.'

Sam was silent for a while. When she spoke, her voice was softer.

'Look, I didn't mean to suggest that anything had happened between you, Jess. You're my oldest friend. I was just taken aback that's all. His mother lives closer to my flat than you do.'

'I wish he hadn't washed up here, Sam. I had plans for this evening. I was going to cook a turkey crown ready for tomorrow, have a few drinks and just chill out with Netflix.'

'Is he still asleep?'

'Yes, he's on the sofa like I said. Are you going to pick... Sorry, you've had a few too.'

'He can stay there for me, the pathetic creature.'

'SAM! He can't stay here. I'm not having you getting any more ideas.'

'I did say sorry, Jess.'

'Only half-heartedly, Sam, don't even joke about me doing something as low as that. You know I wouldn't do anything to hurt you, especially with your boyfriend.'

'He's always fancied you, you know,' Sam replied.

'Don't be ridiculous.'

'He told me. Remember that night we all went out for a meal? The night Calvin tried to hit on me?'

'How could I forget.'

'Well, when we got home, he wouldn't shut up about you. We were both drunk and we started playing a silly game of, who do you fancy. It started out with Brad Pitt, Aniston, famous people, but then I mentioned one of the blokes from his golf club, just as a joke you understand, I wouldn't touch him with a barge pole in real life... anyway, he suddenly came up with your name. I laughed, acting mock-shock, but he doubled down on it and said he thought you were really attractive. I let it go, we were both drunk, as I said, but it was a bit weird. I mean, he knew you'd been my best friend since childhood.'

'Just drunken talk, Sam, he didn't mean it. You can tell how much he loves you just by looking at him when you're out together.'

'He's become obsessed, Jess. It's wearing me down. I feel like I'm suffocating under the weight of his affection.'

'That's a shame, Sam. Look... I really think you two need to sit down and have a long talk about the future.'

'We did that a few weeks ago, love, and then he does this.'

'I still think you need to talk it out. The message hasn't sunk in yet.'

'To tell you the truth, Jess. It's been quite relaxing being at home without him fawning all over me today.'

'I was enjoying my 'me-time' too,' Jess replied.

'Oh, dear. Sorry, Jess, I feel guilty now, this is my problem, not yours.'

'I'm always happy to help when I can, Sam, but I didn't need this today. Tell you what, when he comes to, I'll stick him in a taxi.'

Sam was silent again, then Jess heard her sigh. 'All right, but I hope he sleeps for a few hours yet. I want to be in bed when he comes back, and woe betide him if he wakes me up.'

'I'll tell him to let you sleep before I stick him in the cab. I think he'll be out for a couple of hours yet.'

Sam sighed again. 'Right, I'm going to resume bottle number two. Night, Jess. Happy Christmas.'

Jess put the phone on the table and thought about getting something to eat but realising that if Jamie woke while she was cooking, she'd have to invite him to stay for dinner, she decided to grab a handful of biscuits instead.

'Happy Christmas, Jess,' she said, biting into a digestive.

When Jamie began to make stirring noises at about ten o'clock, Jess made him a strong cup of coffee and shook him by the shoulder.

'Come on, Rip Van Winkle. Get this down you, I'm about to phone for a taxi.'

Jamie sat up, looking perplexed. 'Jess... then his face fell as he remembered the events earlier in the evening. 'I'm so, so sorry. Jess, please forgive me, that wasn't me, I'm not like that, I...'

23

'You were drunk and upset. Let's just forget it ever happened, shall we?'

'I'm sorry... Oh my God, what time is it? Sam will be wondering what's happened to me.'

'I've spoken to Sam. You aren't her favourite person at the moment.'

'You didn't tell her...?'

'No, as I said, we should forget that ever happened, so don't you go confessing to Sam when you're feeling guilty.'

'I won't... thanks, Jess.' Jamie sipped at the coffee and pulled a face. 'Now that's strong,' he said.

'You need it, the state you're in.' Jess walked through to the kitchen, picked up her phone and dialled for an Uber. To her surprise, the operator told her a cab would be with her within five minutes.

'He's on his way,' she shouted, but as the words came out, she saw Jamie appear in the doorway. He held out his arms towards her.

'I don't think that's a good idea,' she said, shaking her head.

'You're probably right,' he replied blowing her a kiss instead. 'Thanks for not dropping me in it and thanks again for accepting my apology.'

'When you get home, Sam will be in bed. Leave her there, don't try to wake her to explain, there will be plenty of time for that tomorrow. Just go straight to the spare room.'

'I will,' Jamie hung his head. 'Jess, I can't tell you—'

'Taxi's here,' Jess interrupted him as two bright lights flashed across the lounge window.

At the door, Jamie stepped out, then turned back to face her. 'Thanks for looking after me, Jess. I'll see you soon. Maybe we can all have a night out in the New Year.'

'Maybe,' said Jess. She watched Jamie climb into the taxi, then giving him a wave, she turned around and went back into the house.

Chapter 3

On Boxing Day morning, Jess pushed a skewer into the turkey crown to check it had properly defrosted, then pulling a face, she laid it on a baking tray and cut it into pieces.

'The foxes will enjoy their late Christmas dinner this year,' she said aloud, and opening the back door, she carried the tray across the yard to the paddock at the back of the barn where she knew a family of foxes congregated. Picking up the pieces of meat, one at a time, she threw them around the paddock, then turned back and returned to the farmhouse.

Jess was restless, she spent twenty minutes tidying her bedroom and lounge before getting changed into leggings and a top that hung just below her bottom. She grabbed her car keys and bag and pulling on her hooded winter jacket, she left the house and drove into town to get a bit of exercise, walking around the shops.

The car park opposite the Uni was almost full as shoppers hit the town to take advantage of the Boxing Day sales. Jess was lucky and found a recently vacated spot near the café, adjacent to the Uni. The last time she had been in the coffee bar was when she witnessed her ex, Calvin, in a shouting match with Tania, a waitress at the Venetian restaurant, the woman he had been having a secret affair with.

The café was closed. On the window was a sign announcing that the premises were under new management and would be re-opening on Monday the 30th.

The weather had changed in the short time since Jess had fed the foxes. The skies had become sullen, thick with black cloud and a fierce, biting wind had picked up. It took her three attempts to get the car door open as she pushed against the strengthening gusts. Once out of the car she pulled up the hood of her coat only to find it blown from her head a few seconds later. Determined not to waste the opportunity to stretch her legs, Jess left the hood billowing behind her head and set off at a brisk pace towards the row of shops that lined the main street.

As she passed the café, she noticed a man struggling to control a roll cage stacked with cardboard boxes. The rear doors of the Luton van he had just unloaded them from, slammed shut behind him leaving him hanging on to the cage as it careered down the short metal ramp that was clipped to the bottom of the van.

'Look out!' he called as he spotted Jess, who was directly in the path of the rattling, rolling, cage. He tried to slow it down, using his heels as a brake but his efforts were only partially successful and the cage swung violently around to the left.

Dropping her bag, Jess took a step to the side, then throwing out both hands, grabbed hold of the side of the cage as it hurtled past her. The man holding onto the back end leaned backwards and dug in his heels again, causing the cage to turn 180 degrees bringing it to an abrupt halt. Stepping forwards, he quickly applied the wheel brake, and puffing out his cheeks, looked around the side of the mesh container to where Jess was sitting on her backside, her feet splayed out in front of her.

'Are you hurt?' asked the young man, full of concern.

Jess grabbed hold of his proffered hand and pulled herself to her feet.

'Only my dignity,' she replied, rubbing her backside with both hands.

'Thanks so much for helping me. I thought it was on its way to the Venetian.' The man pointed across the road towards the restaurant. 'This crockery isn't posh enough for that place.'

Jess smiled. The man was slightly older than her, possibly in his early thirties. His eyes were hazel: brown at the centre with a green tint around the edges. His hair was light brown, at the darker end of blond, longer on top and combed across from a side parting. His beard was short, not much more than stubble. He wore skinny, mid-blue jeans, brown Chelsea boots and a chocolate-brown leather, zip up jacket. When he smiled back at her, he showed off a perfect set of teeth. He held out his hand again, this time in introduction.

'I'm Joshua Seymour,' he said.

His grip was firm, but not too macho.

'Jess Griffiths,' she replied.

The cage suddenly began to rock as another gust of wind hit it.

'I'd better get this inside before it tips over and kills someone,' Joshua said.

'Hang on, I'll give you a hand.' Jess picked up her shoulder bag, dropped it on top of the pile of large, brown boxes and got hold of the side of the cage. 'Where are we heading?' she asked.

'The soon to be renamed, Daily Grind Coffee Bar,' Joshua replied, pointing to the café.

Between them, they managed to get the roll cage into the shop doorway and out of the worst of the wind. Joshua produced a set of keys, unlocked and opened the front door, and together they pushed the cage inside.

'Do you mind if I close the door?' Joshua asked. 'I don't want you to feel awkward about being inside with a strange man.'

'You don't look so odd. I've met stranger ones,' Jess said with a smile.

Joshua pushed the cage to the bar at the far end of the café, passed Jess her bag, then lifted the counter flap and began to carry the heavy boxes of crockery into the kitchen area.

'Do you need a hand with those? They look heavy.' Jess took a step towards the cage.

'No, it's all right, I'll manage, they're not too bad really. I'm just amazed we got them in without smashing the lot.'

Jess looked around. The café had undergone a major facelift since she had last been inside. The place was littered with two and four-seater, round tables Along the sides of the room there were longer, oblong

27

tables, and a long worktop style counter ran the full length of the window. Between the last row of tables and the bar was a twenty-five foot square area of timber-floored space. In the corner, near the bar was an old-fashioned juke box. Jess pressed a couple of buttons on the front of the machine to flip through the songs on offer.

'Blimey, these go back a bit, don't they? I only recognise a few names on here and that's only because my Nana liked Elvis and Buddy Holly.'

'Rock n Roll is only one of the themes,' Joshua replied. 'I intend to have different themed nights. If you push that button on the far right, you'll get a nineteen sixties menu, press again it's the seventies, then eighties. It looks like a real jukebox but it isn't, all the music is streamed from the Internet. I plan to snare the students from the Uni in the evenings, a lot of them are into old sixties music these days. On Saturdays I'll go for the shoppers. I've done my research. I'll get a lot of old folk dropping by for a coffee and a slice of cake at weekends and they love music from the fifties.'

'Seems like you've got it all worked out,' Jess replied as Joshua pushed the empty cage out of the way and stepped back into the café.

'There's nothing like it that I know of,' he replied with a grin. 'It is an experiment though, I'm not sure it will make me a fortune, but it will be a fun journey.'

He walked to the front door and held it open. A strong gust of wind blew a discarded plastic carrier bag into the café. Jess picked it up, screwed it into a ball and looked around for a bin.

'Leave it on one of the tables. I'm back in tomorrow to get all those cups and saucers washed ready for the big opening on Monday.'

Jess dropped the bag on the window counter and stepped across to the door.

'I'll find a Rockabilly dress and drop in for a jive,' she said with a grin.

'Please do. I can jive with the best of 'em. My grandad taught me.'

'I've seen videos of people dancing to Rock n Roll,' replied Jess. 'I'd love to give it a whirl.' She stepped into the doorway and held out her hand towards him. 'It's been a real pleasure, Joshua. I'll catch up with you when you're open, best of luck with it.'

'Call me Josh, please. Only my grandparents call me Joshua. They always say, that's the name on your birth certificate so that's the name we'll use.'

Jess laughed. 'I can hear my Nana using those exact words.' She stepped outside and held down her flapping hood as Josh locked the café door. 'Good luck on Monday. I hope the place is rocking by lunchtime.'

'Look, erm, Jess... are you busy? I mean, is there somewhere you need to be, or someone you have to see urgently?'

'No, I'm footloose and fancy free. I only came into town for a look around the shops. I was bored witless at home on my own.'

'Would you... erm... Could I buy you lunch to say thank you for rescuing my crockery?'

Jess thought about it for all of five seconds. 'You could,' she said, simply.

The Three-Legged Mule, known to the local students as The Wonky Donkey, was situated on the corner of Main Street and the newly built cul-de-sac containing student accommodation, Learner's Way. Owned by one of the major pub chains, it offered cheap beer, mainly aimed at the town's student population and a reasonably priced menu, aimed at local shoppers. Josh checked with the bar staff that meals were available before leading Jess to a corner nook. Everything on the menu seemed to come with chips or rice, so Josh ordered a steak, while Jess, still pleased with herself for giving away her Christmas turkey to the foxes, chose a vegan, five bean chilli with rice and tortillas. Both went for an alcohol-free lager.

'So, tell me about the Daily Grind, is this your first venture in business?' Jess asked.

Josh nodded. 'Yep, I used to work for a marketing company, analysing data for some of the big brands, but I wasn't really happy doing it. I was about to try my luck with one of the medium sized advertising companies when the opportunity to buy the coffee shop came up. My sister was part owner of it but was moving away from the area and needed the money to start up a new business in Dorset. Her partner just wanted a quick sale, so I used my savings and took out a loan to finance the takeover.' He smiled and shook his head. 'Listen to me... takeover... like it's a multi-national or something.'

'I think it's a brave thing to do, especially in the current climate. The High Street is suffering badly at the moment.'

'I'm hoping the students will keep me afloat. I think I stand a good chance if I can get their patronage. My sister said they made up the bulk of her customer base.'

'I love the idea of a dancefloor in a café,' said Jess. 'You wouldn't get too many jiving at once though.'

'I've got a plan for that,' replied Josh. 'There's a big open space upstairs. I believe they used to use it as a classroom when the building was owned by Worker's Educational Association back in the nineteen thirties. It wouldn't take that much to put a counter and a coffee machine up there and turn the space into a larger dance floor.'

Jess laughed. 'You seem to have a plan for everything. You haven't just jumped into this blindly, have you?'

'I've probably overthought a lot of it if I'm honest,' Josh replied.

'Well, I think you've made a great start. I can't wait to come in and have a look when you're up and running.'

'I was going to turn it into an American Diner. A proper fifties throwback, but then I thought the idea of mixed themes might go down better. Not everyone watches streaming repeats of Happy Days.'

'Happy Days?' Jess looked puzzled.

'It's an American import TV series from the eighties. The kids used to meet up at Al's Diner.'

'Ah, I see. That one seems to have passed by my Netflix search.'

'There you go, it would have been a risk. I love the show but it has a limited audience these days.'

'I watch Friends,' Jess replied.

'Oh, me too,' smiled Josh, 'but I don't think a Friends theme would work either, unless I could attract Joey or one of the others to serve behind the counter.' He looked across the table and tipped his head slightly to the side. 'I don't suppose you need a job, do you?'

Jess shook her head. 'No, I've got more than enough on my plate at the moment.'

'What is it you do?' Josh looked genuinely interested.

'I'm a journalist. I write articles for women's magazines in the main, but I'm also researching a novel based on my great grandmother's life during the war.'

'That sounds interesting. I love anything about that era, I think the fashions were fantastic. I really wish I could get away with wearing a double-breasted suit and a Fedora.'

'You'd look like Alice's Gangster Lawyer.'

'Gangster?'

'Godfrey, his name was. He was my great grandmother's lawyer and lover. He drove a car like you see in the gangster movies.' Jess was about to reveal that she had been in the very same car herself with a member of the current generation of lawyers, but bit her tongue and said nothing else.

'This sounds great. What are you using as research material?'

'Alice's memoirs... Alice was my great grandmother, she died recently.' A flash of pain flicked across Jess's face. Josh picked up on her emotions immediately.

31

'I'm so sorry to hear that. You were close I take it?'

'Best friends, she was my mentor. I look just like she did back in the day. Everyone used to say she was a double for the wartime actress, Rita Hayworth.'

'Wow! Then she must have really been a beauty. I've seen a lot of her films. As I said, I love that era.' He leaned forward and studied Jess. 'Yes, I can see it, do your hair in the old-fashioned style, dab on a bit of rouge and you would make a passable Rita.'

Jess laughed, pushed her hair back behind one ear and struck a pose.

'Perfect. You're hired for my next movie,' said Josh.

Jess took a sip of beer and licked her lips. 'This is quite good for alcohol free.'

'So, do you live in town, Jess?'

'I used to until Nana died, she was my favourite person on earth. She was a liberated woman before the term had been invented. She ran a working farm on her own throughout the war, right up until a few years ago in fact. I live in the farm house now though there isn't much land left, she sold it off in plots, over the years. She was ninety-nine when she died.'

'That's a shame, she'd have got the big telegram if she'd lasted another year.'

'She was only a few days short of getting it, not that she was all that bothered. She wasn't a run of the mill pensioner by any stretch of the imagination. She was as sharp as a tack right up to her final breath.'

'She sounds like she was quite a lady.'

'She was... and I miss her terribly. She always had the right bit of advice for any situation.' She looked across the table directly into his eyes. 'Her thoughts on men were particularly insightful.'

Josh feigned concern.

'I think she'd have liked you,' Jess said, smiling.

'That's good. I aim to please.'

Jess looked at her watch, then across the table to Josh.

32

'I'd better be getting back home. I'm miles behind with work. The editor of Femme Fatale magazine is expecting an article about the history of female spies in the next few days and I've only just about fleshed out the outline.'

Josh got to his feet and pulled his wallet from his pocket.

'I'll go halves,' Jess offered. 'You need every penny you've got for your new enterprise.'

Josh shook his head. 'You saved me a fortune in broken crockery today. This is only a small reward really.' When Jess looked like she was going to argue, he slipped his credit card from his wallet and stepping out from behind the table, walked briskly to the bar. 'If you can't accept it as a reward then please let me pay as my treat. If I can't afford to buy a meal for someone as nice as you, then I shouldn't really be in business at all.'

Jess gave in and hung her bag on her shoulder.

'I'll pay next time,' she said.

Josh turned towards her with a grin. 'Next time?'

'Well, if this was a one off, then...'

'No, no... I hope it isn't a one off, I'd love to see you again.'

'Ahem.'

Jess covered a smile with her hand as the waitress behind the bar handed over Josh's card and a receipt. He pushed them both into his wallet and nodded to the girl. As he turned away from the bar she looked towards Jess, winked, then nodded her head twice. 'I would,' she mouthed.

Jess bit her lip and turned towards the door. As Josh opened it, she looked back at the watching waitress and mouthed, 'I would too.'

Outside, Josh zipped up his leather jacket and waited as Jess fastened her own coat.

'The wind's died down a bit now,' she pointed towards the car park on the other side of the street. 'I'm in there,' she said.

They walked to Jess's car chatting about her novel research. When they reached her little Toyota, they stood awkwardly, neither sure how to proceed. Eventually, Jess pressed the button on her key fob and her car lights flashed as the central locking opened. She pulled on the driver's door just as he stepped towards her. They stood, either side of the open door looking at each other in silence, then Jess leaned across and pecked him on the cheek.

'Thank you for a lovely lunch, and good luck on Monday.'

'Could I, er, would you... give me your phone number?'

Jess slipped into the car and looked up at Josh as he took hold of the door handle to close it behind her.

'Next time,' she said with a smile.

Chapter 4

As Jess was pulling away from the car park, a taxi pulled up at the kerb outside the coffee shop and two elderly ladies clambered out.

Martha paid the taxi driver without leaving a tip while Marjorie hopped from one foot to the other excitedly. As the taxi pulled away the driver gave them a look of distaste which, unfortunately for him, Martha had noticed.

'I saw that. Don't start thinking you'll be booked for the return trip.'

The taxi pulled up and the driver stuck his head out of the window. 'Lady, I've been tipped more than I made from your fare today. I'm not going to lose any sleep over it.'

Before Martha could think up a reply, he drove away with a toot of his horn.

'Hurry up, Martha, I'm dying to see what Ogden's have on offer in the sales.'

Martha, who was still glaring after the taxi, turned towards her younger sister.

'There'll be nothing worth buying, Marjorie, that's for certain.'

She marched off towards the department store at a brisk pace leaving Marjorie trailing in her wake. Inside the store she perused the signs that spelled out which items were sold on each floor.

'I hope they have some summer ware in, Marjorie. We'd look ridiculous floating around Thailand wearing that.' She pointed to a mannequin sporting a tweed suit.

They took the escalator to the second floor. Martha strolled quickly past the rails of latest fashion garments while Marjorie stopped to inspect one or two of the dresses. When she looked up, Martha had disappeared.

She hurried along the rails looking right and left as she went. After a couple of minutes, she found herself faced with a row of headless models wearing the skimpiest of bikinis. Marjorie looked around again for her sister, but still excited by the thought of the sales, began to examine the swimsuits.

'Can I help with anything, Madam?'

Marjorie almost jumped out of her skin.

'I was, I want... I... We're going on a cruise and I haven't got a swimsuit,' she said.

The assistant smiled. 'I think I can help you with that. What colour would you like?'

'Red,' said Marjorie without hesitation.

The assistant looked Marjorie up and down to get a rough estimate of her size, then walked along the rail, picking out costumes as she went. Marjorie tagged along behind muttering to herself excitedly.

When the assistant had picked out four swimming costumes, she led Marjorie to a full-length mirror next to the changing rooms and passed them to her one at a time. Marjorie held each one up in front of her before coming to a decision.

'I like this one,' she said, holding up a round necked, high cut, red costume with a floral pattern over the left breast.

The assistant smiled. 'That's a good choice. The colour suits you perfectly. It's a size ten, but it should stretch to a twelve easily enough. I'll just put the others back then I'll take you to the till.'

She led Marjorie back the way they had come, hanging the discarded garments on the rails as they passed. When they reached the till, the girl placed the swimsuit on the counter, smiled at Marjorie, then went to look for another customer to assist. The woman on the cash register looked bored. She picked up the swimsuit and dragged the barcode across the scanner.

'Fifty-four pounds, ninety-nine. Are you paying cash or card?' she asked.

Marjorie began to panic. 'Martha's paying,' she whispered.

'I'm sorry, I didn't hear that. Cash or card?'

'Ooh, I don't know how she's—'

'Marjorie, there you are. Honestly, it's like looking after a five-year-old.'

Martha strode between the rails and stopped at her sister's side.

The till assistant looked from Marjorie to her clearly annoyed, older sister. 'I take it you are Martha?'

'I am she.'

'Fifty-four, ninety-nine,' she said.

'What is?' Martha studied the name tag on the assistant's breast. 'What are you talking about, Colleen?'

Colleen pointed to the swimsuit. 'Fifty-four, ninety-nine,' she repeated.

Martha lifted up the garment and examined it as though she had just found it in her garden on a particularly windy day. 'She doesn't want it,' she said, curtly.

'She might have tried it on, she's got to buy it if she has.'

'Marjorie!' Martha looked sternly at her sibling.

'I didn't... I was just looking... I like it,' she stammered. 'Can I have it, Martha, please?'

Martha examined the costume again.

'No! It's not for you, Marjorie.'

'But I'll need one to swim in the pools onboard the ship, there are four.'

'Swim? You? You can't swim, Marjorie.'

'I can. It's you that can't swim, Martha. I learned when I was in London,' she added as though that made it more official.

Martha blew out her cheeks. 'Well, this costume isn't right for you. It's been made for a much younger woman.'

'I like it, Martha.'

Marjorie's head snapped back as Martha leaned in towards her. 'I said, NO!' she hissed and grabbing her sister by the arm she almost dragged her away from the till. 'Hurry now, the sales will be over before we've had chance to buy anything.'

An hour later, carrying six bags of assorted dresses, tops and knee length shorts, the sisters stood once again on the pavement outside the café. Martha snarled as the first taxi in line pulled up and the face of the driver that had brought them into town appeared from the driver's window.

'Oh, Christ, not you two again.'

Martha gave him a look that would have curdled fresh milk and stomped down the pavement to the next taxi in line. 'Clover Close,' she snapped as she pulled open the back door of the cab. Marjorie scurried around to the opposite side and had to wait for a cyclist to pass before she could open her door. The cab driver looked over his shoulder at them as they pulled on their seatbelts.

'Well? Are we going to sit here all day?' Martha scowled at the driver.

'You're supposed to get in the first cab in line, love,' the driver replied.

'The only thing that man is going to get from me is another piece of my mind and a report to his boss about his behaviour,' said Martha angrily. She narrowed her eyes at the driver. 'Furthermore, I'd like to make it clear that I am not your love. Now, do I have to report you as well, or are you going to take us home sometime today?'

The driver blew out his cheeks and turned back to the front. Starting up his engine he pulled away, shaking his head at the driver in front as he passed.

'And don't expect a tip,' Martha said coldly.

Chapter 5

When Jess got home, she dropped her bag on the table and noticing the unopened Christmas card, she picked it up and turned it over in her hands twice with Sam's words ringing in her head. *Burn it, burn it.*

Ignoring the warning voice, she tore open the envelope and pulled out the card.

Happy Christmas, Jess.
Miss You!
Love
Calvin.
PS I got the deposit together for the flat so you know where to find me when you need to.

Calvin XXXXX

Jess ripped the card in half, then in half again and dropped the scraps into the bag she kept on the back door for recycling.

'Bugger you, Calvin.'

After boiling the kettle she made coffee and sat at the big oak table thinking about her lunch with Josh. He seemed a nice man and was very good-looking with it. She wondered why he was single, or *IF* he really was single. Her recent experience with Bradley had made her a little more cautious about accepting things at face value.

I do like him, she said to herself. *I think I might drop by the café when I'm in town next. Leave it a few days though, Jessica, don't let him think you're desperate.*

Jess took a sip of her coffee and opened up the outline of her article on female spies on her laptop. An hour later she had the first draft of the document written. As she was reading through it she paused at the section she had written about the SOE agents who had been smuggled into France to help the resistance movement during the 1940s. The mention of war made her think of Alice, her great grandmother, who had run a farm throughout the Second World War. The last chapter she had read from her memoirs had been about the Battle of Britain and how Alice had stood in the farmyard with her friend Miriam and two evacuee children, Stephen and Harriet, watching the German bombers flying over like a swarm of locusts.

Unable to concentrate on her article, Jess picked up Alice's hand written memoir labelled '1940' and opened it to September.

Alice. September 1940

During the last week in August, I received an unexpected telephone call from Godfrey who had been stuck in London on government work all through the summer. We had made plans to meet up for a weekend in the capital but he had become so busy turning government diktats into legal documents that we hadn't been able to arrange anything. He hadn't been back home since late January. I wondered how his wife and children were dealing with his absence but he assured me that they were doing fine without him.

'Look, Alice, I know it's short notice for you, but I've actually been able to swing a weekend off. Do you think you could get the train to Victoria Station? I've only got two days, Saturday the eighth and Sunday the ninth of September.'

I thought fast. The harvest was coming up but I'm sure Barney, my foreman, could run things for a couple of days. I shouted into the kitchen for Miriam and she appeared in the doorway thirty seconds later, her hands and forearms covered in flour.

'Can you do without me for the weekend of eighth of September?'

Miriam thought for a moment. 'Yes, of course, are you going to see Godfrey?'

'Are you becoming a mind reader, Miriam, or were you listening in?'

40

Miriam blushed and rubbed her floury hands together. 'Who else gets you into such a state on the phone?' She grinned, winked, then turned away and disappeared back into the kitchen.

'Hello, Godfrey? Are you still there? Good. It's all sorted. Do you have an address? I've never been to London before, I'm not sure I can find my way around.'

'I have a room in a house in Westminster, not too far from the Home Office. Victoria Station is only half a mile away. I'll meet you there. Which train will you get?'

We settled on an early morning train that would get me to the capital by 11 o'clock. The excitement in Godfrey's voice was matched by my own. I couldn't wait to see him. It seemed a lifetime since we had made love in the back seat of his Alvis gangster car.

'Are we staying in your rooms or can you find us a nice discreet hotel for the weekend?' I asked.

'I'll try to get us a hotel room but they're not easy to find these days, there are so many military bods and out of towners working on government business. The Albion is only a short walk from where I'm staying. I'll have a word on the way home this evening. The manager is a decent sort, I've met him in the pub a few times.'

I was already planning what to pack as the conversation went on. I pictured us together, me in my polka dot dress and Oxford heels and my handsome lawyer in his gangster clothes, a navy pin-striped suit and his black Fedora.

'So, let me get it right, I'm staying for two nights, the Saturday and the Sunday and I'll be coming home Monday morning?'

'Correct.' I could visualise him smiling at the other end of the line. 'Don't expect much by the way of fancy food while you're here. You probably eat much better than we do at the moment. Some of the restaurants are doing shady deals with the black-market operators, so we might find somewhere that will dish up a minuscule steak and two veg.'

I wasn't the slightest bit worried about the cuisine. I'd have lived on bread and dripping if it meant a weekend with Godfrey.

'If I bring some steak with me, will they cook it?' I asked, half-seriously.

'You're more likely to be held up at gunpoint at the station,' Godfrey laughed. 'A decent sized steak is like gold dust down here.'

After hanging up the phone I went out into the fields to find Barney and let him know about my trip. I stopped at the paddock on the way and fed a couple of carrots to Bessie, my shire horse and Bray, our retired, ancient donkey who had only been with us a few months but had settled in very quickly.

'The eighth... that's a Saturday, isn't it?' Barney squinted as he worked out the dates in his head.

'That's right, I'll be leaving Saturday morning and coming back on the Monday.'

'That's fine, I'll keep an eye on the place. Don't you worry about that.'

'I'm not worried, Barney. I know you can easily run this place without me.'

Barney nodded, missing the compliment. 'I've been at it long enough.'

I smiled and put my hand on his forearm.

'We'd be lost without you, Barney.'

As I turned away to leave, he spoke again.

'Don't forget we're all going to Old Jack Tanner's funeral tomorrow. They're having a special evening service to allow as many people as possible to pay their respects.'

'I haven't forgotten, Barney. It's not often we get to say goodbye to a local hero.'

'The funeral is taking place at six-thirty. It's family only in the church but we're all allowed to line the path from the lychgate to the front porch. I'll be disappointed if we don't get half the town turning out.'

I walked slowly back to the farmhouse, deep in thought. Old Jack had been almost eighty. He had part-owned a small fishing boat that was kept at Margate. During June, Jack and his younger brother, Cecil, answered the government call and had met up with the rest of Operation Dynamo's little ships at Ramsgate where they sailed across the channel to Dunkirk to rescue our army that were being besieged there. Not satisfied with rescuing a dozen men, as soon as they had disembarked, he set off again to bring back another dozen, but on that trip he caught a bullet in his back, a wound from which he never fully recovered.

On Wednesday evening, we arrived at the church to find hundreds of people lining the pavements waiting for the horse-drawn carriage carrying Old Jack's coffin to arrive. Barney, Miriam, Stephen, Harriet and all of our remaining farm workers, found a place on the paved avenue that led from the lychgate to the church. By the time the hearse arrived the crowd was three deep on either side of the path. We broke into spontaneous applause as Jack's younger brother, Cecil, led Old Jack and his family down the hill towards the church. At the entrance, on either side, a dozen soldiers stood to attention and saluted as the coffin was carried in.

Forty minutes later, the soldiers saluted again as Jack was carried out. By now, as Barney had predicted, it seemed that half of the residents of the town were lining the pathway, or standing among the gravestones to see our own hero off.

No doubt, over the next few years, many a local hero will pass through the lychgate or will be remembered in our prayers at the cenotaph on Armistice Day, but that day was special, we were burying our first.

I had managed to hold it together until, as the coffin passed us by, Stephen, our child evacuee, stood rigid and saluted as though the King himself was standing in front of him. I placed my hand on his back and wept as I thought about the fathers, husbands and sons that Old Jack had rescued and how grateful they and their families must be feeling towards an old man who had done his bit. Then I thought about our farm's own heroes, the lads who had signed up on the first day of war and had been sent off to fight and maybe die in some foreign land. We had heard nothing from any of them since July, when Benny's pregnant wife received a heavily redacted letter saying he was alive and well and looking forward to seeing us all again.

I'm not a particularly religious person, but as Old Jack's coffin was lowered into his newly dug grave I sent up a prayer to God, asking him to receive our hero into his care, then I begged him to ask his angels to keep an eye on our farm boys, wherever they were in the world.

Chapter 6

As Jess was getting ready to visit her mother in hospital on Friday evening, her mobile rang.

'Hello, Jess, it's Bradley.'

'Hi, Bradley, how are you? Fully recovered I hope?'

'I'm fine, I've still got some bruising but at least the pain has eased.'

'Have you heard anything else from the police about the men who attacked you?'

Bradley grunted. 'No, nothing, Jess, but what I went through is nothing compared to what you and your mother have suffered. How is she?'

'I'm just about to visit her actually,' replied Jess. 'Her cuts and bruises are healing but it will take a lot longer for the mental scars to heal.'

'I can imagine. I heard all about it on the lawyer's grapevine. What a brute that man was... Sorry, sorry, Jess, he was your father, it must be awful for you.'

'I've had better times I have to admit.' Jess took a deep breath and sighed.

'They aren't going to charge her with anything are they? I know a really good defence barrister if you need one.'

'I don't know yet, Bradley, we should find out in the next few days. It's very kind of you to think of us and I'll let you know if we need one. She did kill him, so I suppose there's a chance she could be charged with murder or manslaughter, but in reality she was only desperately defending herself. The domestic abuse campaigners will be up in arms if they stick one of those charges on her.'

'I still don't understand how a man can brutally attack his wife like that? Was it all down to wanting a share of the money you were left in the will?'

'Yes, basically it was the money. He was in a lot of debt to people he shouldn't have got involved with. That's his own fault, I have no sympathy there, he was a gambler to the end.'

There was silence for a few seconds then Bradley spoke again.

'I erm, wondered if... have you thought about the phone call I made before Christmas?'

'I have, Bradley, but I'm not sure it's a good idea.'

'Why not, Jess? Please give me a chance to say sorry to your face. I acted despicably the last time I saw you and I really want to apologise for that.'

'You were in a lot of pain; my grandmother had made a formal complaint against your legal practice and you had just found out my father might have been responsible for your injuries. It was an understandable reaction.'

'I was downright rude. The injuries are no excuse. I'm not like that, Jess, I really don't know what came over me. Perhaps it was the medication I was on.'

'You're forgiven, Bradley, don't feel guilty.'

'So, can we meet?'

This time it was Jess's turn to be silent.

'Jess?'

'What about Leonora?'

'What about her?'

'She's still your wife, Bradley. You forgot to mention that when we were in my bed.'

'Technically she's still my wife, but—'

'Technically? You still sleep with her.'

'I don't... well, not for months. It's complicated, Jess. She's a staunch Catholic, as are her parents and my mother. They don't believe in divorce; they have very old-fashioned values.'

'She said that you tell her everything.'

'Jess...'

'Everything, Bradley. I can't believe you'd go into all the sordid details.'

'I didn't tell her *everything*. Not in that sense. I said we'd spent the night together and I told her how much I liked you.'

'She said I'm not like the others and she's going to be keeping an eye on me. Well good luck to her, Bradley because there'll be nothing for her to see.'

'Jess, please?'

'Bradley, I like you, I really do, but I don't need your ex-wife following me around and poking her nose into my business. My life is complicated enough at the moment without her sticking her oar in.'

'She's all talk, Jess, honestly.'

'She's a jealous woman, Bradley and that makes her very dangerous.'

Jess looked at the big clock on the wall and picked up her shoulder bag.

'I'm sorry, Bradley but I have to go now. It's visiting time.'

'Yes, sorry, don't let me keep you, but please, Jess... let me come to see you, or maybe we could meet for coffee, somewhere on neutral ground where you wouldn't feel hemmed in.'

'I don't know, Bradley; it doesn't seem like a good idea to me.'

'Please, Jess. Just half an hour.'

Jess sighed deeply.

'Half an hour and that's all. I'll be going into town next Wednesday. I'll be in the car park outside the Uni at one.'

'Bless you, Jess. You won't regret it.'

'Just make sure you're not followed,' Jess replied before hanging up.

Chapter 7

'Hello, Mum.' Jess smiled broadly as she stepped between the line of beds.

'Hello, love. How are you?'

'Never mind me. You're the one in hospital.' Jess studied her mother carefully. The swelling to her face had almost gone but the purple and yellow bruises remained.

'Mum and Marjorie just left, you only just missed them.'

Jess grinned. 'I know, we planned it. Grandma refused a lift from me. She wanted to make her own way here. How was it? Not too bad I hope.'

'You know your gran, Jess.'

'Oh dear, I hope she didn't lecture you about letting the family down, because if she did, I'll be having words.'

'No, no, nothing like that. She was telling me all about the cruise she's going on. It's always about her.'

'Oh, Mum.'

'I was quite pleased to be honest. I think she knew what she was doing so don't be too hard on her. She was just trying to take my mind off things.'

'Hmm.' Jess wasn't convinced. 'As you said, Mum, it's always about her.'

'Aunt Marjorie is so excited. She could hardly sit still.'

Jess smiled. 'She is looking forward to it so much.'

'She said they went shopping in the sales on Boxing Day.'

'Did they? I bet the shop assistants loved that.'

'Aunt Marjorie said she wanted to buy a swimsuit but your gran said it was too revealing for a woman of her age and wouldn't let her have it. She got her some long shorts and a t-shirt instead.'

Jess frowned. 'Grandma treats her like a toddler. She might be a bit timid, but she can be far more independent than she is allowed to be.'

'She was really disappointed about the swimsuit.'

'Which shop was it in? Aunt Marge can't be more than a size ten. I could see if I can find it.'

'She said it was in Ogden's, it was red... oh, with a flower embroidered on the left breast.'

'I'm on it, Mum. I'm going into town on Wednesday, I'll see if they still have it in stock.'

'It wasn't cheap, Jess. Fifty-five pounds, I think she said.'

Jess laughed. 'She deserves something nice.' She looked around the ward, where only two of the six beds were occupied. 'Have they sent everyone home for Christmas?'

'No, Mrs Jarvis died in the night on Christmas Eve and Mrs Lawrenson has been taken into intensive care. There's just me and Olive here now.' She looked across at the old lady opposite who was happily singing along to Frank Sinatra whilst wearing a set of ear buds.

Jess put her hand on top of her mother's.

'Mum, I know it's not a nice thing to talk about and it's probably the reason Gran went on and on about the cruise, but...'

'It has to be talked about, love, there's no getting around it.'

'Have the police said anything at all about any charges you might face?'

'I've got a domestic violence officer, she's called Val, she comes in every day, but she hasn't heard anything yet. Apparently, they're still liaising with Sussex police, getting some details about what Bi... Owen was up to down there. She wasn't supposed to tell me, but he was living with someone.'

'Well, you knew that, didn't you? When you rang him and a woman answered and asked who you thought you were, ringing her man in the middle of the night.'

'I did a lot of stupid things, Jess. I didn't realise what a hold the booze had over me.'

Jess leaned forward and hugged her.

'Oh, Mum, with all you had to put up with over the years I'm not surprised you needed to use alcohol as a crutch.' She sat back and looked at Nicola. 'You look so much better now you've had the chance to dr...'

'Dry out? It's all right, Jess. I know what I was like. I was insufferable. I'm so sorry for putting you through all that.'

Jess patted her mother's hand, then looked away as a tear appeared in her eye. She blinked it away, then turned back.

'That's all behind you now. All you need to concentrate on is getting better. Have they given you a hint as to when you might be able to go home?'

'The doctor said soon, possibly on Monday.' She suddenly gripped Jess's wrist. 'I can't go back to the house, Jess... I can't. I'd just relive it all the time.'

'You're not going back, Mum. I'm going to get your stuff out of there and let the letting agency know you're terminating your contract. We've got one of Nana's little cottages lined up for you in the New Year, but until then, you're staying with me.'

Nicola's head fell onto Jess's breast and she burst into floods of tears.

When she had recovered, Jess thought a change of subject was in order and picked up three of the four cards that were sitting on the unit next to Nicola's bed, leaving the one she had sent herself, where it was.

'Gran sent you a get-well card? Has Hell frozen over? She only begrudgingly sends birthday cards.'

'I know.' Nicola grinned. 'Have you read the message inside?'

'"Feel better soon. I hope they aren't too hard on you." Oh, for goodness sake.'

'I know. Aunt Marjorie sent the one with the Peppa Pig thing on it.'

Jess laughed. 'The other is from Mrs Kaur from the shop. "I hope you feel better soon. Hurry back, we miss you." Oh, Mum, isn't that lovely?'

'I did get a lump in my throat when I read it,' replied Nicola. 'I thought she hated me.'

'No, Mum, you should have seen her when... you know, when it was all going off, she was very worried about your welfare. She really likes you. She trusts you to run the shop on your own. She only tries to do her best for you.'

Nicola nodded. 'I'm lucky she's keeping my job open for me. I don't deserve it.'

Jess patted her hand again. 'Of course, you deserve it. Now, have the police given you your keys back? I'm going to clear that house tomorrow.'

'I've got my spare set; they kept the originals. They said I can't go back in without their permission as it's still a crime scene.'

'I'll drop in to see them in the morning,' said Jess. She smiled at her mother. 'I can't wait to get you home.'

Chapter 8

At 9.30 on Saturday morning, Jess arrived at the front desk of the police station on Middle Street where she was greeted by a bored-looking young constable who cheered up immediately as she walked into reception.

'Hello,' he said. 'How may I help? Would you like to report a crime?'

'The crime, if it ever was one, has already been committed,' replied Jess.

The constable looked puzzled. 'Really? Do we know about it?'

'It concerns the death of Owen Griffiths. He was... never mind. I believe Detective Inspector Rachel Barraclough is dealing with the case.'

'Owen Griffiths? Ah, the wife beater. I'll get her for you, Miss, erm?'

'Griffiths. Owen was my father.'

'Oh... Look, I didn't mean anything by that comment, it's just... I'll get D.I. Barraclough, wait there please.'

The clearly embarrassed policeman disappeared through a gap behind a tall cupboard. He returned a few minutes later with the detective. She flashed a quick smile at Jessica, then invited her through to her office.

'I thought it best not to discuss this matter in public. Please sit down, Jessica.'

Jessica pulled out a dark-wood seat and did as requested.

The policewoman was in her early fifties with honey-blonde hair tied back in a pony tail. She took off a pair of dark-rimmed spectacles and looked across at Jess through piercing blue eyes.

'How can I help?'

'Well, there are a few things, the most important is whether or not my mum is going to be charged with an offence.'

'I can't say yet, Jessica. We haven't finished the investigation. We're still waiting for a report from the Sussex police force.'

Jess bit her tongue to quell the urge to say, *I know that*. Instead, she held the inspector's gaze and asked another question.

'The doctor said she might be able to go home after the weekend. Will she be allowed to stay with me? You aren't going to chuck her into a cell, are you?'

'Now, I can help you with that one as it's already been decided that your mother isn't a risk to the public.' She held up a hand as Jess leaned forward to speak. 'However, there will be certain constraints. She must live with you or her mother. She will be placed under a strict six pm curfew and she will have to wear an ankle tag so that we can keep an eye on her whereabouts.'

'An ankle tag? You're joking? She's hardly going to get the first flight out of the country. Where would she go for pity's sake?'

This time D.I. Barraclough held up two hands, palms facing Jess.

'Those are the rules, Jessica. It's that or a stay on remand.'

Jess shook her head. 'I don't believe this. She was almost killed herself. She's the victim.'

'A man died, Jessica. We can't just let her return to a normal life until the matter has been fully investigated and the file sent to the CPS.'

'The CPS?'

'The Crown Prosecution Service. They'll make the decision on whether or not to prosecute, not me, not anyone in this building.'

Jess sighed. 'All right, I understand.' She got to her feet. 'Can I pick her up directly from hospital if they release her, or will I have to get her from here?'

'We'll visit her on Monday morning. You can take her home from the hospital.'

Jess nodded. 'Oh, there is one more thing. Can I have the keys to her house, or is it still classed as a crime scene? I promised I'd clear her things out today. She can't face going back there.'

The inspector nodded curtly. 'I'll get them for you.' As she passed the edge of the desk, she stopped and turned to face Jess. 'Please don't think I am unsympathetic, Jessica. I have been in a similar situation myself, though thankfully it didn't end in the same manner. We are only doing the job the public expects us to do.'

Jess looked at her feet. 'I know, and I'm sorry if I appeared annoyed. I just want to get her home and let her try to rebuild her life.'

Rachel took hold of Jess's hand. She smiled warmly. 'I really hope she can.'

Although Nicola had relatively few possessions, it still took Jess two trips in her little Toyota to clear the house. She had rented the property furnished, so the vast majority of the furniture and larger items belonged to the landlord. Jess left the heavy, old-fashioned TV, the ancient toaster, kettle and saucepans behind. If the lettings agency wanted her to remove them she would go back. Nicola's iron had been taken as evidence.

Back home, Jess offloaded her mother's belongings and carried them up to the spare room. She had recently bought a new bed for it and Nicola's bed linen was still in good condition, so she dropped the quilt cover and sheets into the washing machine and sat watching them slosh around as she thought about what the coming days might bring.

When the washing was done, she hung the bedclothes on an indoor line in the parlour and made an omelette for dinner. She had just finished eating when her phone rang.

'Jess? It's Sam.'

'Hi, Sam, I was going to give you a call tonight to see how you both were.'

'How I am you mean. There is no both anymore.'

'What?'

'Jamie's gone back home... to his parents that is. Unless he's about to turn up at your door again.' She gave a harsh laugh.

'Sam!'

'Oh, I'm only joking, Jess. I know where he's gone because I helped him move his stuff out, lock, stock and golf clubs. It's amazing how much room I have in the flat now.'

'Oh, Sam, I'm so sorry. I really thought you two had a forever thing.'

'Nothing lasts forever.' Jess picked up a crack in her friend's voice as she spoke.

'Do you want me to come over or do you want to come here? I've got nothing planned tonight, or tomorrow.'

'No, I wouldn't be any sort of company for you.'

'That doesn't matter, you need close friends at a time like this.'

'I'll just wallow in my own misery for a couple of days, Jess. It's the best thing really. I've stocked up with wine so I won't be alone.'

'Oh, Sam.'

There was silence for a time, then Jess spoke again.

'Was it... I mean... who made the decision, was it a joint one?'

'Me. We talked for ages and it kept coming around to the same thing. What he wants in the near future isn't what I want. In the end there was no room for compromise. He wants a little wife at home, looking after the kids, putting a meal on the table. I want to be out there doing stuff. I'm too young to be tied to a kitchen sink.'

'Oh dear. I suppose that's that then. Poor Jamie. He's very different to a lot of men I know. Most just want the good times, they don't want the domestic drudgery.'

'I'm on their side,' Sam laughed. Jess heard her glug at her wine glass. 'So, I'm footloose and fancy free, just like you, Jess. Give me a few weeks to get over this and we can hit the town. Hey, how about we go to Spain for a fortnight? Maybe the Canaries?'

'That sounds wonderful. I'll keep you to that. It can't be too soon though, I'm going to be looking after Mum, she's coming out of hospital on Monday. She has to stay here and wear an ankle tag.'

'You're kidding me?'

'Sadly, I'm not. I've been clearing her house today. I've got all her stuff here.'

'You should have given me a shout, love. I'd have given you a hand. It must have taken forever in that little tin can of yours.'

'Oi! You leave my little car alone. She does the job.' Jess chuckled. 'Anyway, she hasn't got much. It only took me two trips.'

Jess waited as Sam took another deep drink of wine. It was a full twenty seconds before she spoke again.

'So, what else is new in your world, Jess?'

'Not a lot. I told you about the cruise for Grandma and Aunt Marjorie, didn't I? Apart from th... Oh, there is one bit of news that will tickle your gossip fancy. Bradley rang me again. He wants to meet up.'

'JESS! Stay away. That wife of his could be a serial killer.'

Jess laughed out loud. 'A serial killer? I know she had a quiet word with me but that's stretching it a bit.'

'Listen, sweetheart, you need to be careful with that one. She's creepy.'

'You haven't met her,' Jess replied.

'I don't need to. I can read between the lines. If she was in a murder mystery, she'd be first on my list of suspects.'

'She's a bit strange, I have to admit, but... well she is still married to him, even if it is in name only.'

'Name only? Didn't she tell you she was still sleeping with him, that he tells her all his dirty little secrets?'

'Watch it, Missis,' Jess laughed again. 'I'm no one's dirty little secret.'

'Oh, you know what I mean... anyway. I take it you said no.'

Jess didn't reply. When Sam spoke again, she could hear the disbelief in her voice.

'Come on, Jess. Don't tell me you agreed to see him?'

'Only for half an hour and it will be in the car park near the Uni, not here, or at his.'

'You're a bloody soft touch, Jess. You always see the best in people and it always comes back to bite you on the backside.'

'He's all right, Sam. I feel a bit responsible for what happened to him that's all. We're not going to pick up where we left off.'

'I'll believe it when I see it.'

'Honestly. Bradley is nothing more than my lawyer now. I had to see him again soon anyway. He's sorting out the lease on one of the trust's cottages for Mum. I'm probably going to have to sign something.'

'Tell him to mail it. Jess, I despair, I really do.'

'Don't worry, Sam. It's over between us.'

'It had better be. I'll be ringing you on Wednesday evening. I want a full, blow by blow report.'

'Yes, miss.'

Sam sighed. 'What am I going to do with you? Right, I'm off, I've got an appointment with a bottle of wine and my conscience. Catch you later, hun, and... well, just don't. All right?'

'All right. Enjoy the wine.'

That evening, Jess wrote a second draft of her article and did some extra research on the Internet before finalising her document and emailing it to the editor of Femme Fatale. She found the stories of the brave women who disappeared into the French underground, exhilarating. These women were just as brave, if not braver than some of the men fighting during the war.

Many were captured, tortured and either shot by firing squad, or sent to one of the concentration camps where they were executed alongside the millions of innocent Jews and Gypsies. She was particularly fascinated by a woman called Nancy Wake, who had a price of five million Francs placed on her head. She was known to the resistance as The White Mouse because of her ability to evade capture. On one operation she was spotted by an SS sentry but before he could raise his rifle, she killed him with a single Judo blow to the throat. Nancy survived to see France liberated, but her husband, who never got out of the country, was caught, tortured and executed.

Wake was only one name among hundreds of brave women from all over the world who came to Britain offering their services to help defeat Nazism. The vast majority of them were caught and captured, but it didn't stop more applying for the role. As she posted the article to the editor, Jess thought once again about Alice, the strongest woman she had ever known. She picked up her 1940 memoir, but noticing the time, she placed it gently back down on the table, flicked off the light switch and climbed the stairs to her bed where she dreamt about the heroes that didn't live to collect medals or even get a mention in history until many years after the war had ended.

Chapter 9

On Sunday morning, Jess washed the breakfast dishes then sat down at the table with a cup of tea and picked up Alice's memoir.

Alice. September 1940

After several quite major delays, the train pulled into Victoria Station some forty minutes late. The main hold up had been at Gillingham where the bus station and an area around the train station had been bombed the previous week. The former had been almost flattened by the severity of the attack.

As the train pulled into London, I could see some bomb damage to buildings but a lot less than I had imagined. Back home, we all thought the capital must be lying in ruins. Our RAF boys must have hit the German planes harder than we thought they had in the skies over Kent.

I saw Godfrey waiting patiently, standing by a huge government poster which encouraged us to 'Keep Calm and Carry On.' *That's easy for you to say, Mr Churchill,* I thought. I was having great difficulty remaining calm, knowing that my gangster lawyer lover was only a few yards away.

As I stepped off the train with my little suitcase, it was all I could do to stop myself rushing towards him for a movie-style, railway platform kiss. Instead, although breathing deeply, I walked as demurely as I could across the platform to where Godfrey stood waiting. He was dressed in his usual manner, a gangster hat and pinstriped suit with the extra wide lapels. I kept my aloof demeanour until I was about three feet away, then dropping my case I launched myself at him, throwing my arms around his neck, my lips landing on his with enough force to make his teeth rattle. His arms wrapped around my waist and we stood there, impervious to the other passengers for a good two minutes. Eventually, I pulled my head away, then unable to resist that magnetic smile, I launched a second front, kissing him, then pushing my head alongside his, whispering in his ear, telling him just how much I had missed him.

When I eventually let him go, I noticed we were the centre of attention for many of the passengers who were standing around, waiting for the next train. I glared at their open-mouthed faces belligerently. I was almost twenty-one, my hormones were on fire and I didn't care who knew it.

Outside the station, Godfrey managed to find us a taxi and we chatted about the farm and how the town had been managing since he had last been at home.

'Gillingham caught it bad last week. The bus station has pretty much gone and a lot of houses were damaged. I can't believe the government evacuated kids there from London. Talk about out of the frying pan.' I looked out of the taxi window at the undamaged streets. 'We all thought you were having an horrendous time of it.'

'It's been hit and miss to be honest,' Godfrey replied. 'Sorry about the pun, but parts of the city have fared worse than others. The East End has had it bad.' He paused as he called to the driver to pull over and leaned across me to pay him before opening the back door of the cab.

The Albion hotel wasn't The Ritz, that was for certain, but it was clean and the counter staff were friendly, none of them questioning why a man, obviously approaching forty, would have booked a room to share with a girl young enough to be his daughter.

'Sorry it's a double room,' Godfrey whispered as he took my little case and carried it up the stairs, 'but I was lucky to get it. I asked for two singles but the hotel is full. We only got this one because the manager talked a salesman into taking a room at the pub down the road at a much-reduced rate. The manager is very friendly with the landlady there.' He winked at me and I laughed.

'We could have stayed at the pub, Godfrey. I wouldn't have minded.'

'You wouldn't have like it, Alice. It has a bit of a reputation.' He tapped his nose. 'The clientele is mostly made up of ladies of questionable virtue, if you catch my meaning?'

'No wonder the salesman jumped at the chance,' I said, laughing.

Godfrey opened the door to our room and stood back to allow me to enter first. I wouldn't say it was spartan exactly but there wasn't much in the way of comforts. A dark-oak bed covered in a bedspread that had seen many better days, was the centrepiece. There was a single wardrobe with a wonky door, a wooden chair and a sink with an aging mirror above it in the corner.

'I'm sorry but the bathroom is at the end of the hall,' Godfrey apologised.

I didn't care if it was in the building next door. I was with Godfrey and that's all that mattered. I couldn't wait to get into that bed and feel his arms around me. My face must have betrayed my thoughts because Godfrey suddenly kicked the door shut, dropped my case on the floor and took me in his arms. Kissing me with gusto, he eased me back towards the bed. My hands went to his jacket, I tore it open then grabbed his shirt with both hands and began to tug it from his trousers. My carnal intentions were stymied when we heard a loud knock on the door.

'Bugger,' said Godfrey, tucking his shirt back in.

'Tell whoever it is to sod off,' I hissed, red faced and more than slightly peeved.

Godfrey opened the door, had a ten second conversation, then looked back over his shoulder at me. 'I'm needed on the telephone. Work, I assume.' He smiled at me and winked. 'I won't be long. Don't go starting without me.'

I pointed towards the door. 'Go on then, get it over with and... please hurry back,' I begged.

Godfrey was gone for almost fifteen minutes. When he returned, he found me propped up on the pillows in a sulk.

'I'm so sorry, Alice. Something's come up.'

'Not in here it hasn't,' I muttered.

'I've got to go in, there's been a bit of a mix up. I can't go into details as it's war business, some new regulations that the police will have to enforce. I'll be as quick as I can.' He walked to the side of the bed and took my hand. 'I really am so sorry, Alice.'

'Are you the only lawyer in the office?' I stuck out my lip in a genuine childish pout.

'No, but I'm the most senior, well, one of three, but one has had to go home urgently and the other can't be found after travelling across town to another of our offices in the West End.'

My heart sank. 'How long will you be, have you any idea?'

'It should only take an hour or two, less if Johnny Adlington manages to find a bloody telephone that works in Bow Street.'

I hauled myself off the bed. 'I'll come with you,' I said, making my way across to the sink to tidy my hair in the mirror.

'No, please, Alice. I can't bear to think of you standing around in a busy corridor while I'm in a meeting. I hope it will only be an hour or so, but sadly, it could be longer.'

My shoulders sank.

'I hate this war.'

Godfrey put his arms around me and I sank my head onto his chest. 'I'll be as quick as I can.'

I suddenly made a decision.

'I'm going for a walk. I've never been to London before; I think I'll see some of the sights.'

'But how will I know where you are if the meeting finishes earlier than I anticipate?'

'You won't,' I said with a sly smile. 'I might have met a handsome captain, a Jolly Jack Tar or someone.'

Godfrey feigned shock.

'Have no fear, I only have eyes for you,' I said. 'I'll tell you what. Give the hotel manager a ring, he can call me to the phone if I'm in.'

'And, if you aren't in?'

I looked him in the eyes, licked my finger and placed it onto his lips. 'Then you'll just have to come back and wait here until I am.' I looked at him seductively. 'It will be worth the wait, I promise.'

Godfrey looked at the door, then me, then the bed. 'Dammit,' he cursed. Then giving me a quick peck on the lips, he rushed out of the room. 'Don't get lost,' he called as he reached the top of the stairs.

After Godfrey had gone, I grabbed my jacket and bag, and walked downstairs to reception where I asked a nice young girl called Kathy how to get to Buckingham Palace. Kathy drew a map on the back of a leaflet that warned patrons that 'Walls Have Ears' and pointed in the general direction. In the end I didn't need a map, it was easy. I just had to make my way back to Victoria Station, then up past Victoria underground and onto the aptly named, Buckingham Palace Road.

I couldn't get too close to the palace; it was surrounded by anti-aircraft gun emplacements and sandbags. Huge barrage balloons floated in the breeze on all corners of the building. As I approached, a soldier stepped out from a small wooden hut and held up his hand as a command for me to stop.

'I'm sorry, miss, but you can't go any closer.'

'That's all right, I understand,' I said sadly. I cursed myself for forgetting to bring my camera. I had put it out for packing but had left it on the telephone table in the lounge. Thinking about it now, it was probably a good job I didn't stroll up to the palace pointing a camera at it. There was almost certainly a regulation about it, Godfrey may even have written it himself.

I stepped away as a chugging truck carrying a dozen soldiers pulled up. Seeing all the troops on the streets really brought it home to me how deep into the war we were. I asked directions to the Houses of Parliament from the sentry box guard and instantly regretted it as he immediately asked for my I.D card. Under his suspicious gaze I pulled the brown card from my bag and handed it to him.

He asked me for my name, address, date of birth and then questioned me as to why I was in London when I supposedly lived on a farm in Kent. I thought about telling him the truth, that I was spending the weekend with my married lover, just to shock him, but in the end I decided to lie and told him I was visiting my sister and her husband who was doing important work for the government at the Home Office. I suggested he ring them and ask for Godfrey Wilson who would be in a meeting.

The mention of the government department seemed to ease his concerns and he handed my I.D. card back, and smiling, pointed me in the direction of Westminster.

I took a leisurely stroll along Birdcage Walk and sat by the Houses of Parliament for a good half hour before making my way over Westminster bridge where I found a busy café and ordered a pot of tea. I turned down the offer of cakes as I didn't want to ruin my appetite. Godfrey had gone to a lot of trouble to book us a table for an evening meal and I didn't want to ruin the experience by only picking at my food.

Forty minutes later, I made my way back the way I had come until I reached the Foreign Office where I sat on a bench watching the building for a while, ready to pop up shouting 'Surprise', if Godfrey came out of one of the many doors. I had no idea where the Home Office was but I assumed it had to be somewhere close. The place was teaming with soldiers. Some manning anti-aircraft guns, others marching back and forth in front of the building under the command of a loud-mouthed sergeant, who stuck out his pompous chest as he strode alongside, barking orders.

After half an hour I gave up waiting for him, found my way onto Victoria Street and followed it to the underground station where I turned left and walked past the train station until I came to Pimlico Road where the Albion hotel was situated.

Godfrey had called three times, leaving three separate messages, the last of which said that he wouldn't be back until at least five-thirty. Thankfully, Johnny Adlington had been found and he would be back in the office by then.

Sighing, I went back to the room and after taking off my shoes and jacket, I threw myself onto the bed where I studied the cracks in the ceiling as I cursed the war and everyone involved in it.

Two hours later I was woken by Godfrey gently shaking my shoulder. I sat up, alarmed, then realising where I was and who was waking me, I swung my legs over the bed and stretched my arms above my head. It was dark outside the window. The room was lit by a porcelain table lamp.

'What time is it?' I asked with a yawn.

'It's just after six. We'll have to go soon; I booked the table for seven-thirty and I have to nip back to my rooms first to get changed.'

'Have you only just got back?'

'No, I got back about half an hour ago.'

'Half an hour? Why didn't you wake me?'

'You looked so peaceful; I didn't want to disturb you.'

'I wouldn't have minded, Godfrey.' I got to my feet, put my arms around his neck and kissed him on the lips, then I jerked my head back, breathed into my hand and held it under my nose.

'Bed breath! Oh my God, don't tell me I have bed breath.'

'Your breath is fine, Alice, don't worry.'

'I have to clean my teeth.' I opened my suitcase and pulled out a little leather bag that held my make-up and tooth powder. Grabbing my toothbrush, I rushed to the sink and spent a good three minutes ferociously brushing my teeth.

'Look the other way,' I garbled, without opening my mouth. When he did as I asked, I spat the contents of my mouth into the sink, then rinsed and spat again. Placing my toothbrush and tin of powder on the shelf just below the mirror, I wiped my mouth on the checked towel hanging from the sink and turned around to Godfrey with my arms held wide.

'Now, we can have a proper kiss,' I said, seriously.

'Sadly, a kiss is all we have time for,' he replied with a frown. 'I'm sorry, Alice.'

'You'll just have to make up for it later,' I said, pulling him close.

Forty-five minutes later, dressed in my best polka-dot dress, Oxford heels and silk stockings with my chestnut curls hanging around my shoulders and my gas mask box bouncing on my hip, I followed Godfrey up the stairs to his room on the top floor of a government funded house in Westminster. I was quite surprised at the poor condition of the single room. It was heated by a two-bar electric fire which sat in front of a dingy-looking fireplace. The carpet was threadbare and the wallpaper was peeling. In the corner of the room was a mahogany desk, piled with papers and law books.

'They didn't spend a fortune on you, did they?' I said, looking around.

'No mod-cons at all,' he replied. He opened a wardrobe and pulled out a fresh, navy pinstriped suit and a white shirt. Pulling open a drawer, he selected a red tie and left the room carrying the clothes over his arm.

'My bathroom is along the landing too,' he said. 'I do hope it hasn't been recently occupied.'

I sat on Godfrey's single bed as I waited for him to wash and dress. The mattress was as hard as rock, I don't know how anyone could sleep on it. At the side of the bed was a small wooden table on which sat a terracotta lamp and a photo frame. Picking it up, I immediately felt a lump in my throat as instead of looking at a photograph of his family, I found myself looking at a picture of me, wearing my Saturday night clothes, standing outside the Old Bull. I remembered Amy taking it; I had no idea how Godfrey had got his hands on the picture. I smiled back at my own, smiling image and slid it onto the table as a clean-shaven Godfrey walked back into the room.

'Where did you get this?' I asked, pointing at the photograph.

'Ah, you've discovered my little secret,' he said.

'Well?'

'I persuaded Amy to give it to me. I hope you don't mind, Alice. I miss you so much when I'm stuck down here.'

'I thought you would have a photo of your wife and kids,' I said.

'I have two pictures on my desk at work. I haven't forgotten all about them.' He picked up the gilt frame and looked at the picture, lovingly. 'I kiss this every night before I go to sleep. Is that wrong of me?'

'Oh, Godfrey.' I threw my arms around him and kissed him. 'You old romantic you.'

Chapter 10

Taylor's restaurant was literally a three-minute walk from Godfrey's lodgings. The small pane windows were decorated by crosses made out of sticky tape, or 'scrim' to stop shards of glass flying around during an air raid. Because it was after dark and the blackout was in force, thick heavy curtains had been hung across the inside to prevent any chink of light sneaking out.

Inside, the restaurant boasted a dozen tables, all but one of which was occupied. The clientele was mostly made up of the military, some sharing a table of up to four. Others were taken by men, in the main older than Godfrey, sitting opposite ladies not too much older than myself.

A waiter wearing a stiff collared shirt and a black bowtie, greeted us at the desk and showed us to a two-seater table at the back of the room. He pulled out the chair and pushed it under my bottom as I began to sit down, then he fussed about, handing us a one-page menu and a wine list that was shorter than the shopping list that Miriam took to the market on Saturday mornings.

'I'm afraid we only have a very limited wine cellar and I apologise in advance for the price,' he said to Godfrey, who having eaten in the restaurant before, ordered a Portuguese red without as much as glancing at the list.

The wine was lovely, so much better than the meal itself. The Brown Windsor soup looked like it had been scooped out of a murky pond. The tiny pieces of meat floated on the surface like frog spawn. Although Godfrey had warned me about the portions we would be served up, I was still shocked by the size of the steak. Back home, pre-war, we would have a steak that would almost fill a plate on its own, but since rationing began, we had decided not to be greedy and shared a big steak between two. The tiny portion that was placed in front of me that night was only half the size of the palm of my hand, and it was tougher than an old boot.

The meal came with an assortment of veg and a gravy that appeared to be made of the same ingredients as the soup. I ate it all anyway, I was determined to make the best of it.

During the meal, I told him all about the happenings on the farm and how the whole town had turned out for Old Jack's funeral. Godfrey's eyes never left my face as I waffled on. Eventually I let him get a word in, but he soon turned the conversation back to Spinton.

'It's lovely to hear you talk about our home town, Alice. The only conversations I take part in down here are all about the war, or how a change in regulations might upset the entire country.'

I kicked off my right shoe and pushed my foot towards his. Finding his ankle, I rubbed against it and winked.

He grinned a huge grin, showing off his perfectly straight teeth.

Godfrey skipped desert, but I ordered a bowl of plum pudding, which arrived lukewarm and lumpy. The fruit had been minced to within an inch of its life and the custard, made with powdered egg, was almost as thin as the gravy.

I forced about half of it down, then pushed my plate away. When I saw Godfrey's concerned face, I rubbed my stomach and told him I couldn't manage another bite. It was true enough, but not for the fact that my stomach was full.

We left the restaurant at nine, just in time for the air raid siren to go off. I jumped as the wailing alarm sounded. I had never heard one before; our town having never suffered a bombing raid.

Godfrey grabbed my arm and twisted me around as the huge bright searchlights lit up the sky and the anti-aircraft gunners fired tracers into the night.

'We have to get to the underground station,' he yelled, trying to make his voice heard above the siren.

Just then the first squadron of planes came into view and the bombs began to fall. I held my hands over my ears as the buildings were blown apart on the streets behind us.

'We'll never make it,' Godfrey shouted. He began to drag me back towards his lodgings. 'Come on, we've got to get off the street.'

He took my hand and began to run, I tried to keep up but it was hard to keep up in my heels, so I pulled my hand away from his, and with one elbow pressed against a red-brick wall for balance, I dragged my shoes off and hurried to catch up with Godfrey who had stopped a few yards away.

We reached his lodgings as the bombs began to explode around us. He opened the front door and pushed me inside before slamming it shut. I stupidly made for the stairs but Godfrey snatched at my hand and dragged me through an open door and into the dining room.

While I looked around, panic-stricken, Godfrey lifted the table cloth.

'Remember the advice?' he asked.

I nodded. The government had put out many a leaflet on the subject of how to survive a bombing raid. Most houses were being fitted with Anderson shelters in their gardens but for those without, the advice was simple, if a little basic. Crawl under a table, under the stairs, or if you were stuck upstairs, under your bed.

I looked to the window where the flashing lights from the burning buildings and tracer bullets lit up the night. Then the bombs began to fall on our street.

'That table won't protect us,' I screamed.

Godfrey grabbed my arm and led me out of the dining room and into the hall, opening a small door under the stairs, he pushed me inside, then pulling the door shut behind us, he groped about in the pitch blackness until he found me.

Feeling something soft and warm under my bare feet, I sat down, panting almost as deeply as I had when I gave birth to Martha. Suddenly the cubby hole lit up as Godfrey pulled a box of matches from his pocket and struck one.

The space under the stairs had been used before, that was for certain. The owner of the house had gone to some trouble to make it comfortable. On the floor was a single, but very deep mattress which was covered in a thick eiderdown. There were two pillows, a couple of bottles of water and a biscuit tin which, when opened, contained half a dozen candles and a pocket torch.

Calling out in pain, Godfrey dropped the spent match on the floor before striking up another and lighting one of the candles. Dripping hot wax onto a brick ledge, he wriggled the base of the candle in the hot gloop until it gripped, then slumping down beside me, he waved his burnt fingers in the air.

I took hold of his injured hand and put his singed finger into my mouth.

Godfrey whistled. 'Is this the official treatment for burned fingers?' he asked, drawing in a deep breath.

I nodded, 'Mmmm.'

'I bet Florence Nightingale never tried this on her patients,' he laughed.

We sat quietly for a few minutes listening to the muffled sound of the exploding bombs and the rattling noises coming from the Ack-Ack guns.

'How come the owner of the property isn't in here with us? He, or she, has gone to a lot of trouble only to leave it vacant during the first big attack.'

'It's a married couple,' Godfrey replied. 'Mr and Mrs Latimer. I believe they've gone to visit their daughter in Watford. I hope they're not suffering the same fate as us up there. They're nice people.'

I pulled Godfrey onto the mattress, then moved him onto his back and straddled him. 'Well, I'm happy they aren't here or I wouldn't be able to do this.'

'That racket is rather annoying though,' he replied, reaching up to my breasts. I tutted and pushed his hands away. 'Be patient,' I scolded.

I got to my feet and slid my pants down my legs, then unbuttoned the front of my dress. Reaching behind, I unhooked my brassiere, then straddled him again. As I rubbed myself gently against him, I noticed a dome shaped radio set sitting on the floor behind Godfrey's head. I leaned over him to switch it on, only to hear a repeated warning about the air raid that was taking place around us. I twiddled with the tuning knob until I found a music station, then leaned back again. I slowly unbuttoned Godfrey's shirt and kissed him all the way from neck to navel, then I undid the buttons of his trousers, opened up them up at the waist and slipped my hand into his underpants.

Godfrey moaned. 'Christ, Alice.'

'No, it's just Alice,' I said, quietly. Lifting his hands to my breasts, I lowered myself onto him and by the light of the flickering candle, with the booming and banging of the war dampened by the soulful sound of a jazz band playing My Funny Valentine, we left the dangerous world behind us for a while as we made slow, gentle love.

The next morning I awoke, still half naked, with Godfrey's arms about me. The candle had long burned out, so I eased myself away from my softly-snoring lover and fished about in the biscuit tin until I found the hand torch. Flicking it on, I aimed it towards where I thought the door should be and crawled across the floorboards. Pushing the door open, I stuck my head out into the hall and breathed a sigh of relief when I saw that the house hadn't taken a hit during the night. I straightened up, and holding my still unbuttoned dress together, hurried up the stairs and looked for the bathroom.

When I returned, I walked through to the living room and looked out into the brick-laden street. My heart sank as I saw a woman with her arms around two small children looking desperately at the pile of rubble that used to be someone's home. I let out a little sob and prayed that it wasn't theirs.

Godfrey was just rousing when I flashed the torch back into the darkness under the stairs. He held his hands in front of his eyes as the torch beam pieced the gloom.

'What time is it?' he asked.

I shone the torch onto my wristwatch. 'It's just after seven,' I replied. 'You won't recognise what's left in the street. This house appears to be undamaged. We were so lucky, Godfrey.'

'That's the worst I've ever seen it,' he said, sitting up. He began to fasten his shirt and I pulled my brassiere over my naked breasts, hooked it up, then did up my own buttons. After an increasingly frantic search, I found my pants stuffed down the side of the mattress. As I pulled them on, Godfrey leaned up on his shoulders, yanked up his trousers and fastened the buttons of his fly.

I backed away to the door, then ducking down, still shining the torch beam into the cubby hole, I stepped out into the hall and waited until Godfrey joined me. Once he was out, I reached in, switched off the beam and by the light from the open door, dropped the torch into the biscuit tin.

My bag, and both our gas mask boxes were still lying on the floor of the dining room where we had dropped them the night before. I pulled on my shoes, and made another trip to the bathroom to tidy up my appearance, then we left the house and picked our way through the bricks and broken glass until we found the main road.

By the time we had made our way back to the Albion hotel we were both covered in brick and plaster dust. Godfrey's dirty face was steaked with tears.

'Hitler will pay for this,' he said.

I held him close and put my grimy face against his. 'I do hope so, Godfrey. I really do.'

The Albion had survived the raid unscathed and we went up to our room to catch up on some proper sleep. Neither of us much fancied the idea of going out to wallow in the misery of the poor Londoners who had lost everything overnight. So, when we got up at one o'clock on Sunday afternoon, we went down to the hotel dining room and ordered up a pot of tea and a plate of sandwiches. Godfrey made a twenty-minute call to his office to check for any problems, then we spent the rest of the afternoon chatting with our fellow guests in the hotel lounge as we listened to the surprisingly upbeat newsreader trying to spin some good news into the depressing bulletin.

That evening, we dined at the hotel. The manager apologised before serving our dinners and to a smattering of laughter, paraphrased the pre-meal prayer by announcing, 'for what you are about to receive, may you be well and truly, bloody grateful.'

In actual fact, the meal of stew and dumplings was much nicer than the one Godfrey had paid an over-the-top price for on the previous evening. We washed it down with glasses of warm, bottled beer but all of us agreed that it was the most satisfying meal we'd had for ages.

At eight, we decided to walk over to Godfrey's digs to get him a change of clothes for work on the Monday. I had changed earlier, but poor Godfrey was still wearing the dust-stained suit he had worn the previous evening. We stepped out into the night and walked slowly through the bomb-ravaged streets, stopping now and then to watch firemen and the ARP crews digging in the wreckage in the vain hope of finding someone alive.

When we reached his lodgings, Godfrey changed into clean underwear, a fresh white shirt and the suit he had worn on the Saturday. He folded the dirty one up and stuffed it into a brown paper bag before pulling on a baggy, black, wool-knit overcoat and switching off the lights.

We left his room and made our way back to the hotel, arm in arm, whispering sweet nothings and promising each other the best night of our lives. Sadly, the sweet talk only ever got as far as promises because as we neared St James's Park underground station we were once again treated to the sound of the air raid siren. Searchlights suddenly broke up the black night and the deep hum of heavy bombers broke the eerie silence. It was almost as though the entire city had been waiting with bated breath for them to arrive.

Godfrey took hold of my arm and led me around the corner to join a bustling line of people already queuing to get down the steps to relative safety. By the time we reached the top of the stairs we could hear the explosions as bombs hit the residential streets around us.

In the tunnel at the bottom of flights of steps, we picked our way through the assorted collection of humanity until we found a space right at the end of the platform in front of a cream painted wall. We couldn't hear the bombs or any sort of aircraft noise down there, but there was a steady hum of conversation and the sound of babies crying. Some families had bought food with them and set up impromptu picnics on the floor of the platform. The pungent smell of sweaty bodies wafted along on the warm breeze that swept through the tunnel. I looked at Godfrey and pulled a face, but short of walking along the rails into the darkness, there was little we could do to escape it.

Godfrey took off his voluminous black overcoat and laid it on the platform floor to give us a little bit of comfort, and we sat talking quietly with our backs against the wall, looking over the mass of huddled people that had swarmed into the tunnel. A little further along the platform, a man in a scruffy tweed jacket began to play a harmonica and a couple of minutes later, a man wearing a gaberdine mac joined in on an accordion. I was staggered that someone would take the time to pick up a heavy instrument like that while an air raid was in progress, but as he played it so beautifully, I decided that it must have been of great sentimental or monetary value to him. Other tunnel squatters had brought brass clocks, small paintings and even bird cages, complete with budgies.

As the night wore on, we lay down on Godfrey's overcoat. I pushed my bottom into his groin and he pushed his knees up behind mine and wrapped his arm around my waist. I sighed happily.

'Well, this isn't the weekend break I thought it would be,' I said, quietly.

'I can only apologise, Alice. I wouldn't have put you in danger if I'd known anything like this would happen. We've only had sporadic bombing until last night.'

I wriggled my bottom into his groin. 'I wouldn't change it for the world, Godfrey. I've never had so much excitement in my life.' I paused, then wriggled my bottom again, smiling as I felt a strong reaction. 'I feel I'm part of it all now anyway. What stories I'll take back with me.'

Godfrey grunted and pushed his genitals against my backside.

I raised my head and looked along the platform, most people were either asleep or engrossed in their own thoughts or conversations. We had a few yards of space between me and the first of the masses. I slipped my hands up my dress and pulled my knickers down to my knees before wriggling around as though I was trying to get comfortable, then I dropped a hand behind me and rubbed at Godfrey's trousers.

'Here? Are you sure?' he croaked. He lifted his head to look over me at the crowd of people on the platform.

'I'm sure,' I replied. 'I didn't come all this way for a one-night stand in a broom cupboard.'

Godfrey chuckled, then gasped as I opened his fly and pulled out his penis.

'Oh, God, Alice.'

'No, as I told you, it's just Alice,' I said. My breath came in gasps as I lifted the back of my skirt and guided him into me. Godfrey began to move slowly. I closed my eyes and pushed back against him and for the next five minutes it was as if we were the only people on the planet.

We remained in the station until the next morning when we climbed the steps and blinked in the early morning sunlight.

The bombers had done their worst, yet again. In my head, I made a note of the dates, in the certain knowledge that the 8th and 9th of September 1940 would be etched on my memory for the rest of my life.

I picked up my suitcase from the Albion and Godfrey and I walked through the broken streets to Victoria Station where my train arrived some thirty minutes late.

The station had been hit overnight but the platforms, signals and track were undamaged and a limited service had been put in place. We hugged for what seemed like only a few seconds, but was probably a good five minutes before a uniformed guard blew a whistle and the train tooted its readiness to be off.

'Goodbye, my darling. I'm so sorry the weekend turned into the mess it did.' Godfrey smothered my face in kisses, my tears mingling with his as I struggled to get any words out.

In the end, all I managed was, 'please stay safe, Godfrey.'

He pulled away, holding both of my hands.

'I love you, Alice. I've never felt like this about anyone in my life before.'

I ran the back of my hand across my face to wipe away fresh tears. I snuffled, then wiped my nose on the back of the same hand.

'I love you too, Godfrey. Come home soon.'

'I'll try, sweetheart.' Godfrey wiped his own tears way, then waited as I climbed onto the train. I hurried along the carriage until I found a seat overlooking the platform. Godfrey stepped forward to the side of the train and splayed his hand on the window. I placed mine on the other side of the glass and blew him a kiss with my free hand.

As the train pulled away, I looked along the platform at the forlorn figure in the gangster hat and pinstriped suit, carrying his love-stained overcoat over his arm.

'Au revoir, my darling man,' I sobbed.

Chapter 11

On Monday morning, just as she stepped out of the shower, Jess received a phone call from the police informing her that Nicola was to be released into her care.

'She will have to follow strict guidelines, Jessica,' D.I. Rachel Barraclough informed her. 'You can pick her up anytime this morning but you must bring her straight to the station to complete the formalities of her release. A technician will come to your home to fit her electronic ankle tag and the monitoring unit after our meeting. I'll go through the list of dos and don'ts when I see you.'

Feeling a mixture of excitement and annoyance at the news, Jess dressed quickly and drove to the hospital where she found her mother sitting on her bed with her small travel bag already packed. She got to her feet as Jessica walked around the floral partition that had been pulled around the bed at the end of the small ward. The bruising to her face had begun to fade, her eyes were clear and bright. She looked a good ten years younger than she had a couple of weeks previously.

'Hello, Mum, I've come to spring you from jail.' Jess grinned and gave her a huge hug.

'I can't wait to get out of here. I was beginning to think I'd have to wait until after the New Year before they let me go.' She picked up her bag and marched quickly to the locked ward door. 'Come on, nurse,' she uttered, impatiently. 'I've already signed my release forms. I've got my prescription and I've made sure my bowels are functioning.'

A smiling red-headed nurse came out from behind the desk at the nurses' station and waved an electronic pass across the blinking sensor. The double doors swung open immediately.

'Goodbye, Nicola. Take care of yourself and remember what we discussed. Dry January isn't a punishment, it's part of your treatment.'

'How could I forget,' Nicola muttered as she hurried though the door.

'Mum?' Jessica tugged at her sleeve. 'Say thank you,' she hissed.

Nicola forced a smile and looked back into the ward. 'Thanks for looking after me,' she said, coldly.

'You could have done better than that, Mum,' said Jessica as they followed the exit signs down the seemingly endless corridor. 'It wasn't their fault you were kept in. They were the ones caring for you.'

'Oh, I know that, Jess. Honestly, I'm not ungrateful. I just want to breathe in some fresh air. It feels like I've been locked up for months.'

'We have to stop off at the police station on the...' Jessica paused as a policewoman turned the corner and stopped in front of them.

'Phew, just caught you. Sorry, I'm running a bit late.'

Jessica looked puzzled. 'I thought she was being released.'

'Oh, she is, don't worry. I'm here to make sure you make it to the station. We can't risk her absconding.' She looked along the corridor towards the closed, double doors. 'I was supposed to be in the corridor when you came out of the ward, but, as I said, I was a little late getting here.'

'We won't squeal on you, you're safe,' Nicola said, turning back towards the exit.

The officer looked at Jess, mouthed 'thank you' then hurried after Nicola. 'You'll have to come in the car with me,' she called.

'I'll follow you,' called Jess.

The officer smiled as she looked back over her shoulder. 'Don't get lost now. It's a whole three streets away.'

Detective Barraclough pushed a small stack of forms across the desk and leaned on her palms as Jess picked up a pen to sign. She held out her arm towards a grey suited man who was sitting on a chair by the filing cabinet.

'Jessica, this is Mr Williams from CAPITA, the company the government uses to monitor offenders. He will follow you back to the farm and will fit both the ankle tag and a home monitoring device. Your mother is free to leave the property between the hours of six am and six pm but between those hours she should consider herself to be under curfew. She must report to the police station every afternoon between two pm and five pm. She must never attempt to remove the tag or tamper with the monitoring system. She must abstain completely from alcohol.' She looked directly at Nicola whose head had snapped up on the news. 'I know it's New Year's Eve tomorrow but rules are rules. If you are found to be under the influence of alcohol at any time during your release period you will be remanded in custody until the decision is made on any charges you might face.' She turned back to Jessica.

'She's lucky in a way. In a few months' time, we'll be introducing sobriety monitors which test body sweat for any alcohol content. This one...' she pointed to a silver metal box on the desk, '... is the common or garden ankle tag reader and will just monitor her whereabouts during the curfew.'

'It all seems a little over the top to me,' said Jess with a sigh.

'The law is the law, Jessica. At least you'll have her at home, look on the bright side.'

The detective smiled warmly, then continued.

'By signing these documents, you are agreeing that you will, to the best of your ability, supervise Nicola whenever she is out of the house. You are also agreeing not to provide alcohol for her consumption either at home or in any licenced establishment.'

'It's all right, we're both off the booze. I'll do Dry January with her,' Jessica replied. 'I drank the last of my wine stash last night. There's not so much as an empty bottle for her to sniff.'

She finished signing the papers and slid them back across the desk.

'One other bit of news.' The detective picked up a single sheet of paper from a blue folder. 'The Coroner has opened and adjourned the inquest into your father's death. It will resume when our investigations are complete. The post mortem has been carried out. Your father died from blunt force trauma to the head that caused bleeding to the brain. But of course, we knew that anyway. His body can now be released should you want to arrange the funeral.'

As Jess got to her feet, the detective nodded to the CAPITA officer who picked up his silver case, opened the door and waited until Jess and Nicola had walked through before following them out.

'I'm in the little white Toyota,' Jess called as she reached the front door of the station.

The man waved the silver case at her and chuckled. 'Don't worry, I won't lose you, I've got you tagged.'

An hour later, the monitor had been set up and Nicola had been fitted with a two-tone, grey ankle tag. She lifted her leg and showed it off to Jessica.

'Do you think they'll catch on as a fashion item?' She sighed, then put her foot back on the floor. 'It's a good job it's winter. I'd hate to have to wear trousers all summer long just to hide this bloody thing.'

'It will be all over in a few weeks, Mum, don't worry.' Jess patted Nicola on the shoulder as she passed on her way to the kitchen. 'Fancy a cuppa?'

'Have you got anything stronger than tea?' Nicola called.

'I can do an espresso?'

'You know what I mean.' Jess turned to find Nicola standing behind her.

'I told you, Mum, I drank the last of my wine stash last night. I don't have any booze in the house.'

'It's New Year's Eve tomorrow.' Nicola looked shocked. 'I always have a drink to see in the New Year.

We used to give you a little bit of watered-down wine, remember?'

'Once, I remember getting a bit of wine once, when I was about nine, but that was because you were given a bottle for Christmas that you hid away from Dad. I can't remember any other time.'

'We always celebrated New Year's Eve, Jess.'

'You and Dad did, Mum. You even left me on my own while you both went out to the pub.'

'We weren't gone too long, were we?'

'You came home absolutely slaughtered at four in the morning.'

Nicola flinched as though she'd been hit.

'Once, Jess, once. I know we were in the wrong but...'

'I stayed over with Nana every year after that.'

'Yes, well... Look, all I meant was, it would be nice to have a little drink to see in the New Year.'

'You're not allowed to drink, Mum. Anyway, I'll be in the dock myself if I buy some and let you have any of it. You heard the detective.'

'Nonsense. How is she ever going to know? Come on, Jess. Nip to the offie.'

'NO!' Jess picked up the kettle and angrily turned on the tap to fill it. 'Don't ask me, Mum because I'm not going to listen. You're dry until this mess has been sorted. Do you really want to risk being sent to jail?'

Nicola sniffed. 'No, of course I don't. I just thought we might be able to celebrate me getting out of hospital, that's all. I was only thinking of having a single glass, just to toast the future.'

'There'll be plenty of time for that once the charges have been dropped.' Jess walked slowly across the kitchen and hugged her mother. 'You look so much better when you're sober, Mum. You must feel better too.'

'I feel different, that's for certain.' Nicola pulled away and sat down at the big table. Picking up Alice's memoir, she flipped it open to a random page. 'Still working on this are you?'

'Yes, she was quite a woman, wasn't she?'

'I can't say I knew her that well to be honest. My mother didn't allow me to have much to do with her when I was growing up.'

'You missed out there, Mum. She was a wonderful woman.' Jess pointed to the memoir. 'To go through what she did whilst bringing up a young family and running a business... it's inspirational really. I wish I had her strength and fortitude.'

'She was a tough old bird, that's for sure, but she didn't do a lot for her family.' She looked up at Jess. 'Most of us anyway.'

Jess tutted. 'Now you're sounding like Gran,' she scolded.

'It's true enough, Jess. She kept it all to herself.'

'She earned it. She sweated blood for it... and... she did help you and Dad, but he blew all the money in a week-long gambling session. I can't believe you still stick up for him after what he did. He got us thrown out of our lovely little house and we had to live in a slum. How could you forgive him for that?'

Jess turned away, teary eyes. Nicola got to her feet, followed her to the sink and placed a hand softly on her back.

'I didn't, haven't, could never forgive him for that, Jess. Nor could I ever forgive him for stealing from you. He stole from me too. I had to hide your child benefit book because he would have taken that too and the bit I got from it meant you and I could eat most days.' She patted Jess on the back and looked down at her feet. 'You never saw the worst of him.'

Jess turned and pulled her mother towards her.

'I know you had it hard, Mum. I'm not saying you didn't. I honestly don't know how you got through it. He was a self-centred monster and, while I can't say I'm glad he's gone, there is a big part of me that is very relieved that we won't have to put up with him anymore.'

They held on to each other for a full two minutes before Nicola pulled away. Wiping her eyes, she walked towards the lounge. 'Do you think I should go to his funeral after what I did?'

'I think you should do what you feel you need to do, Mum. I can't imagine anyone else will want to attend. I'm going to ring the funeral directors on Thursday. I'll take any date they've got. The sooner it's over the better.'

She turned away and looked out of the kitchen window, slowly shaking her head. *How had it come to this?* Absentmindedly, she flicked on the kettle. 'Would you like more tea, or would you prefer a coffee this time?'

'Tea will be fine, love. I'll get a dose of the twitches if I have espresso and we don't want to send the wrong message down that monitor.'

Chapter 12

On New Year's Eve, Nicola helped Jess clean up the breakfast dishes before sitting down at the big oak table with a fresh pot of tea.

'I'm worried about my car, Jess, it's been parked outside Mrs Kaur's shop for ages now. There are some really unsavoury types living on that street.'

'Oh my goodness, I'd forgotten all about your car, Mum. I got all the stuff I thought you might need but I didn't even think about the car.'

'I know it's an ancient old thing and I doubt it will pass the MOT this time around, but I wouldn't like to be without it. Cars do come in handy.'

'They do, I'd be lost without mine,' Jess admitted. 'I'm surprised you could afford to keep it running though, Mum.'

'Your grandma used to pay the road tax and MOT which I think was fair, seeing as she used to use me as an unpaid taxi service. I only ever had third party insurance, so that only worked out at about fifteen pounds a month.'

'If it needs a bit of work, I can help you with that this year. You should be able to afford the running expenses now that you're not paying all that money out in rent.' Jess paused and looked quickly up at the clock. 'Which reminds me, I need to speak to Bradley about when I can pick up the keys to your new cottage. I'm meeting him later today.'

'I can't wait to see it,' Nicola said with a smile. 'I'm sure that damp, dirty house was the cause of a lot of my problems. It was so depressing.'

Jess patted her mother's hand. 'Well, you're out of it now, so hopefully your mood will improve.'

'Do you think we could pick my car up later this morning? I really am worried about what those little thugs will do to it.'

'Do you want to go now? I can give you a lift up and you can drive it back.'

'No, not yet, I want to drop in on Mrs Kaur to see about my job, but I've got to work myself up to it.'

Jess smiled. 'Okay, we'll go nearer lunch.' She picked up her phone and dialled Bradley's number. 'Hello, Bradley. I know we're meeting later but do you have a minute to discuss Mum's cottage?'

'Hi, Jess, you must have been practicing telepathy. I was just about to ring you to let you know that the old girl's daughter dropped the keys in at the agency on Saturday. She asked if we'd like to keep the furniture and white goods as it would cost them more money to clear the house than they are worth. I said we'd take a look before making a decision. Normally I'd have asked them to remove everything, but seeing as your mum doesn't have a lot of her own things, it might make sense for her to rent it furnished.'

'That sounds like a plan,' Jess replied. 'When do you think we could have a look at it?'

'I'll take you over after we meet today if you like?'

'Erm, that might be a bit tricky, I have to do a bit of shopping for my aunt. I could meet you there later this afternoon if you could spare half an hour.'

'I'll find time,' Bradley replied cheerfully. 'How about three-thirty?'

'Perfect,' said Jess. 'Mum will be so excited to see it.'

'Oh, you're bringing... Yes, of course she will. I'll get the contract drawn up over the next few days. We'll just set a peppercorn rent so she won't have any problems finding the money.'

'I'd have helped her with it anyway, but thank you, Bradley, you don't know how grateful we are.'

The lawyer was quiet for a moment, then he spoke again.

'We are, I mean, we're still meeting in town, aren't we? I really would like to speak to you on your own for a few minutes.'

'Yes, I'll be in town at one, just as we agreed.'

She could hear the relief in Bradley's voice. 'Great. I'll see you then. I can't tell you how much I'm looking forward to it.'

Jess put the phone down and sighed.

'What's the matter?' Nicola asked.

'Oh, something and nothing, Mum. I'll sort it out later.'

Jess picked up her cold coffee, took a sip, pulled a face and tipped it into the sink. She flicked the switch on the kettle and tipped a spoonful of Barista style granules into her cup, smiling to herself as she thought about the lovely afternoon she had spent by the river with Bradley, how well they had got on and how she had thought she had met someone special. Then she thought about the baggage he came with and her resolve stiffened. Leonora, the clinging wife he had somehow forgotten to tell her about would always be in the background if Jess was to allow their relationship to continue, and she wasn't the sort of person who would be content to remain in the shadows.

I'll just tell him we can't go back to where we were, she said to herself. *I'm sure he'll understand.*

At twelve, Jess drove Nicola to her old street, where they found her mother's Ford Ka in the same condition as she had left it. Jess walked around the vehicle, taking a critical look as Nicola opened the driver's door and slipped inside.

'I don't think I've ever driven this thing completely sober,' she said thoughtfully.

Jess kicked the near side front tyre and pulled a face. 'Don't even joke about it, Mum.' As she walked around the front of the Ford, Mrs Kaur came out of the shop.

'Hello, Jessica,' she ducked down to look inside the car, then rapped on the window. 'Hello, Nicola, I hope you're feeling better now.'

'Hello, Mrs Kaur. Mum was going to drop in to see you.'

Nicola rolled her eyes, then climbed out of the car. 'Hello, Mrs Kaur. I'm much better thanks.'

The shopkeeper's mouth dropped open when she saw how much Nicola's appearance had changed since she had last seen her in the shop. She looked ten years younger, her clothes were clean and nicely ironed, her hair was combed and hung around her shoulders instead of being swept back in an untidy pony tail.

'You look wonderful, Nicola. Well done you.'

Nicola flashed her a quick smile. 'I was going to have a chat with you about my job, if I still have a job that is.'

Mrs Kaur returned Nicola's smile. 'We can't wait to have you back. We've missed you. Come in, have a cup of tea and we'll talk about it. You can ease your way back in if you like. No need to overexert yourself.' Walking back to her shop she opened the door and Nicola heard the familiar bell tinkle.

'Jess, don't you have to be somewhere else?' she asked.

Jess checked her watch. 'I do, but not just yet. I've got a bit of time.'

'There's no need for you to wait. I could be here for ages. Mrs Kaur and I have a lot to talk about, I could be an hour or more.'

Jess pulled a face. 'I don't know, Mum. I'm supposed to supervise you when you're out and about.'

'Oh, Jess, what do you think I'm going to get up to with Mrs Kaur in tow? She can supervise me instead. Off you go. I know my way back to the farm. If I can drive there drunk, I can find my way sober.'

Jess gave in. 'All right, Mum, but be careful. Go straight home when you and Mrs Kaur have finished your chat.'

Nicola gave Jess a kiss on the cheek and turned towards the shop. As Jess moved towards her car, she heard Nicola call out.

'Oh, Jess, sorry. You couldn't give me a few quid for petrol, could you? I know there wasn't much in the tank when I parked it up. I couldn't fill it up because Owen... sorry, Bill, had taken all my money.'

Jess reached into her car, grabbed her bag and pulled a twenty-pound note from her purse. 'Here you are, Mum. That should keep you going for a week or so. You won't need to drive too far because I'll take you anywhere you need to go.'

Nicola took the banknote and slipped it into her pocket. 'Thanks, love.'

'I'll be back in time to take you to the police station,' said Jess.

'Oh, I'd forgotten about that. What a nuisance.'

'It has to be done, Mum. I'll take you at three-ish.'

'I'm not a child, Jess. I can go on my own you know. I really don't need you to hold my hand all the time. Go and do what you have to do, I'll walk to the police station when I leave here, it's only around the corner.'

Jess thought about it. *She's right, I can't stand over her like a prison guard all the time. She has to prove to herself that she can be trusted as much as to me.*

'All right, Mum. I have to meet Bradley then pick up a few bits for Aunt Marjorie from the sales. I'll see if Bradley has time to look over the cottage at lunchtime as he originally planned. I'll drop Auntie Marjorie's stuff off too. I'll be home for three-ish, four if I have to wait to see the cottage.'

Nicola smiled. 'Off you go then... Oh, tell you what. Why don't you pick up a bottle of alcohol-free wine while you're in town? At least we'll be able to see the New Year in with a drink of some description.'

Nicola's chat with the shopkeeper lasted all of fifteen minutes. After drinking two cups of tea and chatting about the goings on in the street while she had been away, Nicola agreed to go back to work, initially for one day a week for the next month, then she'd gradually increase her hours until she was back to her normal shift. As she walked back into the shop, she picked two bottles of red wine from the shelf and placed them on the counter.

'Are you sure you should be having wine, Nicola? You've only just come out of hospital.' Mrs Kaur looked doubtful.

'Jess is having a few friends around to see the New Year in. Don't worry, she won't let me have more than a single glass. She thinks she's my mother now.'

Mrs Kaur laughed and rang the sale into the till. Handing back the change from the twenty-pound note, she pushed the till drawer shut and looked towards the door as a customer entered the shop.

'Goodbye, Nicola, it's wonderful to see you looking so well. Happy New Year to you and Jessica. I'll see you next Wednesday, it will be so nice to have you back at work.'

Nicola waved as she walked out of the shop with the two bottles of wine tucked under her arm. She clicked open the central locking on her car, slipped inside, then put both bottles on the passenger seat. Starting the engine, she put the car in gear and pulled slowly away.

As she turned the corner at the bottom of the street, she pulled into a cul de sac, grabbed one of the bottles, unscrewed the cap and took a long drink. Closing her eyes, she smiled, breathed deeply, then took another long, slow gulp of the wine.

Chapter 13

As Jess turned into the car park in front of the Uni building, she had to wait as a white transit van pulled out before she could find a free spot. As she parked up, a black VW Golf followed her into the car park and reversed into a spot about three rows behind her.

Jess got out of her car and looked around for Bradley's silver Mercedes spotting it on the row in front of hers. He had obviously seen her park up as he got out of his car at exactly the same time as her. He waved a greeting, smiled and nonchalantly locked his car as he walked towards her.

'You're looking fabulous as usual,' he said reaching out both arms towards her.

Jess stepped back, avoiding the intended hug. 'Hello, Bradley.' She looked him up and down. *Was that a new, grey suit?* It certainly looked it. *He's had a haircut too.* She smiled back at him, only too aware of what she had found so attractive about him in the first place.

Bradley's arms dropped to his side but the smile stayed in place. 'So, should we go somewhere a little less open to the elements or are we going to freeze to death out here?'

'I did say we'd talk out in the open, Bradley.'

'You did, but I didn't expect it to be as cold as this.' His arms folded across his chest and he rubbed his biceps for effect. 'We could get a coffee; the café is open... or we could get a soft drink at the Wonky Donkey? What do you think?'

Jessica had begun to feel the cold herself. She had left home thinking she was only making a quick trip to collect her mother's car, but now, standing on the breezy car park, she felt a definite chill in the air.

'Not the café,' she said quickly. 'Let's go to the Wonky Donkey for a quick orange juice.'

The pub was busy, especially the area at the back where food was being served. Jess found a table near the front door while Bradley ordered up fresh orange juice at the bar. He sat down opposite her and placed the drinks carefully on the table. They sat in awkward silence for a few moments, then Jess laughed.

'It's like we only just met, isn't it?'

'In some ways I wish that were true.' Bradley reached across the table and took Jess's hands in his. 'I wouldn't make the same mistakes again. I'd tell you the truth about Leonora. I'd have been a lot more understanding about your circumstances and I'd definitely have been more considerate when it came to your family. What is it they say? You can choose your friends but not—'

'I love my family,' Jess interrupted. 'Look, I know they're not as tight as the Swiss Family Robinson, and I know they are a dysfunctional lot at times, but I love them. They are my blood relatives and I'll back them whenever I can.'

Bradley shook his head. 'Jess, I didn't mean—'

She held up a hand to silence him.

'I know what they are, Bradley. I grew up with them. I went through some hard times, especially in my childhood, but Nana spared me the worst of it. My mother did her best... what she saw as her best at least, and my grandmother and great aunt really could have expected something in the will under different circumstances.' She pulled her hands away from Bradley's, picked up her drink and sipped at it. 'Even my father believed he was doing his best for us by chasing his crazy dream. He wasn't of course, everyone else knew that, but he really did think he'd hit the jackpot one day. I'm sure he went into those casinos or to the illegal card schools dreaming about arriving home laden with expensive presents for us.'

Bradley smiled sadly. 'That dream cost him his life.'

'It did, and it cost you a terrible beating.' Jess reached out and laid her hand on top of Bradley's. 'I would have done anything to stop that.'

Bradley looked across the table with a new hope. It soon dissipated.

'Our relationship can't continue, Bradley. It's not fair on me and it's not fair on your family.'

'To hell with my family.' Bradley slapped the table, spilling juice from his glass. 'Sorry, I'm sorry. I honestly didn't mean to get angry today. I'll sort it out with Leonora, Jess. I'll talk to my mother. I'll let them know that I have no interest in anyone but you. My marriage can't be repaired, it's time Leonora moved on. I can fix this, Jess.'

'Bradley, she's your best friend, you tell her everything. She has the keys to your flat. She does your shopping for you, probably your laundry. You still sleep with her... albeit on very infrequent occasions. She might see other men, but her designs are still set on you.'

'That's not true, Jess. She doesn't love me. She hasn't for years, that's why we split up in the first place. She was seeing other men within a couple of years of our wedding day. She said they were a distraction from the boring life she claimed to lead. A distraction. Can you believe that?'

'She won't give you up, Bradley, she made that very clear when we spoke. Personally, I think she's hiding behind the Catholic distaste for divorce. Her parents, and your mother might feel that way, but they're from a different generation. If Leonora was so devout, she wouldn't have had all those dalliances, wouldn't have jumped into bed quite so easily. No, it isn't her religion. I think she just likes causing mischief. I think she likes to be in control. When she becomes bored of pulling the strings, she'll cut them and let you fall. I'm sure of it.'

'Then help me cut them myself, Jess. Between us we can see off Leonora. It might take a while, but once she sees that she can't win, she'll finally let go and find someone else to manipulate.'

Bradley took hold of Jess's hands again.

'Jess, give me another chance. Please. I'm begging you.'

'Bradley, I—'

'Don't make the decision today, Jess. Take your time, think about it. Remember how good we were together that night? Remember that day by the river? We were made for each other.'

'I don't know, Bradley.' Jess slid her hands back across the table. 'It's not just her. It's your career too. She could quite easily do what grandma did and you'd be hauled over the coals again.'

'I'll step back from the trust. I'll no longer be a trustee. They can't do anything about it then.'

'But I don't want you to step back from the trust, Bradley. I want you as a trustee. I need you by my side whenever difficult decisions have to be made. I know I can trust you to put my best interests before anything else.'

'Of course I would. Regardless of our relationship.'

'There you are then. That's our future, Bradley. The best of friends and close business colleagues.'

'Jess, no, please. I want more than that.' He looked around in case they could be overheard before leaning across the table towards her. 'I love you, Jess. I knew it from the moment we first met.'

'You had a funny way of showing it, Bradley... anyway, as I said—'

'I was angry, confused. I couldn't believe the attack on me had been set up by your father. Please, don't say no until you've had time to think it over. Give me that much... Please?'

'All right. I'll consider it, but don't get your hopes up, Bradley. I really don't want to hurt you, but I can't see any future for us in a romantic sense.'

Bradley smiled thinly. 'At least I have a little hope, albeit a faint one. How much time do you think you'll need?'

Jess sighed.

'I don't know, Bradley. How long is a piece of string?'

'All right, I'm not going to rush you. Take your time, I just hope you come to the right conclusion.'

'I will, Bradley. When I make my final decision, it will be the right one for me.'

Outside the pub the pair stood in awkward silence for a full minute, then Jess spoke.

'Oh, we're supposed to be going to see the cottage later, could you fit it in a bit sooner?'

'Like when?' Bradley checked his watch.

'Like, now. Well, in about twenty minutes, I've got to pick up something from Ogden's for my aunt.'

'I can't, Jess. I've a meeting scheduled, I cut it short to make time for you later on.'

'Oh, that's all right. Don't worry about it. I'll hang around town for a while, then meet you at the cottage.'

'No, that's silly. Look...' Bradley fished in his pocket and came out with a bunch of keys with an address label tied to the chain of the keyring. 'Here, go and look at it on your own. See what you think. I really don't know much about furniture anyway.'

'Are you sure, Bradley? You've made changes to your appointment book.'

Bradley waved her protests away. 'It's fine, Jess. I won't have to rush through the afternoon clients now.'

'Thank you, Bradley. I'll have a look straight after I've been to Ogden's.'

She looked at him, then pulled him into a close hug. 'Don't be sad,' she whispered.

Bradley wrapped his arms around her, then, as she lifted her head from his chest. He turned his face to hers and kissed her on the lips. 'Just promise you'll think long and hard about us, Jess,' he said as he pulled away.

Across the car park, sitting in a black VW Golf, Leonora switched her camera to rapid mode and took shot after shot of the couple. As Bradley walked back to his car, she put the Nikon camera on the passenger seat and smiled to herself. She was about to pull away herself when she saw a handsome man who had been standing in the doorway of the café, walk towards Jessica. She smiled as he approached, there was an attraction there, she could sense it.

Josh came out of the café carrying two twenty-pound notes in his hand, intending to ask the staff of the Wonky Donkey if they could swap them for loose change. The café had run out of pound coins.

Spotting Jess kissing a smart looking man in a grey suit, he hung back in the doorway until the pair had said their fond farewells and the suited man had set off towards the car park before he walked out of the café entrance. Jess spotted him as soon as he stepped out onto the pavement.

'Hi, Josh. How's business?' she asked, cheerily.

'It's been good, thanks, at least, I can't complain. The word hasn't got around yet.'

'I was going to call in for coffee this week,' Jess replied.

'We serve good coffee. You'll enjoy it,' he said as he stepped around her.

'Are you in a hurry?' Jess asked. 'I've got time for a chat if you have time.'

'No, sorry. I've got to get some change for the till.' He waved the two banknotes at her. 'Fliss will wonder where I've got to.'

'Fliss?'

'Oh, sorry. Fliss is my first recruit. I've got a couple of Saturday girls lined up and I still need someone else during the week but I made a great start taking her on. She's attractive, friendly and knows the job inside out.'

'Oh, good, you look like you've landed on your feet then.' Jess forced a smile.

'So do you. Or at least you did a few minutes ago.' Josh flicked his head towards the car park where Bradley was just pulling away.

'Oh, Bradley? he's my lawyer.'

Josh's eyes opened wide. 'Your lawyer? Blimey!'

'What do you mean 'blimey'?'

'Well, it didn't look like you were just finishing a business meeting,' he said.

'It wasn't... Josh, it wasn't a business meeting. We have a very friendly relationship alongside our professional one.'

'I could tell that. It looked very friendly.'

Jess sighed.

'Josh, I don't understand why you're so off with me. Bradley is a good friend, we were close quite recently, but that's over. It didn't work out. That's what our meeting was all about... not that it's anything to do with you.'

Josh stepped back as though he had been slapped.

'I'm sorry, you're right. It has absolutely nothing to do with me.' He nodded to her then stomped off towards the pub.

Jess turned after him. 'Josh... Josh, I didn't mean it to come out as harshly as it soun...'

She broke off mid-sentence as the café owner disappeared into the pub.

Back in her Golf, Leonora clapped her hands with glee. Her instinct had been right. There was definitely something between them. That was a lover's tiff if ever she'd seen one. She smiled to herself, patted her camera, then strapped herself in, started up the car and slipped quietly out of the car park.

Outside the café, Jess thought about waiting to apologise to Josh, but a few seconds later, a twenty-something blonde came out of the café, stood next to her and began to look up and down the street. She was dressed in a short skirt and a thin top that was stretched tight across her ample breasts. She looked at Jess, then back up the road.

'Have you seen a gorgeous-looking hunk with forty quid in his sweaty mitts?' she asked.

'He's in the Donkey,' said Jess.

'I'll have to bend him over my knee when he gets back, I've got customers waiting for change in there.' She looked towards the pub and waved as Josh came back out onto the street carrying a bag of coins. 'Hurry up, handsome.' She laughed and gave Jess a wink. 'I've seen worse bosses,' she confided.

Jess turned away and walked quickly across the pavement towards the department store. She wondered how many applicants had applied for the barista job and whether Josh had bothered interviewing any of them after the busty blonde had turned up.

She was still pondering the subject as she stepped into the lift at Ogden's. *Why was she so concerned about who Josh chose to help run his café? Okay, she was attractive, but she was probably very good at her job too.* Still, her familiarity with her employer had got to her. She felt a mixture of annoyance and disappointment. She thought about dropping into the café when she'd done her shopping, but discarded the idea as quickly as it came into her mind. She had obviously burned her bridges with Josh and she couldn't see any way of repairing the damage. She scolded herself for feeling the totally unreasonable pangs of jealousy. Sighing, she stepped out of the lift and made her way through the aisles of clothing until she reached the beachwear department.

'Men,' she said under her breath. 'They are so predictable.'

Chapter 14

Jess loaded her sales shopping onto the back seat of her little Toyota, pulled out of the car park and drove the short distance to Pepper Hill, a narrow lane that ran between the High Street and Bottom End. The neat, white painted cottage with two lower bay windows was situated about half way up the sharp incline. She drove into the single parking bay at the side of a small, uncut lawn, pulled on the handbrake and picked up her bag from the front seat.

A flagstone path led from the parking bay across the front of the cottage to a recently fitted PVC front door. Inside, a narrow set of stairs led to the first floor while two doors in the hall led to a twelve by ten-foot lounge, furnished with a floral, two-seater sofa and a recliner armchair. There was a nice mahogany coffee table in the centre of the room and a large flat screen TV standing on a unit in the corner. A comfortable-looking seat had been built into the south west facing bay window which meant it would be a nice place to sit and soak up a little afternoon sunshine. There was a good-sized kitchen that contained an oak table and all the appliances Nicola would need. The back door led to a narrow, timber-built conservatory which looked out across an overgrown garden. Jess took a notepad from her bag and made a note to get a gardener/handyman in to sort it out before summer.

The stairs were bare tread, old timber, and led to a short landing with an airing cupboard containing a gas boiler. There was also a modern bathroom with an over-bath shower head, and two good sized bedrooms. The bed in the main room was an old-fashioned double with a coil-sprung mattress that reminded Jess of the one she had found in her own bedroom when she moved into the farm.

Making a note to purchase a new bed and mattress, Jess opened the double sized wardrobe and lifted the lid on an antique ottoman that sat at the foot of the bed.

The curtains and the kitchen window blind were all in good order but Jess would let her mother decide whether to change them or not. All of the rooms were painted in pastel shades which she was sure would add a calming influence.

Delighted with the cottage, Jess let herself out, locked the door and climbed back into her car to drive across town to Martha's house.

She was met at the door by an excited Aunt Marjorie, who led her into the lounge twittering about the things she was going to see on the cruise later that month. Martha was in her usual seat to the right of the TV. She looked up as Jessica entered the room.

'Jessica! To what do we owe this unexpected pleasure?'

'It's only a week since I last visited, Grandma,' Jess replied with a smile. She put the Ogden's bags down at the side of the armchair facing Martha and sat in the armchair opposite her grandmother.

'Tea, Marjorie,' Martha ordered.

Marjorie, who was trying to peek into the bags, straightened up and nodded quickly. 'Yes, Martha,' she said hurriedly.

'No, don't go, Aunt Marjorie, I have something for you.' Jess reached into one of the bags and pulled out a shrink-wrapped bag containing the red swimsuit. 'Here you are, a gift for your adventure.'

Marjorie opened and closed her mouth several times but the only sound that came out was a high-pitched squeak.

'Jessica, I wish you'd have consulted me before wasting your money on that thing.' Martha's lips formed a thin red line.

'Why, Grandma? It's a gift from me. Marjorie wanted it, so I got it for her. You should have let her buy it when you went to the store the other day.'

Martha snorted.

'It was too expensive, it's garish and bordering on the indecent. You might like to flash your backside to anyone who cares to look, Jessica, but Marjorie is seventy-six, she shouldn't be baring it all in public.'

'It's just high cut at the thighs, Grandma. It covers everything it's supposed to cover... anyway, I thought you might object, so I bought this for her too.' Jess reached into a second bag and pulled out a neatly folded, thigh length, white, silk kimono.

Marjorie was once again, speechless. She dropped the swimsuit on the sofa and held the kimono in front of her. 'It's beautiful, Jessica,' she said eventually, then throwing her arms around her grandniece's neck, she burst into tears.

Jess, suddenly feeling very emotional herself, patted Marjorie on the back. 'You're very welcome, Aunt Marjorie. You'll knock them dead at the side of the pool.'

Marjorie pulled away and slipped the kimono on. Twirling like a model on the catwalk, she looked across to her older sister. 'Isn't it beautiful, Martha.'

'It will cover up your backside, I suppose,' Martha said begrudgingly.

Marjorie scooped up the swimming costume from the sofa and rushed out to the stairs. 'I'm going to pack them now,' she trilled.

Jess smiled at her grandmother. 'She's happy, Grandma, you can't begrudge her that, surely?'

'I don't begrudge her anything,' Martha sniffed. 'You do know she's packed her cases already, don't you? She'll have nothing to wear in a day or two. I'm going to have to go through it all before we leave to make sure she hasn't literally packed the kitchen sink.'

Jess laughed, leaned forwards and patted her grandmother's hand. 'I know you look out for her. It doesn't go unnoticed.'

Martha sniffed.

'She's not the stupidest person on the planet, but she should be hoping the person who is, doesn't die any time soon.'

'Grandma!'

'Oh, I'm only joking, Jessica. She is hard work though.'

'She's a free spirit,' Jess said, smiling up at Marjorie as she re-entered the room.

'She's away with the fairies,' muttered Martha.

'All packed away,' said Marjorie, looking pleased with herself.

'I bought something for Grandma too,' said Jess looking at Martha with a mischievous look on her face. She dropped her hand into the third bag and pulled out a black, shrink-wrapped swimsuit.

'You wasted your money, Jessica,' said Martha, refusing to take the proffered garment from her granddaughter's outstretched hand.

'Oh, Grandma, this is a swimsuit specifically designed for the older lady. It's cut longer across the top of the thighs, no bottom can protrude, I promise you. The neckline is cut just under the chin and not a hint of side boob will be on view.'

'I should think not,' snorted Martha, reaching out and taking the transparent plastic bag from Jess.

'Martha can't swim,' said Marjorie quickly.

'She can learn, there will be plenty of time for lessons when she's onboard.'

Martha grunted, tore open the bag and held the garment in the air. 'It's too small. This wouldn't fit a ten-year-old.'

'It stretches, Grandma. It will fit just fine.'

Martha dropped the swimsuit on the side of the chair. 'I'm sorry, it's a very kind thought but I won't be showing my body off to all and sundry.'

'I thought you might say that so I bought you something to cover yourself up with too.' Jess dipped into the fourth bag and pulled out a belted, knee-length, floral patterned, silk kimono. 'This will hide anything you don't want to be on show, and it will keep the sun off you too.'

'Ooh, Martha, that's gorgeous. I'll have it if you don't want it.'

As Marjorie reached for the garment, Martha snatched it away and held it close to her chest.

'It's my gift, Marjorie.'

Jess grinned. 'I want photographs of the pair of you wearing them onboard.'

'Pfft.'

'I've got a camera, Jessica,' Marjorie revealed, 'and Martha has the camera on her telephone. She's taking her computer with her too so we'll be able to have a Zoomer with you and we can Ebail the pictures.'

'EMAIL!' Martha corrected her sister. 'And it's called a Zoom meeting, not... I despair sometimes, I really do.'

Jess reached across and prodded her grandmother's forearm. 'Hey, listen to you, you're getting down with the kids, Grandma. I had no idea you knew what a Zoom meeting was.'

'I do my research. I'm not as stuck in the past as you think I am.'

'I never thought you were. I know you don't like using your mobile though.'

'Those virtual key things are too small. And anyway, I like a keyboard you can feel beneath your fingertips.'

'Martha's been doing some writing on the laptop, haven't you, Martha?'

'Shh. That's my business.' Martha scowled at her sister.

'Come on, out with it. Are you competing with me to get a novel written?' Jess leaned forward, intrigued.

'I have been following in the footsteps of my late mother. I've been jotting down a few paragraphs about my past. Not that anyone would be interested in reading them.' Martha stuck her nose in the air and sniffed.

'I would, Grandma. I don't know much about your early life but I'd love to. Didn't you used to be a nurse?'

'I was, and that's what I've been writing about. I doubt I'll get a dozen volumes out of my life like my mother did but—'

'A dozen?' Jess looked puzzled. 'I've only found six. They cover the war years.'

'There are more, many more. She used to write in her journal most weekends. I can remember her doing it right though the nineteen-fifties, and I know for a fact that she wrote well past the sixties and into the seventies, because she was working on her diary when I went around to see her one Sunday evening, just before Nicola was born.'

'WOW!' Jess's mouth dropped open. 'Do you know where they are?'

Martha shrugged. 'In the attic I suppose, with her Ouija board and the rest of her witch's paraphernalia.'

Jess put her hand to her forehead. 'Oh, Grandma.'

'You might scoff, but... well, we'll leave it there. Strange things happen in that attic.'

Jess suddenly thought about the visions she had seen in the dusty old mirror and said nothing, not wanting to fuel the fires.

'There is no witch's paraphernalia up there. I'd have found it if there had been. It's just a spiteful family rumour invented as a scare story by person or persons, unknown.' Jess looked directly at Martha.

'You haven't found her other memoirs either, have you? So, you don't know what's up there.'

Jess sighed. 'You're wrong about Nana. You always have been. She was a lovely woman.'

'Jessica, if I were to agree with you, then we'd both be wrong and we can't have that, can we?'

Jess frowned as she tried to work out what Martha had said, eventually, she got it, laughed and stood up. 'Right, I'd better be off. I told Mum I'd be home in time to give her a lift to the police station. She has to register every day while she's out on licence.'

Martha shook her head. 'I forgot she was out of hospital. You're taking a risk leaving her on her own, aren't you? It's a good job she hasn't got access to her car or she'd be at Tesco Express loading up with bottles of cheap cider before you could say Jack Robinson.'

'Cut her a bit of slack, Grandma, she's your daughter don't forget. Anyway, she's promised me she's kicking the booze.'

'I'll believe it when I see it,' Martha scoffed.

Jess shook her head and sighed again. Leaning forward she pecked Martha on the cheek, then gave Marjorie a big hug. 'See you soon, Auntie.'

Back outside, Jess climbed into her car, and remembering that she hadn't bought the alcohol-free wine she had promised to pick up, started the engine and set off for the Tesco supermarket.

Chapter 15

When Jess arrived home, she found her mother's old Ford parked sideways across the parking spaces at the side of the farmhouse. Puzzled, she grabbed her shoulder bag, stuffed the bottle of wine she had bought into it and walked up the three stone steps to the front door. Twisting the handle, she found it unlocked and pushing it open she stepped into the hall.

'Hi, Mum, I'm home.' Jess walked along the passage, past the stairs and through the open door that led to the lounge. 'That was a strange bit of parking wasn't...'

Her heart sank as she looked across the room to see Nicola slumped on the sofa with an empty wine bottle at her feet. She waved a quarter-full one at Jess and smiled a lop-sided smile.

'You took your time. Come on, grab a glash, I've saved you a bit.'

'MUM!' Jess looked at the big old clock on the wall. 'Please tell me you've already been to the police station.'

'Pah!' Nicola waved the bottle again. 'Have a drink, Jess. Never mind the police.'

'Mum! It's part of your release agreement... so is steering clear of wine.' Jess pulled the alcohol-free bottle from her bag and showed it to her mother. 'I bought this for tonight. What a bloody waste of time that was.'

'You can have it, Jess. I prefer this.' Nicola took a swig from the neck of the bottle, choked and spat out the wine onto her cardigan. Sticking the damp garment into her mouth, she sucked at it. 'Waste not want not,' she giggled.

Jess put the wine bottle on the coffee table and slumped down in the armchair she used to sit on when Alice was alive.

'What are we going to do, Mum? I can't take you to the police station while you're in that state.'

'Nope. You can't.' Nicola agreed.

'Why, Mum? For pity's sake you've only been a free woman for a few hours.'

'I fancied a drink. It's as simple as that.'

'But you signed a form to say you wouldn't touch alcohol. You promised to follow the rules.'

'Forms, ha! And, aren't rules meant to be broken? Have you always followed the rules, Jess? Weren't you arrested at demos when you were at Uni?'

'That was different.'

'Why was it different? You broke the rules.'

'Yes, but... Look, Mum, I wasn't in danger of being locked up in prison.'

'They charged you with affray, then dropped it when you said sorry.'

'I know, but... oh, come on, Mum, you know how serious this is.'

Nicola drained the bottle, dropped it on the floor and lay back on the cushions. 'Ah, that's better,' she murmured.

'I'll have to ring them, make up an excuse or something,' Jess said, more to herself than her mother.

Grabbing her phone, she walked through to the kitchen where Nicola's release documents were still lying on the table. Picking up the wad of papers, she found the number of the local police station, dialled the number and took a deep breath.

'Hello, Spinton Police.'

'Oh, hello. My name is Jessica Griffiths and I was supposed to bring my mother to the station today to register her whereabouts.'

Jess could hear the policeman ruffle through some papers.

'Yes, I have the report in front of me. Nicola Griffiths. Is there a problem?'

'Yes, well... She's ill. I can't bring her today.'

'Ill? What is the nature of her illness? If she can walk, she ought to be here really.'

'She only got out of hospital yesterday. She took a severe beating. She's not properly over it yet.'

'I see, so she's had a relapse. Have you called for an ambulance?'

'No, it's not a relapse... She's just not very well, she's lying on the sofa, she really isn't up to it today. I'm so sorry.'

'That's all right, Miss, these things happen. Do you think she'll be well enough to attend tomorrow? We'll need a doctor's certificate if she misses two days in a row.'

'I'm sure she'll be better by tomorrow. Will you be open on New Year's Day?'

'We're a police station, Miss. We never close.'

'Of course... sorry.... So, If I bring her in tomorrow afternoon at the scheduled time, will that be all right? Can she sign for both days?'

'I'll check with my superiors, Miss. I hope your mother feels better soon.'

The line went dead. Jessica put the kettle on and made a strong cup of coffee. Lying to the police wasn't something she made a habit of. Her hands were still shaking as she lifted the steaming mug to her lips.

After finishing her coffee, Jess went upstairs and dragged the quilt from Nicola's bed in the spare room and carried it downstairs. After spreading it over her mother's prone body, she picked up the two empty wine bottles and dropped them into the recycling bag she kept on the back door, then remembering the bottle she had bought herself, she retrieved it and put it in the fridge. She was just about to open up her laptop to do a bit of work, when there was a loud rap on the front door. She opened it to see a burly police sergeant standing on the top step. There was another policeman sitting behind the steering wheel of the police car that was parked in the lane.

'Nicola Griffiths? I'm Sergeant Harris, Spinton Police.' The sergeant had a voice to match his bulk.

'No, I'm her daughter, Jessica, Mum's inside, she's not feeling very well. I rang the station to let them know.'

'I'm aware of that, madam, that's why I'm here. Just a routine check you understand. We have to do it; you'd be surprised at the tricks people will try to avoid their daily registration.'

'Mum's ill, Sergeant. She only came out of hospital yesterday.' Jess interlocked the fingers of both hands, hoping to hide the nervous shake that she felt must be so obvious.

'Do you mind if I come in, madam?'

Jess stepped aside and grimaced as the policeman stepped into the hall.

'She's in there.' Jess pointed to the lounge door and sent up a prayer to any deity that might be listening. *Don't let her wake up, please?*

She hurried after the sergeant who had stopped a couple of paces into the room. Jess breathed a sigh of relief as she heard her mother snoring gently under the duvet.

'Do you want me to wake her?' she asked, wondering why the hell she had asked such a stupid question.

'No, that's all right, madam. Leave her to rest.' He turned to face Jess. 'Now, I just have to check that there is no alcohol on the premises.'

'Pardon?'

'One of the stipulations of her release was that there wouldn't be any temptation put in her path. I believe you signed that agreement too.'

'I did, yes, and there is no alcohol on the premises. I've got a bottle of alcohol-free wine in the fridge. You can have a look if you like.'

'Just to be sure.' The policeman didn't smile.

Jess led him through to the kitchen and opened up her American style fridge freezer. Picking up the bottle of wine, she handed it to the officer who gave it a quick glance then handed it back.

'I'm sorry about that, Miss, but we have to be sure. Had your mother turned up today none of these checks would have had to be made.'

'She'll be there tomorrow,' Jess promised as she led the policeman back to the front door.

'Can you be certain? I mean, if she hasn't fully recovered from her injuries, she might not be up to it and then you'll have to produce a doctor's certificate.'

'I've already been informed about that,' said Jess, smiling and willing the officer out of the door.

Instead of walking out the sergeant stopped in the doorway and held out a hand.

'It's been very nice to meet you, Miss Griffiths. I hope your mother makes a speedy recovery.'

Jess's smile turned to a look of horror as she heard a bump from the front room.

'Jess?' Nicola's plaintive call echoed around the hall.

Jess put her hand on the sergeant's arm. 'Goodbye, and thank you for being so understanding. I'd better get back to my mum.'

The sergeant touched his hat and stepped out of the house.

'Goodbye, Miss.'

Closing the door with more haste and force than she had intended, Jess leaned back against it and let all the pent-up air out of her lungs. Then wiping away an angry tear she walked back into the lounge.

'Mum, I had to lie to the police. Do you know how that makes me feel?'

It was an hour later and Jessica was trying to get Nicola to drink a strong mug of black coffee.

'They actually came to the door?' Nicola was astounded.

'They not only came to the door, they came in. Thankfully you were sleeping it off or you'd be in a prison cell by now.'

'Oh, don't be so melodramatic, Jess.'

'Mum, they came to check that I was telling them the truth about you, and I wasn't. I was terrified all the time that man was in the house.'

'All right, Jess. You've made your point.' Nicola took a sip of the sludge-like coffee, grimaced, then put it on the side table with shaking hands.

'It's the last time I'm going to lie for you, Mum.'

'Jess...'

'I mean it. No more lies, no more making up excuses for you. From tonight on, I'm not going to let you out of my sight. I thought I could trust you. You made a promise and didn't keep it.' She bit her lip. 'You're more like Dad than I thought you were.'

Nicola shook her head, then grimaced again as the newly arrived headache kicked in. 'All right, Jess. I messed up. I'll try harder in future.'

Jess rolled her eyes. 'You didn't last twenty-four hours, what chance is there of you making it through the next few days, weeks?'

'I'm sorry, Jess. I truly am. I let you down again.'

Jess swallowed the lump that appeared in her throat and patted her mother's hand.

'It's all right, Mum. I know it's hard for you. Let's put this down to experience, eh?'

She got to her feet, turned away and with tears streaming down her face, walked out to the kitchen.

At midnight, with the sound of Big Ben bonging on the TV, Jess sat alongside Nicola on the sofa and raised her glass of alcohol-free wine. Chinking it against her mother's glass, she smiled and spoke softly.

'Happy New Year, Mum. Let's hope twenty-twenty is a much better year for us all.'

Chapter 16

On New Year's Day, under pressure from Jessica, Nicola donned her short winter coat and the two women went for a brisk four-mile walk along the country lanes that criss-crossed the outskirts of the mainly industrial town.

In the afternoon, they arrived at the police station fifteen minutes early and were made to wait until the clock had ticked onto the hour before a gruff-mannered constable allowed Nicola to sign her registration document.

After returning home, Nicola sat in front of the TV while Jess sat at the big oak table in the kitchen and opened her laptop. She typed a few ideas for an article about how women are treated in the justice system before, once again, picking up Alice's 1940 memoir.

Alice. September 1940

I got up at five as usual on the morning of my twenty-first birthday and by five-thirty I was cleaning out and feeding the pigs. I arrived back in the kitchen at seven thirty-five to find Miriam grinning like the Cheshire Cat from Alice in Wonderland.

'Happy birthday, Alice,' she said, excitedly, producing a card and a birthday present that she had wrapped in newspaper. The wrapping didn't bother me, we were making do and mending after all. I tore open the paper to find a hand knitted sweater with a large letter A on the left breast.

'Thank you,' I said, giving Miriam a hug. I had no idea that she had been knitting it for me. It must have taken her weeks because she had very little leisure time.

Suddenly, unable to contain their excitement any longer our two London evacuees, Stephen and Harriet, leapt out from beneath the table shouting 'happy birthday' at the top of their voices. They presented me with two hand-made cards and, wrapped up in tissue paper, a gilt photo frame containing a picture of them both looking a good few years younger, at the fun fair with their mum and dad. I knelt down and hugged them both.

'We didn't have anything else to give you and we wanted you to have something to remember us by,' said Harriet.

'We brought it with us from London. It was taken at Mitcham fair three years ago,' added Stephen.

Tears flooded from my eyes as I looked at their earnest little faces. They really had arrived with next to nothing. The photograph was the only reminder of their former lives that they possessed. I pulled them both to me and hugged them tight, my tears staining their faces.

'Bless you both, but I can't take this. It's all you have to remind you of your mum and dad.'

'But we want you to have it,' Harriet assured me. 'We don't want you to ever forget us.'

Through my sobs, I managed to tell them that I could never, ever forget them and they would be in my thoughts until the day I died.

When I had recovered my composure, I let go of them, got to my feet and looked around the kitchen. 'I think this gift should be put in a place of importance,' I said, wiping tears from the picture's glass. I moved my favourite pot from its prominent place on the mantlepiece above the old range and put the photograph in its place. Standing back, and with a child under each arm, we studied the mantel with serious faces.

'I think it's perfect,' said Stephen.

'So do I,' agreed Harriet. 'Perfect.'

I gave them each a kiss on the top of the head, and making out I'd heard the telephone ring. I left them in the kitchen while I went through to the front room for another cry.

While I was drying my eyes, the phone did actually ring. It was Amy.

'Happy twenty-one'th birthday, Alice Hussy,' she yelled down the phone.

I looked at the clock. 'Aren't you supposed to be at work?' I asked.

'Shhh, I am. I'm on the phone in the stock room at the Mill. Don't speak too loudly or someone will hear.'

'Amy! Don't get into trouble just to say happy birthday to me,' I said.

'Oh, don't worry, I'll just tell them my gran's been taken seriously ill and I'm checking up on her.'

'Didn't you have a day off for her funeral two years ago when she really did die?'

'Oops, so I did... never mind, I'll tell them it's my other gran. You're allowed to have two.'

I laughed. 'Amy, never change,' I said.

'Right, I'd better go. I'll see you tonight after work. I hope your birthday tea is going to be up to scratch. I'll be skipping dinner at home.'

'I don't know what we're having. Miriam has taken complete control of everything. She's even thinking about coming out with us on Saturday night for the real celebration. It's never the same when your birthday falls on a weekday is it? Especially a big one like your twenty-first.'

'True, the Old Bull won't know what's hit them at the weekend. Better run, Big Nose Beryl is sniffing about. I don't want her reporting me.'

'Bye bye, Amy, thanks for ringing,' I said just before the dial tone came back on the line.

At lunchtime I was treated to a rousing chorus of Happy Birthday to You, and Twenty-One Today, before Barney, my foreman, stepped forward to hand me a card made in the shape of a key.

'Happy birthday, Alice. I wish your mum and dad had been here to witness this moment but as they aren't, it falls to me to do the honours.'

I took the key shaped card, stood on my tiptoes and gave him a peck on the cheek.

'The lads have had a bit of a whip round, we couldn't afford much, but we got you this.' He stepped back and George Foulkes came out from behind the crowd of his fellow workers and passed me a cardboard box that had been tied up with a pink bow.

I thanked him profusely.

'Well, open it then.'

'Oh, sorry,' I replied and removed the bow carefully. Folding the ribbon up, I slipped it into my pocket and pulled the box open. Inside it was another box, then another. In that one was a silver whistle.

I pulled it out and looked around, confused.

'Blow it,' urged George.

I put it to my lips and blew twice. Suddenly the crowd of men parted and Alfie Brown walked through the gap carrying a gorgeous black and white Border Collie puppy. He pushed it into my arms and I sank my face into its soft fur.

'Thank, you, thank you,' I managed to blurt out between the sobs as my already red eyes began to leak again.

'It's a bitch,' said Alfie proudly. 'We bought it from Alsop's farm, they breed champion sheep dogs.' He ruffled the fur on the pup's head. 'I reckon she's a champion already. The farm needs a dog. It's been a while since we had one.'

A minute later, my face still wet with tears, I took the pup inside to meet Miriam and the children. The gift had been so secret none of them had an inkling about it. Miriam cooed and immediately poured the pup a bowl of milk. Harriet and Stephen were even more ecstatic than me. They hopped from one foot to the other in excitement.

'What's his name?'

'He's a her,' I replied, 'and she's so new she hasn't got a name yet.' Putting her gently down on the mat in front of the fire I patted her on the back and announced that she was going to be a house dog.

'She's far too beautiful to sleep in a barn,' I said.

'Isn't she going to work on the farm then?' Miriam asked in a surprised tone of voice.

'The lads would never forgive me if I kept her to myself,' I replied. 'She'll work on the farm in the day, but she can come in with us at night. A dog should have a fire to lie in front of after a hard day's work.'

'But what shall we call her?' Harriet wanted an answer as quickly as possible.

'That's a very good question. Let's all think of a name and we'll vote on what we think is the best one,' I suggested.

'Flash,' Stephen cried, immediately. 'She's got a flash of while on her neck and I bet she'll be really fast when she grows up.'

'I think we should call her... um... Daisy,' suggested Harriet. 'Because she'll be running through the daisies all day chasing the sheep.'

I looked across the table to Miriam.

'Oh, don't ask me. I'm no good with names,' she said.

'Come on, Miriam,' the children shouted together.

'Oh, I don't know, what about... Shadow, because she's mostly black and the sheep won't see her when she's creeping through the shadows to round them up.'

'Very good, Miriam,' I said. 'I don't think I can beat that.'

'Come on, Auntie Alice,' cried Harriet.

'Um... What about... Lass?'

'Nooo,' said Miriam, 'the lads will call her that anyway, she needs a proper name.'

'Oh, all right then, how about... Tess?'

'YES!' the kids shrieked together. 'Tess suits her just fine.'

'She does look like a Tess, bless her little paws,' said Miriam.

And so, it was decided. The puppy would be named Tess. She was the best present anyone could ask for and I loved her from the moment I set eyes on her. Martha loved her too, though she still loved the pigs more and relished every moment she spent with them.

Stephen was sent off to inform the lads of the name we had chosen. He came back grinning from ear to ear and told us that Tess, or Bess, were the two names they had picked out for her.

I struggled to settle in the afternoon. I had to go over the books twice because I couldn't concentrate, always having an ear out for the phone in case Godfrey rang to wish me a happy twenty-first. When no call had arrived by six, I told myself he must be extremely busy with war work and couldn't find the time to ring. That, or the phone lines were out of order because of the bombing. The German bombers had returned night after long night since the weekend I was there. They were calling it the Blitz now, a shortened term from the German word Blitzkrieg, meaning onslaught.

Amy arrived just after six and managed to forget all about the reason she was visiting when she spotted Tess sitting on the mat in front of the fire. She squealed and dropping my card and present on the table, rushed across the room to say hello. It was a full five minutes before she could force herself away from my slobbering, furry present. I stood by the sink with a look of fake annoyance on my face and tapped my foot as she looked up.

'Happy twenty-first, Alice,' she said eventually, giving me a hug and a peck on the cheek.

She picked up her gift and card, handed them to me and tapped her own feet excitedly while she waited for me to open them. I teased her by taking my time reading the card before tearing open the paper bag that contained her gift.

'Come on, come on,' she urged. 'You're going to love this.'

I did love it. Inside was an RCA Victor recording of Glen Miller's, In The Mood.

I rushed into the front room, wound up my gramophone, put the disc on my turntable and Amy and I danced as we played the record five times on the trot.

While we were in the front room, Miriam laid the table for my birthday tea, Martha was put in her high chair and we sat down with Harriet and Stephen to eat daintily cut triangle sandwiches followed by a milk pudding and slices of Miriam's wonderful seed cake.

When we had finished eating, Martha was put into her playpen for an after-dinner nap, while the kids played with Tess in front of the fire. Miriam made a fresh pot of tea, then went into the parlour to catch up on her ironing while Amy and I discussed the latest gossip. We did our best to keep the war out of the conversation, but it did come up eventually when Amy asked me if Godfrey had been in touch.

'No, I thought he might ring today but he must be too busy with his war work.'

Amy pulled a sad face. 'That's a shame.'

'The bombs are still falling in London, Amy. The phone lines might be down but I have to say, I was a little bit disappointed.'

'There's time yet,' replied Amy.

'He'll have to ring us at the Old Bull if he wants to speak to me this evening,' I said taking a quick glance sideways. Amy was wearing a knee length skirt with a blue jumper, not her usual night out attire.

'Dressing down tonight, are we?' I asked.

'It's a week night, that means we can only have a couple of drinks. It's hardly worth taking the risk of getting beer spilled down my best party frock.'

'True enough,' I replied. 'I won't put my glad rags on tonight either.'

Amy looked down her nose at me. 'I'm not going out with you in your smelly overalls, Missis,' she said.

'They're clean,' I said looking down at my working clothes. 'The smelly ones are in the wash.'

'You had better get glammed up, Alice. It is your birthday after all. People will expect it.'

'Who?' I asked. 'The only people we'll see tonight will be Big Nose Beryl and her mates.'

'You never know,' Amy said with a twinkle in her eye. 'Clark Gable might drop in for a beer.'

'Ooh, that will be twice I see him this week then. He'll be on screen at the cinema on Saturday night.'

We were both beyond excited because Gone With The Wind was finally being shown in our backwater of a movie theatre. Amy put her chin in her hands and stared into space with a dreamy look on her face.

'He's gorgeous, isn't he?'

I nodded. Clark Gable was a frequent visitor in my dreams.

'Right,' I said, getting up. 'I'm going to have a quick strip wash.'

'Good,' said Amy, 'because you don't have time for a bath. They close at ten-thirty and you wouldn't be out of it until eleven.'

I threw a tea towel at her and hurried through to the bathroom where I stripped to my undies and washed myself down with a flannel and a lumpy bar of Imperial Leather soap that I had manufactured from the remnants of previously used bars. The government's waste not want not message even extended to the bathroom.

Upstairs, I pulled out a navy, pencil line skirt and a black jumper and laid them on the bed while I sorted my curls, applied a bit of make-up and dabbed a tiny bit of my precious Tabu perfume behind my ears. I changed into a clean brassiere and fresh pair of knickers, and pulled out a pair of black Cuban heels out of the bottom of the wardrobe, then, after checking myself critically in the mirror, I went back downstairs to where Amy was once again, cuddling Tess.

'She's coming home with me tonight. She decided she doesn't want to stay here a minute longer.'

'Noooo, she's our dog,' Harriet yelled.

'Oh, I'm only teasing,' Amy ruffled Harriet's hair and pressed Tess into her arms before turning back to me.

'Is that it?' she asked.

'What's wrong with it? I'm dressed pretty much the same as you.'

'Exactly,' Amy replied, 'but I'm not the birthday girl.'

'Well, it's going to have to do,' I said. 'I'm not getting changed again.'

'Oh, you'll do, I suppose. You'll still make Beryl and co look like they've just come out of the workhouse.'

Amy pulled her coat from the back of the chair and I grabbed mine from the peg. Slipping into the parlour, where Miriam was reading Martha a bedtime story, I kissed my toddler on the forehead and wiggled my fingers at her.

'Be a good girl for Auntie Miriam,' I said.

'She will be, she always is,' Miriam stroked Martha's hair and winked at me. 'Have a lovely time, my lovely,' she said.

Amy and I walked arm in arm up the lane towards the Old Bull, chatting about the goings on at the Mill, the clothing factory where Amy worked as a machinist. The company usually turned-out women's clothing but had recently begun making military uniforms.

The blackout was in place and not a single chink of light crept out of any of the cottages we walked past. Even the telephone box opposite the pub was in darkness. As we drew level with it, Amy stopped dead.

'Oh, bugger, I forgot to put my purse in my bag. I'll just nip back and get it.'

'Don't worry,' I said. 'I've got money. I'll get the drinks.'

'Not on your Nellie, Missis. It's your birthday. I buy the drinks tonight.' She looked over my shoulder towards the pub, then turned away. 'I won't be long. Wait here.'

Amy trotted off. I watched her as she scurried back the way we had come. Suddenly an icy blast of air made me shiver, then a gentle voice came out of the night.

'Hello, Alice.'

I span around, eyes wide. I'd know that voice in a football crowd.

'Godfrey!' I yelled.

He stepped towards me; arms outstretched as the door of the phone booth closed behind him.

'Happy birthday, my darling,' he said, smiling.

I rushed into his arms and we shared a frantic series of kisses. When we finally parted I looked back over my shoulder towards Amy's house.

'She was in on this wasn't she?'

Godfrey nodded. 'It was her idea. I was just going to turn up at the farm.'

'Wait until I see her again. I'll give her what for... I'm so pleased to see you though. It's a lovely birthday surprise.'

We kissed again, then Godfrey took my arm and led me around the corner, away from the Old Bull.

'I take it we're not drinking locally tonight then?'

'No, I thought we'd go somewhere a little quieter,' he replied.

His gangster car was parked in the shadow of a huge elm, he opened the door for me and we climbed inside. Godfrey started up the engine and switched on the headlights. The three-slot masks that had been fitted to the headlamps meant that any light emanating from them was broken up and its weakened, narrow beam was slanted down towards the road in front of the car. Fortunately, because it was night, there were few other vehicles on the road.

Godfrey drove us to a little bar-come-restaurant on the main street of a little village between Gillingham and Chatham. There was only one other couple in the bar, so we got the best seats in the house, two armchairs on either side of a merrily burning fire.

I sipped too many port and lemons while Godfrey took his time over a single glass of malt.

'I have an important meeting at six tomorrow morning, then I have to drive back to London so I have to be careful with my alcohol intake tonight,' he explained, when I queried his abstinence.

Godfrey filled me in about life in London under the endless bombing. Our little hotel was still standing, as were his own digs, but Victoria station had been hit and his office had suffered damage during the previous week.

'I'll come down again soon,' I promised.

'No, Alice, it's too dangerous as things are.' He leaned forward and put his hand on my knee but pulled it away again quickly when the barmaid gave him a reproachful look.

'I'll try my best to get back up here every few weeks even if it's just for a short weekend or something. I can't risk you being hurt, Alice. I'd never be able to live with myself if anything happened to you while you were paying me a visit.'

'I quite enjoyed the sense of danger if I'm honest, Godfrey. It was quite exhilarating.'

Godfrey ignored the barmaid's watching eye and put his hand on my knee again. 'Exhilarating is the word. My God, Alice, I've never felt so alive.'

'When this is all over, I'll come down for a week, or we could go on holiday to the coast,' I said.

Godfrey smiled, sadly. 'I'd never want to come back,' he said.

We stayed in the bar for another hour and a half, then we drove back through the dark country lanes until we hit the main Gillingham Road. Twenty minutes later we pulled up on the asphalt track at the side of the farm.

After a bit of a front seat cuddle, we got out of the car and said goodnight at the farm gate.

'It's been a rare treat seeing you, Alice. I'll be able to face the bombs again now.'

I smiled and hugged him.

'When do you think you'll be able to come back again?'

'I'll try to fiddle a weekend in late November, but failing that I'll be home for a short time over the Christmas break. They can do without me for a couple of days.'

He pulled me to him and we kissed, his hand found its way onto my breast and he squeezed it gently. His other hand ran down over my hip and his fingers grabbed at my skirt.

'No you don't,' I said with a laugh. I pulled away and shook my head as I looked at his disappointed face. 'Godfrey, the next time we do that, it will be in a nice comfortable bed. So far, we've done it on my front room floor, on your desk, in your car, in a cubby hole under the stairs while the bombs were raining down, and on an underground station platform, and while I've enjoyed every one of those experiences, I am determined to do it on a nice soft mattress under a warm blanket.'

Godfrey nodded. 'I understand.'

'Good,' I said, leaning towards him. 'I want to stay in that bed for the entire night too. I want to wake up and find you lying next to me, naked and warm.'

'It would have to be a hotel then, Alice because I can't take you home and we can't use your bed, Miriam wouldn't approve.'

'Miriam wouldn't give a hoot,' I said. 'But it wouldn't be seemly with the kids in the house.' I leaned in close and whispered into his ear. 'We'll find a way.' I kissed him again, then backed slowly away. 'I'd better go in. I'm up at five.'

'Oh, wait a moment. I haven't given you my present.' Godfrey rushed to the car and came back with a glossy, green-coloured gift bag with the name Harrods printed in gold.

'Happy birthday, my beautiful girl,' he said.

I slipped my hand into the bag and pulled out a fancy bottle with a thick knob of a stopper in its neck.

'CHANNEL NUMBER FIVE!' I blurted. 'Oh, my goodness, Godfrey. This must have cost you a fortune.'

'You're only twenty-one once and you're worth every penny,' he said.

I pulled out the stopper and took a deep sniff, then held it out to Godfrey before sniffing it again and reluctantly replacing the top. 'I'll wear this for our first night in bed. Nothing else, just this.'

Godfrey grinned. 'I'll look forward to that, every minute of every day.'

I slipped the perfume into the bag and wrapped my arms around him holding my precious gift against his back.

'Thank you so much for my present, Godfrey, say hello to London for me, and stay safe. I'll be here waiting for you.'

He kissed me gently on the lips. 'Good night, Alice. I'll see you in my dreams.'

Godfrey climbed back into his car and started up the engine, the slatted headlamps lighting up the floor at my feet. He performed a perfunctory three-point turn and dropping his arm out of the open window, he waved twice, then drove away.

Chapter 17

That evening, Jess persuaded Nicola to rustle up her vegetarian chilli recipe. She had tried many times to cook it herself but with varying results. She stood by her mother's side as she prepared the ingredients.

'Mum, I don't get it. I use exactly the same stuff as you, but mine never tastes anything like yours.'

'It's all in the cooking,' Nicola replied. 'I add a few bits while it's simmering away.' She squirted a length of tomato puree from the tube and screwed the top back on. 'The brand Mrs Kaur sells is better than this one.'

As they were chatting about how much chilli powder should be added, and when, Jess's phone rang.

'Hello, Grandma, is everything all right?'

'Why wouldn't it be?' Martha sounded puzzled.

'Well, you don't normally ring me from your mobile for a start.'

'I'm trying to get used to using it. You'll probably get a few text messages from me over the next few days. I Googled a way to make the keyboard bigger.'

'Well done.'

'I've also loaded that Skype computer program thing on my laptop.'

'App, Grandma, it's called an app.'

'It's called an application, Jessica. Why young people have to shorten everything bewilders me. If anyone should shorten things it ought to be old folk because we haven't got so much time to waste.'

'It's because... I don't know why it happens actually, probably to save a few extra seconds in a busy day. I don't use the text talk way of messaging either. I prefer proper English.'

'Quite right too,' said Martha. 'I've seen articles in the paper about that, I mean, why use R and U, instead of the proper words, are and you? It doesn't make any sense.'

'I agree, Grandma, it doesn't. Anyway, I don't suppose you rang me just to complain about text messaging.'

'No, I rang you because I've come to a decision.'

'About what?'

'My house.'

'What about your house?'

'Honestly, Jessica, we only spoke about this the other week. You offered to take the house into the trust, you said I would be given a decent amount of money for using it as collateral.'

'It wouldn't be collateral as such, Grandma. In normal circumstances you would take out a lifetime mortgage in return for a quarter or a third of the value but if you do it via the trust, there is no mortgage. I don't know how much you could be given, it wouldn't be the whole value of the house, but it would be a good amount. I can ask Bradley about it if you like? I can't see there being a problem. I would imagine you would just give your house to me on the proviso that I transfer it immediately into the trust.'

'That sounds all right. I think I can trust you not to sell it and pocket the profit.'

'Erm, thank you, Grandma, that's very kind of you.'

'Oh, you know what I mean.'

'I do, yes.'

'Now, listen, Jessica. I'm only doing this for one reason... well, two reasons. The first is, I'd like to have a bit of money in my bank account. I'm fed up to the back teeth of scrimping and scraping. I want my daily newspaper back and Marjorie is forever nagging me about getting some Sky channels, she wants the Disney channel, of all things. She saw it on one of the big screens at Ogden's and hasn't shut up about it since. I'd also like a decent internet service. Ours is pathetic, it takes forever just to download the Daily Telegraph website and even then I'm only allowed to look at the first couple of paragraphs.'

'It's behind a paywall, Grandma. You have to pay to access the news items.'

'And we were told the internet would mean knowledge was free.'

Jess could imagine Martha's disgusted face as she said the words.

'And the other reason? You said there were two.'

'This may sound brutal, Jessica, but the second reason is the most important. I don't want Nicola anywhere near this house if anything should happen to me.'

'Oh, Grandma, I'm sure she'd look after it.' Jess dropped her voice and glanced across the room towards her mother.

'She'd start by selling off all the ornaments, then the furniture, then she'd let the house go for a song to the first person who offered her money for it.'

'That's not true, she wouldn't.'

'You know her as well as I do. Do you really think she's kicked the booze, or, more importantly, ever will kick the booze?'

Jess thought about the previous afternoon and was silent.

'Exactly. Your silence says it all, Jessica.'

'What about Auntie Marjorie?'

'She can stay, if she outlives me and if she's still fully compos mentis at the time... not that she's holding a full deck of cards at the minute.'

Jess's voice became hard. 'You know what I think about that, I wish you wouldn't be so hard on her. Do you ever let up?'

'It doesn't work, Jessica. She needs to be told what to do, what to wear. She needs a routine, a set of tasks that have to be completed or she goes to pieces.'

'I'm not going to argue but I'm sure she could manage on her own, given time to get used to it.'

'Don't bank on it,' Martha replied.

Jess sighed. 'All right, Grandma, I'll ring Bradley tomorrow. We'll get something sorted out for you.'

'I want to write a will too, so make me an appointment for that. I think Marjorie should write one as well.'

'Why the rush? I know it's a good idea to have a will. Nana made sure... well, you know all about that, but why the concern all of a sudden?'

'We're about to travel half way around the world, my dear. Anything could happen. The plane could crash, the ship could sink. The bullet train might derail... and talking of bullets, we'll be abroad, there are some strange people out there, terrorists, serial killers—'

'Grandma, stop it,' Jess laughed. 'What a doomsday scenario.'

'These things happen, Jessica. I just want to be prepared.'

'All right, I'll get Bradley to give you a call as soon as possible.'

'Good. It has to be all sorted before we leave.'

'All right, I'll tell him... oh and, Gran...'

'Yes?'

'Be nice to him.'

Chapter 18

'Hello, Bradley, it's—'

'Hello, Jessica, I'd recognise your voice anywhere. What can I do for you?'

'Two things. Firstly, when will Mum's contract be ready? And secondly, I have a bit of business for you regarding the trust.'

'Really? That sounds interesting.'

'You might not be so keen when you know who's requesting your assistance,' Jess said with a little laugh.

'First things first then,' Bradley's voice became more business-like. 'The contract for the cottage will be ready later today. It's just a copy and paste job from parts of the old rental contract. We just have to substitute new figures for the rent, etc. I said we'd keep it as low as possible, but we do need to show some income from it so should we set it at, let's see... we don't want her to struggle to find the rent, so... how does, five pounds a month sound?'

'Honestly? Five pounds a month? Mum will be delighted. She was paying £850 for that dump in town.'

'We aim to please,' Bradley replied.

'Well, you've certainly done that.'

'She'll have to find her own council tax, but she'll get the reduced charge because she lives alone. The trust will pay the water rates and any maintenance work that might need doing.' He paused for a moment. 'There are no card meters for the gas and electricity, I know you said she used to use pre-payment cards before.'

'She'll just have to get used to managing monthly direct debits again, Bradley. I'll talk to her about that. We can work out a budget, though I think I might have to help her out as she's only on a part-time wage. She'll still get something by way of Universal Credit.'

'She won't get behind with her rent at least,' Bradley said, then instantly regretted it. 'I'm sorry, I didn't mean anything by that. I was just...'

'I know, Bradley. Don't worry about it.'

'So, what was the second thing? The bit I'm not going to enjoy. It's obviously not the news I was hoping for.'

'No, I haven't' come to a final decision on that yet.' Jessica twiddled with her hair as she spoke. 'Grandma, Martha Crew, that is, would like you to draw up a document that will enable her house to become part of the trust.'

'The trust!'

'That's what I said.'

'Blimey! That's a bolt from the blue.'

'She'd like to be given some money against it. Like a lifetime mortgage, but without the mortgage, if you see what I mean?'

'I understand, and the answer is yes, we can do that, with your agreement of course. We wouldn't be able to give her the full value of the house though, we shouldn't be looking to pay full value in this market.'

'She'd be happy with a decent part of the value.'

'Any idea how much the place is worth?'

'It's a big old house, Bradley. She bought it back in the sixties and living in the area she does, it's got to be worth, somewhere around half a million pounds now.'

She heard Bradley whistle down the phone.

'She's only doing this so my mother doesn't get hold of the place when she's gone. She's not expecting anywhere near the full value, don't worry about that, but she'll drive a hard bargain, I'm sure.'

'I'm expecting nothing less,' Bradley said. 'I'll give her a call this morning. It will be a wonderful asset to add to the trust's property portfolio.'

'It is a lovely house.'

'How soon would she want to set this up?'

'Immediately, I think. She's worried that she might get kidnaped by ISIS while she's off cruising.'

'ISIS?'

'Oh, that or they might hit an iceberg or something. She's covering all bases.'

'It sounds like it,' Bradley laughed. 'Now, back to the contract on the house, shall I bring it over or do you want to come to the office with your mum to sign it?'

'We'll come to the office, Bradley. Are you in this afternoon? I have to give my mum a lift to the police station to register.'

'I'm sorry, I'm not, I have a meeting in Chatham but I'll leave the contract on the desk in reception. I'll need both of you to sign it. Get Melanie on the desk to witness it and I'll add my signature when I get back. She could move in this evening if she likes.'

'She has to stay with me until the police decide whether or not to charge her with any offence,' Jess said, sadly.

'I honestly can't see it, Jess, but then I don't know all of the facts, I'm not her solicitor. Tell you what. I'll ask Jane what she thinks. You could do a lot worse than letting her take the case on, she's an expert on these domestic abuse cases.'

'Thank you, Bradley, that's very kind of you. Ask her if she'll represent Mum if we need her, will you? We've just seen the solicitor the court provides, so far.'

'I'll give her a ring after we finish this call,' said Bradley. 'I need a bit of time to work up the courage to ring your grandmother.'

'Good luck with that too,' said Jess with a grin.

'Mrs Crew?' Bradley's throat suddenly became very dry. He coughed, cleared his throat and waited for her response.

'Yes?'

'Hello, it's Bradley Wilson from Wilson—'

'I know who you are,' Martha cut in.

'Jess, erm Jessica, asked me to give you a call. I believe you have some business to discuss.'

'That's correct.'

'Erm, it's to do with transferring your property to the Mollinson Family Trust?'

'Correct, again.'

'Right, well, I'm calling to let you know that such an arrangement can be set up, but we need to sort out a few details first.'

'Details? I've given Jessica the details of what I'm looking to do.'

'Yes, but it needs to be done legally, Mrs Crew, we can't just say, okay, it's done, after a telephone conversation.'

'I'm not a fool, Mr Wilson. I'm aware of that.'

Bradley pulled the phone away from his face and sighed.

'I've done a quick search on Zoopla to get a rough idea of what your property is worth, but we'll have to send a professional surveyor around to have a proper look before we can settle on a final figure of the house's value.'

'I see. And how much did this Zoopla man say my house was worth, and how would he know?'

'It's an online house selling website, Mrs Crew. They estimate the value from the post code.'

'And how much did the Zoopla estimate?'

'Four hundred and eighty thousand pounds.'

Martha was silent.

'Hello, Mrs Crew?'

'I'm here, I was just a bit shocked that's all... Right. How much will you give me on that estimation?'

'I think we could let you have a third of the value in cash, then we could pay you a sum every year after that.'

'A sum?'

'Twenty thousand or so.'

'We have an agreement, young man. Get on with it.'

'I'll start work on it tomorrow, I'm busy this afternoon. We'll have to start by doing a search on the property.'

'You want to search the property? Do you think we're running a drugs empire from here or something?'

Bradley stifled a laugh. 'No... no, Mrs Crew... It's just a bit of checking we have to do to make sure the land isn't at risk of flooding or of mining subsidence.

We also have to make sure there aren't any debts taken out against the property, whether it's affected by any future planning by the local authority or government. We would want to know if the Ministry of Transport had plans to build a motorway extension through the property for instance.'

'Good grief. Do you think that's likely? We're ten miles from the nearest motorway.'

'No, it's not likely, Mrs Crew, in fact I'd say it's nigh on the most unlikely thing that could possibly happen to your estate.'

'Why mention it then?'

'It was just an example of things we have to check out.'

'I see. And how long would these searches take?'

'Not too long. About ten days is the norm. Make it a fortnight to be on the safe side. I could get the surveyor in within a week though. I know someone who will do it at short notice.'

'What will he do?'

'As it says on the tin, he'll survey the house. He'll check for damp, for structural problems, he'll check the roof, the bathroom... the whole house, really. Then he'll send us a report and valuation.'

'Damp? We have no damp... there's a crack in my bedroom ceiling though, would that make it fail the survey? It's one of the things I'm going to get fixed when I get the money.'

'A crack in a ceiling shouldn't affect the price that much. Most old houses have them, they're generally caused as the house shifts on its foundations over the years. Don't worry about it.'

Martha was quiet for a while, then her voice came back on the phone.

'Supposing everything is all right, when could we expect to conclude the business?'

'I'd say, within four weeks, seeing as there's no mortgage involved.'

'I won't be here in four weeks' time. I'll be in the Far East.'

'I'll do my best to get it done as quickly as possible. There's a chance that the surveyor could come out by the weekend and I can get one of our juniors started on the searches this afternoon. I'll do my best to get it done before you leave. I understand you have concerns about your safety during your cruise.'

'I'm only taking reasonable precautions.'

'Of course. Look, Mrs Crew. I'm sure I can get the paperwork to you before you go, but it will be very tight and the money might not be in your bank before you set off, but it will be transferred as soon as I can arrange it.'

'As long as it's in the bank for when I get back. I don't need much in the way of money on the cruise, everything is paid for really.'

'Yes, Jessica set it up for you, didn't she? That was very generous of her.'

'It was the least she could do, considering... don't think I'm not grateful, I am, but I still say my sister and I should have got more from my mother's will.'

'Yes, well, that's water under the bridge now,' Bradley said, trying to keep a soothing tone in his voice.

'Speaking of wills. That was the other thing I wanted to talk to you about. I want one writing out and so does my sister. I was going to get us one of those fifty-pound thingies, but as you're handy, you may as well do that work too,' Martha coughed. 'Providing you don't charge us a fortune for the privilege, we're pensioners you know?'

'We can use the copy paste service, it's like a pot noodle will. Just add water.'

'What the hell are you talking about, Pot Noodle?'

'I'm sorry, Mrs Crew, I was just making a little joke. What I mean is, we have a standard will that has been pre-written, we just add in any assets you want to transfer on your death. It should be easy enough as the house won't be part of your estate, so we can provide a cheaper service for you.'

'I definitely want those signed and sealed before we leave,' Martha said, sternly.

'I'll get my junior onto it right away.'

'I don't want a junior, I want a proper solicitor.'

'She is a proper solicitor. She recently qualified.'

'She?'

Bradley shook his head. 'Yes, Mrs Crew, SHE. Women do lots of things these days. They don't just cook and clean anymore.'

'Don't be facetious, young man. All I meant was... Look it doesn't matter. Just make sure you check her work,' she was silent for a moment, then said. 'Junior, indeed.'

'My jun... my colleague will ring you later on. She can make a list of your assets and who you want to leave them to, over the phone, then you can drop into the office with your sister to sign them, or my colleague could come to you.'

'Can't you come yourself.'

'I don't do the economy service, Mrs Crew. I tend to do the larger, more complicated wills.'

'Like my mother's?'

'Exactly. Now, if you wanted one as complicated and expensive as that one was. I can oblige.'

'The cheap option will do,' said Martha, grumpily. 'Just make sure it's ready to sign before we go.'

Chapter 19

After lunch, Jessica rang the funeral directors to make an appointment to arrange her father's funeral.

'We have a free appointment tomorrow afternoon. Could you give me the name of the deceased?'

After arranging for her father's body to be collected and taken to the chapel of rest, Jess decided it would be best if she were to go to the funeral director's office herself rather than have them call round while her mother was in and taking the risk of upsetting her.

'Mum? I've got an appointment at Pym's tomorrow afternoon to make arrangements for Dad. I'm not even going to ask if you want to come, but I will have to make sure you aren't tempted to buy more drink while I'm out so I'm going to drop you off at Gran's before I go.'

'For pity's sake, Jessica. I'm not a child. You don't have to organise a baby sitter every time you need to go somewhere. I'm quite capable of looking after myself.'

'I just don't want a repeat of the other day, Mum.'

'Look, Jess. I was in an off licence. I was tempted, all right? I admit it. I won't be in an off licence tomorrow, will I? I won't be within two miles of one. Take the keys to my car. Lock me in, shutter the windows. Put a ball and chain on my ankle but don't embarrass me by taking me to my mother's. Can you even begin to imagine what she'd have to say about it?'

'Mum... Oh, I don't know. I'm really worried about you. The last thing you need is to end up in prison while the police decide what to do, you could be there for weeks.'

'I won't be in prison because I'm not going to get drunk.' Nicola put her hand on Jess's arm. 'Leave your computer on with the webcam active. I'll sit in front of it every twenty minutes and you can log into it from your phone.'

'I can't do that. I don't have an app for it. That's for security cameras really. Anyway. I don't want you to have to do that. I want to be able to trust you.'

'Give me a last chance then, Jess. How long will you be gone? An hour? Two?'

'An hour ought to do it. I have to take you to the police station after. You could come with me and sit in the car?'

'And you'd trust me not to nip over the road to Tesco while you were inside?'

'Oh, Mum. I don't know.'

'One last chance, Jess. If I mess up it'll be on my own head. Anyway, I don't want to disappoint you again, especially not when you're just arranging your dad's funeral.'

Jess thought about it as she filled a bowl in the sink and dropped four potatoes into it.

'All right, Mum, but please, you're letting yourself down as well as me.'

'I wouldn't want to do that, would I?' Nicola faked a look of horror.

'Give me a ring if you're tempted. I can be back home inside fifteen minutes.'

'You won't need to come home, I promise,' Nicola replied.

After signing Nicola's housing contract and registering at the police station, Jess drove her mother back to the farm in better spirits. Nicola seemed to be increasingly confident that she would be able to beat her addiction, even when she was living alone at the cottage.

'Mrs Kaur will keep an eye on me, Jess. You can get her to give you a report every time I'm at work if you like. She'll know straight away if I'm hungover or not.'

'I'm not going to act like the secret police, Mum. I'm going to trust you. I understand that must have been such a temptation for you the other day, but honestly. We don't want the police round here again. We might not get away with it next time.'

At home, Jess cooked dinner while Nicola busied herself changing the bedding upstairs. In the evening, Jess sat herself down in front of her laptop and worked for a while on a work project before closing the lid, placing her notepad and pen in front of her and picking up Alice's memoir.

Alice. October 1940

On the Saturday after my birthday, I bathed and sat in front of the fire in the kitchen, chatting to Harriet, Stephen and Martha, while I dried my hair. Martha wasn't able to add much to the conversation but she liked to be involved when people were talking. She sat on Harriet's knee on the square of patterned carpet while I told them all about some of the adventures Amy and I had been involved in when we were their age.

Earlier that day, I had had the fright of my life when Martha went missing in the farm yard.

Martha was good on her feet and as slippery as an eel to catch when she didn't want to be caught, she could turn on a sixpence and head off in the other direction while Miriam and I groped after her shadow. That morning, I had just finished cleaning out the pigs when Miriam called out to say I was wanted on the telephone. Martha was with me in the yard, so I shouted for Miriam to come out and keep an eye on her while I took the call.

The call only lasted a couple of minutes, but when I walked back though the kitchen I heard Miriam frantically calling Martha's name. I rushed down the steps to find her running into the barn with a look of terror on her face.

'She's not here,' she screamed. 'She must be in with...' Her voice tailed off as I hurtled across the farmyard checking the pig pens as I ran. Suddenly I heard a commotion from the pen where Hector was kept along with his sows. I stuck my head over the fence but all I could hear was the rustling of trotters on the fresh straw and the grunting of porcine throats. Then I saw a flash of blue among the pink bodies and the squeal of an excited toddler.

Screaming her name, I pulled open the gate and leaving it swinging behind me, I lurched into the pen.

Suddenly I was swept backwards as a posse of pigs followed my biggest sow, Bertha, out into the yard. I tried to stand my ground but it was impossible. I felt the weight of five sows on either side of my legs and I was soon lying on my back as the porkers began to explore the yard, sniffing and snuffling for any sort of food they might find. Disorientated, I sat up and looked towards the pen in amazement as Hector, the king of the pigs, came sauntering out of the sty with Martha perched on his back like a rodeo rider. She screamed with delight and hung onto Hector's ears as he sidled past me and began to forage with the rest of the sounder. As Miriam scurried across the yard, I got to my feet and taking five quick strides, grabbed Martha and pulled her off Hector's back. Holding her tight against my chest, I ran for the kitchen with Miriam in hot pursuit. As I reached the steps, Barney came out of the milking parlour to see what all the fuss was about. Seeing my horrified face, he took in the situation and marched quickly across the yard.

'Is the young 'un all right, Missis?'

'I think so,' I gasped, holding her out in front of me. She didn't seem to be hurt in the slightest and as Barney grabbed a length of wood and headed towards the pigs to drive them back into their pen, Martha gave me the dirtiest look I had experienced in my life. Then she opened her lungs, screamed and began to kick at my stomach.

The tantrum lasted a good twenty minutes and nothing I could say, or do, could bring her out of it. Even Miriam and Harriet, who could make her laugh at the drop of a hat couldn't get her to stop. Her temper was truly something to behold.

Once the pigs had been rounded up, Barney, without any instruction from me, brought out ten lengths of four-foot high steel fencing and built a new barrier along the length of the pens, leaving a five-foot corridor which would enable me to complete my feeding and cleaning chores.

I was delighted with his efforts but Martha was disgusted. She loved those animals. I'm sure she would rather have lived with them in the pens than with us in the house. I half placated her by letting her spend some time with the eight-week-old piglets that were being weaned off their mother's milk. When I decided that the piglets couldn't take any more of Martha's love, I walked her back to the house. As we passed Hector's pen, she grabbed hold of the new fence and refused to let go until Hector himself stuck his head through the bars and grunted to her.

Both Amy and I agreed that Gone With The Wind was probably the best film we had ever seen and that Clark Gable and Vivien Leigh were so good it was difficult to believe they had only been acting.

We discussed the Civil War epic as we joined the exiting crowd and made our way along the puddle-strewn pavement towards the bus stop.

'Fancy chips?' I asked. We usually bought and ate them as we stood waiting for the bus.

'I don't to be honest,' said Amy, pulling a face.

'I'm the same,' I said. 'I had a late tea tonight.'

We tried to cram ourselves in with the crowd of women who were huddled together under the roof of the shelter but ended up standing half in, and half out as the rainwater dripped down our necks. Over the road, a group of five young men ate their newspaper-wrapped chips while they checked out the local talent. They were full of youthful exuberance, calling out to the girls, making lewd suggestions. I couldn't be angry at them. Most would be in uniform before the spring arrived. I felt for their mothers.

One of the lads, a fair-haired charmer called Alan, spotted Amy as she raised her hand to pull her sopping collar away from her neck. Thinking she was about to wave at him he turned to face her, stuck out his chest and began to beat on it while doing, what I have to admit, was an excellent impression of Johnny Weissmuller's Tarzan the Ape Man, jungle call.

'Me not Jane,' Amy shouted back. 'She Jane.' She pointed to a mousey-haired girl who was standing about six feet away from him, picking at her bag of chips. Tarzan gave her a quick glance, then shouted back. 'Come on, darlin, it's you I fancy. Run away to the jungle with me.'

Amy shook her head and drops of water fell like pearls from her hair.

'Sorry, love, I'm spoken for.'

'Come on, sweet'eart, I'm off to the war in a few weeks.'

'Sorry,' Amy shouted back. 'I'm married to a copper. He's on the late shift this week. He's probably in the station right now. I'd keep it down if I were you.' Amy actually did have a detective friend called Bodkin who sometimes came to the pictures with us on a Saturday.

The news didn't seem to put the young man off. It was obvious that he'd had a few drinks. He swayed as he took a few steps towards us.

'Don't be mean, darlin,' he called. 'Show us a bit of love. I don't want to go to France a virgin.'

His mates suddenly whooped, hollered and began to shout 'virgin, virgin' at the youth.

He spun around, his face a mask of anger as he swore at his friends.

I thought things might take a nasty turn, but thankfully our bus arrived a few moments later.

As Amy sat in the window seat about half way along the bus, the young man banged his fist on the glass and hurled a mouthful of abuse at her, calling her a whore, a slut and a tart amongst other things. Amy rolled her eyes and shook her damp head.

The youth continued to hammer on the window.

'I'm going to soddin war, you cow,' he screamed.

Amy, as cool as you like, looked straight at him and with the laughter of every woman on the bus ringing in her ears, said. 'Frankly, I don't give a damn.'

The Old Bull was crowded despite the weather. Amy and I sipped our port and lemons while telling the Mill girls about Amy's fabulous response to the young thug. It didn't matter that he almost certainly hadn't heard her, the rest of the passengers on the bus had, and they were made up mainly of women who had to put up with that sort of vile, nastiness every day of their lives. Many men thought women were mere chattels that could be used and abused as a right. Sadly, the law seemed to agree with them, so any chance we had of putting one over on an ignorant, pig of a man was celebrated, remembered and often relived when a crowd of girls got together.

We got soaked to the skin that night as we walked home. We were both on the wrong side of tipsy as we splashed our way through the puddles singing, Somewhere Over The Rainbow. I gave Amy a soppy hug as we said goodnight at her gate and singing the song to myself all over again. I weaved my way home. My chestnut curls lay flat against my head and my feet were sloshing around in my Oxford heeled shoes, but my heart was full of love. As I reached the turn in the lane where I could see the welcoming lights of the farmhouse, I looked up into the dark rainy night and, hoping the strengthening wind would carry my words all the way to London, I shouted, 'Godfrey Wilson, I love you.'

The following day Jess had her meeting with the undertaker at Pym's funeral directors. An aptly named, Mr Burnside showed her a brochure of coffins suitable for cremation and nodded sympathetically as she explained her circumstances.

'So, you'll be the only mourner at the funeral? That's very sad.'

'My father had few friends.'

'I understand why your mother wouldn't want to attend. It's a very delicate situation, isn't it?'

'It is. I feel sorry for Dad but he wasn't a well-liked man.'

Mr Burnside smiled warmly.

'I can find you a few mourners. We've done this sort of thing before. Our pallbearers will stay for the service so you won't be sitting alone.'

'That's very kind but they don't have to stay.'

'Are you having a religious service?'

'No. The last thing Dad would want is a big fuss. He wasn't a believer.'

'Then we'll get a humanist celebrant to conduct the service. There will be no mention of God or Angels or anything like that. He will merely talk a little bit about your father's life and mention his good points.'

'He'd struggle to find any to be honest,' said Jess, quietly. 'How long will the service last?'

'Twenty minutes. I'll get Mr Pyre to give you a call. You'll need to choose your hymns, etc.'

'Hymns? Will I be expected to sing along?'

'When I say hymns, you can of course, choose your own music.'

'Thank you. I'll choose some music this evening. Can you get Mr Pyre to call me ASAP. It might sound a little crass but I'd like to get this done and dusted as soon as possible.'

Throughout the conversation, Jess kept checking her watch, wondering whether her mother was still sober. She hadn't hidden her car keys in the end. Nicola was right, she couldn't treat her like a child. She had to make her own decisions.

Jess rushed home and emitted a huge sigh of relief when she found her mother sitting on the sofa watching Netflix.

Smiling, she walked across to give Nicola a hug. Her mother blew into the air as Jess got close.

'See, no booze, I've been good.'

'Oh, Mum, there was no need to do that. I'd have believed you.'

'All right, sorry, that was a bit over the top.'

'Are you ready to go to the police station? Let's get it out of the way, shall we?'

'I've already been.'

'What?'

'I only got back a couple of minutes ago.' She got to her feet and walked into the kitchen. 'The kettle will have boiled; do you want tea or coffee?'

Sitting at the table sipping their drinks, Jess told her mother what she had agreed with the funeral director.

'Not that it's any of my business but I'm pleased you didn't book a religious service, Jess. God would have speared the place with a bolt of lightning if a man of the cloth had offered up Owen's soul to heaven.'

Jess nodded. 'I think the feeling would have been mutual. He didn't have a good word to say about God, either.'

Nicola pulled a face. 'Let's change the subject, shall we? I'll only get morbid and I'm not at my best when I'm morbid.'

'All right, Mum. What would you like to talk about?'

'You. How are things going with that man of yours?'

'Man? I don't have a man in my life at the moment.'

'What about that lawyer? Has he gone off you?'

'Not exactly... things became difficult.'

'He's not another Calvin, is he? I never did like that little so and so. He gave me the creeps.'

145

Jess laughed dryly. 'Everyone seems to have been able to see through Calvin except me.'

'He was full of his own importance. I doubt he could ever care about anyone but himself.'

'I thought I could change him in time, Mum, it took me a long time to realise that I couldn't. He's a narcissist and you can never change them.'

'Owen wasn't a narcissist; he was a fantasist. He seriously believed he would hit the jackpot one day. He was driven. Nothing could get in the way of the dream.'

'Calvin had dreams, mostly about himself. He had plans for Nana's money. I was just the means by which he would get his hands on it. He was unfaithful at least once, but thinking about it there were probably many other times too. He worked at Uni, surrounded by all that temptation. He used to give private I.T. lessons in the student accommodation and every single student he taught was female. It never crossed my mind that he'd get up to anything. I thought I was the only woman he would ever need. I gave him everything he wanted and did everything he asked me to do, no matter how uncomfortable I felt about it.'

'We all do, love.' Nicola put her hand on top of Jess's. 'We all do the same. We think if we just give in and let them have what they want this one time, they won't ask anything else of us, but they always want more. There's always another demand. Don't blame yourself. I've done it. Mum did it, believe it or not. I'm not sure about Aunt Marjorie, but I'm fairly sure I overheard something about her getting into a fix when she was in London, back in the early sixties.'

'Aunt Marjorie? And Grandma? Martha, you mean? I can't see any man getting the better of her... though there was that man... Roger, was it? The one who took all her money?'

Nicola nodded. 'You see, Jess. It's not just you. It's a family thing. We're a dynasty of daughters. Your great, great, grandmother was one of two girls, she had one daughter. Alice had two girls, Mum had me, I had you

146

and you'll almost certainly only have girls. It's in the genes. We also appear to have a history of producing strong women, but we are only strong because we've been made that way by the men that we allow to come into our lives.' She nodded to the table where Alice's memoirs were stacked up. 'Even the Great Alice. The Ice Queen, was brought to her knees by men. We always choose the wrong ones. It's fate. Give us the choice of any ten men, nine of which are so saintly they could stand at God's side and we'd pick the one that even Lucifer would avoid, every time.'

'I'm sure you're wrong, Mum. Dad was a swine and I don't know much about that Roger, but wasn't Grandma happily married to a banker for years?'

'Have you ever heard her say a good word about him?'

'Well, no, but she's a private person. She never shows her feelings.'

'Her marriage wasn't a happy one, Jess. I'll just leave it at that.'

Jess sighed, then her face brightened. 'Nana's mum had a happy marriage. I read a bit about it in her memoirs.'

'Yes, but even he was a latent alcoholic. That would have come to the fore sooner or later, even if Alice's mother had lived longer. Her death was just an excuse for him to let it take over.'

'They loved each other though. They were soul mates.' Jess smiled as she remembered what Alice has written about them.

'There's no such thing as a perfect couple,' Nicola replied caustically. 'Men are men, they aren't all driven by the same thing, but they're all driven by something, and we are just the poor buggers they use to get what they want.'

'Mum, you're such a cynic.' Jess got to her feet and put the empty mugs in the sink.

'I am what I've been forced to become, Jess. Do you really think I wanted to spend my life in a permanent stupor? My mother used to tell me it was something in the genes that was passed on by your Nana's father, but I know it wasn't preordained. I never touched a drop until I met Owen. Even then it was only a glass or two on a special occasion. I didn't even like the taste of the stuff, so don't listen to your grandma if she ever warns you about booze being in the blood. It's all nonsense, just like her stories about Alice being a witch.'

'I have never believed that story anyway, Mum, and I know why drink became a problem for you. It was the only way you could survive.'

Jess walked slowly across the kitchen and put her arms around her mother's shoulders.

'This is a new chapter we're starting on now. What's done is done, we only ever look forwards from this moment on.'

Nicola patted her hand. 'I don't know how that conversation turned out the way it did. I only asked you about Bradley.' She looked up at Jess, who averted her gaze.

'Bradley is still married, Mum… I nearly added not in the biblical sense, but their marriage only exists because of the bible. Both his wife and his mother are die-hard Catholics, they don't believe in divorce, so poor Bradley is stuck. Leonora keeps an eye on who he's seeing and does her best to mess things up for him. Although she doesn't want to live with him full time, she refuses to let go, so he's in limbo. I really don't want to get stuck in the middle of that tangled web.'

Nicola held her hand out, palms up. 'You see. It's the family's man-curse raising its ugly head again. There's always something wrong with the men we allow into our lives. Even the better-behaved ones come with a set of deep-rooted issues that suddenly become our problems too, and they are, in the main, nasty, ugly issues that suck the life out of us until we are left just an empty shell of the person we should have become.'

Jess sighed again. 'This is all a bit deep, Mum. I thought we were meant to be lightening the mood.'

Nicola stood up and gave her daughter a sad smile. 'Sorry, love. Maybe you'll be the one to break the chain.' She kissed Jess on the cheek. 'I hope so, I really do.'

That night, lying in bed, Jess thought about the letter that Alice had written to her just before her death, and how she had warned her about the men she would likely encounter during her life.

I also wish you good luck in your future choice of men, though as you are pretty much a clone of me, I'm not going to hold what little breath is left inside of me.

Don't fear being lonely, Jessica. Solitude has its benefits.

Jess lay on her back and stared up at the ceiling. Was there really a family curse or was it just a huge coincidence that most of the women in the family had had so much trouble with men?

She fell asleep thinking of Josh and by the morning she had decided to pay him another visit to see if she could patch things up.

Chapter 21

At nine o'clock on Friday morning, Mr Pyre the humanist celebrant, rang Jessica. In a short phone call, she detailed the parts of her father's life that could be reasonably aired in public and chose Nimrod from the Enigma Variations by Elgar as the set piece at the end of the service. Jess could remember her father whistling the tune on many occasions as he chose his horses from the race cards in the newspaper. Mr Pyre also informed Jess that the funeral had been squeezed in at the crematorium for Friday, the following week at 4.30 pm.

At ten, Jess said goodbye to her mother and drove into town, easily finding a parking space on the square outside the Uni building. Standing outside the café she took a deep breath and looking more confident than she was actually feeling, pushed open the door and stepped inside.

Josh was behind the counter with the busty Fliss who was ordering him about as if she owned the place. Jess ordered a latte and looked around at the almost empty café. There were a couple of students in the window seats and an older couple who tapped their fingers on the table as they listened to Buddy Holly singing Peggy Sue.

Josh, who had been busying himself cleaning one of the coffee machines, spotted Jess as she picked up her tall mug. He nodded to her as she smiled.

'Hello, Josh, not too busy yet?'

'No, it generally picks up after eleven. We'll be rushed off our feet by lunchtime.'

Fliss looked at Jess with a critical eye as though wondering where she had seen her before. As another customer entered the café, she gave Jess a curt nod and pointed to the seats.

'Could you move along please?'

Jess shrugged, walked slowly to a table near the juke box, pulled out a chair and sat down. She had just taken a sip of her coffee when Josh appeared at her table.

'Hi,' Jess said, producing her best smile.

Josh nodded. 'What do you want?' he asked.

'I'm sorry?' Jess looked confused. 'I've come for a quick coffee before I go to the library to do a bit of research if you must know,' she replied.

'Ah, good, that's all right then.' Josh looked back to the counter, then pulled out a seat and sat down. Jess followed Josh's glance and saw Fliss glaring at her from behind the bar. She held back a smug smile and turned her attention to Josh.

'Actually, I came in to say sorry about my attitude the other day. I was out of order snapping at you like I did. I am truly sorry. You didn't deserve that.'

'No, I didn't,' agreed Josh.

Jess was taken aback by his demeaner. 'So, can we start over? I'd still like us to be friends.'

Josh blew out his cheeks and let the air out in a gush.

'After what was passed to me the other day, I'm not sure that's possible,' he said, getting to his feet. 'Hang on, I'll show you.'

Jess watched the café owner as he strode purposefully behind the counter and into a room at the side of the kitchen. He returned a couple of minutes later with a buff, A4 mailer in his hands. Fliss watched him with interest as he walked back to the table.

'Yesterday, just before closing, I was wiping down the tables, there was only one customer left, a rather beautiful, refined looking woman in her late twenties. She looked like she should be sipping coffee in Milan, not Spinton. She was well dressed, very elegant, a bit like Sophia Loren. Anyway, she stood up as I approached, gave me a sad smile, pointed to this envelope which was lying on the table, and said, "this is what my husband and your girlfriend get up to behind our backs." Before I could say a word, she blew me a kiss and left. I picked up the package wondering what the hell she was talking about. I thought she might have mistaken me for someone else, you see. Anyway, inside I found these.'

He opened the top of the package, slipped out six, A4 black and white photographs and handed them to Jess.

She grimaced as she saw that the top picture was of her and Bradley, walking hand in hand beside the river. The next one was taken outside the Wonky Donkey on the day that Josh had spotted them together. From the angle the picture had been taken, they appeared to be involved in a passionate kiss. Two were of them holding hands as they looked into each other's eyes across a food laden table. The next was a shot of their cars parked side by side outside the farmhouse and the last one was of Bradley on the top step as he left the farmhouse after the only night they had ever spent together.

'Josh. These pictures don't paint a truly accurate picture of our relationship.'

Josh patted the pile of photos that Jess had just dropped on the table. 'It looks quite convincing to me.'

Jess sighed. 'The woman you saw was Leonora. She is Bradley's wife, but—'

'I don't think you need to say any more, really, Jess.'

'But I do, Josh. Bradley and I did start a relationship, but that was before I knew he was still married.'

'When did you find that out?' Josh asked.

'He was hurt in a nasty attack a few weeks ago, I went to see him at home and met Leonora as I was leaving. Their marriage is over, Josh, they don't love each other anymore but she won't give him a divorce.'

'That's what he told you is it? I'm amazed you fell for that one, Jess.' Josh ran his hand through his parted hair. 'A few weeks ago, you say?' He rifled through the photographs and pulled out the one showing Jess and Bradley in an embrace outside the Wonky Donkey. 'That was taken a few days ago. I was there as it happened. How do you explain that?'

'That wasn't as romantic as it looks here, Josh. We met up at his insistence, he wanted to continue the relationship after I'd called it off, which I did, straight after discovering he was married. I spent the entire meeting trying to let him down slowly. I didn't want to hurt him.'

'When was this one taken? I'm assuming it's Bradley coming out of your house?'

'Yes, it is. As I said we were in a relationship, albeit briefly.'

'You look like you've been together for years in this one.' Josh held up the picture of Jess and Bradley holding hands across a restaurant table. Jess had to admit, Leonora had timed the taking of the photograph perfectly. It was like the cover of a romantic novel, a young couple gazing lovingly into each other's eyes. She wondered how she had managed to get into a position to take it.

'We... Look, Josh, I've admitted that I had a relationship with a married man. But don't you think there's something sinister in the way she just happened to be around whenever we were together? She must have been following us like a private detective. She's very vindictive. She doesn't want him as a husband, but she doesn't want to let go either. I bet she didn't tell you she ran a key down the paintwork of his—'

'I'm not interested in what she did or didn't do, Jess, and for what it's worth, she looked to me like a very emotional woman doing her best to save her marriage. I know exactly what she's been going through as I found myself in exactly the same circumstances not so long ago. When there are children involved it's even worse.'

Jess's brow furrowed. 'Child—'

Ignoring her puzzlement, Josh looked down at the photographs, then back to Jess.

'I'm so disappointed, Jess. I really liked you but it seems that I allowed myself to be taken in. I'm not overly moralistic but when it comes to breaking up a family, well, I have to draw the line at that.'

Josh got to his feet and leaned over to scoop up the pictures but after sliding them across the table, he changed his mind and muttering to himself, turned on his heel and stomped off towards the counter.

Jess shook her head slowly as she looked down at the small pile of photographs, then picking them up, she stuffed them into her bag and with all the self-respect she could muster and with the smirking Fliss watching her every move, she stood up and walked out of the café.

Chapter 22

Late on Saturday morning, Marjorie answered the door to a handsome man in his fifties wearing jeans, a checked shirt and a navy Harrington jacket.

'Hello, I'm Jim Weatherall, your surveyor.'

Marjorie became suddenly flustered. She patted her hair, tugged at the front of her blouse, then patted her hair again.

'Could I, erm, come in?'

'Oh, yes, of course.' Marjorie stepped back quickly and held out her hand towards the lounge. 'Martha's in there, would you like a cup of tea? We've got some biscuits, nice ones.'

'I don't really have time to be honest,' said Jim as he stepped into the hall. He looked around before striding smartly into the lounge. Martha looked up as he entered.

'Ah, you'll be the price fixer,' she said.

'I'm the surveyor. Jim Weatherall.' He put his bag on the table, unzipped it and took out a small instrument in a leather cover.

'Damp meter,' he explained.

'You won't be needing that; the house is as dry as a bone. We've never had a spot of damp in all the time I've lived here.'

'I'm sure you're right, but I have to check anyway.'

Martha grunted as he picked up his iPad and opened a floor plan app. 'Shall I start upstairs?' he asked.

'There's a crack in the ceiling of my bedroom. That's all you'll find wrong up there,' said Martha firmly.

'I'm used to cracks... and pots,' he muttered to himself.

'Take off your shoes before you go up,' Martha said, stiffly. 'We don't want muddy footprints on the stair carpet.'

Forty minutes later, with Martha's incessant questions still ringing in his ears the surveyor left the house, dropped his bag on the front seat and climbed into his car. Pulling his phone from his pocket he dialled Bradley's number and waited impatiently for him to pick up.

'Bradley, ah, good. Now listen, I've got to take the missis to her mother's and I'm already late.'

'Okay.'

'I've just been to survey the Crew residence.'

'Oh, I hope you came through unscathed.'

'Barely, she's a harridan, isn't she? A right old battle axe.'

'Tell me about it,' replied Bradley. 'She... oh, it doesn't matter. Did you manage to complete the survey? I've got a time limit on this job. She's off to meet Bin Laden in a week or so.'

'Who?'

'Never mind.'

'Well, if you need a guesstimate while you wait for the full survey, I'd put the value at four hundred and ninety-five thousand, half a million on a good day. It needs a little bit of work but it's damp free and remarkably well preserved for a building of its age.'

'Great, Kate says the searches are going well so I can't see any major obstacle that might get in the way of the contract.'

'You're rushing this one through, aren't you?'

'I'm doing this as a favour for a special friend of mine if I'm honest. Normally I'd make pushy people like our Mrs Crew wait a few weeks, but...'

'Ah, I see, there's a pretty face behind it eh? Does Leonora know about her?'

'Sadly, yes, and she's doing her best to ruin the relationship.'

Jim groaned. 'A woman scorned and all that.'

'All that with icing on top,' Bradley replied. 'Right, thanks for sorting it so quickly, Jim, we'll have to catch up with a night out soon. It's been too long.'

'You're in the chair, you owe me for this one,' Jim said, seriously.

'Was she that bad?'

'In my ear all the time, telling me how to do my job, pointing out improvements she'd made over the years... and if I hear one more word about that bloody ceiling...'

'That bad, eh?'

'Her sister was even worse. She offered to share her bed with me if I go with them on the cruise.'

'She what?'

'She's seventy-five if she's a day. I know I'm not a young stud myself but for pity's sake... She kept going on about my muscles. I had to put my coat back on to hide my biceps, I swear to God she was going to ask if she could feel them.'

Bradley stifled a laugh. 'Okay, Jim, I'll let you go now, thanks again. Can you get that report to me this week?'

'You'll have it by Thursday,' Jim replied. 'I can't wait to see the back of it.'

After the surveyor had driven away, Marjorie placed a fully laden tea tray on the coffee table and sat down opposite her sister.

Martha was silent for a while but as Marjorie opened her mouth to speak, she let rip.

'Marjorie, you've embarrassed me on many, many occasions, but this time you have excelled yourself.'

'Why, Martha, what have I done?'

'That surveyor. You virtually threw yourself at him.'

'He was nice, I liked him.'

'You like anything in trousers, Marjorie.'

'I don't like Mr Robinson at the newsagents. He's a grumpy—'

'It was cringeworthy, Marjorie. The poor man could hardly do his job with you wittering into his ear all the time.'

'I was only telling him about the cruise, Martha.'

'You told him he could come with us if he liked.'

'I only said—'

'You said he could sleep in your bed.'

'Yes, but... not when I was in it, Martha.' Marjorie blushed.

Martha sighed. 'I hope you're not going to flirt with every man on board ship, Marjorie. You should take a long, hard look at yourself. You're an old woman, the only thing men will ever find remotely interesting about you, is how big your bank balance is.'

'It's not very big, Martha. I gave what I had to you when you... oh, I'm not supposed to talk about that, am I? Sorry.'

Marjorie looked quickly away and picked up the teapot.

'While we're on the subject of money, I have just negotiated a contract with Jessica's trust lawyer, and that means I will soon be receiving a rather large sum of money. That in turn means that I will finally be in a position to pay you back, so you won't have any reason to bring the subject up in future.'

'I don't bring it up that much, Martha.'

Martha sighed again.

'Marjorie, the subject is seldom off your lips, anyone would think you were running the International Monetary Fund.' She held up her hand to silence her sister as she opened her mouth to object. 'As I said, I will shortly be in a far healthier financial position, so, as you gave me twenty percent of the value of my house back in the early nineteen-seventies, I'm going to give you twenty percent of the money that will be arriving in my bank account over the next couple of weeks.'

Marjorie clasped her hands in front of her chest.

'So, you'll be receiving thirty thousand pounds.'

'Thirty thousand? Are you sure, Martha, I only lent you ten thousand.'

'Call the rest, interest accrued,' said Martha generously.

'Ooh, does this mean I'll have money in the bank to spend while we're on holiday?'

'I'm not sure it will arrive by the time we go, but it won't be long after. Consider yourself wealthy, Marjorie.'

'Oh, thank you, Martha. Thirty thousand pounds. I've never been rich before.'

'I said I'd look after you, Marjorie and I meant it. Now, regarding the money. I'll find a nice, safe place to invest it for you, in fact, it would probably be better if I kept it in my bank account. We don't want any of those dreadful Internet scammers to hack into your account and steal it all do we?'

'No, Martha, thank you, it's really kind of you.'

'Don't mention it. As I've said many times, I always know what's best for you, Marjorie. You're my baby sister after all.' Martha leaned back in her cushions. 'Now, make some more tea, that pot will be stewed by now.'

Chapter 23

Jessica spent Friday finishing off the three articles she had been contracted to write. After a final edit, she emailed the documents to the editors of the magazines she had agreed terms with, and sat back with a satisfied grunt.

'That's the bills paid next month, Nana,' she said aloud.

'I can't be called Nana until you have kids, Jess,' Nicola said with a laugh.

'I'm always talking to her, Mum. I'm sure she's hanging around looking out for me like she did when she was alive.'

'Even I give her the credit she's due for that.' Nicola forced a tight smile. 'When I look back...'

'Don't, Mum, it's fine. I'm fine. You don't have to keep beating yourself up about it.'

'I'm not really, Jess, it's just that... well, I could have been a better mother.'

'How? With him taking every penny that came into the house.'

Nicola shrugged. 'I should have kicked him out.'

'And done what, Mum? We struggled enough as it was.' She put her fingers under her mother's chin and gently lifted her head so that their eyes met.

'You did your best. I turned out all right. That's all there is to it. There's nothing you can do about it now, so please don't relive it over and over. That chapter of your life will end in about...' Jess checked her watch... 'an hour's time.'

She turned away and closed the lid of her laptop. 'I'd better get ready. I'm wearing blue, not black. Do you think that's sacrilegious of me?'

'I doubt he'd have expected you to go full Queen Victoria, Jess.'

'I'll wear a black jacket and shoes. I don't want to be totally disrespectful.'

Nicola patted her arm. 'You can wear pink for me, love. He should just be grateful that anyone turned up at all.'

As Jess opened the front door, Nicola called after her. 'Don't forget I'm doing a couple of hours at Mrs Kaur's shop later this afternoon. She's letting me ease myself back in.'

'Are you? I thought you were starting back next Wednesday.'

'I rang her yesterday. I was going to tell you but you've been busy with your writing.'

'Okay, well, good luck with it, Mum. I hope it goes well.'

At 4.15. Jess stood by the entrance to the reception area at the crematorium and waited as the grieving relatives from the previous service read the cards on the floral tributes, or stood around in small groups, laughing or wiping away tears as some distant memory or other was recounted. Jess had the forecourt to herself by the time the hearse arrived at 4.30. Mr Pyre made her jump as he walked up quietly behind her.

'All set then?'

Jess nodded, then stood aside as Mr Pyre wedged open the double doors and four, slight-looking pallbearers carried her father's coffin in the reception hall to the opening bars of Elgar's Nimrod.

Jess followed the coffin with Mr Pyre at her side. 'That's very clever,' she whispered.

'Pardon... Oh, the music.' Mr Pyre pulled out a small, plastic handheld device. 'It's all remote controlled these days.'

Jess sat alone on the front row of seats on the right-hand side as the pallbearers picked seats on different rows on the left, presumably to make the hall appear less empty.

Mr Pyre, unsurprisingly, kept the service short. He spoke for a minute or so about the frailty of the human existence before reading out a couple of short paragraphs about Owen.

Jess was pleased that he didn't wax lyrical about a loving father and husband who would be sadly missed, concentrating instead on his enthusiastic devotion to his life goals, which he set about achieving with an almost religious zeal.

A little more than five minutes after the service had started, Mr Pyre reached into his pocket and pulled out his remote control. A few seconds later an unseen music streamer began to play Nimrod once again and Owen's coffin began to move between the undrawn curtains at the back of the hall. Jess got to her feet, muttered, 'goodbye, Dad' and waited until her father's remains had finished its short, final journey and the curtains had closed before turning away and briskly stepping out of the hall. Outside, she thanked the pallbearers for their diligence and passed a twenty-pound note to the leader of the group, then shaking Mr Pyre's hand she thanked him for conducting the service with such brevity.

'Dad wouldn't have appreciated it anyway, Mr Pyre. A longer service would have been wasted on him. I'm not being mean or disrespectful, but he had no time for pleasantries. Even when he was at his best, which wasn't very often, Dad kept the niceties to a bare minimum. He wasn't one to hand out praise, no matter what anyone had accomplished.'

After saying goodbye to the celebrant, Jess climbed into her car and drove along Main Street until she reached the roadworks that British Gas had set up earlier in the week. The road had been cut back to a single lane for a hundred-yard stretch and was controlled by a temporary traffic light system.

The tea-time traffic was heavy and when Jess looked into her rear-view mirror, she saw a long line of busses, vans and cars had already built up behind her. There was only one car in front, a fifteen-year-old MPV with a deep dent in the right-hand wing.

162

As the lights changed to green, the car in front spluttered into life and a cloud of black fumes shot out of its exhaust. Jess slipped her Toyota into gear and followed the car into the single, coned off lane. About fifty yards further along, the MPV suddenly came to a juddering halt. Jess waited patiently as the driver tried to restart, but her patience began to wear thin when a triple-chinned man wearing clothes straight out of a 1970s TV drama, climbed out of the car, kicked the front wheel, then lifting up the bonnet, began to fiddle around in the engine.

Jess switched off her own engine as the drivers behind began to toot and parp on their horns. After a couple of minutes, the man came out from under the hood of the MPV and wiping an oily hand across his wobbling chins, he climbed back into his car where he tried, and failed to start it. Thirty seconds later he slid from his seat, turned towards Jess and shrugged.

Jess wound down her window and stuck her head out into the cold evening air.

'Electrics have gone,' he said.

'Have you got RAC, Green Flag or someone?' Jess asked.

'No, I can't afford anything like that,' replied the man. 'I can only just about afford the insurance and road tax.'

Jess blew out her cheeks, wound up the window and switched the radio on. The workmen had gone home for the evening and a deep channel had been dug in the road beyond the cones, so it wasn't going to be a simple task to move the car out of the way. Some form of breakdown truck would have to reverse the remaining fifty or so metres through the roadworks to get to the MPV. It looked like being a long wait.

At three forty-five, Nicola parked up her car outside Mrs Kaur's shop and with a familiar tinkle of the bell, entered the shop.

'Hello, Nicola, I didn't expect to see you here today.' Mrs Kaur looked up from the magazine she was reading.

Nicola smiled. 'I know, I need to buy a couple of things so I thought I'd get them here and say hello at the same time.'

'You're always welcome, any time, my dear.' Mrs Kaur got up from her seat. 'Tracey has let me down again. She was due here at three-thirty. I got a call from her at twenty-eight minutes past.'

'I could stand in for an hour to give you a break,' said Nicola. 'I have to report to the police station before five though.'

'You're a star. I'm desperate for a few things from the wholesaler. If I go now, I can be back for four-thirty.'

Nicola held her arm out towards the door. 'Off you go then. Oh, I'd avoid town, there's a breakdown in the roadworks, it's just been on the local radio. Traffic's backing up for miles.'

Mrs Kaur pulled on her coat and picked up her bag. 'Thanks for the warning, I'll take the back road. The wholesaler is only a mile away so even if some of the traffic is using it, I'll still be back in time.'

Nicola stood by the window until she had seen Mrs Kaur's green van drive away before walking smartly to the lockable cupboard behind the counter where the bottles of spirits were kept. Picking up a half bottle of vodka, Nicola ran it across the bar code reader, then dipping into her purse she pulled out her debit card and with bated breath, ran it across the card scanner. Suddenly the till printer burst into life and her receipt was printed. Nicola breathed a sigh of relief, her Universal Credit had been paid in, bang on time. Walking out from behind the till, she stood in the passage between the shop and the living quarters where she couldn't be overlooked by the CCTV camera and with shaking hands, unscrewed the top from the bottle and took three deep swigs.

Mrs Kaur arrived back five minutes before her promised time, and after unloading the various boxes of new stock, she pulled off her coat and relieved Nicola on the till.

'Thank you so much for covering for me, Nicola. I owe you a favour, I won't forget this.'

'You're welcome.' Nicola looked at her watch. 'A quarter to five. Perfect timing.' Picking up her bag from behind the counter she walked slowly towards the door.

'Didn't you want to pick up a few items, Nicola?'

'It's all right, I'd better get round to the police station in case there's a queue at the counter.'

'Okay, well, drop back in on your way home. We can have a cup of tea after you've done your shopping.'

'I'll have to see what time it is. Jess has been to Owen's funeral so I think I'd better get back for her, she might need a shoulder.'

'Ah, I'm so sorry, was that today? I can't blame you for not going after what he did, but I'm glad Jessica went. No one should be sent to meet their God completely alone.'

'I doubt if God will find the time to hang around for him,' Nicola muttered to herself and at the second attempt, managed to find the door handle with her outreached hand. Pulling it open, she stepped into the street and made her way to her car.

Sitting in the old Ford, Nicola reached into the pocket of her coat and pulled out the Vodka. After taking two quick mouthfuls, she slipped the half-empty bottle into the glove compartment and after wiping her mouth on the back of her hand, pulled on her seat belt, started up the engine and drove the few hundred yards to the police station.

'Mrs Griffiths.' The duty constable greeted her and looked up at the big clock on the wall before pulling out her report sheet.

'Sign here please.' The policeman pointed to a dotted line next to the date on the form.

Nicola took the pen and blinking under the bright fluorescent lighting, scrawled her name on the form.

'There's one more thing before you go,' the constable said as Nicola turned to leave. 'One of the stipulations in your release arrangement states that you must abstain from alcohol. Can you confirm that you have stuck to that agreement?'

'I have,' Nicola replied. 'Check with my daughter if you like. She's on the wagon too.'

'That's good to hear. However, the release conditions allow us to ask tagged prisoners to perform a random breathalyser test. Your name came up on the list today, so could you come around the back for a few moments? My colleague will perform the test.'

As the blood drained from Nicola's face, the policeman opened a door at the side of reception and led her through to a small room where a female police officer was sitting behind a desk. She stood up as Nicola entered and came out from behind the desk holding a breathalyser kit in her hands.

'Okay, Mrs Griffiths,' she said with a smile. 'This won't take a minute.'

Chapter 24

Jessica didn't get home until just after five-thirty. Frustrated and tired, she dumped her bag on the big table before putting the kettle on and taking off her coat. She was just pouring water onto the coffee granules when her phone rang.

'Ms Jessica Griffiths?'

Jess knew something was seriously amiss immediately. She closed her eyes and took in a deep breath as she replied.

'Yes.'

'This is Constable Hargreaves from Spinton police. I'm afraid I have some bad news about your mother.'

Jess slumped onto a chair, her heart in her mouth.

'No, please, don't say...'

'No, it's nothing like that, Miss. She's fine, it's just that she has broken the conditions of her release agreement and she's been taken into custody.'

'But, but... look if she didn't turn up this evening it's because she was at work; she's starting back gradually and—'

'She turned up on time, Miss. But she was under the influence of alcohol. She failed a breathalyser test. We have now taken a blood sample and we're waiting for the results to come back.'

Jess sighed. 'Oh, Mum.'

'She'll be kept in a cell overnight and we should have the results in the morning. I must warn you that should the second test prove positive, she will be remanded in custody at a women's prison until the CPS decide whether or not she is going to face charges.'

'Can I see her? I'll come straight over.'

'It's not possible I'm afraid. Should her result be negative, and I have to tell you, Miss Griffiths, having questioned her, that is highly unlikely, then she'll be released to your care in the morning, otherwise she will be remanded to the Bronzefield women's prison in

Ashford. Visiting will be restricted while she settles in, we'll inform you when you can see her.'

'Ashford? That's not too far at least.'

'Erm, I'm sorry to give you more bad news but the prison is situated in Ashford, Middlesex.'

'Middlesex!'

'I'm afraid that's correct. Remand places for Kent females are very limited.'

'How far is Bronze... field, was it?'

'It's about eighty miles or so. I'm sorry, I know how inconvenient that must be but there's not a lot I can do about it.'

'Is there anyone I can speak to? I mean, there has to be a way out of this. After what she went through is there any wonder she weakens at times?'

'I'm sorry, Miss. You can speak to my sergeant, but he's not back until eleven, tomorrow.'

'All right. I'll ring back then. Could you give a message to my mother from me please?'

'I'm sorry but...'

'Please. Just tell her I love her and I'll come to see her as soon as I can.'

'All right, Miss, I'll pass that on. Good evening.'

As the phone went dead, Jess put it on the big, oak table. 'Oh, Mum,' she said, as her head dropped to her chest and the tears began to flow.

At eleven the following morning, Jess had a two-minute phone conversation with an obviously irritated police sergeant in which he informed her that her blood test had showed not only alcohol in her system but enough to put her over the limit to drive. Jess thought quickly.

'And, had she been driving?'

'We don't know for sure, but her car is parked on the road opposite the station.'

'But you don't know for sure if she drove it there? I mean, a friend could have driven her there.'

'Well, no, we have no proof of that but her car keys were in her possession when she was arrested.'

'That doesn't prove she drove there.'

'No... it doesn't but look here, Miss Griffiths—'

'I'll get a cab over and pick up her car. Will the keys be ready for me on reception if I come straight over? I don't want to risk it being vandalised, towed away, clamped or anything while she's in prison.'

'It's outside the police station, Miss, I doubt the former will happen, I can't guarantee the rest.'

'So, can I pick up the keys?'

'I suppose so, I'll leave them on the front desk.'

'And, can I see my mother before she's taken away?'

'No, I'm afraid that's not possible, Miss. She's already being processed into the system.'

After picking up the keys from a surly police constable on the front desk, Jess walked over the road to where Nicola's car was parked. Climbing inside, she sniffed the air for any smell of alcohol then she looked into the back seat and the footwell of the passenger seat before opening up the glove compartment to find her mother's half full bottle of Vodka. Sighing, she dropped the bottle on the front seat and slammed the glove box shut, then, starting the car, she pulled away onto the Gillingham Road and headed to Martha's house to give her the bad news.

'Hello, Jessica, come in, come in.' Marjorie answered the door wearing a summer frock. She shivered in the late morning air and almost slammed the door shut behind Jess as she stepped into the hall.

'Brrr, it's proper metal monkey weather, isn't it?'

Jess kissed Marjorie on the cheek. 'It's Brass Monkey, Auntie,' she whispered.

Marjorie nodded. 'Is it? I see.' A puzzled look came over her face. Jess kissed her again and stepped into the lounge where she found Martha standing at the dining table fiddling about with a bowl of fruit.

'Hello, Grandma. I'm afraid I've got some bad news.'

'Don't tell me the cruise ship has sunk. Marjorie will never get over it.'

'No, nothing like that, the cruise ship is fine and the holiday is still going ahead.'

Martha looked critically at her fruit bowl arrangement. then, after adjusting the position of an apple by about a millimetre, she stepped away and made her way over to her seat.

'Marjorie. Tea,' she ordered.

'Yes, Martha,' Marjorie slipped past Jess and scurried into the kitchen.

'So, what bad news do you bring to brighten our day?' Martha fidgeted about in her chair, then adjusted her cushions before settling back into them.

'Mum's in prison. She failed a breathalyser test at the police station yesterday.'

Martha shrugged. 'It's hardly surprising. I doubt the bookies would even have taken bets on it happening.' She placed her hands on her lap and looked across at Jess. 'Where have they taken her?'

'A place called Bronzefield, it's in Middlesex.'

'MIDDLESEX!'

'I know. It's not fair, is it?'

'Fairness doesn't come into it really, Jessica. She's only got herself to blame. It's you I feel sorry for, having to travel all that way to see her.'

'They won't let me see her yet. She's got to settle in first.'

Martha shook her head slowly. 'The silly girl. I hope these ridiculous charges are sorted out soon. She doesn't belong in prison for pity's sake. She should be getting treatment for her addiction.'

'Oh, Grandma, that's sweet of you. I didn't expect you to show any sympathy for her plight.'

'Contrary to rumour. I do have a beating heart inside my chest, not a swinging brick.'

Jess stood up, walked around the coffee table and gave her grandmother a hug. 'Bless you for caring,' she said, swallowing the lump that had suddenly appeared in her throat.

Martha patted Jess's back then pulled out of the hug. 'Right, that's enough of that.'

Jess laughed. 'Come on, Grandma, you know you enjoyed it. You don't get enough in the way of hugs.'

'Thank the Lord for that,' Martha replied. 'There's too much close contact these days. No wonder all these bugs spread so rapidly.'

Marjorie came back into the lounge carrying a rattling tea tray. Placing it on the coffee table, she picked up a chair from under the dining table and carried it across the room.

'Jessica,' she said as she sat down. 'Could you explain something to me?'

'If I can, Aunt Marjorie. What do you want to know?'

'She doesn't understand how time zones work, that's what she wants to know,' Martha said, rolling her eyes to the ceiling. 'She just can't see why it's light in Japan when it's dark here.'

'It is a bit tricky until you understand it,' said Jess, looking softly at her aunt.

'The sun is the problem,' said Marjorie with a furtive look at Martha.

'For pity's sake, Marjorie, the sun isn't the problem.' Her face sank as she looked towards Jess. 'I've spent all morning trying to explain, I even used fruit from the bowl.'

'Let me have a go, Grandma.' Jess smiled to herself as she walked across the room to pick up the bowl of fruit. 'I think I can remember how it works from when I was at school.'

Marjorie moved the tea tray to one side and Jess emptied the fruit bowl putting the apples, oranges and bananas on her lap. She placed the bowl in the middle of the coffee table and picked up an apple.

'I won't put all the planets in this model as it might get a bit messy,' she said as she pulled a black marker from her bag. 'Right, Auntie Marj, let's pretend that the big fruit bowl is the sun. All right?'

'It's yellow, so that looks right,' replied Marjorie.

'Oh for...' Martha cut her words short as Jess gave her a look.

'Right, Auntie. This apple is the Earth... I know it's green and red, not green and blue, but never mind.' Jess moved the apple in a wide circle around the fruit bowl. 'The Earth orbits the sun; it takes three hundred and sixty-five days to go around it.'

'This is one of the things I get confused about,' said Marjorie. 'Why doesn't the sky go black when we're around the back of it?'

'It doesn't have a dark side, Aunt Marjorie. It's a big ball of fire. It's the same all the way around.'

'So, why does it get dark then?'

Martha sighed.

'I'll show you,' said Jess. She took the top from the marker and held out the apple to Marjorie. 'Right. The bit here, where it was attached to the branch is the north pole and this bit, she turned the apple over and pointed to the core, is the south pole. Okay?'

Marjorie nodded.

'Now, this is where it gets a bit complicated,' said Jess.

'Good luck with this bit,' said Martha, shaking her head.

'The Earth doesn't just orbit the sun, it also spins on its own, like this.' Jess turned the apple around in her hand. 'It's also tilted a little bit... fifteen degrees if I remember correctly.' She tilted the apple slightly. 'Now, let's mark out Japan and the UK.' Jess put a dark blob on one part of the apple and marked it with a J, then moving it around, she put another blob on the other side of the piece of fruit and marked it UK. 'Now then,' Jess tilted the apple again and began to turn it in her hand. 'Can you see which dot is facing the sun?'

172

Marjorie pointed to the J.

'That's right, now, as it keeps spinning, what happens?'

Marjorie leapt out of her seat. 'I can't see the J anymore.'

'So, what's near the sun now?'

'The UK, but where did Japan go?'

'It didn't go anywhere, it's no longer facing the sun, it's in darkness, so it's night time, but the UK is facing the sun, so it's daylight. Do you see.'

'Do it again,' said Marjorie quickly.

Jess turned the apple around slowly so that the J was nearer the fruit bowl. 'So now it's daylight in...?'

'Japan!' Marjorie shouted.

'That's right,' said Jess. 'The thing is, Aunt Marjorie, the sun rises in the east and sets in the west, so as you're flying towards Japan, the earth is still spinning and as it takes twelve hours to fly there, it's going to be dark by the time you arrive because there is an eight-hour time difference, so, if you add together the time the flight takes and the time difference you will find out what time it will be in Japan when you land.'

'I'm confused again,' said Marjorie.

Martha snorted. 'I told you this was a waste of time, Jessica.' She turned to her sister with a scornful look on her face. 'Marjorie, if brains were taxed, you'd be in for a rebate.'

Jess scowled at Martha.

'All right, let's assume you take off from London at eight in the morning and it takes twelve hours to fly to Japan, if you didn't alter your watch, what time would it say when you landed?'

Marjorie did a quick calculation whilst turning her head towards the ceiling.

'Eight o'clock,' she said.

'Well done! It would be four o'clock in London. Now, there's an eight-hour time difference, their time is in front of us, so add that on. What time is it Japan?'

Marjorie did the calculation.

'Four o'clock in the morning?'

'Correct!' Jess beamed at her aunt. 'Do you understand now?'

Marjorie nodded. 'Yes, I think so.'

'Thank heavens for that,' Martha said with a sigh.

'But...' Marjorie looked hard at the fruit bowl, then at the apple. 'It will be past my bedtime when we land... and, I won't be able to sleep with the sun in my eyes, I hope they have thick curtains on the ship.'

'Why would you...?' It was Jessica's turn to look puzzled.

'Because by the time we land the J will be back round to face the fruit bowl.'

'No, no it won't,' Martha was exasperated.

Jess put the fruit into the bowl and put it back on the dining table.

'Just change your watch to Japan time when you land and you'll find it will be dark by bedtime, Auntie.'

'But, how will I know what time Japan time is?'

'YOU LOOK AT A BLINKING CLOCK!' Martha yelled.

Jess nodded. 'It's as simple as that, Auntie Marj. Then when you come back, change your watch to UK time again.'

'Oh, well that's easy, why didn't you say that in the first place?'

Jess stifled a giggle as Martha's shoulders sank.

'You're right, Aunt Marjorie. It would have been simpler.'

Chapter 25

Bronzefield prison was a modern-looking stone and brick clad building with a visitors' welcome centre built away from the main prison block. Jess arrived a good forty-five minutes before her time slot, parked up and walked the short distance from the short-stay car park to a small but comfortably furnished visitors' centre. Because she was early, she was able to present her credentials – her photo card driving licence and a utility bill – at the reception desk, without queuing. Having been recorded onto the system, Jess sat in an armchair where she could look out of the window while she waited to be called.

By the time her name was announced some thirty minutes later, the reception area was full. The visitors were almost all female, some obviously grandmothers, some more likely mothers, but quite a few had brought young children with them. Jess looked on sadly as the young ones played in the soft play area at the back of the room, wondering what sort of life they were living without their loved one playing a part in it.

'Jessica Griffiths?'

Jess got to her feet and was directed through a side door leading to a paved area that ran alongside a steel-tubed car barrier. She followed the pavement until she reached the main entrance to the prison where she was again asked to provide her credentials. Once they had been checked, she stood on a marked spot while her photograph and digital fingerprints were taken. Placing her bag on a small conveyor, she waited as it passed under a scanner before stepping through an airport style, metal detector herself. Inside, she was given a brisk body search by a chunky-looking female security guard.

After her rub down search, she was given a red, plastic tray on which sat a key with a number tag attached. She followed the prison officer's pointing finger and came to a locker room where she opened her assigned locker, took a handful of pound coins from her purse, then placed her shoulder bag containing her phone, purse and car keys in the metal locker. She dropped the coins onto the plastic plate and walked through to the waiting area where she sat for a few minutes until another female security guard opened a sliding glass door to allow her entry to the visiting room.

She spotted her mother straight away, sitting on an armchair well away from another soft play area.

'Hello, Mum.' Jessica hugged Nicola, then turning away, she wiped her eyes before sitting down opposite.

'How are you? Have you settled in all right?' She looked around the room. 'It looks nice enough. I was expecting one of those awful Victorian prisons with the high windows and huge iron-studded oak doors.'

'It's all right, I suppose. It's newish and clean, we get decent food and some time to watch movies or mix with the other inmates.'

'Have you spoken to anyone about how long you might be here?'

'I've seen so many people I've lost count. There are enough social workers to hold their own convention, no wonder you can't get to see one on the outside. I've got friendly with a young woman called Jemima. She's in for persistent shoplifting. When I say persistent, I mean on a daily basis. The poor girl has three kids and she's only just eighteen. THREE! can you imagine what sort of life they have to live?'

'I know, Mum.'

'There are all sorts in here.' Nicola tapped her nose. 'You have to be careful who you talk to. I've already been offered a warm bed at night by two women. One of them is only your age.'

'Oh, dear.'

'It's all right, they took no for an answer. I haven't seen any trouble, everyone's been nice to me so far at least.'

'So, what did your social worker have to say?'

176

'I'm getting treatment for my addiction, though treatment just means sitting in a big circle telling everyone how drink or drugs have dragged us down and how much we'd like to get straight.' Nicola shrugged. 'I can see how some people might get benefit from it but I just tell them what they want to hear, then sit and daydream while the rest are giving up their confession.'

'Mum, it might help if you participated properly.'

'Jess. I'm not airing my dirty laundry in public. I remember your father going to the Gambler's Anonymous gatherings. He'd just talk any old nonsense then come out from the meeting and go straight to a card school.'

Jess sighed. 'Changing the subject, I'm taking Grandma and Aunt Marjorie to the airport on Saturday evening. Marjorie is so excited; she hasn't slept properly for a week. She's still convinced that because Japan is called the land of the rising sun, it never gets dark.'

Nicola laughed. 'That's Aunt Marjie for you. She's nowhere near as daft as she looks, but she does get confused by things.'

'Would you like a coffee? I've brought change.'

Jess walked up to the refreshment counter and ordered up two coffees and two thin slices of chocolate cake. Returning to her seat, she carefully placed her plastic tray on a small table and passed a cup to her mother. A couple of three-year-old girls eyed up their cake from across the room.

'Can we have cake, Gran?'

A poorly dressed woman of about forty-five shook her head. 'I'm not made of money, Brittney. It cost me all I had on bus fares.'

Jess looked at Nicola and pulled a sad face.

'I didn't want cake anyway.'

'Nor me.'

Jess picked up the plate and carried it across to the girls' gran, who was sitting opposite a twenty-something woman with scars across her wrists.

'Excuse me, I've just bought cake for my mother, but she doesn't want it. I hate throwing it away, do you think the children would like it?'

The woman nodded, smiled gratefully and called the girls to her. They grabbed the cake from the plate and began to eat as though they hadn't seen chocolate for months.

'Say thank you to the kind lady,' the grandmother ordered. The girls complied through chocolate covered mouths.

'You're very welcome,' said Jess before turning away and walking back to her seat.

Nicola and Jess spent a further forty minutes together before a prison officer arrived to tell them that visiting time was over. Jess gave Nicola a big hug and once again found herself fighting back tears.

'I'll come back next week, Mum. Hang in there, I'm sure the police will come to their senses soon.'

'Do you know, love, I don't think I care anymore.'

'Mum, don't give up hope, I'm sure this nightmare will be over soon.'

Nicola gave Jess another hug, then wiping her eyes, she walked to the door of the reception room where the prison guard was waiting to escort her back to her cell.

On the way back home, Jess stopped off at Mrs Kaur's shop to tell her that Nicola wouldn't be coming in to work the following week. The shopkeeper was saddened to hear of her mother's arrest.

'She did me a big favour last week. I had been let down by my staff and she watched the shop while I went to the wholesaler. I noticed a half bottle of Vodka had been rung into the till when I got back. Now, I know Nicola has her problems but I always know I can trust her. Tracey would have just stolen the Vodka and more besides.'

'Do you mean you'll still keep her job open for her when she gets out? That's very kind of you,' Jess smiled warmly.

'I'll welcome her back with open arms. In fact, I'll put up some bunting and organise a brass band to celebrate the occasion.' She leaned forward conspiratorially. 'There are very few trustworthy people about these days. Many of my customers steal from me, my staff steal from me and I even found my own grandfather taking a roll of extra strong mints without asking the other day.' She sighed and walked back behind her counter. 'Is she allowed telephone calls? I'd love to speak to her if possible. I might be able to cheer her up a bit.'

'She is, but you have to ring first and book a time slot. I've got the number here.'

Five minutes later, with a bottle of Pinot Grigio on the passenger seat, Jess drove back to the farmhouse. Dropping her shoulder bag on the table she opened the wine and poured a full glass before taking the cigarettes and lighter from the kitchen drawer. Sitting on the top step, she closed the back door behind her and staring up at the star-strewn sky, she lit a cigarette and took a long pull on it.

'Goodnight, Mum, I hope you manage to get some sleep,' she said aloud, then fixing her gaze on the old barn, she took a sip of wine, took another draw on her cigarette and let her mind slip back to the times she spent on the farm as a young girl. Life was simple then, she felt safe, knowing that with her beloved Nana close by, nothing in the world could ever hurt her.

'When did it all get so complicated?' she whispered.

Chapter 26

At 2.15 pm on Saturday, Jessica pulled up in a hired car outside Martha's house to find Marjorie waiting for her in the hall.

'She's been standing there since lunchtime in case you came early,' Martha said with a shake of her head.

Jess gave Marjorie a hug. 'Are you all set to go?'

Marjorie rushed back inside and came out carrying a small suitcase. Putting it carefully on the floor, she extended the handle and walked around the car parking space, pulling it behind her before stopping in front of Jessica.

'I've got a big case too, so has Martha, we got them off the internet, a man delivered them yesterday, I had to repack all my stuff.'

Jess looked at the bright orange, hand luggage trolley and held a hand in front of her eyes as if to shield them from the glare. 'You won't lose that one, will you, Auntie?'

'Why she had to choose that colour is beyond me,' said Martha, wheeling her own, two-tone grey suitcase onto the top step.

'She likes it, that's all that matters,' replied Jess. 'Does the big one match it?'

'It's a matching pair,' said Marjorie, proudly.

'Where's your car?' asked Martha looking puzzled.

'I'd never have got all your luggage and the two of you in my little Toyota,' said Jess. 'We'll all be comfortable in this one.'

Martha helped Jess load the larger of the cases into the extended boot, then piled her own hand luggage on top. She turned around to find Marjorie frantically unzipping and re-zipping the various sized pouches and sections of her wheeled case.

'Don't tell me you've forgotten something, Marjorie. You can't have, you packed just about everything you own.'

'I can't find my sweets... the ones I bought to make my ears go pop on the plane.'

'Are we on a plane at the moment?'

'No, Martha, but...'

'Are your ears likely to go pop in the car?'

'No, but—'

'Then get in the car, Marjorie, we have to get to the airport two hours before the flight takes off and at this rate, we'll miss it by a fortnight.' She stomped across to Marjorie, zipped up the two remaining open sections and dumped the travel case unceremoniously on top of hers.

Marjorie clambered into the back seat of the car and pulled her seatbelt on. She looked back into the extended boot as Martha got into the other side.

'You can pull it along behind the car if you think you'll make it all the way to Heathrow,' Martha said, following her sister's anxious gaze. 'Just forget about the blooming sweets.'

'I was just making sure I'd packed them, Martha.'

'You've checked both of your cases at least four times this morning, Marjorie. Of course, you packed them.'

Jessica, who had just returned to the car after checking that the doors and windows of the house were all locked, listened to her two elderly relatives bickering and shook her head, feeling a surge of relief in the knowledge that she wouldn't be stuck in a cabin with them for the next three weeks. She pulled on her own seat belt, then turned back towards them.

'All set? Have you got your tickets and passports? Good! Airport here we come.'

Jess pulled out of the short drive and turned left onto Mowbray Lane, then switching the sat nav to her pre-entered route, she leaned back in the driver's seat and headed for the A2.

Being a Saturday, the traffic was lighter than it would have been in the week and they made good time until they reached the M25 where all the lanes were busy. Jess checked the time on the car's console and satisfied at the progress they were making, pulled into the middle lane and sat at a safe distance behind a London tour bus.

As they neared the Clacket Lane services, Jess asked the two old ladies if they needed a toilet break. Martha shook her head and looked sideways at her sister.

'Are you sure, Marjorie? We can pull in if you need to go.'

'I'm fine, Martha. I went before we set off and I haven't had any tea since then so I won't need to pee.'

'Don't you dare ask to go as soon as we've passed the turn off.' Martha looked sternly at her younger sister.

'I won't.' Marjorie looked back belligerently.

Five miles past the services, Marjorie leaned forwards and tapped Jess on the arm. Jess took a quick glance over her shoulder and then focussed on the road.

'What is it, Auntie?'

'Don't tell me you need the lavatory,' Martha spat.

'No, of course not. I was just going to ask—'

'And don't you dare start asking if we're nearly there yet.'

'No... well, yes, I was going to ask that.'

'We're over half way there, Auntie Marj,' said Jessica.

'Ooh, half way, that's good, isn't it?'

'We're making good time,' Jess replied.

'So, there's no need to ask every five minutes,' added Martha.

'You can work out how far we have to go by the road signs, Auntie,' said Jess. 'Just follow the signs for Heathrow, some are only there to tell us we're on the right road, but others will tell you how far we still have to go.'

'Ooh, this is exciting,' Marjorie said as she leaned between the two front seats to get a better view of the road signs.

182

As they approached junction 14, Jess's sat nav, which had been silent for quite a while, suddenly rapped out an instruction.

'After eight hundred yards, take the exit.'

Marjorie clapped her hands in excitement. 'Isn't it clever, Jessica?'

'It's very clever, Auntie.'

'But… how does it know?'

'It knows because it's been here before and it remembered the route,' said Martha, dryly.

'It has a good memory then,' Marjorie replied.

'It has maps built inside, and it uses a satellite, Auntie, don't listen to Grandma.'

Marjorie looked at Martha and screwed up her face. 'I didn't believe you anyway,' she said.

Jess pulled onto the slip road at junction 14 and navigated her way around the roundabout until she saw the turning for Heathrow, then turning off, she went back to her sat nav instructions and followed the sign for Wayfarer Road.

Twenty minutes later, Jess parked up in the short stay car park at terminal 5, got out of the car and stretched before opening the boot and helping Martha pull out their cases.

Marjorie looked skywards as a jumbo jet came in above their heads. She covered her ears with her hands and looked at Martha with wide eyes.

'I hope it's not that noisy when we're sat inside ours,' she said.

Martha ignored her and placed the bright orange travel case on the floor. Jess looked around and found an abandoned trolley close by. She loaded the big cases on, then locking the car with the remote button on the key, she waited patiently while Marjorie carefully extended the handle on her travel case.

'Everyone ready,' she said with a grin.

Marjorie nodded eagerly and set off in the wrong direction. Jess called her back and pointed to the entrance. 'We're going in there, Auntie.'

As they entered the building, they passed several policemen carrying sub machine guns. Marjorie skirted them nervously but Martha strode confidently past, nodding to each one in turn. Once inside the vast terminal, Jess walked past the lines of queuing passengers looking for the Japan Airlines check-in desk. Finding it unattended and with a propped-up sign on the main counter, informing her that the desk would open at five-twenty, she led Martha and Marjorie to an open-air café where she ordered tea for them and coffee for herself.

They sat in silence for a while, each wound up in their own thoughts, then Marjorie spoke.

'It's like an ant's nest here isn't it? All these people scurrying about like little ants.'

'That's a perfect description of it,' agreed Martha. 'When you think of all the planning that must go into running this operation... it's mind boggling.'

'We saw a programme on Heathrow airport on the TV, didn't we, Martha? It showed what happens behind the scenes. My mind was boggled all right.'

'It generally is,' Martha said. She looked away quickly as Jess gave her a narrow-eyed look.

At five-ten, Jess led her family across the concourse to join a rapidly forming queue in front of the JAL check-in desk, and at five-twenty precisely, two uniformed women came out from behind a large, logo dominated screen and sat down in two seats facing the queue. Smiling at the people at the front, they logged onto their computers and motioned the first of the passengers to step forward.

The JAL staff worked quickly and they were only in the queue for about ten minutes before being asked to approach the desk.

Martha handed over their tickets and passports, and waited as the desk clerk typed some information into the computer.

'I'll print your boarding passes for you, but it would have been easier if you'd printed them yourself at home.' The desk clerk smiled sourly at Martha.

'I wouldn't want to do you out of a job,' Martha replied. 'Just think, dear, if passengers did all the work, you wouldn't have anything to do, and they'd replace you with a machine, we wouldn't want that now, would we?' She looked down at the clerk's name tag. 'Angelica.'

Angelica gave a thin smile. 'Place your bag on the scales.'

'Please?'

Angelica ignored the remark and pointed to the scales again.

Jess grunted as she lifted Martha's case onto the metal platform. Angelica checked the weight, then looking slightly disappointed, printed off a label, wrapped it around the handle before dragging the case off the scale and sliding it away from the rear of the desk. 'Next one,' she said.

Jess placed Marjorie's case on the scale and stood back. Martha eyed up Angelica as she checked the weight. 'It's under the limit. I weighed them myself this morning and my bathroom scales are digital, so don't try to get us to pay excess.'

Angelica looked from under her eyelids and said nothing. A few seconds later she wrapped a label around the handle of Marjorie's bright orange case and dragged it off the scales.

'You won't lose that one, will you?' she said, returning to her seat.

'We've heard that joke already,' muttered Martha under her breath.

A few minutes later, armed with their passports and boarding passes, Jessica walked the old ladies to the sign marked 'Departures' where they would have to go through a security check.

Jess gave them both a long hug before making sure they knew what to do next.

'Right, have a lovely time, you two. Once you're through security you can go to your boarding gate, the number is on your passes but...' Jess looked at her watch, 'your flight doesn't leave until seven-twenty so you'll have some time to kill. Inside you'll find the duty-free shops and there'll be restaurants and coffee bars with big screen TVs so you'll easily find something to do. Make sure you're at the boarding gate a good twenty minutes before your flight is called though.'

'We aren't children, Jessica. We have flown before,' Martha said.

'I know, but this is a lot busier than East Midland's airport, Grandma.'

'We'll be fine, if we get stuck, we'll find a man.'

Jessica stuck her thumbs up. 'Great. Now, when you get to Tokyo, you'll find a man waiting for you when you come out of customs with your bags. He'll have a sign with your name on it so don't go outside without him. He'll drive you to your hotel, then the company he works for will transfer your main luggage to the cruise ship terminal. It will hopefully be in your cabin when you get on board.

'You're going to be really tired after a twelve-hour flight, but I've booked you into a nice hotel overnight, then after breakfast on Monday, another driver will take you to the bullet train. You'll be met again at Yokohama train station. That driver will take you to the check in at the harbour, then, after you hand over your tickets, you can board.'

Marjorie opened her mouth to ask a question but was silenced by Martha.

'Don't worry, Marjorie. I've got all that.'

'Please don't go anywhere without finding your driver, Grandma. Tokyo is a big city and you'll easily get lost.'

Martha nodded. 'I understand, Jessica.' She leaned forward and pecked her on the cheek.

'Thank you for organising all this, we're both very grateful,' she smiled her thin smile, 'and please don't worry about Marjorie. I'll keep my eye on her... both eyes in fact.'

Martha checked their boarding passes again, then her eyes turned once again to Jess. 'Oh, I knew there was something else. Marjorie and I have signed our wills, that junior from Bradley's firm rang me yesterday to say that everything was in order so if anything happens to us, there won't be any problems with our estates. I'll tell you now, Jessica, I have left everything to you, via the trust of course, I think my mother might have been onto something when she set it up.'

'That's very kind of you, Grandma.'

'Who else would I leave it all to... a cat's home?'

'Well, there's Mum,' Jess replied.

'No,' Martha said firmly, with a shake of her head.

'There is one more thing. You have the keys to the house, don't you?'

Jess patted the pocket of her jacket and nodded.

'Good. On the coffee table in the lounge there is a blue folder. Inside you'll find the notes that I've been typing up on the laptop these last few weeks. I'm warning you now, you won't find them as elegantly written as my mother's epic tomes but I hope you will find them of interest. They detail my life from when I left home up to the time my first husband died. I may continue it on the voyage, I have the laptop in my case and I should have plenty of time, when I'm not keeping my eye on Marjorie, that is.'

'Ooh, that will be an interesting read, I'm quite looking forward to that, Grandma.'

Jess kissed Marjorie again and waved them off as they stepped through the entrance into the security section.

As they disappeared from view, she turned away and walked back out of the building to the car park. Waving her pre-printed parking pass at the scanner, she took her receipt, switched on her sat nav and headed towards the M25.

Looking back towards the terminal in her rear-view mirror, she shook her head slowly and spoke to Alice as if she were sitting next to her.

'Japan has to deal with tsunamis, earthquakes and typhoons, Nana, but I wonder if it's ready to face these two?'

She laughed to herself as the sat nav gave out a fresh set of instructions, and taking the first turn off on the roundabout she drove up the slip road towards the motorway.

Chapter 27

On the way home, Jess squeezed the hire car into the last parking space on the asphalt at the side of the farmhouse and yawning, she walked through to the kitchen and studied the contents of her fridge. Settling on the leftovers from the previous night's pasta, she put the bowl in the microwave and heated it for three minutes on full power. Taking a spoon from the drawer she went through to the lounge, switched on the TV and watched the BBC news channel for twenty minutes while she ate her food.

Just before eight, her phone rang. It was Sam.

'Hiya, have the dragons flown then?'

'Yep,' Jess looked at her watch, 'they should have taken off about forty minutes ago, they'll be somewhere over Europe by now, I imagine.'

'Let's just hope the pilot doesn't have to make an emergency landing in Moscow to hand them over to the police for disrupting the flight.'

'Oh, Sam, they aren't that bad.'

'I know, but Martha can be very... how shall I put it... forthright.'

'Martha can, that's for sure, but she's got Marjorie to look after so she may not be as demanding as you fear.'

'So, how's your love life? Have you made up with that lawyer of yours yet?'

'No, that's over, Sam. I know he's married in name only, but he's still married, and that Leonora has already been up to her tricks.'

'Ooh, do tell.'

'Not now, I'll tell you when I see you next.'

'When will that be? Fancy a night out now your rellies are all out of the way.'

'You heard about Mum, then?'

'Yep, it's on the grapevine, Jess. I did mean to call you but I've had all sorts on at work. I've not been getting home until after nine most nights. How is she?'

'Mum's all right. She's away from temptation in prison. She's in therapy classes but she isn't taking them seriously.'

'To be honest, I wouldn't either,' Sam said seriously.

'You'll be just like Mum in a few years if you don't slow down,' said Jess.

'Well, love, you'll be in the Betty Ford clinic with me because you like the old vino as much as I do.'

'Hey, I've been good recently. I've had to be for Mum.'

'So, are you really telling me there's no wine in the fridge?'

'Erm, no, I'm not going to lie. I've got half a bottle of Pinot Grig in there. It won't be there much longer either.'

Sam laughed. 'Right on, sister.' She paused for a moment. 'Now, the reason I called... I've met a new bloke. He's drop dead gorgeous, has his own business and he's unattached, which is incredible really. Looking like he does you'd think every woman in town would be following him around with their tongues hanging out.'

'Really! It didn't take you long to get over James, did it?'

'You know me, love. Heartbroken one day, full of the joys of spring the next... and talking of springs, I'd let him test my bedsprings out any time he wanted.'

'Sam! You're incorrigible.'

'Always. Incorrigibility is my forte... is that even a word?'

'Yes, it's a word and it was made especially for ladies like you.'

'I reckon I could shag for GB at the Olympics,' said Sam.

Jess laughed. 'So, who is this Adonis? What does he do? He sounds too good to be true, are you sure he isn't married? Just remember Bradley.'

'He says he isn't so... I'll believe him unless or until I find out differently.' Jess heard Sam take a sip of wine.

'Okay, so...'

'I only met him today. He's taking me for a meal in the Venetian tomorrow night.'

'Very nice, he has good taste then.'

'Apparently so. He's just taken over a café in town, the one near the Uni. The coffee is great and there's an old-fashioned juke box. There's also a blonde girl working there, big eyes, big boobs and a big mouth, but there's nothing going on between them. I know because I asked him... his name is Josh by the way.'

Jess sighed.

'What's up, love? You don't seem too happy for me.'

'It's nothing,' Jess replied. 'I know who you mean, I met him a couple of weeks ago... Look, have a lovely time tomorrow, I'm sure you'll get on like a house on fire.'

'I'll give you a snog-by-snog report on Monday,' Sam replied.

'I'll look forward to it... Night, Sam, I've got to go, I'm tired out from all the driving.'

Jess pressed the red button to end the call, dropped her phone onto the arm of the sofa and leaned back into the cushions.

'Bugger,' she said.

Chapter 28

Feeling down, and not entirely sure why, Jess carried Alice's memoir into the lounge and sat in the armchair opposite the one Alice used to sit in when she visited. Taking a gulp of wine she placed her glass on the old lion's foot coffee table and opened up the notebook.

Alice. November 1940

November was one of those months when the weather gods couldn't make up their minds what to send us. The early part of the month was a mixture of sunshine and heavy rain. A 60-degree weekday was followed by a 30-degree temperature with howling winds and torrential rain. On the 15th we got news of a ten-hour bombing raid on the city of Coventry which had left it pretty much flattened.

Because of the rain we couldn't really do much on the farm, but because our land was so well drained and the rain held off for a day or two, we managed to continue harvesting the late-autumn veg crop.

On the 30th, the council organised a fundraising event in the church hall to raise money to help replace some of the 800 planes we had lost during the Battle of Britain. We raided our wardrobes to find clothes we didn't use any more and handed them in on the second-hand stall that was run by a fussy lady called Violet, who examined the garments forensically before slapping a price tag of sixpence or ninepence on each item. One of my mother's dresses was marked up for two and sixpence which, although the dress was in excellent condition, I thought to be a little excessive as it was fifteen years old and hardly a fashion statement.

The vicar and three other men lucky enough to have escaped the call up, were busy decking the place out with union flag bunting and government posters which encouraged us to Make Do And Mend, or to Keep Calm And Carry On.

After dropping off the clothes, Barney gave Amy and me a lift back to the farm for lunch and a change of clothes before returning to the hall for the afternoon event which we would follow up with our usual Saturday evening at the pictures.

The fundraiser was superbly supported by the townsfolk and there was a steady stream of people in and out of the hall all afternoon. At five, a posh-looking woman wearing an expensive dress and a fox-fur stole, climbed the steps to the stage and stood behind the microphone that the Housey Housey host used to call out the numbers to a packed hall most Wednesday evenings.

The adults hushed as she tapped the microphone to make sure it was working. The kids ran around shouting and shooting at imaginary Red Indians until the vicar leaned in front of the woman to ask the parents to control their offspring.

'Ladies and Gentlemen,' the posh woman began eventually. 'It is my great pleasure to have been asked to speak to you today.'

The woman was hatless and her dark brown hair had been formed into a rolled, updo. She wore a string of pearls around her neck and her make-up had been administered expertly. I put her at about forty years old. She was still attractive but her thin lips and brown eyes that didn't narrow at all when she smiled, made it look, to me at least, as though her words of gratitude to the local populace weren't as genuine as they might have been.

After her short speech, she stepped down to a round of polite applause and was replaced by the ARP man, William Tannersley, who held a sheet of paper up to his face, squinted at it, then announced that the evening had raised the princely sum of fourteen pounds, twelve shillings and eightpence. The remaining clothing and other items would be packed up and sent to London to be handed out to the homeless, and people who had lost everything during the bombing.

I stood on the right-hand side of the hall with Amy, sipping fizzy lemonade, applauding with the rest as William announced the total. Suddenly, Amy nudged me and nodded towards Violet who was busy rolling up my mother's dress and sticking it into her bag while the rest of the excess clothing was being piled into hessian bags ready to be transported to the poor of the capital. I sauntered over to her, smiled and flicked my head towards William who had just left the stage.

'We've done well, haven't we? That's a decent amount, though I doubt it will even pay for a single wing.'

'We did our best,' Violet replied, looking down at her bag guiltily.

'Did you really pay two and six for that dress? I thought it was a bit much, I'm not surprised it didn't sell.'

Violet suddenly developed a coughing fit.

'Do you want me to tell William to add half a crown to the total?' I asked, trying to hide a smirk.

'No, I mean, look, it was left over, and I'll be honest, I had my eye on it since you handed it in. It's far too nice to be used as a day dress so the poor of London wouldn't have much of a use for it, would they?'

'I tend to agree, Violet, but you ought to pay something for it, think about all those cockpits that need to be built.'

'I've worked hard here all day,' she blustered. 'I deserve something for my efforts.'

'The money raised is to help with the war effort. No one is being paid for helping out today.' I caught William's eye as he picked up his half-drunk glass of lemonade from a table nearby and beckoned him over. 'Violet has a little extra to add to the total,' I said, fixing her with a tight smile. 'She decided to buy a leftover dress at the last minute, isn't that kind of her, especially after the effort she's put in today.'

Violet glared at me, but when William began to thank her, she rummaged in her purse and came up with a shiny sixpence and a threepenny bit. Dropping them into William's hand, she turned on her heel and marched out of the hall.

Amy, who had witnessed the whole thing, was grinning at me as I walked back carrying the dregs of my lemonade.

'She's a miserable old so and so. She did the same thing at the Bring and Buy charity sale we had when we were raising funds for the church roof. No one pulled her up that day, so well done you.'

I was about to air my thoughts on Violet when I heard someone clear their throat behind me. I turned to find the posh woman standing about three feet away.

'I'm sorry to interrupt what must be a very important conversation, but I'm rather pushed for time and I'd like to have a private word with you if that's all right?'

Amy and I exchanged glances, she nodded and mouthed, 'go on', then feigning interest in a table covered in children's clothes, she stepped away.

The woman took my arm and led me to a quiet corner where she looked me up and down with a critical eye.

'You're the Mollison girl,' she said, eventually.

'I am, but I don't think we've been introduced,' I replied.

The woman considered it. 'I wouldn't have thought so. We mingle in different circles.' She smiled that thin smile again, her eyes wide, showing the lie behind it.

'Oh, I don't know,' I said. 'I've mingled with a few toffs in my time.'

She gave me a look that could have curdled milk and looked down her nose at my best Saturday night frock.

'I'm Virginia Wilson, I'm the wife of Godfrey, director of Wilson, Kendall and Beanney, Associates.'

'Ah,' I said, wondering what the hell was coming.

'Ah, indeed, Miss Mollison... It is still Miss, isn't it?'

I nodded and feared the worst.

'You are more attractive than I imagined. I tend to picture you in overalls covered in pig... slurry when I think of you, but I have to say, I'm moderately impressed.'

'Thank you,' I replied, with a slight edge to my voice. If she was trying to provoke a response from me, she was going the right way about it.

She picked up the aggressive note in my voice and laid her gloved hand softly on my arm. 'Now, now, dear, there's no need to get angry. I was paying you a compliment of sorts.'

'If that was a compliment, I'd hate to hear you insult someone,' I said, quickly.

'Let's start again,' she said, smiling that fake smile of hers. 'I merely wanted to let you know that I am aware of your relationship with my husband, and have been for some time.'

I groaned inwardly. 'Mrs Wilson...' I began.

'Please don't try to explain, or make up some falsehood or other, my dear, I'm not a fool. I know what you've been up to.'

I stepped back and looked around, hoping no one else was in earshot.

'He has a thing for beautiful young women and I have to admit, you do fall into that category, albeit at the less refined end of the scale.' She looked me directly in the eyes. 'There, is that a better compliment?'

I turned away; I'd had enough, but she put her hand on my arm again.

'I'm sorry, I honestly didn't mean to offend you. Listen, Alice, isn't it? I'm not here to warn you off or create a scene, that's why I wanted this private word.' She looked down at my breasts, then back up to my face. 'The thing is, I am a little concerned this time. I think he's allowed you to get under his skin and that's something I'd rather not have happened.' She smiled again, looking like a cat that had cornered a mouse. 'I am willing to allow this... dalliance, to continue, but I must have your word that you won't attempt to lure him away from his family. We don't believe in divorce, you see.' She paused as she glanced up towards the big, wall clock. 'I know he's quite a catch and you must be very taken with him, what with his background and all. But, Alice, my dear, you can never have him... not in the full meaning of the phrase. He will never leave us.'

'I've never asked him to leave you, but he...' I bit my tongue before telling her that he had, indeed offered to.

'That's very wise, my dear.' She looked over her shoulder to make sure we couldn't be overheard. 'The thing is, and this is a very personal thing for me to admit... the thing is, Godfrey is a very physical man and he has certain needs, like all men. Unfortunately, there were complications after the birth of our second child, complications that meant I could no longer enjoy the physical side of our marriage, it is too... uncomfortable, shall we say?'

I shook my head, 'I really don't need to know—'

'I merely want you to understand why he has these... flings. In every other respect, our marriage is sound. He wants for nothing in that sense.'

'I'm sure you have the perfect marriage,' I replied, 'and I hope it remains that way until the day you die. I do not and never have, intended to come between you and Godfrey, what happened was a—'

'Don't apologise, my dear. You aren't the first to be taken in by that smile of his and I'm sure you won't be the last.' Ignoring my attempt to butt in, she continued. 'Now, I have to rush, I have an important engagement tonight and I'm expecting a call from Godfrey, so I'll just say this, so you don't feel so guilty about things. I'm happy for you to spend time with my husband. If he is happy then I am happy. As I told him on the telephone yesterday, I have decided to allow this little affair to continue, you are my gift to him.'

'Your GIFT! Now listen here... I am the only person who will ever decide who I give, or don't give, myself to. I'm not a cheap trinket to be handed over as a present. I own a farm; I am a business woman and in my own way

I am doing my bit for the country. I also have my wants and needs but I will make up my own mind who I share my bed with.' I glared at her, lifted my arm and pointed towards the door. 'Now get out of my sight, and never, and I mean, never, come within half a mile of me again.' I turned quickly away, angry tears in my eyes, but then I swung myself around to face her again. 'And you can tell Godfrey the same,' I spat.

Victoria stared at me, open mouthed. I gave her an icy stare and flicked my head towards the door.

'Didn't you have an important engagement?' I said, calmy, then tossing my head, I turned away and ignoring her protests, walked slowly across to Amy.

Chapter 29

Martha and Marjorie walked along a narrow, screen-lined corridor until they came to the security area where they joined a short queue to have their passports and boarding passes checked again, before a large-framed security guard lifted their travel cases onto a conveyor belt that passed under a scanner. As instructed, they took off their watches and metal jewellery and place them into a plastic tray which was then placed on the conveyor. As their bags were being checked they were motioned to step through the metal detector after which they were given a light rub down search by a female security officer.

Marjorie was visibly excited by the whole experience and giggled when the guard ran her hands under her armpits. Martha accepted the intrusion into her privacy with alacrity. 'Thank you for keeping us and the plane safe,' she said after her rub down.

Safely through security, they walked along another screen-lined corridor until they came out into the huge duty-free area. Marjorie's jaw dropped as she saw the shops, bars and restaurants laid out before her. She rushed to the nearest open fronted-shop and picked up a London policeman doll.

'Ooh, look, Martha, a London policeman, he's even got his helmet on.'

Martha took the cellophane wrapped box from Marjorie's hands and put it back on the display.

'These dolls are for foreign visitors, Marjorie. We see policemen in helmets every day of our lives, they're nothing special.'

Marjorie wasn't listening; moving to her left she picked up a Beefeater doll.

'Ooh, Martha, a Beefeater doll. That would look nice on my chest of drawers at home.'

Martha sighed. 'If you must have one, Marjorie, buy it on the way back, that way you won't have to cart it half way around the world.'

Marjorie looked disappointed. 'Are you sure they'll let us buy them coming back? They'll know we aren't foreign tourists.'

Martha opened her mouth to explain, then knowing where this type of conversation usually ended up, decided to say nothing, and putting the doll back on the display she took hold of Marjorie's arm and marched her away from the shop.

'We've still got an hour and a half before the flight goes, let's get a cup of tea and a slice of cake.' She pointed to a café with a dozen empty tables outside. 'There, that one will do.'

After ordering their tea and paying what Martha told the waitress was an extortionate amount for what was essentially two tea bags and a couple of slivers of fruit cake, the pair took their tray out to a round table and sat down to watch the world, or at least many of its inhabitants, go by. Martha had only just sipped at her tea when Marjorie got to her feet and rushed across the concourse to a kiosk which had boxes of cigarettes piled up outside. Martha sighed, got to her feet and followed her sister into the shop. Inside, she found Marjorie picking up small boxes of perfume.

'Oh, Martha look, Yves St Laurent... Black Opium, ooh that sounds decadent, doesn't it? And look... Dior... Pure Poison... Oh, Martha we have to get some.'

'Expensive rubbish,' spat Martha. 'What's wrong with your Lily of the Valley all of a sudden?'

'I've been wearing that since you bought me a bottle from Avon in nineteen seventy-three,' Marjorie replied. 'I just fancy a change. Please, Martha, let me buy some, I want to smell nice at the cabaret.'

Martha grunted and pulled the box of Armani, Oud Royal from Marjorie's vice-like grip. 'All right, I give in, you can buy some, but we are not paying two hundred pounds for a small spray bottle.'

They moved along the line of fragrances slowly, Martha slapping her sister's hand every time she reached for an expensive bottle. Away from the counter they found some cheaper perfumes. On the second shelf, Marjorie picked out a pink box of Hugo Boss, Femme, priced at £35. At the side of the unopened boxes was a sample spray bottle. Marjorie snatched it up and sprayed three, long squirts onto her neck. Martha grabbed the bottle and held it at arm's length, out of Marjorie's grasping reach.

'You're supposed to put a little bit of it on your wrist, Marjorie.' She took hold of her sister's hand and pushing up her sleeve, squirted a small amount onto the inside of her wrist. 'Now, leave it a few seconds, then have a sniff at it.'

Marjorie waited impatiently until Martha gave her a nod, then lifting her wrist to her nose she took in a deep sniff.

'Oh, Martha, that's beautiful,' she said, and inhaled again as she took a second sniff. 'Can I have it, Martha? Please. I won't ask for anything else?'

Martha nodded curtly, picked up a cellophane wrapped box and carried it to the counter. The assistant dropped it into a shiny, World Duty Free printed bag and waited while Martha tapped her debit card pin into the machine.

Marjorie almost snatched the bag from the assistant's hands as she passed it over the counter.

'Excuse my sister,' Martha told the assistant. 'She doesn't get out much.'

At the far end of duty-free, the sisters followed the signs for their departure gate, going down an escalator and across an open area until they found the travelator that would take them to their destination. The moving walkway seemed to go on interminably, but eventually, they stepped off the end, pulling their onboard cases behind them, and walked the rest of the way to their departure lounge.

Martha checked her watch with the big digital clock above the departure's information sign and satisfied that both were correct, found a couple of spare seats by the boarding gate.

'We've still got fifty minutes, Marjorie. Shall we splash out on another cup of tea? There's a ladies toilet over there should you feel the need.'

Marjorie hugged her precious duty-free bag to her chest. 'I'll go soon. Can I get a magazine, Martha?'

'That's the most sensible thing you've said today,' Martha replied, leading the way to a newsagent's kiosk about thirty feet away. She was delighted to find a paperback by Hilary Mantel that she hadn't read while her sister picked up a copy of The People's Friend and a dot to dot, puzzle book.

Thirty minutes later their flight was called, and after looking around carefully to make sure they hadn't left anything behind, the sisters joined a queue and waited until their seat numbers were called. After handing in their boarding passes and having their passports checked one final time, they walked along a wide corridor where they were greeted at the plane's entrance by two hostesses wearing smart, JAL uniforms. Martha waited while Marjorie fussed about, packing her perfume into her onboard case before stretching and loading both their bags into the overhead storage compartment.

Marjorie hopped from one foot to the other in excitement. 'Can I have the window seat, Martha,' she begged.

To her surprise, Martha didn't argue. 'In you get then, I'll have the aisle seat.'

Marjorie slipped into the seat, and immediately began to fiddle with her seat belt. 'It won't fasten, Martha, I think it's broken.' Her face was a picture of concern.

Martha reached across and snapped the belt closed, then sat back in her own seat and looked sideways at the family who were just getting settled into their seats on the opposite side of the aisle.

'Fasten your seat belt, Martha. You have to fasten it or we can't take off.'

Martha sighed and did as she was bid. Marjorie was excited enough without tipping her over the edge.

When everyone was in their seats, they looked to the front as a stewardess went through the safety procedures, explaining how to fit the emergency oxygen mask and where to find their life vest and whistle.

Suddenly the engines began to make a low rumbling sound, Marjorie sat bolt upright and reached out to grab Martha's hand. She looked across at her big sister with a fixed grin on her face.

The grimace remained in place as the plane taxied along to the runway. When it began to pick up speed, she shut her eyes tight and listened to Martha murmuring a prayer. She took a quick look out of the window as the plane hurtled past the airport buildings but closed her eyes again as the aircraft built up enough speed to ensure they could achieve the required lift.

As the plane continued its steep rise, Martha finished her prayer and looked sideways at her sister who was staring fixedly ahead.

'Are you all right, you don't want to be sick, do you?'

'No, Martha,' Marjorie muttered. 'I don't like heights, that's all.'

When the illuminated sign came on, informing them that they could release their seatbelts, Martha unfastened hers, then reached over and did the same for her sister.

'Would you like to change seats?' she asked.

Marjorie turned her head an inch towards the window and glanced down at the motorway lights as they passed over.

'No, I'm all right now, Martha.'

'Well, don't think you're going to hog that seat for the full twelve hours,' Martha replied. 'I'd quite like to see the mountains when we pass over them.'

'It will be too dark to see them,' said Marjorie. 'Unless they're in Japan, where the sun is.'

Two hours later, after the pair had finished eating their first meal of the flight, the stewardess pushed a drinks trolley along the aisle. When she reached the sisters she placed two patterned bowls on their trays and held up an ornamental tea pot that looked more like a kettle.

'Green tea?'

'Not likely,' said Martha bitterly. 'I've had that stuff before; it tastes like old socks.'

The stewardess smiled patiently and put the bowls back on the trolley. 'Could I get you anything else?'

'We'd like a cup of proper tea,' Martha informed her. 'English tea.'

'Actually, there's no such thing as English tea, it's all grown in India or—'

'Don't try to be clever, my dear.' Martha gave the stewardess one of her looks. 'You know exactly what I mean.'

'Carly has the tea and coffee trolley. She'll be along in a minute.'

Ten long minutes later, Carly arrived at their side. 'Tea or coffee?'

'What sort is it?' Martha asked. 'I'd prefer PG Tips, but I'll settle for Tetley's, Yorkshire if I absolutely have to.'

'It's Twinings,' Carly replied.

'Well, I suppose that will have to do, as long as it's not like cat's piddle.' Martha watched carefully as the tea was poured. Marjorie waited until her big sister had tasted it before picking up her cup and taking the tiniest of sips.

'It's quite nice, isn't it, Martha?'

'It'll do,' Martha replied. 'The cups could be bigger though.'

After another hour, Marjorie tapped Martha on the shoulder and eased herself to her feet.

Martha, who had been dozing, jerked forwards in her seat.

'What!'

'I'm just going to walk around the plane for a bit,' Marjorie said.

Martha got to her feet and stepped into the aisle so that Marjorie could get out. 'Go to the toilet while you're up. I don't want disturbing again in half an hours' time.'

'You should take a walk with me, Martha. I was reading about it on the internet last week. Pensioners especially should walk up and down the aisle for fifteen minutes every few hours or they could get a vain trombonist.'

'A what?'

'A trombonist.'

Martha thought for a few moments, still not quite properly awake.

'Thrombosis, you mean deep vein thrombosis... trombonist indeed.'

When the man in the seat opposite began to laugh, Martha fixed him with a steely glare until he looked down at his knees.

'Off you go, Marjorie... don't forget to use the toilet.'

Martha only managed a couple of hours of fitful sleep as Marjorie laughed her way through an old Marx brother's movie on the small screen in front. When the film had finished, and after discovering a package consisting of a blue blindfold and a pair of thin slippers, she fell asleep and slept non-stop for almost five hours. When she woke up, dinner was being served.

The landing was without incident but Martha and Marjorie again held hands as the plane descended at Tokyo Haneda airport. Marjorie missing the chance to see the snow topped Mount Fuji out of the window.

After leaving the plane, the sisters joined a long queue at the immigration desk. Martha handed over their passports and waited patiently, turning her face left, then right, as the official checked the passport photograph against her features. Two minutes later they were waved on and they passed through a door to find themselves in the luggage reclaim area.

Martha's case arrived relatively quickly, but as other passengers pulled their bags from the conveyor, there was no sign of Marjorie's.

After ten minutes, they found they were the only people left. Martha tapped her foot and cursed under her breath.

'How could they possibly lose that monstrosity,' she muttered. 'You could spot it from the moon.'

Suddenly, a bright orange blob came into view at the far end of the conveyor. Marjorie pointed to it and hopped about in excitement. 'Here it is, Martha, they didn't lose it.'

'You couldn't,' Martha muttered as she helped Marjorie drag the big orange box off the carousel. Once the suitcase was on the floor, she looked around for a trolley to load their cases onto and sighed in relief as an airport worker came in through the door marked Customs pushing a long line of them.

Unsure as to whether the man would understand English, Martha pointed to a trolley and said, 'Me take?'

'Of course, madam,' said the elderly man with a bow. 'Take, take.'

He pulled one of the trolleys from the line and lifted their cases on to it.

'That's a bright one,' he said with a smile as he slid Marjorie's case onto the trolley.

They passed through the Nothing to Declare line in the customs check and walked along a tight corridor until they came out into the main airport arrivals area. Sitting on a bench seat about fifty feet away from them was a uniformed man with a handwritten sign on his lap. He stood and bowed to them as they approached.

'Mrs Crow?'

'Crew, it's Crew,' said Martha.

'Crow... repeated the man, and Mrs Morrison?'

'It's Mollis—'

Marjorie was cut short by a dig in the ribs from her sister.

'That's us,' said Martha, as the man bowed again and took hold of the trolley handle.

'You not lose that one,' he said, smiling as he pointed to Marjorie's case.

Fifteen minutes later, they arrived in reception at a four-star hotel. The ultra-polite lady on the check-in desk made sure their cases were booked onto the shuttle before handing over their room keys and pointing the way to the lift.

'Everything is arranged,' she told them in perfect English. 'Dinner will be served between six pm and nine. You will receive a telephone alarm call at seven-thirty in the morning. A taxi has been booked to take you to the train station at nine-thirty. Breakfast is served from six. She smiled at them. 'Enjoy your stay.'

Chapter 30

On Monday morning, Jess drove over to Martha's to pick up the signed documents that would hand over ownership of her house to the Mollison Farm trust. She found them on the coffee table alongside a blue folder, exactly as her grandmother had said she would. Intrigued as to what the folder might contain, she put her shoulder bag on the seat Martha usually sat in, opened the folder and pulled out a thick wad of printed A4 paper. The top page was titled: My Life. 1955-1977. Underneath was a hand written note, advising Jess that the document was for her eyes only and not to be used as background for her novel.

Jess took a sip of water from the bottle in her shoulder bag, then leaning back in the armchair, she made herself comfortable and began to read.

Martha. July 1955

I never got on with my mother. We had nothing in common apart from a love of pigs. I found her domineering, uncaring and at times downright cruel. Oh, she never hit me or anything like that, I was well fed and clothed but there was never a real bond between us, it was like the stork had dropped me off at the chimney of the wrong house. I grew up telling myself that somewhere in the town was another woman bringing up a child who was having the same problems trying to fit into the wrong family. I know my mother was busy trying to run a farm, but I can only ever remember coming second to anything that was work related. I still find it odd that rather than inviting other toddlers around to the farm to play with me she just stuck me in with the piglets. As I grew up, she used to tell me that I had a problem bonding with people. It should hardly have been a surprise to her really.

I was about four when Marjorie was born. She was, and still is, a timid creature. She grew up with no personality of her own so she latched onto me and tried to share mine. She always preferred my company to my mother's or our live-in housekeeper, Miriam's. We even shared the same bed for a few years, not that she didn't have her own bed, she did, she just preferred to sleep in mine. She felt safe if I was around.

Her dependency lessened a tad as we were growing up and she found some friends of her own at school, but at home she was never more than a few feet away. It was quite claustrophobic at times.

When I hit thirteen, I let her know in no uncertain terms, that as I was now becoming a woman and as she was only nine, her constant need for my attention would no longer be welcomed or tolerated. There were tears and tantrums, but for once, both my mother and Miriam were on my side and between us we encouraged her to develop her own personality and interests. It worked to a degree, but whenever she was troubled, she would come into my room at night, tug on my nightdress and beg for my advice or assistance. I never failed her, I had words with a few people at the school gates and she was seldom bothered by any of them again. I think it was about this time that I began to suspect my mother of having something to hide when I found her on her hands and knees on the parlour floor, nailing down the trapdoor that led to the cellar. She flatly refused to say why she had sealed it off, Miriam made some lame excuse about there being a lot of rats down there, but I was never really convinced. Friends at school speculated that she could be hiding a body and I couldn't find it in me to argue.

It was around that time that I began to have problems with my scalp. My mother, instead of taking me to a specialist in such problems, decided instead to use a home-made remedy that stank of paraffin. It did stop the scalp problem in its tracks but my hair never really regained the lustre it had shown previously and I have been plagued with thin, limp hair ever since.

I had my first proper boyfriend at fourteen. He was a farm worker's son, his father worked on the farm

209

further along the lane. He was a weak-willed lad, not bad looking but after a few weeks I began to think I had replaced Marjorie with a male clone, so I dumped him and set my cap at a seventeen-year-old called Walter. He wasn't the slightest bit interested in me, but, stubborn as I was, I kept at it. One evening, following a loud argument between him and his real girlfriend, a red-headed girl called Janet, we found ourselves alone on the lane just below our farm. Walter, who must have still been aroused by his aborted attempt to seduce Janet, set to work on me. I happily accepted his kisses and promises of undying love, but when his hand went up my skirt, I responded with what was literally a knee-jerk reaction which left him rolling around on the floor, his hands cradling his testicles, whimpering like a whipped cur. In my naivety I thought I might have done him permanent harm, but after a few minutes he got to his feet, called me something I won't repeat here, and walked slowly up the lane, stopping now and then to check that his crown jewels were still in place.

I left home at sixteen. I just couldn't bear to be there any longer. I had attained a distinction in my School Certificate, which meant that I stood a good chance of getting a reasonable job in an office instead of working in the local factories with the majority of my classmates.

I didn't have many what I would call, close friends. I found most of my female peers to be shallow creatures, besotted with clothes, movie stars and singers, none of which held the slightest bit of interest to me. I was more interested in argument and debate. My mother said I should continue with my education and try to get a place at university, or at least enrol in adult education, but I wasn't really interested in any of the courses on offer, so, I ended up spending a whole year moping about the farm, trying to ignore my mother's persistent demands to muck in and do a bit to earn my keep. In 1955, after my best friend Celia, who was a year older than me, announced that she was

210

leaving home and moving into a flat with her sister in Maidstone, I begged and pleaded with her to allow me to go with them. As there was an attic room in the property, the sisters acquiesced to my pleas and on August 23rd 1955, I packed a single suitcase and without a scintilla of regret, caught the train to Maidstone, the county town of Kent.

The attic room was small with just enough room for a single bed, a single wardrobe and a tall, thin set of drawers. The lone window was built into the slope of the roof and light leaked through in the early hours in summer, no matter what I did to try to cover it.

Initially, I thought I was moving in with two like-minded, teenage girls to have a little fun and explore the night life of the town, but it wasn't long before I realised that I had been mistaken. Both Celia and her nineteen-year-old sister Clara, had jobs to go to. Celia with a firm of local solicitors and Clara, at Oaklands Asylum where she dealt with patients' records. I was expected to contribute towards my keep, so I took a job in a clothing factory where I worked five and a half days, running between the machines collecting finished garments for the princely sum of twelve shillings and sixpence a week. The sisters took my wage packet from me every Friday and handed back a shiny half-crown which would have to pay for my toiletries, clothes and lunch in the canteen at work. I was always penniless by Wednesday and either had to borrow sixpence from Mary, the line supervisor, or go without anything at all for lunch on the Thursday. As the only thing I had eaten all day was a boiled egg before I set off to work, the borrowed sixpence was often needed. After about three months I was offered a few extra hours on Saturday afternoons, but after mentioning it to Clara one evening and discovering that she would take the extra money from my wage packet on a Friday night leaving me no better off, I turned down the extra hours, deciding instead to start a Sunday morning newspaper delivery round for which I was paid a shilling a week. The round covered a large area and the papers were heavy, but I enjoyed being out in the open air and the extra shilling went a long way.

Celia and Clara went dancing on a Saturday night and used to arrive home more than a little tiddly with their lipstick smeared all over their faces. I would beg them to take me along too but they always flatly refused.

As my eighteenth birthday approached, I decided I'd had enough but with a flat of my own being little more than a pipe dream, I decided to apply for nurses training at West Kent Hospital in the town. Trainee nurses lived in a dorm onsite and were fed well and their uniforms were provided free. The hours were long and the work dull but I earned twenty-one shillings a week whilst training and because most of my weekly needs were catered for, it meant I had money to spare every weekend. Not that I could do much with it. We were trained under the watchful eye of a Matron who could have easily made a career in the Gestapo had she lived in Germany a few years earlier. She was sharp tongued, eagle eyed and was, to all intents and purposes, our legal guardian. As we didn't reach our majority until we were twenty-one, she acted as a surrogate parent to us. My own mother would have ranked a poor second to her in the disciplinary stakes. She decided when we could go out, what time we would be back in and even where we were allowed to go. Training was all done in the hospital building and consisted mainly of cleaning bedpans, cooking toast and boiled eggs for patients' breakfasts, taking temperatures and changing disgusting bandages stained with all sorts of detritus. Some of the older men took great liberties when we gave them their bed baths but if we complained about it, Matron would just tell us it was part of the job and we should treat it as such.

One afternoon, I was told to give a patient called Alfred Briggs a bed bath. Alfred had recently had an operation to remove his appendix, so he wasn't particularly needy, but I did as I was told without argument. I had recently spent a week doing nothing but bedpan cleaning because of a tiny breach of the rules and I didn't want to spend another one off ward. As soon as I had closed off the screen and greeted the licentious old sod, I pulled back the sheets to find he had already removed his pyjama bottoms to show off an enormous erection. Leaning back into his pillows he leered at me and winked.

On my trolley, as well as the soap, flannels and towel, I had a bowl of steaming hot water and a pitcher of cold to make things more comfortable for the patient. Ignoring the cold, I dropped one of the flannels into the still simmering water, then, with a lightning move, whipped it out and slapped it onto the head of his member. The last time I had heard a squeal like that was from one of the piglets on the farm when it got its head stuck in the sty gate.

The ward sister, another little female Hitler, was on the scene in a flash. Alfred's naturally purple head was now at least three shades darker and he was in a lot of pain. Sister Marks took all of five seconds to understand what had happened, and calling for a Staff Nurse, she ordered me to wait in her office.

I fully expected to be dismissed or at least disciplined but all I got was a lecture on how to check the temperature of liquids when used to bathe patients. Sister Marks said that Alfred was a dirty old so and so who had upset more than one trainee nurse. More experienced nurses, it turned out, could dampen a patient's ardour with a quick flick of the back of their hand. I was advised to learn that technique as quickly as possible.

A few months into my training I was waiting at the ward door when a tall, white coated man, who I assumed correctly to be a doctor, strode purposely along the corridor and came to a halt at the side of me. Peter Ross, as I later found him out to be, was in his forties, handsome and carried an air of friendly superiority. He smiled at me and looked through one of the port-hole windows in the door of the ward. 'How are you getting on with the old battleaxe?' he asked, flicking his head towards the doors.

I was flabbergasted to find myself being spoken to by someone as far up the hierarchy as a doctor, so I just nodded and mumbled. 'Okay, thanks.'

Back then, a Sister ruled the ward like a despot. We weren't allowed to address them without her speaking first and even doctors and surgeons waited until they had been invited onto the ward before walking through the doors.

I stood, looking lost, while the Sister showed the doctor around the ward. When their inspection was over, they had a quick conversation at the swing door, then he came out, striding his long stride and winking at me as he went by. Sister Marks finally turned her attention to me and barked out a few instructions, the first of which was to run after Doctor Ross to return his stethoscope which he had inadvertently left on a patient's bed.

I had to run along two long corridors before I managed to catch him up. I almost shouted to him as he turned a corner up ahead, but I had been trained well and I knew my place in the system.

I finally caught up when he stopped to talk to a pretty Staff Nurse called Erica something. I stood, red-faced and silent while they laughed about something or other that had happened in the canteen earlier that day. Eventually, he noticed me and dismissing Erica with a smile, he turned towards me. Unable to speak through my panting, I bobbed a courtesy and handed him the stethoscope.

He thanked me, then to my astonishment and delight, he asked my name.

'I'm Martha, I'm a trainee.'

He told me he could tell that by my uniform and I blushed through my already, red face. He then asked me where I hung out at the weekend as he hadn't seen me in any of the local pubs that the nurses frequented. I said that Sister Marks hadn't given me permission to go to the pub and he laughed.

'So, where do you go?'

I told him I and a couple of friends (I use that term lightly), frequented a coffee bar in the town where they had a juke box. Doctor Ross asked for the name of the café, then winking at me again, he strode off towards the operating theatres.

On the following Saturday, I found myself alone in the coffee bar after Glenys and Joy, my usual companions, had both cried off, one with her monthlies, the other, having attracted the wrath of Matron after being found talking to a porter, had been grounded for the week.

I sat alone in a window seat, tapping my foot mechanically as Frankie Vaughan explained to us what delights awaited on the other side of the Green Door. I was just about to pick up my bag and walk the half mile home, when a man's mac was draped over the back of the seat at the side of me. I looked up to see the grinning face of Doctor Ross. He asked me if I'd like another coffee and not wanting to offend someone of his status, I nodded, although I'd already had two.

Peter, as I was ordered to call him when off duty, was entertaining, funny, and made the evening the best I'd had since I moved into the town. At nine he said we should move on to a pub, as he always had a beer or two on a Saturday night. I said I couldn't go with him because I hadn't had permission from Matron and I had to be in for ten. He shrugged and said he wouldn't tell her if I didn't and as the pub was only a couple of hundred yards from the nurses' quarters, I could easily be in on time. He dug into his pocket and handed me a half empty roll of peppermints so that my breath wouldn't stink of alcohol if she checked.

The pub was packed, and he had to raise his voice so that I could hear him above the sound of Elvis Presley's Blue Suede Shoes, a tune that seemed to be the only song on the jukebox. I sipped my gin and tonic, the first I'd ever tasted, and laughed obligingly as he recalled funny stories from his youth.

At five to ten, he pointed to the door and told me I'd better get home before Matron sent out a search party. He took my empty glass from my hands as I searched around for somewhere to put it and asked if I'd like to do the same thing next week. I told him I'd have to be careful because the rumours would erupt in the nursing home if Glenys and Joy told everyone who I was talking to in the coffee bar. He said that couldn't happen if we skipped coffee and went straight to a pub. I didn't think twice. I didn't know if he was married, I didn't know how much older than me he was, and I didn't particularly care. I was flattered by his attentions and I also knew that any one of my colleagues would have jumped at the chance had they been in my position.

'Of course, I'll come,' I told him.

We arranged to meet outside the library in town, at seven-thirty. It took all of my willpower to stop spilling the beans about my secret during the week, especially after Rita Smart, a blonde with a reputation as long as the main street, started taking the mickey out of my appearance, saying I'd never get a man with hair like that.

I nearly came a cropper on the Friday when Sister Marks almost caught me reading a copy of Woman magazine when I was supposed to be collecting bedsheets from the laundry but I managed to slip it into a pile of pillowslips as she came barging through the door.

I had a long, leisurely bath early on Saturday evening, wearing a towel for a turban so I didn't damage the hair do I'd forked out for that afternoon. My hair was never going to be my crowning glory like my mother's, but Sarah at Snips had made the best of a bad job and it looked almost as good as anyone else's. By six-thirty I was made up, dressed and ready to go. I sneaked out of the quarters without Matron noticing and got the bus to the coffee bar where I sipped at an espresso until it was time to walk over to the library. I still couldn't believe I was going on my first date, and with a doctor of all people. My mind kept playing tricks on me, telling me I'd be stood up, that he'd only asked me for a laugh and that when I arrived at the library, the entire nurses' home would be waiting for me, laughing at my embarrassment.

None of that happened of course. Peter was actually waiting for me as I crossed the road.

Chapter 31

After leaving Martha's house, and with her grandmother's blue folder on the passenger seat of the Toyota, Jess drove the mile and a half to Wilson and Beanney's offices where she found Bradley leaning over his receptionist's desk, pointing out something in his diary that needed changing. He greeted her with a smile as she entered the reception.

'Hello, Jess, what a lovely surprise.'

Jess returned the smile and ignoring a hostile look from Melanie, who was obviously enjoying the close encounter with her boss, she waved the plastic folder containing Martha's legal documents at him.

'Martha's trust documents, signed, sealed and delivered,' she said. 'Her signature was witnessed by her local councillor; she took it to the Town Hall and refused to leave until she got his attention. I'm amazed she knew who her representative was, she's usually so scathing about them. Still, it seems she found a use for him for once.'

Bradley pulled a face as he took the folder from her. 'I wonder if the councillor has recovered from the experience yet.'

'That may take some time,' Jess said with a laugh. 'Not many people forget their first encounter with Grandma.'

'Speaking of Martha, did they get off all right?' Bradley asked.

Jess nodded. 'Yep, I dropped them at Heathrow on Saturday. I would imagine they're on board the cruise ship now, they're eight hours ahead of us.'

'I hope they enjoy the cruise. It was very generous of you to pay for it.'

'They haven't been able to afford a decent holiday for a few years. It was the least I could do after my own good fortune.'

218

Bradley grinned. 'I don't envy the crew I have to admit. I can imagine Martha summoning her servants with a beckoning finger.'

Jess wagged a finger at him. 'Oh, she's not that ba... Well, she can be rather demanding at times but the Japanese are a polite race, I think she'll appreciate that.'

'Did you warn the Captain that she's boarding? She'll be wanting a seat at the top table.'

'I don't know if they do that on the larger liners, Bradley. There are about two and a half thousand passengers on board. He... or she, can't really meet and greet them all.'

Bradley smiled. 'I wasn't being totally serious, Jess. I just hope she's got a nice view out of her cabin porthole or whatever they have nowadays. I wouldn't want to be on the other end of the conversation if she hasn't.'

'They have a cabin with a good view, and one that's near the lifts so they can explore the ship without walking too far... oh, and there aren't any portholes, they're more like French windows.'

Bradley checked his watch. 'Do you have time for lunch? I can take an early one, I've only got telephone appointments until two o'clock and most of them are just advisory ones, so won't take long.'

Jess took Bradley's arm and led him away from the receptionist's desk where Melanie was pretending to tidy some paper files whilst obviously listening in.

'This is all very conspiratorial,' said Bradley as Jess stopped near the big glass doors at the front of the office.

'I just wanted to tell you in person, rather than by phone or text... Look, Bradley, I'm sorry, but I've made up my mind and I'm afraid that I can't continue with our relationship. I'm so sorry, but Leonora has made it impossible. I can't go through life wondering what sort of mischief she's going to get up to next.'

Bradley's face dropped. 'What has she done now?' he asked, quietly.

219

'She's been following us around taking photographs for one thing. Honestly, Bradley, she should be working for one of the tabloids, or maybe MI5.'

Bradley groaned. 'How do you know?'

Jess looked over his shoulder to make sure that Melanie couldn't overhear before continuing.

'She completely got hold of the wrong end of the stick and dropped a stack of pictures off at the coffee bar in town. She mistakenly thought the owner, Josh, and I were an item, but the truth is we've only ever had lunch together once. Now, I like Josh, we might become good friends one day, but Leonora handing over a folder of photos while playing the victim of an adulterous husband and his wanton bit on the side, really hasn't helped in that department.'

Bradley groaned again. 'It's not the first time she's done it, Jess. She's quite an accomplished actress. I'm sorry if she's ruined a potential relationship for you and I understand how angry you must be.'

'I have no idea whether that friendship would have resulted in a relationship and I don't suppose I'll ever find out now. I think he has issues with adultery.'

Bradley shook his head. 'Relationships... you can't live with them and you can't live without them.'

He looked intently into Jess's eyes.

'I accept that this isn't the right moment for us, Jess, but please don't rule out a future relationship. Leonora won't always be there to complicate things.'

'If you were divorced it would make things easier, but as that isn't even remotely on the horizon I can't see how things will ever be any different between us.' Jess put her hand on his arm. 'I like you, Bradley, I really do and I hope she won't come between us as friends or business partners, but I'm afraid that has to be the extent of our relationship.'

Bradley nodded. 'Karma will kick in one day. She's got a lot of payback coming.'

Jess kissed the lawyer on the cheek and turned away towards the door, then, making an instant decision, she turned back.

'She was the one that ran her key down your lovely old car.'

'Leonora? I thought it was your ex... Calvin?'

'It wasn't him; he would deny if of course, but in this case he's innocent. Leonora did it.'

'How can you be so sure?' he asked.

'She told me. On the day I came round to your flat to see how you were after the attack. She seemed quite proud of it.'

Bradley's face became a mask of anger. 'My mother still hasn't totally forgiven me for that. She'd have plenty to say to Leonora if it's true. She doesn't particularly like her anyway, it's only the religious element that keeps her in favour.'

'It's true, Bradley. I wouldn't make something like that up. I wasn't going to tell you if I'm honest.'

Bradley began to pace back and forth across the plush carpet.

'I'm glad you told me, Jess.' He punched a fist into the palm of his other hand. 'She'll get what's coming to her for this... starting with the bloody bill.'

Jess smiled softly and laid her hand lightly on Bradley's arm again.

'It seems that Karma is about to respond,' she said.

That evening, after a meal of beans on toast, Jess received a call from Sam.

'Hello, darling, how are you?'

'I'm all right, thanks, Sam. How did the big date go?'

'Erm, I'm not sure how it went to be honest. We're not exactly kindred spirits.'

'Oh dear, what went wrong?'

'Nothing spectacular, it just wasn't one of those evenings you'll look back on in later life with a great deal of affection.'

'I'm sorry about that, Sam. I know you said you fancied the pants off him.'

'Oh, I did, and still do, and all is not quite lost. We're going out again on Wednesday and it will be on my territory. We're off to the Carpenter's in Gillingham. It's music night so there'll be a band, a DJ and stacks of people. I'll be in my element. I'm not really one for cross-table heart to heart chats as you know.'

'Oops, is that what it turned out to be?'

'Sort of… it's difficult to describe it any other way. We had a nice meal and some nice wine and we chatted about our work but as I loosened up a bit… as the wine flowed… Well, you know what I'm like, Jess. I'm a flirt, I always have been and I always will be. I was designed for fun, not deep, meaningful conversation.'

'So, your flirting got you into trouble again, did it? It's hardly the first time.'

'It was only a waiter… oh, and the two businessmen on the next table, but that was hardly anything.'

Jess sighed as her best friend laughed down the line.

'I can see your disapproving face in my mind's eye.'

'Not so much disapproving as disappointed. You really will have to grow up one day. How did Josh take it?'

Sam paused. 'Let's just say he wasn't overjoyed.'

'Poor Josh. But at least he'll know what to expect on Wednesday.'

'I'm just going to be myself, hun, he can take me or leave me.' Sam sipped noisily at a glass of wine.

'Good idea, no point in trying to be something you're not,' Jess replied.

'Your name kept cropping up. He seemed more interested in you than me, which is probably why I ended up flirting so readily.'

'My name?' Jess was puzzled.

'I brought you up to start with, you just came up in my half of the conversation, but he jumped in with both feet when he found out I knew you. I wouldn't say he was obsessed, but he did ask a lot of questions.'

'What sort of questions?' Jess asked, a little too eagerly.

'Oh, you know, how old you were, how long we've been friends, whether you're in a relationship or not, what type of knickers you prefer.'

'WHAT!'

Sam laughed hard. 'Oh, Jess, you're such an easy target. Of course, that wasn't mentioned, but he was really interested in your life. I told him about your break up with Calvin, not all the sordid details of course... I didn't mention him attacking me, but I gave him the basics. He was quite sad when I said how much you'd been hurt.'

'He seems a sensitive sort of bloke,' Jess replied. 'I think he has a heart.'

'It's been broken badly, at least twice.'

'Oh dear! Poor Josh. Did he tell you about it?' Jess asked.

'Did he ever. I felt like an agony aunt for about an hour.'

'So...'

'His ex, twice over, actually, used to mess him about. He was with her for eight years and they had a daughter together, she's five.'

'Twice, over? I don't understand.'

'They were together for a couple of years, but then she met someone at work and moved in with him for about six months. Josh had her back when it all went wrong. The guy was married you see and when he'd had enough of, erm, Katy, he used the old excuse of getting back together with his wife, so that was the end of that. Anyway, she obviously hadn't learned her lesson because eighteen months ago, she met another married guy and left Josh again, taking her daughter with her.'

'Poor Josh,' Jess repeated.

'Poor Josh indeed. To make it worse he was accosted by the deserted wife outside his house. She was

223

almost hysterical, blaming him for his wife's infidelity, saying that if he'd been any good in bed she'd probably never have felt the need to look elsewhere for her kicks.'

'It was hardly his fault that this Katy couldn't keep her knickers above ankle level.' Jess began to feel genuinely sorry for the café owner.

'Quite, and her abusive tirade wasn't limited to just that one occasion. She followed him around, begging him to somehow persuade Katy to come back. She said that she had two kids herself and she couldn't understand why her partner had ditched his own children to look after someone else's. She told him she was having suicidal thoughts and that the Social Services were looking closely at her mental state and that she might end up losing her children.'

'Oh, my goodness!' Jess exclaimed. 'How long did all this go on for?'

Sam sipped at her wine again and smacked her lips. 'Ooh this is nice... Erm, well, in the end, Josh sold up and moved away, that's why he ended up in our little backwater. He said he still had nightmares about that poor woman's tear-stained face.'

'The poor man. He didn't deserve all that dumped onto him, he'd lost everything that mattered to him too.'

Sam's reply wasn't quite as sympathetic as Jess expected it to be. 'Yes, but... well, maybe he ought to try counselling or something. He's really got a thing about infidelity. To be brutally honest, Jess, unless he lightens up a bit, I can't see the two of us ever getting it on. I'd end up more like a Samaritan than good old Sam.'

'So, why bother with Wednesday night then?' Jess enquired.

'Because he is very fanciable and I'm hoping he's got it all out of his system now.'

'So, you still think there's a chance for the two of you?'

'Not if he's in the same frame of mind on Wednesday.'

'Let him down gently, Sam. I know you won't lead him on, but don't let him think there's something there when there isn't.'

'You know me, love. I'm always kind to dumb animals.'

'SAM!'

'Ha-ha, I'm only joking. I'll tell you this though, if your name comes up more than mine again on Wednesday, I'm going to stick him in a taxi and send him round to the farm.'

'Don't do that,' Jess said with a nervous laugh. 'I've only just got rid of one male with a problem woman in the background.'

'You told him then? How did he take it, was he devastated?'

'Not so you'd know it. He was disappointed and he said he understood my reasons.'

Sam's voice suddenly acquired an edge. 'That bloody wife of his has a lot to answer for, just like Josh's. It's not always the man's fault, is it? They just seem to accumulate baggage.'

'I told him it was Leonora who keyed his old car, that was a bit naughty of me really.'

'Rubbish,' Sam spat. 'He deserves to know what sort of a cow he married.'

'I think he knows that without me harping on about it,' Jess replied, 'but the identity of who scratched the car was a surprise to him. I wouldn't like to be Leonora when his mother hears about it. I'd love to be a fly on the wall.'

'Karma,' said Sam. 'Right, I'm off to find something on Netflix. I'll call you on Thursday for an update... Oh, I meant to ask. Have you heard from Martha and Marjorie?'

'No, nothing yet, but I'm expecting an email once they've settled into their posh cabin.'

'Well, I hope the servants aren't playing up. Night, Jess, sleep well.'

Jess put down the phone, poured herself a glass of wine, then taking her dwindling supply of cigarettes from the drawer, she pulled on her coat, sat on the top step and thought back to her last meeting with Josh.

Chapter 32

Martha and Marjorie were met at the hotel reception by a uniformed driver who, just like their previous one, carried a placard with the word 'Crow' written on it. They arrived at the station, which looked pretty much the same as the airport terminal they had left the night before, without incident and only had to wait a few minutes before the sleek, gleaming train arrived.

The sixteen-carriage Bullet train was white with a blue stripe and had a long sloping front end that looked to Marjorie to be something of a cross between a dolphin's nose and an eagle's beak. The Shinkansen guide that they had been given with their tickets, however, described how the re-designed nose of the train had actually been inspired by the Kingfisher's ability to enter the water, barely making a splash.

Inside, it looked more like an airliner than a train. Marjorie was fascinated as she watched a passenger swing around a pair of seats so that it faced the rest of his group. Although it resembled the inside of a Jumbo jet, there was much more by way of leg room between the seats and the sisters were able to stow their travel trollies on the floor in front of them without feeling cramped.

The journey itself took a mere eighteen minutes from the moment the train pulled away from the platform in Tokyo to when it pulled up in Shin Yokohama station. About a third of the way into the trip, Marjorie got to her feet and as the telegraph poles and pylons whizzed by in a blur, she began to walk up the aisle between the seats.

'How fast are we going, Martha?' she called.

An American gentleman, who was sitting on the front row of seats in the carriage, pointed to a round dial above the door.

'One hundred and fifty miles an hour,' he reported.

227

Marjorie rushed back to her seat; her eyes wide. When she sat down, she was silent for a few moments as she tried to work something out.

'Martha, you know when I was walking just then... was I walking at a hundred and fifty miles an hour, or was I walking faster than the train?'

'For pity's sake, Marjorie, how am I supposed to know that? I'm not a mathematician.'

'I was just thinking...'

'Please, don't do that, Marjorie, you know what problems it causes.'

At Shin Yokohama station there were several uniformed drivers holding up placards and shouting out various names but Martha couldn't see or hear one calling for them. Telling Marjorie not to even think about moving from the spot where she left her, Martha walked along a shortening line of hire-car and taxi drivers as they met up with their target passengers. She was just about to turn back towards her sister when a short man in a navy uniform came hurtling onto the platform looking up and down the concourse in panic.

'Crow,' shouted Martha as he got closer.

'Not Crow, Crew... Crew...' The man looked up and down the platform again.

Martha stomped towards him. 'I'm Crew,' she said. 'Not Crow?'

'Not Crow,' Martha repeated. She turned to Marjorie and made a beckoning motion with her hand. 'This is my sister. We are travelling to Yokohama to board the Paradise Pearl.'

'Ah, Paradise Pearl. Yes.'

The driver bowed and reached out to take charge of their trollies. Martha shook her head firmly, pointed to the exit and followed their driver to the parking bay in front of the station. Fifteen minutes later he deposited them at the doors of the harbour terminal. Martha averted her eyes as he waited for a tip after taking their cases from the boot and placing them on the pavement outside the entrance to the terminal.

'Thank you,' she said, as the driver bowed, looking at her from under his eyelids.

Marjorie gasped as she turned around to see the huge bulk of the Paradise Pearl looming above the roof of the terminal. 'It's like a floating city,' she whispered.

Even Martha was impressed, and taking her phone from her bag, she found the camera app and took a series of photographs of the ship as it dominated the skyline.

The check-in was smooth and efficient and after walking through a security checkpoint similar to the one they had seen in London, they handed in their tickets to a smart, polite woman who handed them two credit card style passes and a guide book for the liner.

'The cards are not only your ship boarding passes, they also work as your electronic cabin keys and as a sort of credit card for use in the bars and restaurants. You must use your own credit cards in the shops or if you wish to purchase a massage, or any of the other services not included in your package.'

After a short wait in a holding area, the sisters heard their cabin number called and alongside twenty other passengers they were shown through a sliding door and led along the quayside to one of the many walkways leading up to the ship.

They followed their guide until they came to the Atrium, a vast area filled with shops, bars and cafés. From the centre, long flights of stairs ran upwards in all directions and pairs of glass plated lifts with gold domes ran up and down continuously. They followed their guide to the lifts and travelled to deck six, where she led them across an open seating area and down a long, narrow corridor to their balcony suite.

After inserting a master card into the electronic lock, the guide pushed the door open and stood back to allow the sisters to enter.

As Martha reached into her pocket to pull out her room pass, the young woman mistakenly thought that she was about to be tipped, and smiling, held out her hand, but Martha just made a 'tsk' sound and stepping out into the corridor with the puzzled guide, pulled the door shut and inserted the card. When she heard the door lock click, she removed the card, pushed the door open, then turning to the guide, muttered, 'thank you, that will be all,' and stepped smartly back into the room, closing the door behind her.

Inside the plush, carpeted suite were two, three-quarter sized beds, and two large, built-in wardrobes, where they found their larger cases had already been neatly stowed. There was a desk with an internet connection point and electrical sockets that accepted the various adapters that were lined up on a small shelf at the side. Above the desk was a decent-sized square mirror and above that, angled across the corner was a thirty-two-inch, flat-screen TV. In the far corner was a fridge-come-drinks cabinet holding several bottles of soft drinks and mineral water.

The bathroom was equipped with a sink, a toilet and a walk-in shower with a large silver head.

'No bath and no bidet, that's a disappointment,' said Martha with a shake of her head.

'It's lovely though, despite that.' Marjorie was entranced. Walking to the huge glass doors she pulled them apart and stepped out onto the balcony.

'Ooh, Martha, we've got our own sunbeds... and we've got a picnic table,' she trilled.

Martha stepped outside and tested the strength of one of the sun lounges by pressing on it, then nodding to herself, she looked out over the balcony to the harbour where people were milling about like ants. Turning back, she looked into their cabin and nodded again.

'It'll do,' she announced.

It took them over an hour to unpack, bickering between themselves over who had which drawer or whose toiletries were taking up too much space on the bathroom shelves. Eventually, with Marjorie pestering her to take a walk around the ship, Martha held out both hands in front of her and shook her head.

'Marjorie, we have three weeks to explore the ship. I'm worn out after all this travelling so I intend to take a nap. I advise you to do the same or you'll be nodding off over dinner, and we don't want that, do we?'

'No, Martha,' Marjorie agreed.

Choosing the left-hand bed that had the best view of the balcony, Martha kicked off her shoes and lay down on the cream coverlet. Twisting her head, side to side to make a dent in the memory foam pillow, she closed her eyes and was asleep within minutes.

She woke up almost two hours later to the rumbling of the ship's engines. Blinking, she sat up, rubbed her eyes and looked around the room.

There was no sign of Marjorie.

Chapter 33

Martha quickly pulled on her shoes and, pausing only long enough to pick up her card pass, hurried out of the door. Racing down the corridor as fast as her eighty-year-old legs allowed, she stopped, undecided about where to begin her search. Looking out onto deck six, she thought that would be the most sensible place to start, and finding a door leading out into the cold sea air, she stepped through and walked quickly around the perimeter of the deck. Finding only a few passengers on the viewing platform, she turned and rushed back inside.

Panic setting in, Martha entered one of the lifts and descended to the Atrium where she found a male crew member giving directions to a group of European passengers.

'Excuse me, and I'm sorry for butting in, but I have an emergency situation. Could I borrow this gentleman?' Without waiting for a reply, she grabbed hold of the crewman and spun him around.

'Do you speak English?' she asked, then noticing the man's name badge, she quickly added, 'Serge.'

Serge nodded, then replied in English with a thick, French accent.

'I will only be a moment, Madame.' Turning back to the passengers, he pointed across the Atrium floor and gave some directions. Smiling, they thanked him and walked away.

As he was turning back to her, Martha grabbed his sleeve and began to drag him towards the lifts.

Serge put on the brakes and stopped dead, Martha's grip slipped and she carried on a few paces before stopping herself.

'What is the nature of the emergency?' Serge asked, brushing down his crumpled sleeve.

'It's my sister, Marjorie, she's gone missing.'

'How long has she been missing?'

Martha looked in the air and sighed. 'I don't know. I fell asleep not long after we boarded and when I woke up, she wasn't there.'

'How long were you asleep?' the crewman asked.

'An hour, no, two, two hours. My God, she could be anywhere.'

'I'm sure she's fine, Mrs?'

'Crew, I'm Martha Crew, and my sister is Marjorie Mollison, she's seventy-six, very timid, she could get lost in a lavatory. We're from Kent in England,' she added.

'What was she wearing?'

Martha thought for a few moments. 'She had her pink winter jacket on, it's one of those ridiculous puffer jackets, with padding that looks like muscles.'

'Ah, I have one of those, they're very warm in the cold weather. You should get one.'

'Never mind the damn coat. What can we do to find her?'

Serge smiled and led her between two souvenir shops to a small room with a single desk, a computer and a microphone. Flicking a switch, he picked up the mic and spoke into the P.A. system.

'Would a Miss Marjorie Mollison from Kent in England please make herself known to a crew member or make her way to the Atrium where her sister is worrying about her.'

Serge waited a few seconds, then repeated the announcement. After three minutes, he repeated it again. Suddenly a voice came back through the tannoy system.

'Hello, crew member, nine-seven-nine, Bhatt reporting that I have successfully discovered the missing English lady. I will return her to the Atrium immediately.'

'Well, that was highly efficient, I must admit,' said Martha.

Serge switched off the P.A. and smiled.

'Crisis over,' he said. 'This happens at the start of every voyage, the situation gradually improves as people get to know the layout of the ship, but we still get missing person alerts right up until the day we return to Yokohama. Taiwan seems to be the place most people go missing ashore for some reason.'

Serge led Martha back to the Atrium and a few minutes later, a clearly flustered Marjorie, led by an Asian crew member, hurried in from the lower deck. They were followed by an elderly man wearing a white captain's hat with the Paradise Pearl logo on the brim.

'Marjorie, for pity's sake, where the hell have you been?'

As Marjorie looked at the floor, Serge shook hands with his Bangladeshi crewmate and with a nod to Martha, they walked briskly through the crowd of passengers wandering about the Atrium.

'She was in good hands.' The elderly gentleman touched the peak of his cap and held out a hand which Martha studiously ignored. 'We haven't been introduced,' he said.

'Nor are we likely to be.' Martha dismissed him with a look.

Unfazed, the man stuck his hand in the pocket of his jacket and spoke again. 'My name is Henry Farthingale, I'm from Kent, a bit further south than you, though I do know Spinton, I was there many years ago.'

Martha ignored him and switched her attention to the cowering Marjorie. 'Well, what have you got to say for yourself?'

'I was just waving, Martha. You were asleep and I went to look out from our balcony as the engines started up. There were lots of people on the quayside waving to the ship, so I waved to them, but they were all tiny little dots and they couldn't see me.'

'So, you decided to come all the way down here without letting me know?'

'I'm sorry, Martha, you were asleep and you know how you hate it when I wake you up.'

'She was in good hands,' Henry repeated. 'I would have brought her back to her cabin.'

'Or your own.' Martha glared at him.

'I can assure you that my intentions towards Marjorie were, and will always be, honourable,' Henry replied, tersely.

Martha looked at him as if she didn't believe a word of it. After a long, narrow-eyed stare, she turned her attention back to her sister.

'Now, Marjorie, when you got down to this deck and looked over to the quayside, did you see anyone you recognised?'

'No, Martha.'

'No, Martha,' Martha echoed. 'But nonetheless the people on the quayside were waving. Who do you think they were waving to?'

Marjorie shuffled her feet. 'The other passengers, Martha.'

'The other passengers, Martha.'

Martha pursed her lips. 'So, none of them were actually waving to you?'

'No Ma—'

'Hang on a minute,' Henry interrupted. 'I was waving to the people at the quayside too and I didn't know anyone.'

'Then you're as barmy as she is,' Martha spat.

'Mrs, erm, Martha, if I may call you that? Waving when a ship sails, is something most passengers do. The people on the quayside do it to wish the ship Bon Voyage and safe passage. The staff who work in the terminal all come out to wave, it's a traditional thing. It happens all over the world whenever a ship sets sail.'

Martha spun around to face him.

'Mr Fartingale... Farthin...gale, you have no idea the amount of concern this episode has caused. You don't know my sister. She suffers from anxiety. As I just told the staff member a moment ago. She doesn't feel comfortable out on her own, she could get lost in a... telephone box. Now, if you really were about to see her safely back to *our* cabin, then accept my thanks, but if you see her out and about again on her own, whether it's on deck six where she belongs, or anywhere else on this enormous vessel, please hand her in to a crew member and tell them to send her back.' She looked sideways at her sister. 'Come along, Marjorie, you'll need a nap before dinner or you'll be crabby.'

'Did you say you're on deck six?' Henry asked.

'I did, what of it?'

'Oh, nothing. It's just that I'm on deck six too. I don't have a balcony suite like Marjorie said you have, but it's a nice little room. I'll be in for my meal and the after dinner show this evening.' He bowed from the waist. 'I hope to see you there.'

'Wonderful, just blooming wonderful,' Martha muttered as she led Marjorie to the lift. 'You were on board all of ten seconds and you've got a man chasing your money.'

'I haven't got any money, Martha, you have it, remember?'

Martha stepped into the lift and almost dragged Marjorie in after her.

'Now, listen to me. You are not, and I repeat, not, to have anything more to do with that gentleman, do I make myself clear?'

'But, Martha, he was so nice, he's been on this ship before and he knows—'

'I don't care if he's the blooming Captain, you are not to speak to him again.'

Marjorie giggled. 'I thought he was the Captain too, Martha, but he isn't. He bought that hat in one of the shops.'

Martha sighed as the lift system announced that they had reached deck six. She was about to give her sister a lecture on elderly men, when a group of Chinese passengers brushed past them. Steering her towards the corridor where their suite was situated, Martha pursed her lips, then decided now wasn't the time. Pulling her pass card from her pocket, she unlocked the door and pushed it open. Pointing towards Marjorie's, bed, she let the door close behind her before barking out a set of short one-word orders.

'Bed. Shower. Dinner.'

'Can we stay for the cabaret, Martha?'

'Only if you promise not to chase everything in trousers,' Martha replied, sourly.

Chapter 34

On Tuesday morning, Jess woke up to find a short email from Martha.

Arrived in one piece. Cabin fine, Marjorie her usual self. Dinner and cabaret tonight. Nothing else to report. Will email when there is.

Martha

Jess laughed to herself. Martha's emails, rare as they were, always read like telegrams. She replied in kind.

Glad all is well. Mostly good here too. Have handed in trust forms. Reading memoir.

Love to both.

Jess

After eating a bowl of muesli, Jess made coffee and answered the rest of her emails. The editor of Female Futures had written, asking for a follow up to her previous submission about cracking the glass ceiling, while Mslexia, to her great delight, had accepted a short story she had submitted just before Alice had died.

Sitting back in her chair, Jess gave a little whoop.

'That short story was the one I read to you a couple of weeks before you left us, Nana,' she said quietly. 'The Lamplighter's Daughter, remember?' Jess whooped again and picked up Alice's memoir from 1942.

'Let's see what the new year brought you, Nana.' She turned to a new page in her notepad, clicked the top of her pen, wrote, 1942 and opened the book at the first page.

Alice. January 1942

The early January weather was mild with temperatures up to 50F and we managed to get a lot of preparatory work done, ready for spring. Later in the month we were hit by a heavy snow storm that left the fields blanketed in a foot of snow.

One late January morning, after feeding the pigs, I was sitting in the kitchen, chatting to Miriam about her marriage-averse boyfriend, John, when I received a telephone call from the military.

'Mrs Mollison, I'm Captain Formby, Giles, not George. I'm stationed at the POW camp just down the road from you.'

'Oh, this is a surprise. Have you had a mass breakout or something?'

Formby laughed. 'No, nothing like that. I was wondering if I could pop over for a chat. I've already rung the other two farms close to you but they weren't interested in my proposal.'

'Proposal? What are you proposing, Captain Formby?' I was intrigued.

The officer hesitated. 'I'll wait until I can explain face to face if you don't mind. I think asking the other two farms by phone might have been a mistake. Do you think I could come over this afternoon?'

'If you can make it through the snow. It's pretty deep around here.'

'My staff car will get me through a bit of the white stuff, no problem,' he replied. 'Would two-thirty suit?'

Captain Formby was a slender, good-looking man who looked like he could do with feeding up. He sported a mop of unruly, dark hair, and wore an angry scar on his left cheek. He took off his cap as he entered the kitchen and shook hands with both me and Miriam. Nodding eagerly at the offer of tea, he pulled off his khaki greatcoat and looked around for somewhere to hang it. I took it from him and hung it on the back of the door, it must have weighed almost as much as he did and it took me three attempts before I managed to get it onto the hook.

Miriam placed two steaming mugs of tea on the table and nodded acknowledgment as the captain thanked her. Picking up the mug in both hands he held it for a few seconds before taking a sip.

'That's hit the spot,' he said, continuing to hold the mug. 'I left my gloves in the office.'

'What are the roads like?' I asked. 'Barney, my foreman has to take the truck out to one of our suppliers in a few minutes.'

'It's pretty hairy in places,' the captain admitted. 'It's okay if you take your time though. My Humber Sprite staff car struggled on the bends.'

'Barney will be in a big, heavy truck, if a car can get though, that will.'

Just then, Stephen and Harriet came in from the front room where they had been doing an arithmetic test I had set them. The school was closed due to the snow.

Stephen looked carefully at Formby's scarred face.

'How did you get that?' he asked.

'Stephen!' I shook my head quickly.

'It's all right,' the captain replied, touching the scar gently as though it was still healing. 'It's a shrapnel scar. I was on the beach at Dunkirk.'

'Did you kill any Germans?' asked Harriet.

I sighed and shook my head again. 'I'm sorry, Captain.'

Formby held up a hand. 'As I said, it's fine. Children's questions should be answered. It's their war too.' He turned to them both and smiled a warm smile. 'The truth of the matter is, I don't know. I shot at a lot of soldiers but I don't really know if I hit any.'

'When are we going to invade? Are you going back to fight?' asked Stephen.

'That's up to Mr Churchill, young man. I will go back to fight if they ask me to, but at the moment, I'm in charge of the POW camp. I was in hospital for a long time after I got home so I don't really know if they'll send me back.'

Stephen lined up an imaginary rifle and pointed it at the back door. 'I'm going to fight when I'm old enough.'

Formby pursed his lips. 'Don't look forward to it too much. It's not as much fun as you think.'

As Stephen began to fire imaginary bullets, I took the chance to change the topic of the conversation.

'So, Captain Formby... Giles, not George... what can we do for you?'

'Well, I've been doing a little digging,' he began.

'You'll fit right in here then, we do a lot of that.'

The captain laughed. 'I'm sure you do. That's the reason I'm here as a matter of fact.' He sipped at his tea again and put the mug on the table.

'You haven't been assigned any Land Army girls yet, though my sources tell me you should be hearing from the ministry about this a little later in the year. Kent has a shortage it seems.'

I had heard about the WLA, an army of some two hundred thousand women who had been called up to help replace the men who had left the farms to fight.

'They have half a dozen at Lambley's farm a couple of miles away. I thought they might have loaned one or two out to us but when I asked, they refused. They were given a tractor too,' I said, jealously.

'Your turn will come, I'm sure,' said Captain Formby. 'For the moment though you're understaffed.'

'We're all right at the moment, we just about get by, but that's because there's less work in winter. Come spring, we might struggle as a lot of the local women and retired men who might have helped us out have been offered better paid, and less arduous work in the factories.'

'That's the reason I'm here.' Formby looked from me to the kids, then back again. 'How would you feel about having a couple of POWs to help out on the farm.'

'GERMANS!' spat Miriam. 'I don't think so.'

'I'm not sure I like the idea either,' I replied. 'We've got the children to think about and I really don't think the lads in the fields would allow it. Not with some of their own involved in the war.'

'It would be two, ex Luftwaffe officers,' Formby said, soothingly. 'They are both very well-bred young men. One lived on a family farm before the war began, he knows all there is to know about farming.'

'We're having no Nazis on this farm.' Miriam looked at Formby with a steely glare. 'When I think of what they've done to those poor Jewish people...' her voice broke and she tailed off.

'Please, let me assure you, the two young men I'm talking about are no more a Nazi than you or I. They are so anti-Hitler in fact, that instead of flying bombing missions over London, on their first flight, they landed their plane in a field and handed themselves in to the authorities. They've been here since nineteen-forty.'

Miriam threw her wet dishcloth into the sink. 'No,' she said, simply.

'Richard and Dieter are both only twenty years old. Richard in particular has as good a reason to hate the Nazis as you do...' he paused. '...But that's his story to tell, or not, so I won't go into that in detail here. Suffice to say, that members of his family were detained for resisting the SS. I've got to know them well over the last few months and I can guarantee that if we allowed the pair of them to climb into a Spitfire and fly off to protect our coastline, they'd do it in an instant.'

Miriam was unshaken in her hostility to the idea, but I was thinking ahead to the spring when we would be struggling for labour and getting two extra pairs of hands in, with no wages to pay, was a tempting offer.

'How can we be sure we'd be safe?' I asked.

'You can't be serious!' Miriam exclaimed. 'Think of the children.'

'They won't be goosestepping their way here carrying machine guns, Miriam,' I said. 'I assume they will be supervised in some way?'

'Two of our chaps will be keeping an eye on them.' Formby smiled at Miriam reassuringly. 'They will be armed with rifles. They'll arrive by eight, and we'll take them back to the camp before dark. In the summer, if all goes well, they'll work the same hours as your chaps.'

'If you're that sure about them you wouldn't need to have them guarded all the time.' Miriam was not to be convinced. She beckoned the wide-eyed children towards her and put a protective arm around their shoulders.

'We need extra workers until the ministry send us some of the WLA workers, Miriam.' I looked hard at Formby. 'You promise that I'm not putting us all in danger by agreeing to this?'

'I promise, Mrs Mollison.'

'Alice,' I said, quickly.

'I promise, Alice. I would trust these men with my own family. You won't regret this I assure you. The men are going crazy locked up in the camp with nothing to keep them occupied. We have to keep them segregated from the real Nazis, though to be fair, there are very few die-hard ones in the camp. Most are just happy to be out of it.'

'I want to meet them first,' I said carefully.

'Of course, I'll bring them over in a few days' time, I'll get the paperwork sorted first.'

'We're going to get some Germans,' Stephen said excitedly. 'Wait until I tell the kids at school. Can they all come around to see them, Auntie, Alice?'

'It's a farm, not a zoo, Stephen,' I replied.

Miriam shook her head. 'I hope you know what you're doing, Alice,' she said.

I closed my eyes and blew out my cheeks.

So do I, I thought.

Chapter 35

On Tuesday afternoon, Jess paid her weekly visit to her mother in Bronzefield prison. Nicola seemed to be in better spirits. The improved diet and forced abstinence from alcohol was having a remarkable effect on both her body and her mood. Because the bruising had now completely disappeared, she looked healthier than Jess had seen her for years.

'Mrs Kaur's phoned me twice this week, Jess. I know I used to moan about her but she really has got a heart of gold.'

'She's a lovely woman, Mum. What did she have to say, if it's not too personal, that is.'

'We're cooking up a plan for when I get out,' Nicola replied. 'We've worked out that if I do slightly longer hours, but for just three days a week... Monday, Wednesday and Friday for instance, and I restrict or curtail my drinking on the nights before my shifts, it could work out for both of us.'

'What do you mean?' Jess asked.

'Well, if I only drink on Monday, Wednesday and Friday evenings, I'll always be sober at work. Saturdays, you and I could maybe do something together, but I'd have to abstain on Sundays as part of the plan.'

'It sounds good, Mum, but wouldn't it be better if you abstained completely?'

'We both know that's never going to happen, Jess. I like booze. I enjoy it.'

'I know, Mum, but it's not good for you.'

'Cigarettes are no good for you, Jess, but you started smoking again. I remember what you said when that swine, Calvin forced you to give them up. You said it was like a bereavement. Well, I feel the same about alcohol. Trying to give it up completely won't work. I know it in my heart, but I'm positive that I can manage my drinking... once all this mess has been cleared up that is.'

Jess patted her mother's hand.

'All right, Mum. I think it's definitely worth a go, and I don't know about every Saturday, but I'd really enjoy your company for a night out now and then.'

'You can keep your eye on me. Make sure I don't go overboard.'

'That sounds good. Don't take your purse, I'll buy on our nights out.'

'That's a deal.' Nicola leaned across and hugged Jess.

'I've been told I may be getting good news from the police very soon,' she whispered.

'MUM! that's great, why didn't you tell me straight away?'

'I was saving it up. I wanted to savour it. I nearly didn't tell you in case I jinxed it.'

Jess hugged her mother again. 'Oh, Mum, I've got everything crossed for you.'

Nicola pulled away and put her finger to her lips.

'Mum's the word, Jess. It's not official yet.'

Back in Spinton, Jess stopped off at Tesco Express to pick up a couple of bottles of wine and a pack of cigarettes. She was just fishing for her car keys in her bag when she heard a male voice behind her.

'Hello, Jess.'

'Ewan? How are you?'

'I'm good thanks. You?'

'Well, I might have just had some wonderful news, so yes, I'm good too.' She looked around the lamplit street. 'How come we only ever meet outside of Tesco.'

Ewan shrugged. 'It won't happen again... not for a while anyway.'

'Oh? Why's that?'

'I'm going back to Africa. The charity has offered me a supervisor's role. I couldn't turn it down really.' He gave Jess a sad look. 'There's nothing for me here.'

Jess patted him on the arm. 'I'm sorry, Ewan, sometimes things just aren't meant to be.'

'My African magic spell didn't work, not that I thought it would, but you have to try, don't you?'

'African what?' Jess looked confused.

'The scarecrow type figures I left on that bed you put out to be recycled.'

'That was you? Oh my God, Ewan, I blamed Calvin.'

'He wouldn't have cared enough about you to do that.'

'I... why did you do it? I can see what it was meant to signify, but I don't see where Africa comes into it.'

'The village Babu taught me how to do it. I just had to make figures representative of the two of us, and cast a spell over them and then we'd become inseparable.'

'Babu, who's Babu?'

'It's what they call the village wise man... the healer. In the west we called them Witch Doctors, but that's doing them a disservice. They do good work in the community. The villagers swear by them.'

'It's just mumbo-jumbo, surely you can't believe in it, Ewan.'

Ewan snorted. 'Well, it didn't work for me.'

'Perhaps you got the spell wrong.' Jess smiled. 'I'm sorry, Ewan. I don't mean to make fun of you, but it is all a bit silly, isn't it?'

'I've seen it work... but maybe it only works in Africa,' he replied.

'That's the answer then. Get back to Africa and get those spells cast. Find yourself a nice African woman. She'd be lucky to have you.'

'It was the last throw of the dice, Jess. I finally began to realise you didn't feel anything for me.'

'I always liked you, Ewan,' Jess said softly, 'but not in that way. You're a very nice man, but we aren't really suited.'

'I've loved you since school.' Ewan turned his face away and wiped away a tear.

'Oh, Ewan.'

'It's all right. I'm pretty much reconciled to it now.' He turned back to face her and forced a smile.

'When do you leave?'

'The second week in February. It's a three-year posting.'

Jess stood on her tiptoes and kissed him softly on the cheek.

'I hope it goes well. Drop me an email now and again, let me know how you are.'

'I'd better not do that, Jess,' he replied, looking away again. 'I'm going to do what the Foreign Legion soldiers do. Try to forget.'

'That's so sad, Ewan.' Jess felt herself tearing up, so she turned towards the car and pressed the key fob. 'Work on that magic spell, there'll be someone out there for you.'

She climbed into the car, switched on the headlights and pulled on her seatbelt. Looking out of the window, she smiled, waved, then checking her rear mirror, indicated and pulled out into the road.

Chapter 36

There were two dining rooms on deck six, the Rising Moon and the Setting Sun. Martha tossed a mental coin and when it came down heads, she guided Marjorie into the former and waited by the door until a waiter led them to a table in the centre of the restaurant. Martha looked around and spotting a table in the corner of the room where they wouldn't be the centre of attention, demanded that the waiter show them to that one instead.

The meal was delicious, even Martha had to admit it and after eating every morsel on the plate, she asked the waiter to pass her regards to the chef, or chefs.

Declining desert herself, she ordered a bottle of wine and sipped it as she watched their fellow passengers come and go. Marjorie tucked into a plate of ice cream and wild strawberries before taking her first sip of wine.

'I don't want this cruise to ever end,' she said.

'Don't drink too much of that,' Martha advised as her sister took another large sip. 'You're still on breakfast duty you know?'

'Oh, Martha, I'm on holiday too. I thought the serv... erm the stewards would cook breakfast for us.'

'They will, Marjorie, they will, but I want to eat it in bed, as I normally do, so I can plan my day at leisure. To that end, I've ordered room service for us. The stewards will deliver our breakfasts at seven-thirty. You can plate it and serve it up, just like you do at home.'

'Martha...'

'Routine, Marjorie. You need a routine, even on holiday. It's not asking too much, really, is it? And it does add a bit of structure to your day, as will packing the dirty laundry into a bag and leaving it for the cleaning team to pick up every morning.'

'So, I don't have to do the washing myself.'

'Don't be ridiculous, Marjorie. Of course you don't.'

'I hope they use the right detergent, Martha. Remember when we tried a different one, you came out in a rash.'

'Good point, Marjorie,' Martha replied. 'I'll have a word with the staff first thing in the morning.'

'I hope they set the egg timer right too,' Marjorie added.

Martha pursed her lips. 'Remind me to set the alarm half an hour early. I'll ring the kitchen to let them know.'

After dinner, the sisters strolled through the casino to the far end of the deck where the theatre was situated. Finding aisle seats on the lower level, they sat down and waited for the show to start. Within a few minutes, Martha was regretting her choice, when other passengers arrived and they had to frequently stand up to allow access to seats further along the row.

At nine, the house lights dimmed and a compere arrived on stage, cracking a few mildly amusing jokes before bursting into a rendition of Rod Stewart's hit song, Sailing. Next up were a troupe of female dancers wearing, as Martha put it, 'hardly anything'.

'You see how much of her backside that blonde woman is exposing? That's just like your swimsuit, Marjorie, so think on before you wear it in public.'

As the dancers were being applauded off the stage, Martha felt a presence at her side and looked up to see Henry Farthingale standing in the aisle.

'Would you mind? Thank you.'

Martha sighed as Henry slid past wearing a black suit and a bow tie. Marjorie's eyes shone in the dimmed lighting as he sat down next to her.

When they were all seated again, Martha leaned across in front of Marjorie and fixed her gaze on Henry.

'I'm watching you,' she hissed.

The next act was a female country and western tribute act who called herself, Polly Darton, and actually looked and sounded almost as good as the original.

Marjorie swayed from side to side in her seat and clapped along to the music as she belted out Nine to Five. Martha, who had been a country and western fan since the days of Hank Williams, applauded loudly when Polly was joined on stage by the compere for a full-throated rendition of Islands In The Stream.

She left the stage to a standing ovation and after two encores, which were equally rapturously received, she was replaced by a mentalist act called Brian Brain who immediately asked for volunteers from the audience.

Marjorie, who was twelve rows back, wriggled in her seat, desperate to take part, but was too nervous to stand up in public. She looked in askance to Martha who shook her head, firmly.

'Marjorie, I've spent the last forty years trying to work out how your mind works. That poor man has about twenty minutes, what chance does he stand?'

Henry, who had heard the comment, tutted and looked disapprovingly at Martha, but when she raised a questioning eyebrow, he turned back towards the stage.

Brian Brain's act was professional, sleek and totally bewildered Marjorie who was fully taken in by the performance. During the interval, she quizzed both Martha and Henry about his amazing ability to read a series of passenger's minds. When Martha suggested some form of trickery, or card marking had been used, Marjorie flatly refused to accept it.

After the finale, during which all of the evening's acts had come back to the stage to wave and bow, the sisters got out of their seats and joined the slow queue that appeared out of nowhere the moment after the curtains were drawn across the stage. Outside the theatre, as small groups of people headed off towards the bars or the casino to finish off their night's entertainment, Henry fell in step alongside Marjorie.

'Could I buy you lovely ladies a nightcap before you turn in?' he asked.

'I don't think so.' Martha was adamant.

'Just a quickie? I'm in the chair. How about a cocktail?'

'Ooh, cocktails. I've never had a cocktail,' Marjorie replied, excitedly.

Martha stopped dead and turned to face the elderly gentleman, fixing him with her usual, narrow-eyed stare.

'Firstly, Mr Farthingale. We are not late-night drinkers, in fact, we are usually in bed well before now. Secondly, your offer of buying us cocktails is completely bogus, as anything we consume on board this ship, is free.' She waved her pass card at him and taking Marjorie's arm, led her into the corridor towards their cabin.

'I'll see you tomorrow, hopefully,' Henry called after them.

Martha looked back over her shoulder. 'I wouldn't get your hopes up.'

After breakfast the following morning, Martha and Marjorie, wearing their winter coats and thick tights, stepped out onto deck six to find leaden skies and a bitter northerly breeze.

'Brrr, I thought it was going to be warmer than this,' said Marjorie. 'I haven't had a chance to wear my swimming costume yet.'

'Thank heavens for small mercies,' Martha replied as she set off on the first of what they had agreed would be three laps of the deck. 'The weather will turn soon, the further south we go, the warmer it will become.'

Marjorie pulled the collar of her coat tighter and held it in place with her hand.

'I wish I'd brought my gloves, Martha. If we were at home, we'd stay in on days like this.'

'Walk faster, Marjorie,' Martha said as she put on a spurt, and with the sea spray stinging her eyes, she dipped her head and marched into the biting wind.

Chapter 37

On Thursday morning, Jess got the news she had been eagerly awaiting when she received a phone call asking her to call into the police station, after eleven, that morning.

'Ask for Detective Sergeant Christopher Kent. He'll fill you in with the details. I can't go into it over the phone, but rest assured, we have good news for you and your mother.'

Jess spent the morning clock watching as she willed the time to pass. She was dressed and ready to leave by nine-fifteen and spent the next hour and a quarter trying to find things to do. Eventually she gave up and sat on the back step, smoking the remaining two cigarettes in the pack.

At ten-thirty, unable to wait any longer, she drove to the police station where she parked up and sat in the car listening to the radio for a few minutes, then, as the heavens opened up, she got out of the car and made a dash for the entrance.

A dark-haired policewoman looked up as she hurried through the doors.

'Is it raining?' she asked.

'Just started,' Jess replied. She looked floorward and ran her hands through her dripping hair.

'How may I help?' the policewoman asked.

'My name is Jessica Griffiths, I've an appointment with Detective Kent.'

The officer checked her computer screen and clicked her mouse. 'Take a seat please, he'll be with you shortly.'

Jess sat down on the long, wooden bench and pushed her damp hair out of her eyes. Although she tried to avoid the clock, she found herself glancing up at it every few seconds. After what seemed an eternity, a door opened at the side of reception and a brown haired, ruggedly handsome man wearing a navy suit, white shirt and red tie, stepped through.

'Jessica, is it? I'm D.S. Kent.'

Jess held out her hand and the officer took it in a firm grip.

'You've got the perfect name for these parts,' she said.

Kent smiled. 'It has been noted on more than one occasion. Follow me please.'

Jess followed the sergeant to an untidy office containing a desk almost overflowing with files.

'They're keeping you busy by the looks of it,' she said, looking at the piles of folders.

'We're two officers down, they've been seconded by the Gillingham force, so I'm picking up the pieces, which is why I have the good fortune to be with you today.' He looked into her eyes and smiled. 'It's not that often we get to hand out good news. Usually, it's a caution or an arrest warrant.'

He motioned to Jess to sit down in the seat on the other side of the desk before sitting down himself. Picking up the folder in front of him, he opened it and pulled out a small sheaf of papers.

'The CPS had decreed that as they are not confident of winning a court case based on the evidence available, all charges against your mother are to be dropped.'

Jess looked down at the desk as the tears of relief began to flow.

'Thank you so much,' she sniffed, wiping her eyes on the back of her hand.

'To be honest, it was a foregone conclusion. There's no way a jury would ever convict her of murder or even manslaughter on that evidence.' He opened a drawer, pulled out a box of tissues and handed them to Jess. 'She was fighting for her life, she's lucky to still be here.'

'But why was she ever charged in the first place?' Jess dabbed at her eyes with a tissue.

'We have to investigate, Jessica, especially when someone has been killed. We can't just make assumptions based on the initial, visual evidence.'

'I understand.' Jess nodded and forced a smile. The detective looked genuinely sorry for what Nicola had been put through. 'When will she be released? I've got to get over to Bronzefield to pick her up.'

'She'll be out sometime today, I would imagine. The prison governor was informed at the same time as you were.'

Jess got quickly to her feet. 'Oh, my goodness, I'd better get my skates on then.'

'Wait a moment, I'll give them a ring to see what's what.'

The detective looked up a number and dialled it into the landline telephone on the desk, after a brief conversation he put the handset down and looked across at Jess.

'It's too late, the bird has flown the coup.'

'She's out already?' Jess looked towards the door, then back to the policeman. 'Poor Mum, she'll be wondering where I am.'

'She was given a train ticket and money for her bus fare from Gillingham to Spinton. The prison van will take her to the train station at eleven-thirty this morning to put her on the twelve o'clock train. She should be arriving in Gillingham just after one. You've got plenty of time to get there.' Kent smiled and got to his feet. 'I'll show you out, shall I?'

Outside, the rain had eased to a light drizzle, to the south the clouds were beginning to break up revealing a thin patch of pale blue sky.

Kent walked with Jessica to her car in silence. When they reached the white Toyota, Kent cleared his throat.

'I erm, I know this is a bit forward of me, but could you make time for a coffee? I'd love to hear the background story of what happened to your mum. We are finally beginning to take domestic violence seriously and anything you can tell me about what led up to the incident would help me immensely. Witness statements don't really tell us everything. We have to be able to spot these cases when the victim first calls in with a complaint.' Kent looked at Jessica seriously. 'If you are happy to go over it all again, that is?'

Jess nodded slowly. 'I don't mind. If it's going to help in the future, it will be well worth while. It's just that... well, this news was so unexpected and exciting, I don't think I'm in the right mindset to remember it all. It goes back for years you see.'

'I understand completely,' said the officer. 'We could arrange another time for that... but, erm... the thing is, I'm in court this afternoon... an ABH trial, I'm going to be there until late and I won't get a chance to eat... So... well, the offer of a coffee still stands. It would be nice to have a chat to someone without it being crime related. You wouldn't believe how long it's been since I sat down with an attractive woman to talk about everyday things.' The policeman pushed away a stray lock of hair as it fell onto his forehead.

Jess looked at Kent's rugged face, his piercing blue eyes held hers for the most fleeting of moments before she felt she had to look away.

'I can't, not today. I daren't risk missing Mum at Gillingham. I'm a bit concerned as to why she hasn't given me a ring to be honest. They'll have given her mobile back.'

Kent was obviously disappointed. Jess checked her phone, then looked up at him again.

'Oh, I'm sorry, I didn't mean to be rude. I'd love to have a coffee with you, but can we make it another time? I wouldn't be much in the way of company today anyway; I'd be thinking about Mum all the time.'

Kent brightened. 'Great... look,' he reached into his pocket and pulled out a white card. Call me any time, leave a message if I don't pick up straight away. I might be in court, or busy shining a bright light into a criminal's eyes as I interrogate him.'

Jess took the card and opened the door of her Toyota.

'Thanks again for being the bearer of such good news. I can't thank you enough.'

'Just make sure you give me a call,' said Kent. 'That will be all the thanks I need.'

Jess watched Kent walk back to the station as she pulled on her seatbelt. He looked good in a suit, even a slightly crumpled one. He looked comfortable in it, the way some men did in a sweat shirt. Jess put him at a tad under six feet tall, his shoulders, while not overly broad, gave him an appearance of strength. He ran his hand through his hair as he reached the top step, then he turned and looked back at her.

'Damn, he caught me looking,' Jess muttered. Flashing an embarrassed smile, she looked down at the console of her car and twisted the key in the ignition. As she pulled out into the street she glanced sideways again, he was still there, smiling. She took her right hand off the steering wheel and waved with her fingers. Kent's smile broadened as he raised his arm and waved back.

As she turned the corner from Middle Street onto the Gillingham Road her phone rang. Jess glanced down at the screen, then grabbing the mobile with her left hand, she swerved sharply across to the side of the road, slipped the car out of gear and pulled on the hand brake.

'Mum! Oh, Mum, I'm so, so happy for you.'

'It's such a relief, Jess, I can't even begin to explain.'

'Why didn't you call me as soon as they let you out?'

'I wanted to surprise you, so I didn't ring from the prison, then, once I was out, I regretted it, but I had no credit left on my phone, so I had to wait until I got to the shop at the railway station to top it up.'

'I'll be waiting for you at Gillingham station, so don't go getting a bus to Spinton. Oh, Mum, I can't tell you how pleased I am. I've just come from the police station. They called me in to inform me about the CPS verdict, why they couldn't tell me on the phone I don't know.'

'Data protection probably, love. I even had to put up with it in Bronzefield. They used to ask for my prison number, name, and date of birth before they'd tell me anything. They have to make sure they have the right person before they divulge anything, I suppose.'

'I didn't get asked for my I.D. when I got there... still, it doesn't matter now. You're free, and your actions have been vindicated. I can't wait to get you home.'

'Get a nice bottle of wine in for the celebrations tonight, Jess... tell you what... make it two. I'm buying.'

'Not likely, Mum. I'll provide the wine; you just concentrate on putting all this behind you.'

'All right, love. I'll hang up now. The train will be here soon. See you about one-ish.'

At two-thirty, Jess drove onto the asphalt parking bay outside the farmhouse, pulled on the handbrake and turned to Nicola.

'I can't stop looking at you,' she said, her eyes beginning to mist.

Nicola slipped off her seatbelt, then leaned across to pat Jess's hand. 'You'll be sick of the sight of me before long.'

'Never, Mum.' Jess threw her arms around Nicola and snuggled into her shoulder. After a full minute, she pulled away, then wiping her eyes, she opened the car door and climbed out. Her phone alerted her to a text message as she pushed the key into the front door lock.

Hi, sorry for the delay in replying, was in a meeting. Brilliant News! So happy for you both. We'll have to organise a night out, just the three of us. Will call later. News update on Josh. Luv, Sam.

Jess walked through to the kitchen and put the two bottles of wine she had bought into the fridge, then filling the kettle she switched it on to boil.

'Bet you're ready for a proper cuppa, Mum.'

'I've been dreaming about it all the way home. The tea in there was dreadful, so was the one I had on the train, like cat's pee.' Nicola put her hand on Jess's arm. 'And there's you thinking I'd be dreaming about the wine.'

'No... well, I could understand if you were.'

'All right, I was licking my lips at the prospect of that too, I'll admit it.'

Jess grinned. 'Shall we have a takeaway tonight? Make it a proper girl's night in.'

'Anything but chilli,' Nicola said. 'I've had so much of that lately, I'm off it for life.'

'Chinese, then... Indian? What about a Thai curry?'

'You choose, Jess. I'll be happy whatever you decide.' She stretched and yawned. 'I'm going up for a nap after my tea. I feel really drained all of a sudden.'

Jess pouted. 'You're bound to, Mum. The adrenalin rush will have worn off. Do you want to go now? I'll bring it up to you.'

Nicola nodded, then yawning again, she turned and walked slowly out of the kitchen. 'It will be so nice to lie down on a comfortable bed.'

Just after six, Sam rang.

'Hi, darling, how's the ex-con settling in? Give her a hug from me.'

'She's here if you want a word?'

'No, it's okay, I'll nip over at the weekend and say hello properly. I've got a bit of work to do later so this call will be a quickie. I just wanted to let you know how it went last night.'

'Okay, how did it go?'

'Flatter than a witch's boob with a puncture,' Sam replied.

'Oh, dear, that bad?'

'Worse. He left after an hour and got a taxi home.'

'Bugger. You didn't click at all then?' Jess asked.

'We're not the slightest bit compatible, Jess. He doesn't like the music I like; he doesn't find silly things funny like I do... you know me, a girl tripped and fell flat on her face carrying a tray of drinks, I was in hysterics. He just wanted to help her up.'

'Hmm, I think I would have too.'

'Exactly.'

'Hey, I have a sense of humour too, I just don't fall about at someone's misfortune.'

'It was bloody funny, the tray went up in the air, it was like an old Buster Keaton movie scene.' Sam began to giggle at the memory.

Jess sighed and waited until her friend had recovered her composure 'Sometimes I wonder how we get on as well as we do.'

'Opposites attract... sometimes... Not in this particular case though. I don't know what he's looking for, Jess, but I'm not it, that's for certain.'

'Did he go on about his ex, again?'

'He tried, but I just kept changing the subject. Your name came up again, so, if you fancy playing the Tricia Goddard agony aunt role, I'm sure it would be appreciated.'

'Poor Josh,' Jess said quietly.

'Poor me, you mean. He almost ruined my night out. Luckily a couple of old mates came in just after he'd gone, so it wasn't a total disaster.'

'I'm pleased about that, Sam, but Josh...'

'He's bloody hard work, Jess. You have the patience of a saint, but even you would struggle with him for longer than half an hour. He needs therapy, really. I'd bet money that if he ever does get into a relationship again, and Katy offered to come back, he'd ditch the new partner like a shot.'

'Well, there is his daughter to consider.'

'There is, but that would hardly be fair on the new partner, would it?'

'Is this meant as a warning to me, Sam?' Jess laughed half-heartedly.

'Only if you're daft enough to be thinking of taking him on.'

'Well, I'm not, so you don't have to worry.'

Sam whooped. 'Good, now, I've got to run, but how about we meet up for lunch and have a proper catch up?'

'Sounds good to me,' said Jess, 'where shall we go? Not the Wonky Donkey.'

'No, God no... I don't want to risk meeting up with him again. I'd need anti-depressants.'

'Sam!'

'All right, he's not quite as bad as that but, no, not the Donkey.'

'How about the Casa Blanc? It's really nice there, do you know it?'

'I know of it. I've never been, isn't it a bit pricey?'

'It's not too bad, but they do have a really good menu. It's my treat anyway.'

'Sold,' said Sam. 'When shall we meet? I'm fine tomorrow, or Wednesday and Thursday next week.'

'Tomorrow is good for me. I can't wait to see you, Sam, it's been ages.'

'Tomorrow it is, I'm really looking forward to seeing you too. What time?'

'One?'

'Done, are we drinking or driving?'

Jess ummed. 'You drink, I'll drive. I'll pick you up in town, outside the library, you won't have far to walk then.'

'Fab. See you tomorrow,' Sam replied. 'All the best to your mum, tell her I'm chuffed to bits for her.'

'We're having a girl's night in. The wine will flow, hence me not drinking tomorrow.'

'Have a lovely evening, Jess. Get rid of all those pent-up tears the pair of you.'

Chapter 38

Jess was up and about early on Friday morning. Still suffering the after effects of Thursday's wine, she went for a long walk around the local lanes. The rain had ceased during the night and she was treated to a weak, watery sun as she walked briskly along the narrow, muddy tracks trying to avoid the deeper of the water-filled pot holes.

When she got home, Nicola was still in bed, so she showered and with a towel turban around her head, made coffee, then standing at Alice's big, oak table in the kitchen, she pondered over whether to read Alice's next chapter or to continue where she left off with Martha's history. Deciding on Martha, she picked up the blue folder and carried it along with her coffee to the lounge. After taking a sip of the hot liquid, she put the mug carefully down on the coffee table, then pulling her legs beneath her, she pulled out the wad of A4 paper from the folder and settled back to read.

Martha. August 1956-57

The Saturday date nights became a regular thing and I looked forward to them immensely. Peter was charming, funny and very handsome and I soon found myself falling hopelessly in love with him. Being seen with him in public also raised my standing amongst not only the trainee nurses but some of the qualified ones as well, and I was often asked if Peter had a friend he could bring along for one of my colleagues. No one seemed to care about the age difference, or the fact that he was married. Affairs between doctors and young nurses were a common occurrence, the more mature ones seemed a more attractive proposition to the overworked, junior doctors on the wards. As long as Matron remained ignorant of our courtship, everything seemed rosy.

Nothing had happened between us by this point, apart from a hasty, frenzied kiss and grope session behind the bus shelter near the gates of the nurses' home. He did ask me if I could sneak him inside once, when he'd had one or two pints more than usual, but I managed to persuade him that it wasn't worth the risk. One night, bowing to pressure, I agreed to go to the park with him, but when we got there the gates were locked, so it was back to the bus shelter again for more clumsy petting.

By mid-August I could tell that he was getting frustrated and he was beginning to take interest in other nurses in the pub, so I told him I'd lie to Matron and tell her I was going home the following Sunday for my grandmother's birthday if he could manage to find us somewhere to go.

The somewhere, turned out to be his friend's flat, part of a large house in Aylesford, a small town about three miles away.

I was buzzing all week, daydreaming about movie-style seductions. I had never promised to save myself for a future husband, but I was quite picky about who I would allow to take my virginity. Peter was mature, eloquent and beguiling. He was knowledgeable about art and music, not that I knew much about anything. I was easily impressed.

On the Saturday, after my midday finish, I got the bus into town and bought a slinky, black negligee, new underwear, a black suspender belt and two pairs of nylons. I considered buying some perfume too, but my budget was limited and the stuff I could afford to buy seemed cheap and tarty, so I decided to stick with my precious bottle of the aptly named, Grande Affair from Coty.

I packed my newly purchased items in the bottom of my small suitcase and covered them with my daily use underwear, skirt and jumper in case Matron became suspicious and decided to do a spot check before I left. I had, once again, paid for a hairdo that afternoon and to belay the suspicions of Matron who must have seen plenty of nurses heading out for illicit liaisons over the years, I only half did my makeup, finishing it off in the ladies lavatory in the coffee bar.

We met outside the library as usual, but this time, instead of heading for his local, we climbed into a taxi and made the three-and-a-half-mile drive to Aylesford where I dropped off my bag, touched up my hair and makeup in a very posh bathroom, before taking Peter's arm and walking the short distance to a pub that overlooked the river.

Peter was full of surprises and had telephoned the pub in the afternoon to book us a table. The unexpected meal was welcome as I'd skipped lunch to go shopping earlier in the day.

After the food, he led me to a quiet bar at the back of the pub where we listened to piped music and chatted about things in general. At ten, we left the pub and took a leisurely walk back to the flat.

The night was everything I dreamed it would be. Peter was an experienced and attentive lover. I had heard so much about how I would feel a bit of pain as I lost my virginity but there was none. I was tense initially, but my lover knew how to relax me and I soon found myself wrapped around him as we made warm, tender love.

We didn't get much sleep that night, merely dozing between making love, but eventually, I did fall into a dreamy sleep just as the sun was coming up.

I stayed in bed until twelve o'clock when Peter brought in a tray of bacon, eggs and hot tea and we sat up listening to the Family Favourites show on the BBC Light programme.

In the afternoon, we walked by the river, before going back to bed for more lovemaking, then, at seven, Peter called for a taxi and we travelled back to Maidstone.

After saying goodbye at the gates of the nurses' home, Peter climbed back into the taxi and I reported to Matron, unpacked my bag, then lay on my bed and relived my overnight experience.

Over the next three months we spent every moment we could together. I even sneaked out of the nurses' quarters at midnight one Wednesday night to spend a happy hour cavorting in the back seat of his car, down a local lover's lane. By December, his ardour seemed to cool with the winter weather and I didn't see much of him at all. I asked him whether I'd done something wrong when we bumped into each other in the corridor at the hospital one afternoon, but he assured me, in whispered tones, that I hadn't.

Things picked up again in January and I began to think things had returned to normal, but on the last Saturday of the month I was left standing in the rain outside the library. I waited a good hour before finally understanding that he wasn't going to turn up. On impulse, I trapsed through the rain to the pub, where I found him in the company of a pretty trainee nurse who had only recently joined the hospital. He didn't appear to be put out in the slightest when I confronted him, treating me to a shrug of his shoulders before turning back to Bella. She seemed to be more interested in me than in what he was saying to her, but after giving me a glare, he whispered something in her ear and she looked me straight in the eyes and laughed.

As it turned out, his fling with Bella didn't last long. She was caught sneaking into the nurses' quarters in the early hours once too often and was dismissed by Matron. By the summer, I'd almost completed my first year of training and had taken my second exam, which I passed with flying colours. By now I was spending most of my time on the wards and I was much more confident around the patients. There was also the bonus that I was no longer the general dogsbody. Oh, I was still a dogsbody of sorts, but it was now the job of the newer recruits to sluice the bedpans and clean the puke from the patients' sheets. I spent more and more of my time actually caring for people. Although the regular SENs still looked down their noses at me, I had finally climbed off the bottom rung of the ladder.

Becoming a second-year trainee didn't mean my life was any easier, the hours were still long and the restrictions on my private life were just as draconian as they ever had been, but overall, I was happy enough. I got friendly with a porter, called Stan, who used to throw paper planes with hidden messages inside onto the table I shared with six other trainees in the canteen. Stan was a tall, stringy lad with lank hair who suffered frequent, and profuse, acne attacks. He had a great personality though, and nothing ever seemed to get him down. He wasn't my type, far from it. At times I found him infuriatingly childlike, but when he was in a more serious mood we got on quite well. We used to meet up in the coffee bar in town on Saturday nights where he would always insist on paying for my drinks, even though I was earning a little bit more than him and had no living expenses to find. One night, he asked me out on 'a proper date' as he put it. I told him I'd think about it, but that was only really a delaying tactic so that I didn't have to embarrass him by refusing immediately.

At nine, he left to meet his mates at the bowling alley and I was just finishing my second coffee when I heard a familiar voice behind. I spun around on my seat to find Peter smiling down at me.

'Fancy a beer?' he asked, as if nothing had changed between us.

Stupidly, I nodded, and the affair was back on again.

At Christmas, and after half a dozen glorious nights spent making love in his friend's flat, I found out that I was pregnant. I don't know why I thought he'd be decent about it. Although I was so nervous about telling him, I held on to a ridiculous notion that he'd leave his childless, apparently loveless, fifteen-year marriage, and marry me. I couldn't have been more wrong.

It took me most of a long Saturday night in the Chequers pub in Aylesford to bring the subject up. When I did, he immediately got to his feet, called me a 'stupid cow' and stormed out of the bar. I grabbed my coat and ran after him, begging him to stop. When he did, he told me in no uncertain terms that we had no future together and if I had any sense at all, I'd make plans to get rid of the child before it was too late. Shoving a half crown into my hand, he flagged down a taxi, shoved me inside and gave the driver instructions where to drop me off. I looked out of the back window of the cab through tear-stained eyes as I watched him turn away and walk back to the pub.

My mind was in a permanent state of confusion over the next two weeks. I knew I'd have to either do something about my situation or own up to Matron and be sent packing from the job I was beginning to enjoy. In my despair, I even considered taking up with Stan and try to talk him into a quick marriage, but in the back of my mind I knew that wouldn't work.

In the end, it was Peter himself who came to my rescue, if you can call it that. He certainly saved my job and my reputation, I suppose.

He came looking for me in the café one Saturday night in the January of 1957. I turned my back on him as he came through the door, thinking he'd come in to meet someone else, but a few seconds later I felt his hand on my arm and he asked me to step outside for a moment.

I'll never forget that night. It was cold, drizzly, and I was already feeling utterly miserable, even before he asked me whether I'd done anything about the baby yet.

'You have to sort this out now, Martha. You have no idea what sort of life lies ahead for you, or the child if you don't.' He dug into his pocket and pulled out a ten-pound note and a scrap of paper with an address written on it.

'Don't leave it much longer,' he snapped. Then he turned and walked away.

The rain came down heavier as I walked slowly home. I was grateful for it as my dripping hair and wet face hid my tears as I reported in at the nurses' home. My first thought was to burn the scrap of paper on the gas stove and pocket the ten pounds to put towards my keep after I was thrown out, but though I actually lit the hob and held the paper above the flames, I couldn't will myself to set it alight, and turning off the gas, I went back to my room and stuffed the address in my purse with the money.

The terraced house was in a poor part of town. The street was dirty and I could smell rotting food from a line of overflowing dustbins that lined the doorsteps. I raised my hand to knock on the faded, red door, three times before I finally managed to do it. I looked back to the bus stop and told myself that I could make it back onboard before the bus departed, but as I backed away from the step, I heard the ring of a bell and the green double decker bus drove off.

A scrawny woman with untidy hair and a cigarette hanging from the corner of her mouth opened the door, looked me up and down and obviously noting my terrified face, understood my situation immediately. Her demeanour suddenly changed and she smiled a sad smile at me.

'Come on in, love,' she said, stepping away from the door.

The house wasn't what you'd call sterile, but it wasn't filthy either. She ushered her three kids away from the table in the kitchen then sat me down, poured me a cup of tea and tipped a generous measure of cheap gin into it.

'That'll steady your nerves, girl.'

She told me to call her Nora, but she admitted that it wasn't her real name. She asked me if I had the money and I showed her the ten-pound note. Her eyes widened at that and she said that she couldn't give me change. I told her she could keep the lot, I just wanted it over and done with.

After the tea, she evicted her kids from the landing where they were playing a game of marbles and opened the door to a bedroom where I found a double bed covered in a thick, woollen blanket. I sat on the edge of the mattress, shaking like a leaf while she spread out a few clean-looking towels and told me to take my knickers off and lie down.

She returned about ten minutes later with a bowl of steaming water and three, thick syringes filled with what I later learned was a scalding hot, carbolic soap mix. 'Now, love, if this doesn't do the trick by tomorrow, come back and we'll do it again. You should be okay, but there was one woman who had to come back three times before she bled.'

I lay back, screwed up my eyes and as the tears squirted down the sides of my face, Nora went to work.

A short time later, we returned to the kitchen where I handed over the money and she poured more tea.

'Don't forget, come back in a few days if it doesn't work. Don't leave it too long.'

'That was better than I thought it would be,' I said tearfully. 'I've heard awful stories... about knitting needles and crotchet hooks.'

'Desperation stakes,' Nora said with a shake of her head. 'We haven't got to that stage yet.'

When I left the house, I walked blindly around the streets having no idea where I was, or where I was going. I half expected God to take revenge by throwing down a thunderbolt, but his eyes must have been elsewhere that night because I got home unscathed some two hours later. When I woke up in the morning, I found blood on my sheets. A lot of blood. Pulling them off the bed, I screwed them up with my nightie inside and took them straight to the laundry where I dropped my nightgown into the medical waste bin and shoved the sheets into a pile of soiled washing that some unfortunate trainee would have to boil wash later that day.

After that, I decided that men were more trouble than they were worth. I met Peter a few times on the ward after that but he always ignored me or I'd make myself busy with something or other.

I finished my training in the summer of 1958 and was given my State Enrolled Nurse certificate at a ceremony in the hospital. Peter attended and applauded politely as I stepped forward to pick it up.

Chapter 39

The late January sun seeped out of the thin veil of high cloud looking as though it had been captured in a water colour painting. Although it was lunchtime, the early frost had managed to cling on to the plants in the shadier parts of the restaurant garden. Jess shivered as she walked between the skeletal rose bushes that lined the stone path. She felt the welcome heat from the over-door air curtain and began to unbutton her coat as she walked into the restaurant. Sam was already inside and waved to her as she entered.

At the table, the friends hugged, then Jess removed her coat and handed it to the waiter who had followed her across the room.

'It's a bit posh in here, isn't it?' Sam said as Jess took her seat. 'You don't get coat removal service at Maccy D's, do you?'

'They do a nice veggie burger here,' said Jess.

'They shouldn't be able to call them that, it's sacrilege, a burger is a burger. It's made of beef, it's traditional.'

'I haven't had a real one for over a year now,' Jess admitted.

'Shame on you,' replied Sam with a look of mock horror on her face. 'We used to live in Maccie's when we were students.'

'I'm trying to be good, but you keep dragging me back to the dark side.' Jess admonished her with a wagging finger. 'I'd weaned myself off bacon until you turned up at the farmhouse.'

'Farmhouses should smell of bacon, especially yours,' said Sam, unperturbed by the accusation. 'Especially that particular farmhouse. Pigs were bred there for centuries.'

'A century, in the singular,' Jess responded. 'Nana stopped breeding them in the nineteen-seventies.'

'Semantics,' said Sam. 'There was a plethora of pork until you took over.'

270

'And it will remain a pork free zone as long as I live in it, give or take the odd sandwich lapse,' said Jess. She picked up the menu as the waiter came back.

'I'll have one of your splendid veggie burgers, as recommended by my vegan friend here,' Jess said, smirking over the menu at Sam.

'What do you do with pork?' Sam asked, sticking her tongue out at Jess.

Jess ordered a bottle of Pinot Noir and a bottle of sparking water for herself and the pair were soon engrossed in their usual, gossipy conversation. Jess had just pushed away her plate after finishing her burger when she heard a familiar voice call her name from the reception desk.

'Jess!'

She turned to see Bradley hurrying across the restaurant towards her. When he reached their table, he grinned widely at her, then nodded to Sam, who was looking him up and down with an appreciative eye.

'Hello,' Jess smiled warmly, and held out her hand towards her friend. 'Bradley, this is Sam, my best friend and conspirator, I think I've mentioned her a few times. Sam, this is my friend and lawyer, Bradley.'

Sam got to her feet as Bradley stepped around the table, sticking out her hand as Bradley offered his, never taking her eyes from his face. 'So, you're the legal eagle that Jess speaks so highly of.'

Bradley nodded and tried to pull his hand away but Sam clung on.

'I'm sorry,' she said as she finally released it. 'I was just trying to think of some legal trouble I might need advice on... I'm sure there must be something.'

Her eyes shone as she looked directly into his.

'I'd be delighted to represent you, whatever the situation,' he replied.

The lawyer sat down between the girls, ordering a Danish sandwich and a bottle of still water as the waiter arrived to clear their plates. Sam took a sip of wine and winked at Jess, mouthing 'nice' as Bradley unscrewed the top of his water bottle.

'What brings you here today?' he asked as he poured the liquid into a glass.

'Just a girlie lunch, nothing important,' Jess replied.

'Well, I'm delighted you chose today to have it.' Bradley looked from one to the other, his eyes remaining on Sam for a moment longer than they might have.

Sam stretched out her leg under the table and rubbed her foot against the lawyer's ankle.

'Not half as delighted as me,' she said.

Jess shook her head and smiled to herself. She was used to Sam's flirty ways.

Ten minutes later, she realised that she hadn't uttered a single word since she had greeted Bradley. He and Sam were getting on like a house on fire. Sam giggling at his weak jokes, Bradley showing off like men do when they know an attractive woman is interested in them. Smiling to herself, she got to her feet and picked up her bag. To her slight annoyance, her two friends didn't notice.

'I'm, err… I'm just going to powder my nose,' she said eventually.

Sam looked up and smiled, then focussed on Bradley again. Bradley shot her a quick glance and nodded to her before turning his full attention back to Sam.

Jess walked away smirking. A full ten minutes later, she returned via the bar where she paid for both their own meals and Bradleys, then taking her phone from her bag she strode briskly back to the table.

'Sorry, I've got to rush, I've just had a call.' She held out the phone out as evidence. 'Will you be all right getting home, Sam?'

Sam nodded eagerly. 'I'll get an Uber, Jess.'

'No, please. My car is outside. I can give you a lift home, it's no trouble.' Bradley's eyes looked almost pleadingly into Sam's.

Sam looked up and made an 'ooh' expression with her mouth as Jess rolled her eyes heavenward. 'Right, I'll be off then, have fun, you two.'

'Oh, I'm sure we will,' Sam replied, placing her fingers delicately on Bradley's hand.

Jess arrived home fifteen minutes later to find Nicola making a late lunch in the kitchen.

'Hi, Mum, how's your day been?'

'To be honest, I haven't been up all that long,' Nicola replied with a sheepish grin. 'I didn't realise how poorly I must have slept in Bronzefield.'

Jess gave her mother a hug. 'It's been an incredibly stressful time for you, Mum, please don't apologise for catching up on your sleep.'

'How was lunch?' Nicola asked.

'Bradley turned up; he appears to have fallen under Sam's spell. It was hilarious. I'm sure she slipped a love potion into his drink. He's already besotted with her.'

Nicola looked at her daughter closely.

'Does that bother you?'

'No, Mum. I had made up my mind about Bradley and I'm not going to change it. That ex-wife of his poisoned any chance we ever had of forming a relationship.'

'She'll be turning her attentions to Sam now then. Have you warned her?'

'Sam can handle herself, Mum. It's Leonora you should feel sorry for. She has no idea what sort of hornet's nest she'll be kicking if she starts all that nonsense with her.'

'You could have handled it too, love.' Nicola patted Jess on the arm. 'I think you pulled away for other reasons.'

'Possibly.' Jess frowned as she thought. 'Possibly,' she repeated as she picked up Alice's memoir. 'I'm just going to take a trip back to nineteen forty-two. Do you want to watch TV? I'll read it out here if you do.'

'Read it wherever you feel most comfortable,' Nicola replied sliding a fried egg onto a piece of toast.

'I'll stay out here then, Mum. You have the lounge. I'll read Nana's diary in the place where she probably wrote it.' She looked around the old kitchen and patted the big oak table. 'I feel a bit guilty about having new units put in now. They'll be fitting them in a couple of weeks. I hope it doesn't change the atmosphere in here, it's just so warm and inviting. When I'm reading the memoir, it feels like I am sitting at the table with her.' She looked across at Nicola as she picked up her plate and turned towards the door to the lounge. 'Do you ever feel that?'

'I can't say I do, Jess. But then, I was never made as welcome as you.'

'I'm sorry you feel like that, Mum. I don't think Nana held any particular grievance against you.'

'I used to think she did, but that was probably my mother's influence. Anyway, that doesn't matter now. I'll be out of here soon. I was thinking of moving into the cottage next week if that's all right with you.'

'Of course it is. I wish you'd stay a bit longer though. Get a bit more rest before you move.'

'Give my liver a bit more rest you mean,' Nicola said with a laugh. 'Let's make it the first week in February then, that's the week after.'

'That sounds good, Mum.' Jess smiled and turned back to the table as Nicola pushed open the door to the lounge.

'Right, Nana,' she said quietly. 'What have you been up to since last we met.'

Alice. February 1942

We had just finished breakfast when Captain Formby arrived at the back door accompanied by two rifle bearing soldiers and a tall man in a black-dyed, RAF greatcoat.

The officer rubbed his red hands together as he stepped into the kitchen. 'Forgot my gloves,' he said.

'That's becoming a habit,' I said, smiling at them each in turn. One of the soldiers nodded in reply, the other, a round-faced man with droopy eyes and acne scars, flashed a set of tobacco-stained teeth as he looked me up and down.

'Could you leave the rifles in the car, or at least in the shed outside?' I asked.

The droopy eyed soldier replied before the captain had a chance to.

'He's a Nazi, miss. He's dangerous. He's likely to grab a knife or something and—'

'That will do, Courtney,' Formby cut in.

'You can't trust him, Sir,' the soldier replied belligerently.

'I won't have guns in the house when the children are here,' I said looking sternly at Courtney. 'I even keep my own shotgun locked away.'

'Don't tell him that, Mi—'

'Enough, Courtney!' the officer hissed.

I put my arms around the shoulders of my evacuees. 'I mean it, Captain Formby. I won't have guns in the kitchen when the children are here. Stephen already has an imaginary rifle; I'd hate to see him tempted to pick up a real one.'

'I understand completely,' Formby replied. 'Courtney, take Robinson's rife and wait in the yard.'

'It's bloody cold out there, Sir, I—'

'Then wait in the barn, man.' He glared at the private. 'That is an order.'

Courtney sniffed and gave me a glare as he took Robinson's rifle and stomped out of the kitchen, slamming the door behind him.

'Right, down to business. We haven't been introduced.' I held my hand out towards the German officer. 'I'm Alice Mollison.'

'Richard Perle,' replied the German in perfect English with just a hint of an accent. He was a tall man with neatly parted, brown hair. His handsome, but slightly weather-beaten face showed off a pair of bright blue eyes. He was obviously an outdoor type. I felt an immediate connection with him.

I shook his hand, much to the disgust of Miriam, who had taken my place with her arms around the children.

'This is Miriam, she is both my housekeeper and my very good friend, we'd be lost without her.'

Richard held out his hand to Miriam but noticing the look of distaste on her face, he withdrew it and bowed stiffly, instead.

'This is Stephen and Harriet, our evacuees from London.'

'They're only here because of the likes of you,' spat Miriam. 'They should be with their parents but you blew their house up.'

The children looked up at Miriam with puzzled looks on their faces.

'Did he drop the bomb, Auntie?'

'As good as,' Miriam hissed.

'I can assure you; I have never dropped a bomb on a house in my life. I flew my plane to England and gave myself up before the first bomber flew over here.'

'So you say.'

'Miriam, please. Let's just hear what Richard has to say before we condemn him, shall we?' I smiled at her sadly, then looked back to the pilot. 'Miriam has missing family in Germany, Mr Perle. She has a right to be suspicious.'

Richard nodded in understanding. 'Miriam. I grew up with a lady of the same name, I was fortunate to have her as my nanny.'

Miriam's face remained a mask of hatred.

'Please sit down, I'll make tea,' I said, trying to ease the tension in the room. I turned back to Stephen. 'While I make a brew, could you nip out to the milking parlour and ask Barney to bring the lads in please. I'd like them all to be here when the decision is made. They will have to work with Richard, after all.'

I picked up the huge metal tea pot we used when we had a gathering of the men and loaded it with a dozen spoons of tea leaves, then put it in the sink and sat it under the Ascot gas boiler until it was full. Making my way across the kitchen, I put a couple of cut logs onto the fire and gave it a poke. Richard got to his feet and began to unbutton his greatcoat. 'Do you mind if I take this off? It's rather warm in here.'

He pulled off the heavy overcoat and Captain Formby took it from him and hung it on the back door before hanging his own coat next to it. Robinson removed his khaki coat and laid it across the back of his chair. Wiping a line of sweat from his forehead, he looked at Hattie and said, 'phew.'

Stephen came back in at the head of a line of farm workers as I was about to pour the tea into two long rows of mugs. They wiped their muddy feet on the coconut mat as they entered, then stood in a group behind Miriam and the children as I passed around the steaming mugs of tea.

'This is Richard Perle,' I said when everyone was settled. 'Captain Formby has asked if we would take him on as an extra, unpaid, labourer for a while.'

The men stared at Perle with looks that ranged from confusion to outright hostility, their demeanour didn't change as I explained what Richard had already told us about how he had ended up in Kent.

'It's all right him saying he gave himself up, but he could just be a Nazi coward,' said George Foulkes, one of the workers that was too old to be asked to fight himself. Others muttered in agreement.

'How old is he?' asked Alfie Brown. 'He only looks about twenty, that means he grew up under Hitler. How do we know he's not just a spy?'

'Let's let him talk, shall we?' I suggested. 'I'm sure he'll explain all about himself, given the chance.'

277

Richard put his mug on the table and got to his feet. He was wearing a British army uniform that had been dyed black. On the tunic, front and back were brightly covered patches, denoting his position as a POW. 'I will tell you all about myself, but please, not in front of the children. They are too young to hear some of the things I have to reveal about my life under the Nazis. I'm hoping that when I finish my story, you will understand why I did what I did, but some of the details are too horrific for such young ears.'

I nodded in agreement. 'Children, please go into the lounge and carry on with the schoolwork I set you yesterday. We'll call you back in later. You will have a say in the decision we make.'

As Stephen and Harriet left the room, Richard took a sip of hot tea, and nodding in appreciation to me, began his story.

Chapter 40

'More coffee, Jess?'

An hour later, Nicola stepped into the kitchen with her tea cup and an empty plate.

Jess held up a hand as she read the last paragraph of Alice's chapter. 'Sorry, Mum, I was totally engrossed in that. You ought to read some of Nana's memoirs. You would learn a lot about her and I'm sure it would banish a few of those myths.'

'I'll wait for your novel, Jess. I'm too old to start banishing memories. True or false they're part of me now. I know a lot of them were made up by my mother, they were always too ridiculous to be true and I can understand why she was so reluctant to give us money, knowing what Owen would do with it. At the time, it just seemed mean, but I was under a lot of pressure to get her to donate to his gambling fund. I stupidly thought you and I would get at least a few pounds to buy some shopping or pay the electricity bill.'

'I know, Mum but you and Dad seemed to be joined at the hip and were the architects of your own downfall. She knew that any money she gave you would end up in his pocket, albeit for the shortest time imaginable.'

Nicola sighed, 'I should have been stronger.'

'You tried, Mum, you did get him into Gambler's Anonymous for a while, that was a big achievement, really.'

'It wasn't enough though. I should have left him when he lapsed.'

'As Dad said when I reminded him of his past treatment of me, that's water under the bridge now. We should only ever look forwards.'

Nicola smiled sadly. 'You're right. In future when we talk about the past, let's just try to remember the good times, few as they were.'

Nicola placed Jess's coffee on the table and sipped at her own tea as she stood looking over her shoulder.

'Are you coming in for Cash in the Attic? There's a repeat on the Yesterday channel.'

'I'm going to read another chapter of the memoirs, thanks, Mum. There are so many things I knew nothing about.'

'She was a deep one, Jess. She knew how to keep a secret.'

'Well, they're all coming out now,' Jess replied, tapping the cover of the book. 'I wonder where this episode is going. There's a German pilot on the farm.'

'Really! A German? I'm surprised Mum didn't bring that one up.'

'She wasn't even four at the time. I doubt she'll remember anything about it.'

Nicola laughed as she walked back to the lounge door. 'Mum? You're kidding, aren't you? I think she can remember being in the womb. She's got the collective memory of a herd of elephants.'

Jess laughed along, then, after sipping the steaming coffee, she picked up the memoir again.

Alice. February 1942

I cut short the last entry deliberately, as I wanted to take my time to remember every tiny detail of what we heard that morning. It has been a week since we crammed into my kitchen to listen to Richard as he took us through the heart-breaking events of his late childhood. A week on, I still sob when I think about how those black shirted monsters ruined his life.

'I was lucky to be born into one of Germany's oldest families. A family that used to own great swathes of land in Westphalia, for one reason or another, over time, that was reduced to about two hundred acres. The farm was much like this one, we grew wheat, barley, corn and beet, but we also had a healthy herd of cattle, we produced pork and even a few horses, which at one time, we used to sell for their meat, but by the time I arrived on the scene, we only produced animals for the farming community.

Because of the reparations placed on Germany by the allies at Versailles at the end of the first world war, the majority of the German people were living in real poverty. There was no work, little food and the Nazi party took advantage of that, blaming the French, the British but mostly the Jews for every problem they encountered in their lives. Living on a farm as we did, we were isolated from much of it, we had plenty of food, we had good housing and we were well educated, at first at home, then at one of the top schools in Cologne. Our main problem was protecting our livestock from being stolen and butchered to sell in the markets around the area.

I lived on the farm with my father and brother, Wilhelm, my mother had died of tuberculosis in nineteen twenty-seven. My father employed a nanny called Miriam, who had a beautiful raven-haired daughter named Rebecca who I had been in love with all my life.

In thirty-three, a few months after Hitler had come to power, the government set up an SS training camp on the outskirts of Cologne. One sunny afternoon, I was cleaning up the farm yard when a band of a dozen or so black-shirted soldiers drove into the farm on the back of two lorries.

They pulled up in the yard, and their commander, a man who introduced himself as Major Fuchs, asked to speak to my father, who was in the barn at the time. When he came out, they questioned him about our farm labourers, demanding to know whether we employed any Jewish workers.

We had all heard what had happened a few weeks before, when Jewish businesses had been attacked in some of the major cities and many of their owners were either forced to leave or had suffered beatings, threats and intimidation. My father refused to answer the question and was hit across the face by the commander for his transgression. Two soldiers then forced him to his knees and as one pointed a gun at him, the other hit him across the shoulders with the butt of his rifle. When my father refused to answer a second time, the commander grabbed me by the shoulder and asked me the same question. As a terrified twelve-year-old I was dumbstruck and couldn't reply, so the officer pulled out his pistol, put it to my head and asked my father again if we had any Jewish workers on the farm.

Just then, Rebecca came out of the kitchen to see what all the fuss was about. As I have said, Rebecca was the same age as me and was just becoming a woman, the soldiers leered at her as she rushed across to my side. Handing me over to one of the soldiers, Fuchs took off his hat and made a sort of mock bow to her.

'Now then, pretty girl, what is your name?'

'I'm Rebecca,' she replied in a shaky voice.

'Rebecca...' He took off his gloves and ran his hand through her long, black hair. 'So very pretty...' his hand dropped to her breast and he squeezed it hard, making her flinch. 'No, tears? you like it then... I bet you do, you little harlot.'

The major dragged poor, terrified Rebecca across the farmyard to the barn where he threw her face down onto a hay bale, tore her dress up the back and raped her to the cheers of his troops. I shook off the soldier holding onto my shoulder and ran towards the barn but I was tripped by the booted foot of one of the troops and ended up lying in a pile of dung. The SS man dragged me to my feet and holding me by the biceps, forced me to watch as one by one, the band of soldiers took their turn with her.

I was screaming her name, despite the punches that were rained down on my head. I struggled to get free, but only God knows what I thought I could do. I would happily have given my life for her but I was helpless.

As the troops were lining up to take their turn, Miriam came into the yard carrying a basket of washing.

She'd been at the back of the farm and hadn't heard the commotion.

Miriam was in her thirties and you could easily see where Rebecca got her looks from. As she saw what was happening, she ran towards the barn screaming at the men to stop. One of the soldiers waiting impatiently for his turn with Rebecca, hit her with the butt of his rifle as she ran past him. She fell to the floor, blood oozing from the wound on the back of her head. When she came to, she forced herself to her knees and began to crawl towards her sobbing daughter, crying out her name, begging God to send down his angels to stop this abomination. The troops laughed even harder, then one of them, an ugly, square-jawed sergeant, kicked her in the stomach, stomped on her back, then lifting his rifle, put a bullet into her head.

I sank to my knees; I was in total shock. My father, who had been screaming that he would report the major to the authorities, was silenced by another swipe from a rifle butt, knocking out several of his teeth and breaking his nose.

The horrific events continued for a full hour before Major Fuchs decided he'd had enough enjoyment for one day and ordered his men back onto the trucks.

'Bring her,' he said, pointing at the prone figure of Rebecca.

'Leave her alone, haven't you done enough,' I cried as they lifted her poor, bruised body and threw her over the side of the truck.

Fuchs just laughed at me and said that there was a whole camp of soldiers in training who hadn't seen a woman in months.

I received another round of blows, then the soldiers climbed back on the lorries and drove away.'

It was obviously difficult for Richard to relive those moments. Tears streamed down his face and his voice broke as he told the horrific story. He wasn't the only one in tears. Miriam fell to her knees and wept. Barney, his face a mask of anger, helped her back to her feet and held her as Richard continued.

'My father went straight into town, his face a mask of blood. He reported the incident to the authorities only to be asked if he was a party member. When he replied negatively, he was told that he had no status and that his complaint would not be looked into. The Mayor then informed him that if he hadn't joined the party by the end of the month, and if he couldn't produce his membership documents, then the land that had been in our family for generations would be forfeited.

So, my father joined the Nazi party, he had little choice really. It was that or destitution for his family. Wilhelm and I were enrolled in the Hitler Youth and spent our evenings and weekends, singing patriotic songs as we were taught how to become model Germans. The training was tough, almost as tough as the regular army faced, and within a year I was learning how to shoot a rifle and throw a grenade. My training went well and I threw myself into it, not letting on how much I despised them all. Every time I shot at a target, in my mind I was shooting at either Hitler himself, or Major Fuchs. I never missed.

I continued to work on the farm throughout the next five years, but then, in nineteen thirty-eight, just before my eighteenth birthday, I was told that I had been selected to join the Luftwaffe and I was to train to become a pilot. My father was pleased, as although it would be a dangerous occupation, I wouldn't be stuck in the trenches fighting for a month to gain a yard of mud, as he had done in the first war.

My training went well and I began to formulate my plan of escape. My navigator, a man named Dieter Haas, who you will meet when he has recovered from appendicitis, was of a similar mind. The Nazis had bankrupted his father when he had refused to join the party back in thirty-six and he hated them almost as much as I did. On our first reconnaissance flight during which we were merely supposed to fly along the coast of Kent to take photographs of the air defences, we decided we could serve our country better by handing over our aircraft to the RAF, and we landed in a field just along the coast from here and we surrendered to a local farmer, armed only with a pitchfork.'

Richard had been speaking for about half an hour, nonstop. He paused and took a sip of cold tea, pulled a face, then carried on in a quiet voice.

'I will never forgive the Nazis for what they did. I loved Rebecca, it was no secret, both of our families knew that when the time was right, I would marry her. I still see her when I close my eyes at night, though I try hard to concentrate on her beautiful face, not her bruised and abused body we found in a ditch at the entrance to our farm a few days later. I still see Miriam, my nanny, a woman who was there at my birth and who had long been a surrogate mother to me, crawling through the muck to try to save her daughter. I see myself, standing, helpless and hopeless, doing nothing to protect them. Some mornings I cannot look myself in the face in my shaving mirror. I still feel the shame of my inaction, my impotence. I begged the local RAF commander to allow me to fly, to fight, to try to ease some of the shame I still feel, but he wouldn't hear of it, and I've been stuck in the camp for almost two years now. I want to do my bit, something, anything to hasten the end of that regime. If that means digging a ditch on an English farm, so be it. Nothing can ever take away the pain I feel and nothing will ever diminish the hatred I feel for those people. I just want to be able to tell myself that I'm doing something, no matter how small.'

When Richard sat down, I looked around the room and I can't remember seeing a dry eye. Alfie, who had been listening, sitting down with his back against the wall, suddenly got to his feet, and shouting, 'he's still a bloody

German, don't forget we have some of our own out there fighting scum like him,' he stormed out of the kitchen. I was told later that he shut himself in one of the storage sheds for half an hour, kicking and punching the door.

When Stephen and Harriet came back into the room it was obvious that they had been listening through a crack in the door. Harriet looked directly at me and asked me what rape was. I told her that it meant that the soldiers had hurt Rebecca and she nodded her head slowly and turned to face Richard.

'I'm so sorry you couldn't stop her being hurt, but you shouldn't really blame yourself. You were only as old as Stephen.'

'I'd have grabbed a gun and shot them all if they'd done that to Harriet,' Stephen boasted.

'I wish I possessed your courage, young man,' Richard replied seriously. 'I should have done something, anything...'

'What could you do?' said Miriam, still wiping tears from her cheeks. 'You were little more than a child.'

'All right,' I said, when she had finished speaking. 'It's decision time. I want everyone to think long and hard about this because it will affect us all. I have no idea what the townsfolk will think of us if we decide to allow Richard and Dieter to work here, and I know you'll be the ones who take all the flak for it in the Old Bull, so this is your decision as much as mine and I'll agree with whatever you decide.'

Barney was the first to speak.

'I know the Nazis are a despicable lot, but I never realised just how despicable. I just thank the Lord that we don't have a similar regime running this country.' He paused for a moment and looked hard at Richard. 'Young man, my heart goes out to you. No one should have to witness the things you have, especially as a child. I for one, welcome you to the farm. We could do with another experienced hand, but I will say this before I finish. If Mr Perle is going to be doing the same work as the rest of us, then he should receive the same wage

286

as the rest of us, otherwise he'll be little more than a slave, and I'm not having that. We're fighting a war against that sort of thing.'

Barney's speech was received with a ripple of applause, but no one else stepped forward to speak.

'Okay then,' I said with a quaking voice, 'let's have the vote. Hands up those who think we should allow Richard and Dieter to work on the farm.'

The show of hands was unanimous, Hattie sticking both hand in the air as she jumped up and down excitedly. Each of my men nodded to Richard or offered to shake his hand as they left the kitchen. When they had all returned to work, I made more tea and the remainder of us sat around my big oak table where all the farm's big decisions were made, and discussed the result of the vote.

'I don't think we can actually allow you to pay the men to work, Alice,' Formby said with a shake of his head. 'The Ministry of War won't allow it.'

'I'd happily work for nothing,' said Richard.

'I'm not having you work for nothing. I agree with Barney, there has to be some way around this.'

'Give the wages to charity,' Miriam suggested.

'Good Idea!' I exclaimed, 'but which one? Would you like to decide, Richard? they're your wages after all.'

'Any charity that helps defeat the Nazis,' Richard replied. 'Is there such an organisation?'

'We have a Spitfire fund in the town,' I replied. 'We raised enough money to buy a wing or two last year. I'm sure they'd welcome a couple of pounds a week extra.'

'Spitfires,' said Richard dreamily. 'How I'd love to fly in one. I think you have made the perfect choice, Alice... do you mind if I call you, Alice?'

He looked into my eyes and held them for a few seconds and I knew then that our connection was more than one just formed by a love of the soil.

Chapter 41

On Saturday the 25th of January, Martha and Marjorie stepped out onto their balcony to find themselves bathing in glorious, warm sunshine and instead of winter coats and gloves, they took on the three-lap tour of the deck wearing shorts and polo shirts.

Later that morning, as they were lounging on their sunbeds on the balcony, they heard a message over the public address system advising them that they would be arriving in Hong Kong in a matter of hours and that a guided tour had been arranged for them that would last throughout the afternoon and into the evening. *'You won't want to miss a trip across Kowloon harbour, the Temple Street night market and the laser light show after the sun goes down.'*

'Ooh, Martha, a laser light show? We have to see that.'

'They're like firework displays, Marjorie, when you've seen one, you've seen them all.'

'Have you ever seen one, Martha? I don't think they have them in Kent.'

'Don't try to be clever, Marjorie,' Martha said with a curl of her lip. 'I've seen them on TV.'

'I bet it's better in real life though. Henry says it's quite spectacular, he's seen them three—'

'Henry, is it? He was Mr Farthingale a few short days ago.' Martha looked down her nose at her sister.

'He told me to call him that.'

'When was this exactly, Marjorie? I haven't seen hide nor hair of the man since we went to the theatre for the variety show.'

'Erm...'

'Give me some credit, Marjorie. I know you sneak out to see him when I have my afternoon nap.'

Marjorie's mouth dropped open.

'And stop doing your impression of a goldfish. Their attention span at five seconds is twice as long as yours.'

'I like him, Martha, he makes me laugh.'

Martha sighed.

'Well, are we going ashore this afternoon? Henry says he'll give us the tour.'

'We have already been invited on a tour, Marjorie, it was announced on the P.A. system five short minutes ago.' She looked up from her sunbed at her sister as she stared out over the side of the balcony towards the hills of Hong Kong. 'I was only joking when I mentioned the goldfish, but it seems my analogy was eerily accurate.'

'Yes, but Henry says you have to pay for the tour and he said he would show us around for free.'

Martha's eyes narrowed. 'Hmm, that might be an offer we can take him up on. It seems he might prove useful for once.'

By three o'clock the temperature had reached 22 degrees Celsius and the sisters finally managed to put on their summer outfits for the trip ashore. Martha wore a mid-blue shirt and a pair of wide, white trousers cut just above the ankle while Marjorie pulled on navy, knee length shorts she had worn for the deck walk that morning and a white shirt with a leaf motif on the right breast.

They found Henry waiting for them in the Atrium, wearing white shorts, a pilot's shirt and his captain's hat.

'Ladies,' he said. 'I am your humble servant,' and offering them an arm each he turned to face the exit. Marjorie took his arm instantly but Martha just rolled her eyes heavenward and set off at a brisk pace towards the disembarkation gate.

Even Martha had to admit that she had an enjoyable trip. After crossing Kowloon harbour, they arrived on Hong Kong Island where Henry was true to his word and showed them the sights. The highlight was a ride on the Peak Tram funicular railway to Victoria Peak where they stood for a while taking in the amazing views over the Hong Kong city towers and Kowloon harbour.

At six, they returned to Kowloon and visited the famous Temple Street night market, where Martha haggled over the price of a silk shawl and a gold bracelet and Marjorie bought a satin, dragon patterned robe and, to Martha's amazement, another, white bathing costume.

'Why on earth do you need a second costume, Marjorie?' she asked.

'Because my other one will have to go in the wash and I won't have anything to wear at the pool.' Marjorie replied with a pout.

'At least that one will cover your backside,' Martha quipped as she put her credit card into the machine.

After leaving the market, they ordered a meal in one of the many Victoria harbour restaurants. Marjorie ate oysters for the first time in her life as they watched the sun go down in spectacular fashion. At eight o'clock, the laser light show began and the Hong Kong skyscrapers were lit up in blazing colour to the backdrop of loud Chinese music.

At nine, they returned to the ship at the Kai Tak cruise terminal and paid a visit to the poolside bar on deck twelve, where they sipped cocktails, ordered up by a very tipsy Henry. At ten, Martha announced that it was time they were heading up the wooden hill and after leaving Henry chatting to the bar staff at the poolside, they took the lift to deck six and returned to their cabin.

At eleven the next morning with the ship still moored at Kai Tak terminal, the sisters retraced their steps of the night before and returned to the terrace pool at the aft end of deck twelve. The day before they had checked out all three pools and the terrace was much quieter than the others.

They found sunbeds at the side of the bar and Martha adjusted hers to a position where she could overlook the pool while reading the novel she had bought at Heathrow. She wore the black swimsuit covered with the mid-thigh kimono that Jess had bought her. Marjorie, under some pressure from Martha wore the white swimsuit she had bought at Kowloon. Covered by the shorter kimono that Jess had bought, she stretched out on her sunbed and looked up into the almost cloudless sky.

'Not enough cloud to make a pair of sailors trousers,' she said happily.

Martha looked over her sunglasses at her.

'Blimey! that takes me back, Marjorie. I haven't heard that saying since we were kids.'

'It just came to me, Martha. It's true though, look at that lovely sky.'

'I'd rather not burn out my corneas thank you.' Martha returned to her book.

After half an hour, Marjorie climbed off her sunbed, pulled on her bathing cap and walked down the corner steps into the pool where she performed a stylish breaststroke, swimming lengths for a good fifteen minutes. As she reached the shallow end for the last time, she saw Henry waving to her from a sunbed at the far end of the pool. Marjorie swam over and took his offered hand to assist her up the steep steps. Once out of the water, she sat on the edge of a seat and accepted the striped beach towel that Henry held out to her. After drying some of the water from her arms and shoulders, she lay back on the sunbed next to Farthingale's and closed her eyes. They were not closed for long however.

'Marjorie, for pity's sake, that costume has become transparent, cover yourself up, you silly woman.' Martha threw Marjorie's kimono at her. 'Hurry now, people can see everything you've got.'

Marjorie sat up in panic and covered herself with the striped towel as she awkwardly slipped into her kimono.

'You should take that swimsuit back and demand a refund,' Martha said with a shake of her head. 'It's indecent.'

'It's not a swimsuit, it's a bathing costume, at least that's what it said on the label.'

'Probably just meant for sunbathing then. Honestly, Marjorie, can't you get anything right?'

Martha stormed back to her sunbed where she pulled a lever to lower the headrest, took off her sunglasses and lay down, adjusting her own kimono so that she was covered down to her knees. Pulling the brim of her sunhat over her eyes, she wriggled her body to get comfortable and a few minutes later she was fast asleep.

She woke up an hour later with her kimono flapping against her thigh, a strong breeze had got up while she had been dozing. She raised her head to find that she was the only person on the sunbeds around the edge of the pool. She looked for Marjorie but she was nowhere in sight. Getting to her feet, she walked quickly to the bar, where a group of middle-aged women were sitting.

'Have you seen an elderly woman in a white costume?'

One of the women nodded. 'If you mean the giggling old girl, she went off with Captain Birdseye about forty minutes ago.'

'The silly...' Martha held up a hand in thanks, then picking up her book and sunglasses she hurried to the lifts. On deck six, she was lucky enough to find a pair of English tourists coming out of the corridor where most of the cabins were situated.

'Excuse, me,' she began, 'would you happen to know where I can find a chap called Henry Farthingale?'

'Is that the old boy with the captain's hat? If so, he's in cabin number four.' The male of the pair pointed back down the corridor.

'That's the very man, thank you.' Martha hurried past the couple and quickly found Henry's cabin. Hammering on the door she called out her sister's name.

'Marjorie. I know you're in there. Come out this instant.'

After ten seconds she began hammering again. 'Marjorie, come out. I know you're in there.'

292

The door opened slowly and Martha was treated to the sight of Henry, wearing only a baggy pair of Y-fronts and his captain's hat. Martha blew out her cheeks, then barging past him, she stepped into the room.

'Marjorie, I won't tell you again.'

The top of her sister's head eased out from under the crumpled duvet that lay across the double bed. Her eyes peered over the colourful, double stitching on the edge of the cover.

'It's not what it looks like, Martha.'

'Then what is it, Marjorie, what are you doing in Henry's bed... sightseeing?'

'I was... we were...'

'Just get out, Marjorie.' She pointed to her younger sister's white bathing costume that lay neatly folded on a chair next to the bed. 'And get dressed too.'

'I'm not getting out while you're watching,' Marjorie pulled the duvet down to her neck.

'For God's sake, Marjorie. I've seen you in the bath at least a hundred times.'

'I know, but there aren't any soap bubbles in here.'

Shaking her head, Martha turned around and faced the door. Looking to the side, she grabbed hold of Henry's shoulder and pulled him around so that he was facing the same way as her. 'I blame the oysters you had for dinner last night. They obviously worked as an aphrodisiac. They have turned you into a sex crazed wanton.'

Two minutes later, Marjorie tapped Martha on the shoulder and announced that she was ready.

Martha grabbed hold of her sister's hand and almost dragged her out of the cabin, giving Henry one last glare as she brushed past him.

'Don't expect a repeat performance tomorrow. Seafood is off the menu.'

Back in their cabin, Martha pulled the balcony door shut and slumped down on her bed. Marjorie seemed unperturbed by her elder sibling's outrage and sitting down on her own bed, she began to examine her nails.

'For pity's sake, Marjorie, who loses their virginity at seventy-six?'

Marjorie looked up from her nails with a puzzled look on her face.

'Not me,' she said, quietly. 'I lost mine when I was twenty-one.'

Chapter 42

'Are you sure? I can't remember anything about this, Marjorie.'

'You weren't there, Martha.'

Martha sighed. 'I know that for goodness' sake. I was just remarking on the fact that you've never mentioned it.'

'Why would I? It's private, and anyway. It was my secret.'

'Would you like to share that secret now?' Martha asked. 'Who was it? Not that blooming Gary Manchester? He used to follow you around when you were in the cottage?'

'No, not him, although... no, not him. It was when I was in London, Martha.'

'And...'

'His name was Garfield. He was from Jamaica.'

Martha's hand went to her brow. 'Jamaica?'

'Yes, what's wrong with that?' Marjorie sat bolt upright.

'Nothing, nothing at all, you know me, Marjorie, the last thing I am is a racist. Some of my best friends were from the Caribbean when I was in the nursing home.'

'That's all right then. Some people in London hated them, there were signs up in bed and breakfast windows, saying no blacks.' Marjorie looked out onto the balcony with a wistful look in her eyes. 'People used to call me names when they saw me out with him. They called him names too, but he was stronger than me, I used to get really upset but he'd sing a song called 'My Girl' to me as we walked along and their foul words didn't matter.'

Martha pursed her lips as she studied her sister. 'Shall we have tea while you tell your tale?'

'That would be nice, Martha.'

'Righto, you know where the kettle is.'

Five minutes later, the sisters sat on their beds facing each other, sipping hot tea. Martha put hers down on the bedside table, piled her pillows up behind her and swung her legs onto the bed.

'Right, Marjorie, out with it.'

'Like I said, it was when I was in London.'

'Why did you go to London in the first place, Marjorie? I honestly can't remember.'

'I left home. I told Mother I was going to stay with you.'

Martha frowned. 'But I was never in London. Was this in nineteen sixty-three?'

Marjorie nodded.

'I was still working in the hospital at Maidstone then. I had no idea you were in London. I thought you moved straight into the cottage when you left home.'

'No, Mother let me have the cottage when she brought me back from London. I didn't want to go home, so she let me have one of the houses she owned. I still had to pay a bit of rent though. That's when I was working as a dinner lady at the school.' Marjorie smiled to herself and sipped at her tea. 'I loved that job. I was there for ten—'

'Never mind the dinner lady job, Marjorie, what happened in London, why on earth did you go there on your own?'

'We hadn't heard from you for over six years, apart from the odd Christmas card. You didn't even send me a card on my twenty-first.' Marjorie pulled a sad face. 'Anyway, the last thing we'd had from you was a postcard of Guy's Hospital with no message on the back. We assumed that's where you were working.'

Martha narrowed her eyes as she racked her brains. 'Ah, I went there on a course, it only lasted one day.'

'Well, that's where we thought you were, so I told Mother I was going to stay with you for a couple of weeks. She obviously thought I'd find you easily enough because she gave me a lift to the station and paid for my open return train ticket. She gave me ten pounds for the trip too.'

'Oh, Marjorie, you silly old thing. What happened?'

296

'I got off the train at Victoria Station and someone stole my handbag. It had my money in it, my train ticket home, they left me with nothing.'

'Did you telephone Mother?'

'I didn't even have twopence for the phone box.'

'You could have reversed the charges and... oh never mind... so, what happened then?'

I sat on my case in the station and began to cry. People walked past me, no one seemed to care, then a man crouched down and asked me what was wrong. When I told him, he helped me to my feet and took me to the café in the station and bought me a cup of tea and a slice of cake. His name was Garfield and he was such a nice man, he calmed me down and even made me laugh.'

'Weren't you ever told about stranger danger?'

'Yes, but Garfield was so nice. Anyway, he wasn't a dirty old man, he was only twenty-five.'

Martha shook her head, then decided against saying anything.

'After tea, he offered to give me the money to ring home, but I said that would be too embarrassing. I wanted to stay away for at least a few days. When I told him about you, Garfield took me round to Guy's and we asked at reception, but no one had ever heard of you, so we sat on some seats at London Bridge for a while, then Garfield offered to put me up for a few days. He was living in a squat in Peckham, just off the Old Kent Road. I remember that because of the square on the Monopoly board game we used to play when we were growing up.

'It was a big house with a hole in the roof and the windows had been smashed on the first floor, but the ground floor rooms were okay. They had somehow connected the electricity to the mains so they had free lighting and power for cooking. It was cold in winter though.' Marjorie paused and smiled to herself as she remembered the building. 'There were eight people, not including me. Garfield had the back room of the house facing out over an overgrown garden. He had two really good friends who lived there, Leon, who was from Jamaica like him and his girlfriend, Suzy, who had come down from Nottingham. They made me feel so welcome. That first night, they cooked a stew and we all sat around a Formica table to eat. They didn't have a TV but they had this radio service that was cabled in from somewhere and that was on all the time.

'Garfield was such a gentleman. He used to sleep on a mattress on the floor and he let me have it while he slept on his tatty old sofa. The next day, he went off to work with Leon and Suzy showed me around the area. I got to know her really well over the next few weeks. She understood that I was the nervous type and did her best to make me feel safe. She made me telephone home to let Mother know I was all right. I lied to her and told her I'd got a job at the hospital with you.

'I did get a job as it turned out. Suzy used to work part time as a cleaner in the evenings at the adult education college and she had a word about me with someone in the kitchens and before I knew it, I was working nine to five in the college canteen and earning a steady wage. I used to chip in for food, and the bottles of cider and wine we bought, but apart from that, most of my money went on clothes or paying for my round in the pub.

'It was after a night in the pub that I lost my virginity. Suzy and Leon were staying over at a friend's house so Garfield and I were alone. We were both pretty drunk when we got home and he started larking about, tickling me and what have you. Anyway, the next thing I know, we had taken our clothes off and he was lying on top of me. I was so nervous, but he was very patient with me. I remember that night like it was yesterday, Martha. It was blissful, I had never felt so alive, so wanted.

'After that, we were an item, and outside of work we did everything together, then one day, about three months after I moved into the squat, he took me down to the cellar where Leon and Suzy were standing at a

298

table with a big bag of pills, a roll of kitchen foil and a foot long box of what looked to be dried leaves.

'He told me it was weed. Leon must have seen my puzzled look because he tried to explain by using the word grass. I didn't understand how anyone could make money out of selling weeds and grass and when I said that they all laughed. Not at me, they never once made fun of me.

'A couple of days after that, Garfield said that it would be a good idea if I had a bank account, so we went to the local Lloyds Bank branch and opened one in my name. After that he used to give me money two or three times a week to pay into it. Sometimes twenty or thirty pounds, sometimes as much as a hundred. In no time at all there was a thousand pounds in there and by the time I left there was more than ten thousand.

'We were so happy in the house, Martha. No one bothered us, we used to have some great parties. Leon had a record player and we used to dance at night to reggae and soul music. I was happy.

'Everything was fine for nearly two years, then, one night, Suzy came rushing in and told me we had to split... that means get out. She said the police might be round to bust up the place so we got our stuff and went around to her friend's house. We stayed there for a couple of nights, but then Suzy vanished off the face of the earth. I went back to the squat but there was no sign of Garfield, so I went looking for him. I knew he sold his stuff all around the city but he spent a lot of time around Victoria Station which is why he was there on the day that he met me.

'I didn't find Garfield, but I did find another Jamaican called Kenny, who knew him. It was then I found out that Garfield was dead. He had been shot by members of a drug gang. Leon had been shot too and he had died in hospital. I was distraught, Martha, I didn't know what to do, then Kenny told me I'd be safer if I got out of London because the drug gang might come looking for Garfield's... I think he called it a stash... or his money. I was terrified. I rushed back to the squat and hid in one of the upstairs rooms. I jumped out of my skin every time I heard a creak. I felt so alone, Martha, when the realisation of Garfield's death finally hit me, I decided I didn't want to live anymore.'

'Marjorie... You didn't?' Martha looked sternly at her sister.

Marjorie's face crumpled.

'I knew that Garfield kept a bag of pills in the cistern above the lavatory, so I fished it out, tipped a handful onto the table, and took a dozen or so of them with a bottle of cider. I can't remember anything after that until I woke up in a mental hospital. Someone had discovered me; I don't know who to this day.

'The pills, whatever they were, had a bad effect on my mental state. I was always a nervous person as you know, Martha, but after that I had real anxiety, I was having suicidal thoughts. They kept me in for six months, then one day, Mother turned up to take me home. I was only at the farm for a couple of weeks, I didn't want to be there anymore and she knew it, so she let me have my little cottage and I got the job in the kitchens at the school not long after.'

It was now Martha's turn to do the goldfish impression. She sat, open mouthed and silent for a full two minutes before speaking.

'Marjorie, I had no idea. I'm sorry you were put through all that, but you are your own worst enemy at times. Why have you never told me any of this? I knew you left home in the mid-sixties and came back a couple of years later, but I assumed you'd been working away. For some reason, I had it in my mind that you had been working in a nursing home.'

'You were never interested really, Martha. When I came back you were married to Thomas and you didn't want to have anything to do with me. It was only after he died and you got into trouble with money that you remembered I was your sister.'

'Marjorie, that's not true.'

'It is true, Martha.' Marjorie stared at her belligerently. 'I had a bit of money and you needed it.'

'I did need the money, that's true, but... well, I had my own life to lead. I had troubles enough of my own.'

'I helped you out though, didn't I, Martha?'

'Here we go again. Tell me again how you gave me your money to pay off Roger.'

'Oh, it wasn't my money, Martha. I didn't have any of my own. That was Garfield's money. There was a Lloyd's branch in Spinton, and I just went to them with my bank account number and they gave me the lot.'

'You mean... you mean to say that my house was... my house was paid for with drug money?'

Marjorie nodded happily. 'Garfield was dead, he couldn't spend it and I didn't have anything to spend it on, so I thought you might as well make use of it.'

Martha's face became a mask of anger. 'Marjorie. You shouldn't have kept me in the dark.'

'But you never asked where it came from, Martha. I didn't think it mattered.'

Martha grunted.

'Wait a minute, what about Gary Manchester? Were you seeing him when you lived at the cottage?'

'Oh, yes. And his brother, Martin, then there was—'

'Marjorie! Spare me the sordid details.'

'I like men, I always have, Martha. You hate them.'

'I have good reason, Marjorie, but as it happens, I don't hate all men, just the ones that have come into my life. None of them were any good.'

'I was lucky with Garfield, Martha. He looked after me.'

'He was a dru... Never mind, Marjorie.' Martha adjusted her pillows and lay back into them. 'Right, I'm going to have my nap. Don't abscond while I'm sleeping. You'll wear the poor man out.'

Chapter 43

On Saturday, Jess and Nicola got an Uber and spent the night in and out of the busy wine bars and pubs that were situated every hundred yards or so throughout the busy town centre. Early on, Jess kept a wary eye on the amount that Nicola was consuming, but by ten o'clock, matching her drink for drink, she gave up counting. In the Startled Saint, the Karaoke was in full swing and Jess joined her mother on the microphone to belt out a high pitched, quite tuneless version of Shania Twain's hit, Man I Feel Like A Woman. Managing to build up enough will power to walk past the kebab shop, they finished the night in the White Cow where they bumped into a couple of Jess's old friends and shared stories from their youth that Jess, in a sober state, would never have wanted her mother to hear.

Back at the farm, Nicola had to support Jess as she stumbled on the top step, trying to insert her key, and after leaning on the door to steady her hand, she fell into the hall in a giggle fit as the weight of her body forced it open.

As Nicola pulled a bottle of wine from the fridge, Jess threw open the back door and vomited into the farm yard. Staggering, holding her head, she waved away the offer of a night cap, weaved her way across the kitchen and after three steadying stops on the stairs, managed to find her way to her bedroom where she collapsed onto her back and fell into a dream-laden sleep.

The following morning, with a head 'like a box of frogs' she stirred a fizzing glass of Berroca and sat in the kitchen listening to the radio news until a cheerful Nicola got up at ten o'clock.

'Fry up?' she offered as she breezed into the kitchen.

Jess pulled a face and shook her head.

'You must have the stomach of a concrete rhino,' she said.

'Years of experience, my dear,' her mother replied, dropping three rashers of bacon into a pan of sizzling oil.

Jess gagged as the smell of frying bacon wafted across the kitchen. 'I'm going in the lounge, please eat that out here, Mum.'

Jess slumped into a chair and holding her stomach, she muttered 'never again' as she leaned back into the soft cushions. Then as quickly as she had sat down, she got to her feet and raced to the bathroom where the fluorescent, orange Berroca, and what was left of the previous night's wine, came back up with a vengeance.

At one o'clock, still wearing her pyjamas, she came downstairs for the second time feeling much better. As she stepped into the lounge, Nicola waved to her from the sofa.

'Hello again, love. That was quite a night, wasn't it? I think we should make it a regular thing, don't you?'

Jess shook her head, turned away and headed for the kitchen.

'I need coffee,' she said. 'Lots of it.'

At two-thirty, Jess opened up her laptop and two minutes later she received a Skype call from Martha. She beamed as she clicked the button to accept the call and a few seconds later, her grandmother's face appeared on the screen.

'Hello, Grandma, how are you both? I hope you're having a lovely time. Have you been ashore yet? I'm so jealous.'

'If I could get a word in, I'd tell you,' Martha replied.

'Sorry, I was just excited to see you. How's the ship, how's your room...? Sorry.'

'The room is adequate for our needs. Thank you for the balcony, it really is nice to sit out in the open air.'

'You're welcome.' Jess grinned. 'And the food. How's Au...? Sorry.'

303

'The food is excellent I have to say. Marjorie is Marjorie, no need to go into further detail there, except to say that she has hooked up with a man in a sailor's hat.'

'A sailor? You mean one of the crew?'

'No, this is an elderly man who wears a captain's hat all the time, even when he's undressed.'

'Undressed? Oh, do tell, Grandma, how did you get to see him in such a state?'

'It's a long story, Jessica and...' the screen flickered and locked before Martha's voice came through again. '...when we get back.'

'I didn't get a lot of that; you're breaking up a bit.' Jess frowned at the screen.

'I have been told to expect that, Jessica. It's something to do with... bandwidth, whatever that is. I think it's someth... a lot of peo... ...at the same time.'

'Ah, I see. Did you go ashore in Hong Kong? I hope you were there in the evening, that laser show is incredible, isn't it?'

'It was very nice, yes. Marjorie bought another costume... it was like glass when she went swimming in it.'

Jess put her hand over her mouth to stifle a giggle. 'Poor Auntie Marjie.'

'Oh, she didn't care, the hussy. She lay on a sunbed flaunting it for all the world to see.'

'Good for her,' Jess laughed, unable to control it any longer.

'It was embarrassing, Jessica. I didn't know where to put my face.'

'Never mind, Grandma, I hope the costumes I bought for you are a little less revealing.'

'Hmm, debatable, but I suppose I'd rather see her backside hanging out of it than having the rest of her bits on show.'

Jess laughed again. 'Sorry, Grandma.'

'Right, let's get down to brass tacks. Has that lawyer friend of yours completed our business? I thought I might have received an email by now.'

'It's all done. I spoke to Bradley about it the other day. We thought it would be a good idea to pay the money into your account on the day you get back rather than risk the account being hacked or something while you're abroad. You did say you were worried about security.'

'That sounds like a good idea. What about the wills?'

'They're all done too.'

'Good. Right, I'd better see what Marjorie is up to. Every time I turn my back she disappears.'

As if summoned, Marjorie suddenly appeared on screen behind Martha's shoulder. She waved excitedly at Jess. 'Hello, Jessica, I'm in... where am I, Martha?'

'We're in the South China Sea, heading for Taiwan,' said Martha, stiffly.

'The South China Sea, I never, ever thought I'd be talking to you from the South China Sea,' Marjorie said, her eyes wide.

'I've been hearing about you and Captain Jack Sparrow, Auntie.'

'His name is Farthingale, Jessica and he's... ...captain he just... a hat.'

'You're breaking up, Auntie.'

'We're going now, it's time for bed here,' Martha butted in.

'YES! We do have night time over here, Jessica,' Marjorie added.

Jess shook her head and laughed. 'Goodnight, you two. Have a lovely cruise. Enjoy Taiwan.'

'Goodnight, or good day, whatever time it is over there. I'll Skype you again in a few days,' Martha said shushing Marjorie, who took the hint and waved instead.

'They're having a high old time by the looks of it, Mum,' Jess said as she closed the lid of her laptop.

Nicola smiled. 'I heard. God help Martha if the weather gets bad. Imagine being stuck in a cabin with Marjorie for more than a few hours. You'd go stir crazy.'

'Did you hear the bit about the old guy she's snared? Good on her.'

'And God help him,' Nicola added, rolling her eyes heavenward.

At nine, Jess announced that she was going to have an early night, and picking up Alice's memoir for 1942, she kissed Nicola on the forehead and took herself up to bed.

Alice. July 1942

Richard hadn't been exaggerating when he had said he knew what he was doing around the farm, he was especially good with the animals. Most years we lost a couple of ewes during the lambing season but this year we didn't lose a single sheep, he seemed to be able to coax out the most reluctant of lambs. It was the same with the cattle, this was the first year in memory that we didn't have to call in the vet to supervise a difficult birth. One morning, I ventured into the milking parlour to find Richard, elbows deep in a cow, it was amazing what that man could do with a bucket of warm, soapy water and a length of rope. Even Barney, a man who had witnessed the arrival of scores of calves was impressed.

'Can we keep him after the war, Missis? we'll never need the vet again,' he told me on one of our regular, kitchen table meetings.

After a cool April and a changeable May, we were treated to above average temperatures right from the start of June. During late spring I had taken to visiting the lads in the fields during their lunch break, treating them to drinks of homemade lemonade and slices of Miriam's wonderful fruit cake, made with Golden Syrup instead of sugar. She could still use butter in her baking because she made her own on the farm. During those lunchtimes, I used to sit on the end of the trailer and join in the conversation as the lads discussed everything from the progress of the war, to politics, to the weather. They seemed to be getting on well with our new workers. The two men were supervised by Barney, but watched over by two, rifle-bearing soldiers. The men were as different as chalk and cheese. One of them was a man called Tullow, he was a tall, black haired, stringy man whose beard shadow became darker as the day went on. He was a lazy man, often found taking forty winks in the back of the trailer, or leaning against a fence post, his rifle lying at his side. The other was an oval-faced, bespectacled man called Felix Chambers who belonged in a library, not the army. He would sit with his rifle across his knees and his nose in a book, even when he was supposedly keeping an eye on our alien workers. Nothing pleased him more than a tea break discussion about the work of the romantic poets, or some obscure, Russian author with the very well-read German pilot.

Richard and I took to walking laps of the field while the lads lay on their backs, soaking up the sunshine. I found him incredibly interesting and articulate. He could talk with authority about anything from astrology to astronomy, he could recite full length poems by Keats, Wordsworth and Tennison and his knowledge of world politics put mine in the shade. He was also a movie buff.

One lunchtime, in the second week of June, Richard and Dieter were working the bottom pasture with Barney, Alfie and George, accompanied as usual by Tullow and Chambers. The bottom pasture was boggier than the rest of the farm and boasted a large, natural, reed pond on the bottom right edge. It was a beautiful spot, the perfect place for a half hour rest. A light, cooling breeze ran across the surface of the pond, rustling through the reedbed. Above, a red kite circled, looking for lunch.

I was sitting on the back of the trailer, dangling my bare legs over the side, listening to Richard and Felix discussing an author called Dostoevsky. The trailer had been unharnessed from Bessie to allow her and her inseparable companion, Bray, to find some nice, tender grass shoots for their own lunch. The animals had been tethered to the wheels of the wagon with enough spare rope to allow them some freedom.

Suddenly Bray began to buck, her eyes were wide with fear, ears flat against her head. Barney leapt to his feet to try to soothe her but his efforts were in vain. Bray kicked back against the side of the trailer and tried to bite through her tether in a desperate attempt to escape.

Richard got to his feet and walked calmly across to the terrified animal as Barney tried to avoid her flailing hooves. Glancing down at the grass, he stepped up to Bray's side and whispering comfortingly in German and placing his hand softly on her head, he stroked her face, then her ears, then her mane. As Bray began to calm down, he untied her tether and led her away from the trailer. The lads sat with open mouths as they watched the spectacle, then after only two or three minutes, Richard handed the tether to Barney and walked quickly back to the spot where Bray had been grazing. Bending over, he pushed the long stalks aside, and quick as lightning, he reached into the grass and pulled out a three-foot-long snake.

'For Christ's sake,' Tullow threw himself backwards and reached for his gun. 'Quick, put it down, I'll shoot the bugger.'

Richard lifted the snake in front of his face and still holding it at the back of its head. Pursed his lips and kissed it.

'Holy shit,' shouted Tullow. 'Do you have a death wish or something?'

Richard held out the dangling snake towards the soldier. 'Would you like to hold him? It's quite safe.'

'I'd rather smooch with Adolph.' Tullow edged further back on the trailer.

'It's a grass snake,' Richard said, offering it to the lads. 'It's not poisonous.'

'He's right,' said Barney.

Alfie nodded. 'It's a grass snake all right. Adders have a zig zag pattern; this has stripes down the sides.'

'It's still a bloody snake,' said Tullow, unconvinced by its identification. 'I'll have nightmares about this.'

Richard walked around the side of the pond and laid the snake down gently into the grass. 'Go find a frog for lunch,' he said, softly.

When he returned, Alfie had pulled out a tube of peppermints and was handing them around. As Richard arrived, he held out the packet to the pilot.

'Could I take two?' Richard asked, reaching forwards.

'If you must,' sniffed Alfie, shaking his head as he looked at the others.

'Thank you.' Richard pulled two round mints from the tube, and fed one each to Bessie and Bray, who munched on it while still looking warily at the spot where she had been grazing.

'That does it,' Alfie said loudly, and getting to his feet he marched across to Richard, holding out his hand. 'Anyone who will put an animal before himself is all right with me.'

Smiling, Richard took Alfie's hand and shook it vigorously. The rest of the lads looked at each other, grinning and winking.

'You'll do,' said Alfie as he returned to his patch of flattened grass. Pulling a harmonica out of his pocket, he led the men into a rendition of 'Hitler has only got one ball'. A delighted, laughing Richard, who had picked the words up from the soldiers at the POW camp, was the loudest and most enthusiastic singer of the lot.

By the end of the month, I began to realise I was developing what would probably be described by my neighbours as an unhealthy attraction to Richard. He was on my mind most mornings as I was cleaning out the pigs or going through the books. I had to force myself to walk slowly and demurely across to whichever field he was working in, while my brain was screaming at me to run. One Friday, he was working in the east field, an area that boasted a small copse of trees that ran across the northern tip. Leaving Tullow sleeping and Chambers reading a novel by a nineteenth century French writer I had never heard of, Richard and I set off for a lap of the field. No one as much as looked up as we set off.

As we walked slowly around the perimeter, I found that I couldn't take my eyes off him, even when, twice, he stopped talking to look sideways at me. A couple of years ago I'd have stared down at my feet in embarrassment, but I am a stronger person now. I understand my body and my feelings and I knew damn well what they were saying to me. As we entered the copse I looked back to make sure we couldn't be seen, then dropping my hand I took hold of his and squeezed it gently.

'Alice,' he said, looking back the way we had come. 'If someone sees...'

'No one can see,' I replied with more confidence than I felt. I knew it was risky, but my head had been battered into submission by my heart. I got onto my tiptoes, held his face in my hands and kissed him softly on the lips.

His face was a mask of concern. 'Alice, this isn't...'

'Shhh,' I whispered, and kissed him again, this time I let my lips linger a little longer.

'We can't stay in here too, long,' he said, looking over his shoulder again. Then, turning back, he wrapped those strong, bronzed arms around me, held me so tight that I thought my ribs might break, and kissed me long, hard and deep.

Happily, no one had noticed our absence as I copped a dozen frantic kisses in the copse, and we walked out of the other side, both breathing heavily, but looking as innocent as we had when we first walked in.

That weekend I could think of nothing else but Richard. I lost my appetite; I could barely concentrate. I had never been as fixated on a man, not even Godfrey. The last time I could remember being in such an emotional flux, was when I was fourteen and I developed a teenage crush on a young stand-in teacher at school.

On the Sunday, I was hosing out the pigs, harbouring thoughts that would make a courtesan blush, when I noticed that the drain was backing up and a thick stream of sediment was pouring into the yard. I quickly switched off the hose and shouted for Barney, who was clearing out the stable with Richard.

Taking in the situation immediately, and before Barney had the chance to do anything, Richard stripped to the waste and stuck his bare hands into the gloop to pull up the two-foot square drain cover. Barney rushed to the shed where we kept a set of long bamboo poles, similar to the ones sweeps use, and carried them across to Richard.

'You don't have to do this, son. It's not expected of you.'

Richard took the poles and began to screw the lengths together. Taking a deep breath, he pointed to the hose pipe I had dropped on the floor.

'Just be ready with that when I've finished.'

After half an hour of pushing, twisting and pulling there was a loud gurgling noise and the drain suddenly emptied. Richard, who had been lying on his stomach as he fed the rods into the drain, got to his feet and after heaving twice, threw up into the foul-smelling gunk that covered the farmyard.

It was obvious that even after being hosed down, Richard couldn't spend the rest of the day working in his slurry-covered clothes and I wouldn't have thought about asking him to. Instead, I told him to take off his boots, then I led him into the house, through the kitchen and parlour and into the bathroom that I had installed a couple of years previously. Stephen and Harriet held their noses as he passed by.

'Pee-ew,' they said together.

After his bath, Richard stepped back into the parlour wearing just a towel wrapped around his waist. I had dumped his filthy, work shirt, pants and trousers into the big Belfast sink where I scrubbed them to within an inch of their lives.

'Alice. What am I supposed to wear now?' he asked.

As I turned to look at his sun kissed body, my heart skipped a beat. A mop of wet blond hair was stuck to his forehead. A thin rivulet of water ran down his broad, sun bronzed naked chest and his long, elegant fingers held the white towel at his waist as if fearful it might slip.

I gulped as I tried to force myself to look away, knowing it was always going to be an impossible ask.

'I've got an old set of overalls, the ones I wore when I was pregnant, they were my father's so they ought to fit you,' I said, eventually. Desperately fighting the urge to invite him up to my bedroom where they were lying, neatly folded in the bottom of a wardrobe. I reluctantly averted my gaze and with eyes closed, trying to keep the vision of manliness in my mind, I hurried up the stairs to collect them.

When Richard was dressed, I finished washing his stinking work clothes and hung them onto the line to dry. As they flapped about in a warm breeze, I invited Barney, Tullow and Chambers into the kitchen and made them bacon sandwiches and steaming hot mugs of tea.

I spent that night tossing and turning as I encountered the most vivid, sex-fuelled dreams I'd had since my teenage crush years. This time however, they were far more explicit, and I woke up on Monday morning bathed in sweat, feeling absolutely exhausted.

Chapter 44

On Saturday February the first, Martha and Marjorie were enjoying the warm sunshine on their balcony when a message came over the P.A. system.

Ladies and Gentlemen, due to sickness aboard ship, the visit to Taiwan has been cancelled and the Paradise Pearl has been asked to return to Yokohama. To limit the spread of the illness, passengers are asked, for now, to remain in their cabins and balcony areas. Further advice will be given later today. We appreciate that this news will be a disappointment to you but there is little the company can do other than follow the guidance of the World Health Organisation and the Japanese government. Thank you for your understanding during this difficult time.

Martha sat bolt upright as she listened to the news being relayed over the tannoy system.

'This really isn't good enough. We paid a small fortune for this cruise.'

'Jessica paid a small fortune, you mean, Martha, we didn't—'

'Don't be pedantic, Marjorie, you know exactly what I meant.' Standing up, she slipped her kimono over her shoulders and stomped into the cabin. Snatching up the phone she dialled nine and listened as the same recorded message she had just heard, was played back to her. Slamming the phone down on its cradle, she crossed the room and threw open the door. Outside in the corridor twenty or so angry passengers were berating a single crew member who backed away towards the lifts with his hands in the air, promising to come back with some answers as soon as possible.

Martha slammed the door and walked back to the balcony, her face a mask of wrath.

'Honestly, Marjorie, you'd think they would give us a snippet of information at least. After all we could all be in danger. What if it's the Bubonic Plague or the Black Death? We could all be dead by Monday.'

313

'Henry did have a bad cough the last time I saw him. He says he got it off the Chinese gentleman he used to have dinner with in the evenings. He left the ship at Hong Kong.'

'Marjorie. I doubt a cruise ship of this size with three and a half thousand people on board would have its journey cut short and be ordered to sail back to port immediately, just because someone had a cough.'

'I was just saying.'

'Well, don't. It isn't helping.'

'But...'

'But what, Marjorie? Come on, let's have it. Are you going to tell me he had diarrhoea too? That wouldn't surprise me with all the raw fish he eats.'

'I was about to say, I haven't seen him for three days now. I knocked on his door yesterday, but he didn't answer. I tried ringing his cabin when you were having your afternoon nap but there was no reply. I thought he might have got bored with me or something.'

'I doubt there's any something about it, Marjorie. He had what he wanted from you and now he's moved on. It's what men like him do.'

'He's not like that, Martha, he's a gentleman.'

'Gentlemen don't try to lure vulnerable, silly old women into their beds,' Martha spat.

Marjorie stuck out her tongue. 'He didn't, as it happens. I asked him to take me to bed.'

Martha's mouth gaped.

'The sea air has brought out the worst in you, Marjorie Mollison. I hardly recognise you anymore.' Martha spun around on her heel and headed for the cabin. 'I'm going to see if I can get in touch with Jessica. Maybe she can shine a bit of light onto this.'

A few hours later, Jessica came downstairs to find a series of increasingly angry emails and Skype requests on her laptop. After reading through them, she typed out a quick reply telling Martha she would do a bit of digging and get back to her as soon as possible. Jess switched on the BBC twenty-four-hour news channel, then did a search on Google for the Paradise Pearl. As she was clicking on the first link, a breaking news report appeared on the TV screen.

Breaking!

The Cruise ship, Paradise Pearl, was denied permission to dock in Taiwan yesterday after reports of Coronavirus on board. A Chinese passenger who left the ship in Hong Kong on the twenty-fifth of January later tested positive for the virus and was admitted to hospital where he is now being treated in intensive care. The unnamed passenger had recently been in the Chinese city of Wuhan which has been in lockdown since January the twenty-third.

Passengers on the ship have been asked to remain vigilant and to avoid crowded places until the ship returns to its home port of Yokohama. Unverified reports suggest that ten of thirty-five people tested so far, have contracted the virus. Symptoms include a new, continuous cough, a high temperature and a loss of the sense of taste and smell. A source from the ship's owners told the BBC that the passengers may face at least fourteen days in quarantine when the Paradise Pearl reaches port.

More to follow.

Jess sat down at the table and typed out a more expansive email to Martha, detailing the facts as she understood them. A few minutes later she received a reply.

My God, Jessica, what have you got us into? Whoever is responsible for these things has turned off the news channels on our TVs. All we have now are movie channels, endless celebrity chat shows and children's cartoons. Even the radio has been switched off. All we get is piped music and the same message repeated on the hour every hour. The lady in the cabin opposite ours says she managed to talk to a crew member who told her that an update will be issued this evening.

If you hear any more news, please forward it.
ASAP!
Martha.

At six o'clock that evening, a new message came over the P.A. system advising passengers that they could assemble as usual in the dining areas, theatres and the casino. However, the Captain had asked everyone to mingle as little as possible with strangers. Outdoor pursuits would carry on as normal until the ship docked in Yokohama.

'Well, that was a waste of a day,' Martha said after listening to the latest announcement.

Marjorie brightened. 'I wonder if Henry will feel well enough to come to dinner tonight?'

'Keep him well away from me if he does,' Martha warned. 'I don't want to risk catching this blooming flu bug.'

Over the next two days, life went on pretty much as usual on board, though the sisters did see, and did their best to avoid, scores of coughing passengers. On the morning of the third day, a steward walked into the corridor as Marjorie was knocking on Henry's door.

'Are you looking for Mr Farthingale?' she asked.

Marjorie nodded. 'Yes, I haven't seen him for days. I've tried ringing his cabin on the phone but no one answers.'

'He's not there, that's why, Madam. He was taken to the ship's sick bay three days ago. He's very ill.'

'Oh no.' Marjorie, put a hand to her mouth. 'Can I visit him?'

'I'm afraid not. We're hoping Mr Farthingale will be transferred to hospital when we dock at Yokohama this evening.'

Marjorie walked forlornly back to the lifts, rode to the 12th floor and made her way to the small swimming pool where Martha was sitting with her book and a soft drink.

'Henry is in sick bay. He's really poorly.'

Martha shrugged. 'It could be worse, Marjorie, it could be me.'

Marjorie slumped down onto a sunbed. 'You can be mean at times, Martha. You know I like him.'

'It was just an observation, Marjorie. There was nothing malicious behind it.' Martha sipped her drink, put it down on the deck at the side of her and turned a page in her novel.

'They're taking him off to hospital when we dock.'

'Really. When is that by the way? I haven't heard anything on the P.A.'

'This evening, or so the steward said.'

'Good,' replied Martha. 'They'll hopefully offload all the sick passengers and allow the rest of us to resume the cruise.'

At seven o'clock that evening a new message came over the P.A. system.

Ladies and Gentlemen. Due to the ongoing sickness onboard. The Paradise Pearl has been refused permission to dock at Yokohama. We will instead be docking off the coast of Daikoku Pier as we await instructions. Further information will be relayed to you as we get it. In the meantime, please feel free to enjoy all of the ship's facilities. Thank you for your patience.

'Oh my goodness,' cried Marjorie on hearing the announcement. 'They won't be able to take Henry to hospital now.' She pouted as she looked at her sister. 'Poor Henry.'

'Poor us, you mean,' Martha replied with a look of annoyance. 'If we can't dock until tomorrow that will be another day's cruising lost.'

At dinner that evening, whilst chewing on a piece of crusty bread, Marjorie suddenly went into a violent, coughing fit. When she continued to cough after taking several sips of water, Martha got up from her seat, walked around the table and hit her several times on the back with the palm of her hand. When the coughing didn't stop, she asked a steward if any of the crew knew how to administer the Heimlich manoeuvre, but as a middle-aged crew member approached the table, Marjorie's coughing fit ceased and she took another gulp of water before fanning her face with the menu.

'It's all right, I'm not choking. I swallowed the food before I started to cough.'

Martha looked at her sister with distaste. 'Marjorie. If that Henry Farthingale has given you his flu, and I catch it from you, I'm going to dance on his blooming grave.'

The steward crouched down at the side of the table and looked from Martha to Marjorie, his face a picture of sadness. 'I know you were friends with the old gentleman, and I'm sorry to be the bearer of such bad news, but Mr Farthingale was extremely ill, there was nothing the doctor could do for him. Sadly, he died this afternoon.'

Chapter 45

At six o'clock on Saturday afternoon, Nicola walked into the kitchen towelling her wet hair.

'Shower's free.'

Jess shut the lid on her laptop, got to her feet and stretched. 'I've been waiting for an update on Grandma and Aunt Marjorie, but I suppose no news is good news. Auntie Marj might just have had a frog in her throat.'

'Fingers crossed,' said Nicola, rubbing her hair vigorously with the towel. 'Come on, get your shower or the bars will be rammed by the time we get into town.'

'I'm not sure I want to go, Mum,' Jess replied quietly. 'I'm worried about those two, stuck on a boat on their own.'

'They're hardly alone, Jess. There are three and a half thousand people on that ship including the crew.'

'I know, and it seems that half of them have this blooming virus.'

Nicola stopped rubbing at her hair and patted Jess on the arm. 'Stop exaggerating. How many were ill at the last count? Ten, was it?'

'Sky News said there have been another sixty-five cases announced, and three passengers have died.'

'How old were those passengers?' Nicola asked.

Jess thought quickly. 'The dead ones? Two in their late eighties. Marjorie's friend was eighty-three. Martha told me that in her last email.'

'All a fair bit older than Marjorie then?'

'Yes, but not all that much older than Grandma.'

Nicola snorted. 'If that bug has any sense, it will stay well away from my mother. She has the constitution of someone half her age. I wouldn't worry too much, love.'

'I feel so guilty. I paid for their trip. I wish I'd sent them somewhere else.'

'Stop worrying, Jess. It's only a form of flu, isn't it?'

'Flu-like,' Jess replied.

'There you are then. Give all the passengers a flu jab and the virus will be wiped out inside a fortnight. Mum and Aunt Marj have had the flu jab anyway, it's bound to give them some protection.' She pointed to the big round clock on the wall. 'It's two in the morning over there, Jess. They're hardly likely to be sending emails through the night. Come on, get showered. A night out will take your mind off it.'

Jess thought for a moment. She didn't want to let her mother down. Nicola had been careful with the amount of alcohol she had been consuming throughout the week. A bit of a supervised binge on a Saturday night was a fair reward for her efforts.

'All right, Mum. But we're not drinking as much as last week. It took me until Tuesday to get over it.'

After her shower, and applying the bare minimum of makeup, Jess slipped into her favourite black mini dress and a red jacket that was just an inch or two shorter. After pulling on a matching pair of red shoes, she stood in front of her full-length mirror, turning this way and that as she made a critical examination of her appearance. Finally satisfied, she grabbed her bag and walked down the stairs to where Nicola was waiting impatiently in the lounge.

'Good timing,' her mother said. 'I've ordered the Uber.' Nicola grinned as the bright beam of headlamps flashed across the front window.

Jess picked up her phone from the old lion's foot coffee table and checked it for messages before slipping it into her bag.

'So far so good, Mum. Let's hope they have a quiet night.'

After a quick drink in the almost deserted, Happy Farmer Inn, Jess and Nicola crossed the road to the much busier, Devine Wine bar where it took them a full fifteen minutes to be served. Sipping their cocktails, they eased their way through the crowd at the bar and found a space near the door where they just managed to finish their drinks before a crowd of boisterous students arrived. Moving on to the Flag, the pair found a table at the back of the bar, beneath a large screen TV showing nonstop, pop videos.

At nine-thirty, they left the Flag and walked the two hundred yards up the hill to the Startled Saint, where the Karaoke was in full swing. As they were about to climb the two steps to the entrance, Jess heard her name called. She turned around to see that a sporty Volkswagen Golf had pulled up at the side of the road. The window was wound down.

As Jess stooped to peer into the open window, the interior light came on and she found herself looking into the smiling face of Leonora Wilson. Bradley's Italian wife.

Leonora leaned across and pulled the lever to open the passenger side door.

'Hop in for a moment,' she said, still smiling.

Jess turned back to Nicola who was waiting on the top step, she rummaged in her purse and came out with a twenty-pound note. 'Get them in, please, Mum. I'll be there in a moment.'

As the doors closed behind Nicola, Jess slipped into the passenger seat of the Golf and pulled the door shut behind her. Leonora flicked the switch to close the window, then turned sideways in her seat to face Jess.

'It's lovely to see you again, Jessica. I was hoping we'd bump into each other.'

'Why?' asked Jess, bluntly.

Leonora reached across and patted Jess's exposed wrist. 'Don't be like that. I'm not a total monster you know, and I do actually quite like you.'

Jess sighed. 'What do you want, Leonora? I'm on a night out with my mother, I don't have time to play your games.'

'I was really pleased to see she had been released from prison,' Leonora said with a concerned look on her face. 'It must have been an awful experience for her... and you.'

'We've had better times,' Jess replied. She turned and reached for the door catch. 'If that's it...'

'No, no, please?' Leonora grabbed Jess's wrist, then immediately let it go. 'I'm sorry about that. I just wanted to talk to you for a few minutes.'

Jess turned back towards her. 'Well, I'm waiting.'

'Look, I just wanted to tell you that I'm sorry about what I did. My heart rules my head at times.'

'What you did was despicable,' Jess replied with a steely glint in her eyes. 'That poor man has been trying desperately to get over his wife and daughter leaving him for a married man and you led him to believe that you were in the same dire straits as he was.' Jess glowered at Leonora. 'Josh and I had only just met. We weren't even in a relationship. There was absolutely no reason for you to hurt him like that.'

'I'm sorry, I truly am. I wasn't aware of his family situation or I wouldn't have—'

'Yes, you would,' Jess cut in. 'You can't help yourself.'

Leonora held up both hands, palms towards Jess. 'I admit I got it wrong. I was angry with you for seemingly being able to get on with your life so quickly.' She lowered her hands and placed them demurely on her lap. 'I see Bradley has moved on anyway. He has reverted to type. He's with a blonde bimbo now. She's flirty, outrageous, and almost certainly not as intelligent as you, and while I don't see her as a real threat, I have begun to take measures, just in case. I don't think I'll need to push too hard though, in a few weeks' time this flirtation will be over. I've seen the likes of her off more than once.' She paused, looking intently at Jess. 'You, on the other hand, had me seriously worried. I've never seen him like that with anyone before. I really thought you might be able to take him away from me, and I couldn't allow that to happen. I'm surprised you gave in so easily though. I was expecting more of a challenge.'

Jess, who had been looking out of the windscreen as Leonora spoke, pursed her lips then turned her head

322

and looked directly at Bradley's estranged wife. 'Firstly, that blonde bimbo is my best friend and I'm telling you now, if you think she is unintelligent, then you're in for a huge surprise. She's also as tough as old boots, so if you are planning on playing your little games with her, you should think again. If you try, she will chew you up and spit you out in tiny pieces.' Jess paused to let the message sink in, then spoke again, this time in a softer tone. 'Secondly, I split with Bradley because he kept your marriage a secret. Had he told me about you from the start, things might have been different, but as it was, I felt that if he could lie to me about something as fundamental as that, he could lie to me about anything. You see, to me, trust is the most important thing in a relationship. I liked Bradley... I still like Bradley, but I have my red lines and he crossed them.'

Leonora spread her hands and shrugged in typical Italian fashion. 'Bradley is just a man; he has his faults as they all do. They like to think they're in control of things, they think they understand us, but they don't really.' Leonora shifted her position slightly and leaned towards Jessica. 'I knew you were a strong woman when I first spoke to you, Jess... do you mind if I call you Jess?' Without waiting for a reply, she continued. 'When Bradley and I met, he saw me as something different, someone who would take him outside of his comfort zone. Did he ever tell you that I like women as much as I like men? I think that was one of the things he found so interesting about me. Like all men, he fantasised about having two women in his bed, having two women make love while he watched. It didn't happen of course.' Leonora reached out her hand and placed it gently on the top of Jessica's leg, her fingers curled into the gap between them. 'Are you the curious type, Jessica?' She moved her head towards her, lips slightly parted.

Jess turned her face away as Leonora moved towards her. Gently taking hold of her hand, she lifted it from her thigh and pushed it away.

'I don't really know why I should give you an answer to that question as it's a very personal thing, but I will say, in general, that I think almost all women are curious when it comes to female attraction. I also think all women have fantasised about it at some point in their lives, in their teenage years, for certain, but not all of us want to play out those fantasies. That's where I sit, Leonora. I'm flattered by your interest, but I'm afraid, that's as far as it goes.'

Leonora smiled, sadly. 'That's a shame, Jessica. I think we would make beautiful love together. We might even have played out Bradley's fantasy. I am offering to share him with you when he's finished with this friend of yours.'

Jess snorted. 'That, wouldn't happen, regardless.' She flicked the lever on the door and pushed it open before sliding off the seat.

As she was about to shut the door, Leonora reached into her pocket and pulled out a bright pink, business card. She placed it lightly on the passenger seat and blew Jess a kiss. 'If you ever change your mind...'

Jess shook her head and closed the door firmly. 'Thanks, but no thanks,' she muttered, then smiling to herself she climbed the two wide, stone steps and pushed open the door of the pub.

Chapter 46

On Sunday morning, Jess got up early and managed to get a five-minute Skype meeting with Martha before the signal got so bad the connection became unusable.

Relieved that Marjorie was no worse than she had been on the previous day, she wrote a quick email, wishing her a speedy recovery before making coffee and sitting in front of the big screen to watch the latest news programme, hoping to find a bit of extra information to pass on to Martha but the reporters were just rehashing the bulletin from the day before, the only change being the increase in the amount of people who were ill.

Nicola came downstairs as Jess was making her second hot drink of the morning.

'Coffee?' Jess offered already knowing the reply.

'Tea for me, please,' Nicola said, picking up the frying pan and waving it at Jess. 'Will you be joining me? You can't be too fragile this morning, we hardly drank anything last night.'

'Not for me, thanks, Mum, I'm trying to be good, though be warned, if the smell of frying bacon gets too irresistible, you might have your sandwich snatched out of your hands.'

'You'll need to be quick,' Nicola replied meaningfully, dropping three rashers into the hot pan. 'I'm so hungry, this little lot won't touch the sides on the way down.'

To help ease the temptation of asking her mother to drop in another two rashers, Jess took her new pack of cigarettes and her disposable lighter from the top drawer and grabbing her coat from the back door, she sat on the top step sipping her coffee and blowing smoke rings across the yard as she mapped out her day. Twenty minutes and two cigarettes later, she stood up and walked back into the kitchen. She had just dropped her cigarettes back into the drawer when her phone rang. It was Sam.

'Hi, Sam. How's stuff?'

'I'm bloody furious, Jess, that's how stuff is.'

'Why, what's the matter? Don't tell me that Bradley—'

'No, we're fine, we're getting on like a house on fire actually. Speaking of fires, he's hot stuff, isn't he? He stayed over in the week and again last night. I'm shattered, the man is insatiable.'

Jess suddenly remembered the one night she had spent with Bradley and only just managed to stop herself agreeing with her best friend. Pushing the memory to the back of her mind she tried to steer the conversation away from her former lover.

'So, what are you so furious about?'

'That bloody ex of his, Leonora.'

'Why, what's she been up to?'

'I know you said I'd have to watch out for her, Jess but I didn't expect her to stoop to such depths.'

Before Jess could reply, she continued. 'She's only printed my picture on a load of flyers and stuck them through every bloody letterbox on my street.'

'Oh dear...'

'Oh dear indeed. She even stapled them to telegraph poles and stuck them on lampposts. There was one superglued to the front door of my block of flats. All my neighbours have had one pushed into their external mail boxes. Hang on, I'll send you a pic of it.'

A few seconds later, Jess's phone buzzed. She opened her WhatsApp and clicked on the picture that Sam had uploaded. Above the photo that Leonora had obviously taken without Sam realising, was the word, *SLUT!* printed in 40-point red coloured font. Underneath the picture, it read, *DO YOU KNOW WHERE YOUR HUSBAND WAS LAST NIGHT? I KNOW WHERE MINE WAS, HE WAS WITH THIS HARLOT. KEEP A CLOSE EYE ON YOUR MAN IF YOU LIVE NEARBY!*

'Good grief,' Jess gasped. 'I know she said she'd begun to take measures but... well, this is beyond the pale.'

'What do you mean, she said? Have you seen her, Jess?'

'I have, sadly. She ambushed me outside the pub last night. She offered me... oh, never mind. Let's just say I refused.'

'So, she's boasting about her disgusting behaviour, is she? Well, Jess, my darling, she's picked on the wrong slut this time.'

Jess nodded to herself. 'I did warn her, not that I said you were a ... well, you know... but I did advise her that she was biting off more than she could chew.'

'I'll make her choke on that mouthful, Jess. You see if I don't.'

'What are you going to do? Don't go too far, Sam, she's not worth it.'

'It's best you don't know, Jess, then you can't be dragged into it. Let's just say that she won't be the flavour of the month with Bradley's mother. I'm going to meet her in the week, oh, and I managed to persuade Bradley to give me the name of her priest. I can't wait to stick a note in his confessional.'

'Blimey, this is moving fast, regarding Bradley, I mean,' Jess said with a laugh. 'Aren't you rather throwing yourself in at the deep end?'

'I do like him, I like him a lot, we seem to have built up a strong connection although we've only just met, but no, don't worry. I'm not the marrying kind and he's already in a marriage he can't get out of, so it's win, win, really.'

'Well then, watch out Leonora. Karma is about to rear its ugly head,' said Jess.

'And she has teeth like a Great White shark,' replied Sam, with feeling.

Jess laughed again. 'Enjoy your plotting. See you when I see you.'

'Oh, there's just one more thing,' Sam replied hesitantly. 'I err, that is Bradley and I dropped in for a cup of coffee at Josh's place yesterday afternoon. We ended up having quite a long chat with him. Bradley explained all about his relationship with you and how Leonora had spun him a yarn about their marriage, how they had no children and had been separated for years, etc. Anyway, Josh was really upset about being duped like that and wants to call you to put things right. Now, I know I might live to regret it, knowing what baggage he comes with and all that, but I gave him your phone number... Sorry, love, I think you can expect a call before too long.'

'That's all right, Sam. I do like Josh, I'm not sure I need the baggage though. I've got enough going on in my life as it is.'

'I know, love,' Sam replied softly. 'How's the invalid? Better, I hope? I read your text last night.'

'She's no worse, that's the good news. There's no sign of her being taken off the ship yet though.'

'Send her my love when you speak to them next. I've got everything crossed for her.'

'I will, Sam, thank you.'

'I hope that bug doesn't find its way over here,' Sam said firmly.

'Oh, I can't see it,' Jess replied. 'We'll have treatments for it, surely.'

'Yeah, we will have. The flu jab might even sort it... Right. I'm off to plot. Have a lazy Sunday, Jess. Love you.'

'Love you too, Sam... Be careful.'

Jess put her phone down on the big, oak table as her mother came back into the kitchen carrying her breakfast plate.

'How's Sam? I heard you mention her name.'

'She's fine, Mum. Her and Bradley are getting along famously.'

'Oh, Jess, that can't be easy for you to hear.'

Jess shrugged. 'The Mollison man curse strikes again?'

'You might mock, but it's a fact, Jess. We Mollison women are doomed to a series of failed relationships. We always pick the wrong man.'

'I wasn't mocking, Mum, in fact, I'm beginning to think there might be something in it. According to Sam, I'm about to receive a phone call from a seriously dishy man carrying a mountain of baggage.'

'Take my advice, Jess. When he rings, just hang up and block the contact.'

Jess sighed. 'You know me, Mum, I'm a sucker for a sob story.'

'So was I, Jess. I heard thousands of them.'

When Nicola had gone upstairs to shower and dress, Jess picked up Martha's folder and carried it through to the lounge. Pulling her legs up beneath her, she sat on the sofa, opened the folder and took out a wad of papers that had been stapled together at the top right-hand corner.

'What Martha did next,' she whispered as she began to read.

Chapter 47

Martha. 1963

I left nursing and what had become my home in 1963 after a bust up with Matron. It had been building up for weeks and I had become heartily sick of her almost stalking behaviour. There had been an off-duty argument in the laundry when I stopped by to pick up the clothes I'd left with one of the trainees earlier in the day. I know we were supposed to do our own washing, officially, but it had been a long-established practice that juniors would do the more experienced nurses' laundry when asked. I had done it in my time and I'm sure that Matron had in hers. The mistake on this occasion was made by the junior, a spotty girl called Janet, who had stupidly washed my clothes whilst leaving Matron's underwear and nightgown unwashed, in a basket on top of the machine.

Instead of taking the hit and moving on as I had become accustomed to doing, I snapped and asked why it was that she could have her washing done by someone else but I could not. After that she became almost leech-like, sticking to me wherever I went. At times it seemed that I was wearing a human cloak. I would find her at the door of my room ten minutes before I was supposed to be on duty. She'd plonk herself down at the side of me in the canteen at meal breaks and spend the time looking between my face and her fob watch. She would regularly refuse me permission to go out on a Saturday night, citing some misdemeanour or other, and she constantly put me down on the ward in front of the junior nurses. If I had possessed a modicum of sense, I'd have apologised to her in front of witnesses and all would have been forgotten, I was, after all, a top-notch nurse, and she knew it. She could hardly afford to lose me, but her pride was at stake, she was like a fighting dog with its jaws clamped onto his opponent's hind quarters and she wasn't going to let go.

It finally came to a head one Saturday afternoon. I wasn't on duty and I had a hot (or as hot as it got for me) date that evening with a Junior Doctor called Rufus. I had just got out of the bath and was sitting in front of my mirror trying to do something with my awful hair, when she stormed into my room without knocking.

'Mollison. Stop what you're doing, get into your uniform and onto the ward. We need an extra pair of hands tonight.'

'I've done an extra half shift today already,' I complained. 'I'm tired out.'

'Just do as you're told,' she spat at me.

I shook my head and returned to brushing my hair. 'I've got something on tonight.'

She stood there, stupefied. 'Doctor Rufus will have to find other ways to entertain himself. I'm sure there will be plenty of nurses willing to stand in for you.'

I never did find out how she knew about my date, but it was the last straw for me. I'd had enough. I got off my stool, turned towards her and gave her the biggest mouthful she'd had in her life. When I had finished, and after gawping, opening and shutting her mouth like a goldfish for a full two minutes, she told me that I'd be up on a disciplinary on Monday and I should expect to have my pay cut and be demoted to junior nurse level at a bare minimum. My reply took up just two words and I won't repeat them here.

The date wasn't all I had hoped for, but I went back to his room with him anyway just to spite Matron and on Sunday morning, without a modicum of regret, I wrote out my notice and slipped it under her door. Before she even had time to read it and demand that I stick to my contract by working a four-week notice period, I had packed my stuff and moved out.

I had only got as far as Woolworths in Maidstone town centre when I began to regret my hastily made decision. Within twenty-four hours I had gone from being someone with a steady job, future prospects and secure, if restrictive, living arrangements to an out of work twenty something with nowhere to go.

Being a Sunday, there wasn't a lot open but I managed to find a copy of the Saturday edition of the local paper in the newsagents and sat in the bus shelter as I scoured the accommodation and job columns.

After jotting down the contact details of three bedsits and the phone numbers of two prospective jobs which I would chase up on Monday, I deliberated for a while about where I would spend the night. Going home wasn't an option although it was only a short train journey away. I would rather have spent the night on the damp streets of Maidstone than admit to my mother that I had made a mess of things. The few friends I had, if I could call them that, all worked and lived at the hospital so I couldn't ask any of them for help. I was almost resigned to spending a night on a bench in the park or hanging around inside the station with the local prostitutes, when I remembered Gillian.

Gillian had started nursing at the same time as me but had fallen foul of the prison camp rules after sneaking her boyfriend of three months into the nursing home one foul, winter's night. Summarily dismissed and frogmarched out of the hospital in the middle of the night with the boyfriend that dumped her the following week, she had reinvented herself as a till operator at the very Woolworth's store I had been standing outside of earlier that day. I had bumped into her once or twice over the last two years and she had told me that she had found a flat in the seedier district of town, quite near to the place where I had undergone my abortion. I wracked my brains trying to remember her address and as if to confirm my memory hadn't let me down, two minutes later, a bus arrived that would take me to the very street where the miscreant nurse had set up home.

Gillian Whitehall was an attractive woman, prone to putting on weight. She greeted me at the door of her ground floor flat, still in her nightgown with a mass of unbrushed, auburn hair flopping over her eyes.

'Hello, Martha,' she said sleepily.

'Hello, Gill, have you got a minute?'

Gillian yawned spectacularly and nodded. Stepping aside, she let me into an untidy hall with too many coats piled onto the pegs and a heap of unread mail that had been pushed behind the open door. A bucket, half full of dirty water in which floated a grimy floor cloth, was sitting against one wall. Noticing me looking at the pile of mail she laughed.

'Not mine, love. I think there must be at least half a dozen people using this address for one reason or another.'

'Do you think they might live in the flats above?'

'No idea, I don't mix with that shower. Bloody inbreds the lot of 'em.'

Gillian led me through a black painted door into the front room of her flat.

'Charlie! I've got a visitor, so make sure you put some underpants on before you get up,' she called.

I flashed her a quick smile. 'Is Charlie the man you—'

'God, no. That was Ken. I was well rid of him. He had some very peculiar... never mind. Let's just say that's the reason I got caught.'

She laughed and winked at me, so I laughed too.

'So, what brings you here on a Sunday?' Gillian filled the kettle, lit the gas hob and set it to boil.

'I've erm, suffered the same fate as you, although there wasn't a man involved... well, there was, but not inside the home. Basically, I went out for my date when Matron wanted me to work an extra shift. I ended up telling her where she could stick her job, hence...' I looked down at my battered old suitcase. 'There's no going back, but as things stand, I'm out of work and for tonight at least, I have nowhere to go.' I waved the Saturday edition of the paper at her. 'I do have some bedsits to look at tomorrow and there are a couple of jobs I think I might stand a chance of getting.'

'I've got a spare room, you can stay for a few nights if it helps, Martha. Just be aware that Charlie is... how should I describe it... very energetic... and quite noisy in the night... if you get my drift.'

She led me through to a box room containing an ancient single bed with a striped, flock mattress and a single wardrobe without a door, pushed against the wall.

I thanked her profusely. The battered old bed with the rusty springs and the stained mattress was preferrable to a night with the street girls, that was for sure. There was no bedding, but I had my thick winter coat to use as a blanket and I rolled up a couple of towels that Gillian handed me to improvise a makeshift pillow.

She hadn't exaggerated about Charlie either. My sleep was interrupted at least three times by the loud squeaking of bedsprings and the banging of their headboard against the wall at the side of me.

On Monday, I telephoned the first of the job advertisements and arranged an appointment with a lady called Mrs Johnson at Falstaff's bank on the High Street on the Wednesday of that week. The job was in the accounts department, not on the cashier points. I'd had enough of facing the miserable public every day.

The first two bedsits were filthy, too expensive for what they offered and not in the part of town I'd have chosen if I hadn't been so desperate. The third was on the wonderfully named Knightrider Street which was situated near the town centre. The top floor bedsit was quite large, clean and only a short flight of stairs away from the shared kitchen and bathroom. Below me was a young, unmarried mother who shared her two rooms with a smiling Irishman and their teething toddler who would scream the house down most nights. My bank account was quite healthy at that time and I paid a month's rent in advance and was issued with a set of keys, a pair of clean-looking pillows and a set of single sheets, two woollen blankets and a thin, threadbare eiderdown. There was an iron and an ironing board in the kitchen along with a gas meter that always seemed to need a shilling whenever I cooked a meal. There was a similar electric meter in my room.

I moved in that same afternoon and after stocking the meter with coins, I visited the nearby chip shop, then sat on my bed and ate lunch whilst flicking through the pages of Woman's Weekly with my greasy fingers.

Mrs Johnson was a stern looking woman with a thin face which made her long nose look witch-like. Her already narrow eyes became mere slits as she perused the application-form I had just filled in. She checked my school and nursing certificates carefully, then suddenly asked me a few random mental arithmetic questions. Seemingly satisfied with my answers she asked me if I had ever done any ledger work. I answered her honestly and said that I had done a bit on the farm under the instruction of my mother. Again, the answer seemed to satisfy her and I began to feel quite confident of being offered the job. My hopes were realised a few seconds later when a portly man of about forty years entered the room. He puffed as though the effort of opening the door had been a strain.

'Mrs Johnson, I wonder if...' he paused and looked at me carefully. Stroking his double chin and adjusting his spectacles he smiled and wagged his finger. 'I know you,' he said eventually. 'You helped nurse me back to health after my first heart attack.'

'Mr Crew,' I said, getting to my feet. 'I remember you. How's the old ticker now? Better I hope.'

'Not so you'd notice,' he replied. 'But it still ticks.' He offered his hand and I shook it before sitting down again.

He thought for a moment. 'Nurse... Mollison, is it?'

I nodded. 'No longer nurse. That's why I'm here, I'm applying for a job in accounts.'

Mr Crew, who I soon found out was the area manager of the bank, beamed at me before turning to Mrs Johnson. 'She's got the job,' he said, simply.

'Yes, Mr Crew.' Mrs Johnson scooped her pile of papers and pushed my certificates across the table. 'You start on Monday. Eight-thirty, sharp.'

And so, that was that. I now had my own private room and a steady nine to five job that paid better than the all-hours, skivvying, nurse's job. They only needed to give me one full day's instruction on debiting, crediting and balancing customer accounts. I took to it like a duck to water, it was, after all pretty much the same as the ledger my mother used on the farm for her monthly incomings and outgoings.

I enjoyed my time at the bank. My colleagues generally left me alone unless they had a reason to speak to me. Mrs Johnson, who at first had checked my work with an almost religious zeal, soon began to trust my intelligence and spent most of her time berating the office junior, Clarice, who couldn't add two and two together but had the face and body to match that of the French movie star, Brigitte Bardot, so she was very popular with the all-male management team.

Mr Crew, who was based at the branch, used to pop into my shared office at least two or three times a day when he'd perch his ample backside on the corner of my desk and reminisce about the three occasions he had been treated in hospital for his ailing heart, or talk about his photography hobby. Something I soon realised he was immensely keen on.

'I've got my own dark room at home you know? I develop all my own films.'

One bright, autumn afternoon, he asked me if I'd pose for him while he took a few shots. 'Pull your skirt up a bit, you've got lovely legs, you really should show them off.'

So, I sat at my desk with my legs crossed, then uncrossed, then crossed again, showing off my shapely knees and a good deal of my thighs while he clicked away happily. A few days later, I arrived at work to find an envelope on my desk with a couple of the photographs inside, and I have to admit, he had made me look like a professional model, even my hair looked reasonable. Underneath the photographs was an invitation to the Christmas party that he held at his home every year for his favourite members of staff.

Later that afternoon, he dropped into my office and asked me if I intended to accept the invitation.

'Please say yes,' he begged, then whispered. 'Most of the guests are real stick in the muds, the only topic of conversation will be banking.' He beamed when I said, 'thank you, I'd love to come.'

'Put your glad rags on. I'm claiming the first dance.'

The area manager's house was a large, Georgian building that sat on a steepish rise. Enclosed by tall trees on three sides, it overlooked the small estate of detached houses that had been built around it in the 1950s. The large farmhouse that I had grown up in would have easily fitted into it twice over. Mr Crew lived there alone; his wife having left him some ten years before.

On the Saturday of the party, I went into town and bought a new blouse and after agonising over it for almost an hour, a Ya Ya skirt which was the forerunner of Mary Quant's famous mini skirt. I tried a couple of them on. One of them, four inches above the knee and the other, an alarming five inches. I bent over, stretched and sat down crossing and uncrossing my legs to see just how much of my thighs, or my underwear, would be on show. Satisfied that at least the tops of my stockings were hidden away, I took the plunge and bought a black one. It was expensive, but I was out to impress.

I enjoyed the party and the attention I received from many of the management team, much to the disgust of their wives. I got a bit tiddly quite early on after being showered with compliments and having flute after flute of champagne thrust into my eager hands. I

337

had half expected some dull, background music allowing the banking conversations to take place but instead, Mr Crew stacked his top-quality record player with singles by Johnny Kidd and the Pirates, Billy Fury and a newish group called The Beatles. As requested, I gave him the first dance, then the third, fourth and fifth and by the time the slow ballads were put on at around ten o'clock, right up until the party began to break up at eleven, he was my sole partner and I received many a whispered endearment as he pushed himself against me, his hands performing feats an octopus would have been proud of.

Thomas, as I had now been instructed to call him, was not only a semi-invalid, he was as rich as Croesus. The house had six bedrooms, three bathrooms, a kitchen to die for, and sat in an acre of land. I think, if anything, I was more interested in snaring him than he was of snaring me. After the party, with sore breasts and a bruised, heavily pinched bottom, I lay in bed fantasising about the kind of lifestyle that the vast majority of women could only dream of. Okay, he was fifteen or so years older than me, he was fat, he was so unfit that he probably got out of breath just thinking about sex, but I could see the bigger picture. I would almost certainly outlive him by a great many years, and, if I played my cards right and became the bank manager's dutiful little wife, then in time, all of his worldly goods would be mine. I figured that with all I had been through, I deserved it.

Within two months, Thomas and I were an item. I was promoted to his office, becoming his personal secretary and a couple of weeks after that, I had an engagement ring on my finger.

Chapter 48

Martha. 1964

    We got married at a registry office one bleak Wednesday afternoon in March. There were only six guests, none belonged to his family, or mine. He chose a Wednesday afternoon because it was half day at the bank. We both went back to work on the Thursday.

    To say my wedding night was forgettable would be an understatement. I can't say I had gone out of my way to spend my hard-earned cash on lingerie either. I had a feeling it would have been a waste of time though the dirty old bugger did ask if he could take some snaps of me in my skimpy, lace-trimmed, baby doll nightie. The look on my face gave my reply without having to use words.

    We had sex once on our wedding night. There was little to no foreplay and the entire act lasted less than two minutes which was a good job because with the state he was in, if it had lasted for three, I would have almost certainly become a bride and a widow on the same day.

    I have to admit, I was really worried about him. After he had done his thing, he rolled off and lay gasping, staring purple-faced at the ceiling. I did ask him if he wanted me to call for a doctor but he shook his head and wheezed, 'no.'

    When he finally began to breathe a little more easily and his flabby chest (his breasts were almost as big as mine) stopped heaving, he patted my thigh and said that he was a bit out of practice but it would get better with time. Being an ex-nurse, and knowing what I knew, I seriously doubted that.

    I moved into my new home after work the following day. If I thought that my new husband would be eager to get in some much-needed practice in the bedroom I was mistaken. Over the next few weeks, we settled into a Saturday night pattern where we'd watch Dixon of Dock Green and Wells Fargo on the BBC before flicking over to watch the crime drama, Gideon's Way. As we watched our black and white TV, I'd sip a couple of glasses of more than decent wine, while he'd have two shots of single malt whisky. As soon as the final credits of the police drama rolled across the screen, I'd go up to bed while he busied himself checking the doors and windows before puffing up the stairs to perform his two-minute, purple faced showstopper.

I was surprised when, after only a few weeks of marriage, he suggested that I should give up my job as he didn't consider it seemly that the wife of a man in his position should go to work. It sent out the wrong message apparently. I argued that I needed to work so that I had my own income, money to spend on the odd luxury, nice clothes, and underwear etc, so he set me up with a monthly allowance that matched the wages I had been earning at the bank. I also had a housekeeping budget that far exceeded the amount I needed, no matter how expensive a bottle of my nightly tipple was.

That summer, I received a telephone call from the chairwoman of the W.I. asking if I would consider joining their happy little band. I accepted, because although I would much rather be a stay-at-home wife than a working one, I was starting to become a little bored in the daytime. After the morning tidy up as I listened to the radio, there was little apart from magazines to fill my time, so any distraction was to be welcomed.

Mrs Harlaxton-Smythe-Jones was a bespectacled woman with a slight frame that was more than made up for by her iron-willed personality. She had been chairwoman for almost thirty years and as she told me, God willing, she'd like to be in the same position in thirty years' time. I wouldn't have put it past her either although she was already in her eighties. She told me that as a well-respected woman of my social standing, I ought to make being member of such an august organisation, a priority. As a bit of a bribe, she offered me the branch secretary's post.

'Mrs Morten has sadly had to leave us to look after her invalid husband,' she confided.

I thought about Thomas's heart condition and wondered how long I'd last in the role myself.

Anyway, I allowed myself to be persuaded and over the next few months I attended the weekly Wednesday night meetings and almost all of the weekday guest speaker talks and the big summer fete, where our jams, cakes and biscuits were judged and later sold. By the autumn of that year I was a respected member of the group and my standing, socially, had moved up a level.

Being the area manager of one of the big banks, Thomas was always being invited to opening nights at the theatre or being asked to chair, or at least sit on the panel of many of the local business groups. We went out to dinner at a restaurant or as the invited guest at the homes of the local rich and almost famous at least once a fortnight. We even held little dinner parties ourselves where the likes of Mrs Harlaxton-Smythe-Jones, buttered up Thomas in the hope of receiving a donation to whatever good cause was being promoted that month. Mrs Harlaxton-Smythe-Jones was always accompanied by her 95-year-old husband, who owned a body even frailer than hers. Walking at a snail's pace and held up on two thick walking sticks, he was famous for falling asleep at the dinner table. I once had to lift his face out of the soup before he drowned.

Wednesday night was also Thomas's Photography Club night. I never did find out where the club held its meetings, but he always left on foot, carrying his camera bag, returning half an hour or so after me, smelling of whisky and smiling like the cat who found himself locked in at the dairy.

Thursday evenings would be spent in the attic developing the pictures he'd taken on club night. I was never invited into the loft; it was his sanctuary and I wasn't the slightest bit interested in his hobby anyway. The closest I ever got to a camera was to smile into the lens of a junior reporter as he took pictures of local events and celebrities for the evening paper.

I only went up the final flight of stairs to the attic on one occasion during our first year of marriage and was greeted by a red light and a red-faced husband shouting, 'get out,' as I pushed open the door to ask him what he fancied for supper. He later apologised and explained that any outside light could ruin his photographs as they were developing.

In 1967, I went on the pill. Doctors would only prescribe it at that time to married women who wanted to restrict the size of their families. Society was concerned that single women might take it on themselves to become sex-crazed wantons as their risk of pregnancy was minimised. As I didn't have children, my own doctor was reluctant to hand over the prescription but, as my monthlies were becoming irregular at best and sometimes lasted for up to a fortnight, he finally relented. Within a couple of months, all was back to normal and I felt stronger than I had done for a couple of years.

Because Thomas and I had taken no precautions during sex I assumed that either his little tadpoles were poor swimmers, or the abortion I had undergone back in the day had damaged something internally that was stopping me having children. I wasn't bothered in the slightest and Thomas, whose weekly Saturday night exertions had by now been reduced to a fortnightly fumble, didn't seem to care either. He spent more time in his darkroom where he began to develop films for a few of his clubmates.

I did ask him once what he got up to at the meetings and he told me that they mostly took pictures of inanimate objects, or, if the weather was fine, they'd go out to the woods to take wildlife shots. Now and then they'd pay for a life class model to sit, sometimes male, sometimes female. He then began to wax lyrical about shutter speeds, f-stops and apertures, and my brain turned to mush. I only ever mentioned the subject again when I asked him if he'd had a good time on his return.

Now and then, he'd ask me to pose for him but I always refused, arguing that he saw me naked at least twice a month as it was and I couldn't see any reason why he would need a naked photograph. His argument was always about the artistic side of things. He claimed that if he could practice on me, the photographs he took of models under different lighting conditions, would improve dramatically.

I told him I'd think about it.

I finally gave in after weeks of nagging. As it was his birthday and I'd forgotten all about it until he returned home from work with a handful of cards, I decided to pretend that I was giving him a private photo session as a gift.

So, he set up his tripod and put rolls of film into his two best cameras and I drank half a bottle of wine and ran a bubble bath. As I dropped my towel to climb in, his flashgun began to pop. I wasn't happy about that as I had been bending over the side of the bath and he must have had an eyeful of my private parts. Thomas just told me to relax and not to worry as he'd discard anything too revealing when he developed the pictures.

I gave him fifteen minutes as I posed, mostly covered in bubbles, but he continued to click as I climbed out of the bath, and being on the tipsy side, I stupidly allowed him to take a few more of me on the bed.

The next morning at breakfast, feeling ashamed of myself, I demanded to see the pictures he had taken, so he spent that evening developing and enlarging them. The ones he showed me were quite artistic I had to admit. When I asked him what he'd done with the one of me bending over and the ones he had taken mid pose on the bed when I was more exposed, he told me he had destroyed them and I, like a fool, believed him.

In 1969, I met a man called Mick in a café in town. I had dropped into the coffee bar with a handful of W.I.

flyers promoting a Bring and Buy sale we were promoting and he was holding the fort while the manageress nipped to the lavatory. Mick was a late entry art student come poet. He was a tall man in his mid-twenties with hair down to his shoulders, he wore a pair of faded, denim jeans with a flare stitched into the bottoms of the legs, and a grandad vest... one of those collarless things with buttons at the neck. He wasn't exactly Roger Moore and he would never have fitted in at one of our little dinner parties, but he was funny, bright and confident.

'How old are you?' he asked as I reached into my bag for the leaflets.

'A bit older than my teeth,' I replied. 'Why do you want to know?'

'Because you look about my age but you're wearing a tweed skirt so you must be at least fifty.'

He grinned at me and pointed to the coffee machine. 'Can I tempt you? I'm in the chair.'

I think it was the grin that did it. I nodded and tried to hand him the flyers but he just turned away and poured coffee into two, clear glass cups. 'Come on, Tweedy,' he said, walking from behind the counter. 'Let's have a natter.'

'Tweedy,' I snorted. 'Tweedy.'

We sat in the café, chatting for well over an hour. It was a bit of a release for me, talking to someone of my own age for the first time in ages. Most of the people I met socially were well into their fifties or even older.

The time flew by as we sat talking about anything and everything, my stomach ached with laughing. As I got to my feet, he leaned back in his chair and looked me up and down. 'That tweed has to go, Martha, don't wear it next time.'

'Next time? So, you think there's going to be a next time, do you?' I looked at him, my head tilted to the side. 'You're a cocky one, I'll give you that.'

Mick shrugged. 'Same time, same place?'

'We'll see,' I said looking over my shoulder as I opened the door.

'Bye, Tweedy,' he called after me.

The following week I arrived at the café wearing a peasant blouse and a pair of new jeans that I bought from a market stall on the previous Saturday.

'Tweedy!' he called out loudly as I entered the café. 'Sandra, two of your finest Kenco's please.'

'That's my name now, is it? I will henceforth be forever known as Tweedy.'

'It suits you,' he said, grinning that wicked grin of his.

Our coffee mornings became a regular thing after that and we got to know each other quite well. I was in no real danger of being spotted with him as none of the members of the W.I. would be seen dead in that part of town. I really used to look forward to our meet ups. Nothing had happened between us at that point, he wasn't pushing it and neither was I, although I wouldn't have declined had he offered to take me to bed. To anyone who did notice us, were just two, youngish people who enjoyed each other's company.

About six weeks after we first met, we were having our usual morning chat when he suddenly looked out of the front, plate glass window and muttered, 'shit'. Hurriedly reaching into the pocket of his denim jacket, he slipped a black, felt bag under the table and dropped it on my lap. 'Hide it, quick,' he hissed.

As I slipped the miniature sack into the linen carrier bag that I had brought in with me, two burly policemen burst into the café.

'Well, if it isn't Marijuana Mick,' said one of the policemen, stepping towards him as the other one guarded the door. 'You know the form, up against the wall... hurry up, we haven't got all day.'

I slid across the bench seat to allow Mick to get out from behind the table and watched as he was forced up against the wall and patted down.

'Nothing! Not so much as an aspirin. What's up, Mick, have you found God or something?'

Mick turned away from the wall with a grin on his face. 'Not bloody likely,' he said.

The taller of the two policemen then turned his attention to me. 'Now, miss, what are you doing, associating with such low life? You look far too decent to be hanging around with the likes of him.'

Mick's face sank as I reached into my bag, but instead of pulling out his little black bag, I produced a wad of W.I. leaflets instead.

'We're having a coffee morning for the Spastics? Can I interest you in a leaflet?'

The policeman looked at me as though I'd offered him a cup of hemlock tea.

'Come on, Harris, crime won't crack itself.'

When they had gone, Mick told me to 'hutch up' and sat down at the side of me. Taking a quick look out of the window to make sure the police officers had gone, he patted my thigh and thanked me for saving him.

'Are you a drug dealer?' I asked in a disappointed tone.

'No, what you have in your bag is for my own use. I buy in once a month, or whenever I have a few quid spare. They help me when I'm working late.'

Mick got to his feet, walked to the door and checked the street.

'Could you do me a huge favour? Could you keep the gear in your bag until we get back to mine?'

'I wasn't aware we were going back to yours,' I replied with a glint in my eye.

Mick's flat was a two-room affair at the top of a three-storey building not far from where my own flat had been. It was untidy rather than dirty with torn out notebook sketches on the floor lying next to discarded clothing, some of which was female. In the corner of the room, beneath the skylight was an easel holding an almost finished painting of a pretty girl wearing nothing but a smile. Mick scooped up a pile of sketches from the threadbare sofa and invited me to sit.

'Do you, er, live here with someone?' I asked, pointing to the matching bra and pants set on the floor whilst trying to keep the disappointed tone out of my voice.

Mick looked puzzled, then spotting the underwear he shrugged and kicked at it.

'No, I live alone these days... well, since last week. I was involved in a short-term relationship with the woman in the painting,' he pointed to the portrait in the corner, 'but she erm, well, let's just say she wanted more out of life than I could reasonably afford to give her.'

'Ah,' I said. 'You couldn't live up to her expectations.'

'Financially no. Her father owns an investment company.' He pointed to my shopping bag. 'Could I have my stuff back now. Please?'

I fished the little black bag out and handed it to him.

'I'm rather disappointed in you, Mick. Why do you bother with that stuff? Isn't it harmful?'

'I couldn't work without the contents of this bag, Tweedy,' he replied. 'In here I've got a few tabs of speed, a few downers and half a dozen wraps of weed.'

'You lost me at speed,' I replied.

'Speed are amphetamines, stimulants, they keep you going when you'd normally need sleep. I use them when I've got an art project to hand in and I need to work all night on it.'

'Ah, I understand. I used to be a nurse. I know about amphetamines, but downers?'

'Barbiturates, they calm you down when you need to sleep after taking the speed.'

I shook my head. 'The things you learn... and the weed?'

'Marijuana. Surely you've heard about that. It just allows you to space out and chill.'

'I see.'

347

'Would you like to turn on?' he asked.

'Turn what on... the radio?'

He laughed. 'Yourself. Would you like to try a joint? He pulled a little square of foil from his bag. I can roll one up if you like.'

'I'll stay turned off thanks, Mick,' I replied.

Mick dropped the foil wrapped drug into the bag and sat down close to me. Sliding his arm around my shoulders he put his mouth next to my ear and whispered, 'there are other ways of turning you on.' The next thing I know we were indulging in a deep, French kiss and before long, my underwear had joined his ex's forgotten lingerie on the floor.

Chapter 49

'Mum, I've had an email about your new bed.'

Nicola appeared at the top of the stairs as Jess called up. 'Yes?'

'They're delivering it today instead of Saturday. We had better get over there this morning and dismantle the old one.'

Nicola hurried down the stairs with an excited look on her face.

'Great, I'll be able to move in this afternoon then.'

Jess pulled a sad face. 'Are you in that much of a hurry to leave?'

Nicola patted her on the arm. 'No, love, it's not that, but... well, I am looking forward to being independent again. You'll get your own life back as well.'

Jess laughed. 'I do know what you mean, but you are always welcome here, Mum, you know that.'

Nicola put the kettle on and pulled two mugs from the mug tree. 'What time are we going over? I've got my stuff packed already. I'd like to get a bit of shopping in later on too. Stock up my new cupboards, get some cleaning stuff, toothpaste etc.'

'Great, can you get me a few bits too while you're there. I've left a list on the worktop.'

Nicola picked up the scrap of paper, glanced at it and stuffed it into her pocket. 'Benson and Hedges, top of the list.'

'They're my one weakness,' Jess said with a grin. 'It's a good job Calvin can't see me when I sit on the back step, he'd have a fit.'

'Bugger Calvin,' Nicola replied with feeling.

As she sipped her coffee, Jess checked her emails, there was a short one from Martha informing her that Marjorie was no worse. After typing out a quick reply, saying that she was pleased to hear it, Jess closed the lid of her laptop and still swallowing the last dregs of her coffee, she opened a base unit in the parlour and pulled out a spray can of WD40 and an adjustable spanner.

349

'God knows how long that bed has been there,' she said to herself.

It took them just over half an hour to dismantle the bed and stack the various parts against the wall in one of the spare bedrooms. The WD40 had come in handy as most of the wingnuts that held the frame of the bed together had rusted in.

'Right, Mum, the email said they'd be here between one and five, so you've got a bit of time to kill. Do you want me to keep you company or shall I go home?'

'Go back to the farm, love. I'm only going to be unpacking my stuff anyway. I don't need any help with that.'

Back at the farmhouse, Jess made a quick lunch, then settled down in her armchair and picked up the last few pages of Martha's memoir.

Martha. 1970-1975

Mick and I met up at his flat every week for about a year after that, then my monthlies problem returned with a vengeance, so some weeks we'd just sit and put the world to rights or I'd sit on the sofa while he sketched me.

'One day, when I've finished my course, I'll do a nude portrait of you.'

I thanked him but said that there was no point as no one but the two of us could ever be allowed to see it.

When I visited my doctor to complain about my seemingly never-ending period, he did a few tests, then said he'd try me on a different brand of contraceptive pill but that I'd have to come off the one I was on for a few months first.

After three months, my monthlies were almost back to normal so, stupidly, Mick and I resumed our activities without using any protection and in the summer, I found myself pregnant, Mick's rhythm method having failed us both.

I didn't tell him to begin with, fearing that being the decent sort of man he was, he'd demand to play an active role in the baby's life. I did tell Thomas however. To say he wasn't best pleased would be an understatement.

One good thing to come out of it was that his Saturday night, two-minute wonder sessions, ended. He actually told me that he found the thought of pregnant women, repulsive.

When I finally told Mick, however, he had no hang ups about it and our rampant sex sessions went on much as before. He did ask about the baby's future a couple of times, but I told him firmly that as far as the rest of the world was concerned, Thomas was the baby's father. He accepted it with a fixed smile, but never brought the subject up again. Our affair ended when I was seven months' pregnant and I began to find sex uncomfortable.

Nicola was born in the late summer of 1971. It was a long, lonely labour lasting for over forty hours and by the time she finally arrived, kicking and screaming without being slapped, I was absolutely exhausted and not the slightest bit interested in bonding with my new-born.

That changed over the next few days as I began to realise that I was in danger of turning into my own mother, and so, not wanting my child to have to endure the same indifference as I had been shown, I forced myself to feed, bathe and cuddle my new daughter until I found myself worrying about her in the night, picking her up to make sure she was breathing.

Thomas wanted nothing to do with his 'daughter' and exiled himself in another part of the house, appearing merely to eat or to climb the stairs to his dark room. He slept in one of the bedrooms in what he called, the East Wing of the big house.

Life pretty much went on as it always had but with Thomas spending more and more time with his photography club members. After a few months of suffering new mother syndrome, when I'd take Nicola out in the middle of the night in all weathers in an attempt to get her to sleep, things improved and she began to settle into a regular nocturnal routine. Not long after that I resumed my W.I. secretary duties, taking Nicola with me to both the day and evening meetings. I never once had to pick her up to comfort her at the W.I. as there was always a willing pair of hands ready to perform that task. There were even heated arguments between the mostly elderly committee about whose turn it was to change her nappy or give her a spoonful of gripe water.

Nicola accompanied me to the Wednesday night meetings until she was about eighteen months old, when it was reluctantly agreed by my peers that she should really be at home, asleep long before the meeting ended. So, I took up the offer of Joanne Briggs, a W.I. member and close neighbour, to babysit Nicola while I attended the gatherings. Thomas reckoned that she only offered so that she could snoop around the house to see what we owned and warned me to check the silver when I got home.

This arrangement went on for about three years before Joanne told me that her mother had suffered a stroke and would be moving in with them. She was to be her carer. I thought about asking her to look after Nicola at her house and I'd pick her up after the meetings but it wasn't really a practical idea. The W.I. was my only release from the drudgery of motherhood in those days and I was reluctant to give up my hard-earned position in it. Young as I was, I had been tipped to take over as chairwoman on a temporary basis later that year.

Luckily, the daughter of Joanne's sister's neighbour was looking to earn a bit of extra cash. She was thirteen and a fashion fanatic. She was already doing two paper rounds and had an illegal Saturday job working at a local stable. She was a pretty girl, her body just beginning on the journey towards womanhood. She lived about a mile away on the council estate. She was friendly, cheerful and loved Thomas's new stereo equipment and record collection. She also, I later found out, liked to sample the contents of our wine cabinet.

One hot summer Thursday evening, Thomas received an urgent telephone call from the police, informing him that the bank's alarm system had gone off and they couldn't get in touch with the manager. Thomas stormed out of his dark room, grabbed his car keys and puffed and panted his way to the car leaving me, the harbinger of such bad news, standing on the landing outside his studio. I couldn't help myself. Looking over the banister to make sure he wasn't on his way back up the stairs, I pushed the door open and stepped inside. The room was brightly lit with two long strings of curtain wire hanging from the ceiling with a dozen or so wooden clothes pegs clipped onto them. There was a wooden bench running along one wall with a large white sink built into the middle of it. Pushed up against the opposite wall was an old fashioned, roll top desk. I pushed at the lid to see what was inside, but it was locked and there was no sign of a key. Pulling open one of the drawers, I found a stack of pornographic magazines. Not really caring how he got his kicks, I picked up the top one and flicked through it, stopping, horrified on the section labelled 'Readers' Wives'. There, laid out in a four-photo group were some of the pictures that Thomas had taken of me on the night of his birthday. They were not the semi-decent ones he had shown me either. They were the ones he had assured me he had destroyed; the highlight of the set was a large picture of me bending over the bath showing off my womanhood so clearly that a gynaecologist could have used it to make a diagnosis.

Furious, I tore out the offending pages, folded them up and stuck them in the pocket of my pinafore.

'Just you bloody wait, Thomas Crew,' I fumed.

He got back an hour later, angry, red-faced and sweating. I had drunk a few glasses of a 15% proof wine by then and I was ready and waiting. I thrust the offending magazine pages into his face and gave him both barrels. He wasn't the slightest bit ashamed. Instead of apologising he fell back on his old argument about it being 'art'. He told me I should be grateful that he found my body attractive enough to share with other men. I was gobsmacked.

'I could go to the police with these. You didn't have my permission to publish them.'

'If you did, there would be a scandal,' he replied, calmly. 'Do you really want that? Imagine what the newspapers would make of it.'

I was snookered and he knew it. There was no way I could complain without the pictures being reproduced in the Sunday newspapers, albeit with tiny black stars covering my intimate bits. I told him that as far as I was concerned, our marriage was over. He looked at me smugly and said it had been over since Nicola was born and if I wanted to leave, I could, but he would make sure that all the sordid details of our photo session came out at the divorce hearing. Angry and frustrated, I tossed the glossy pictures into the fireplace and lit them with his cigarette lighter.

'That's the end of those,' I said, smugly.

'I'll just order a back issue,' he replied, looking equally smug. 'I'll order one tomorrow in fact. I do like looking at those shots, they were particularly good, the lighting was just perf—'

I picked up the big crystal ashtray and hurled it at him. He ducked and it smashed against the wall showering him with slivers of glass. 'Get out of my sight you perverted bastard,' I screamed.

On reflection, I had no choice but to put up with the situation, but things took a dramatic turn one Wednesday night when I suffered an appalling headache and returned home early from the W.I.

For three out of the four previous Wednesdays, I had arrived home to find Ella, our babysitter, had already gone home. When I asked why, Thomas said that the photo club had been finishing early because they had been shooting outdoors and the light wasn't good enough to continue until their usual finish time.

This particular week, I had only been out of the house for half an hour and I was surprised to find three cars parked on the drive when I arrived home. As soon as I opened the front door I could hear the sound of raised men's voices coming from upstairs. Puzzled, I left the front door open and without so much as removing my coat I stepped quickly up the stairs. The door to my bedroom was wide open and as I stepped inside my heart sank. Standing around my bed, cameras at the ready were four, fifty-plus men, calling eagerly to my naked thirteen-year-old babysitter, demanding that she, 'spread 'em wider, you little slut.'

Ella lay sprawled across the bed, legs akimbo, trying to pull a Marylin Monroe pout. Her arms were lying across her stomach pushing up her small, pert breasts. It was instantly obvious that she had been plied with wine. There was a half empty bottle on the table at the side of the bed. Her clothes were littered across the room.

Thomas, who was kneeling at the foot of the bed to get the best angle, called out to her as he wound on the film for the next shot. 'Come on, Ella, get those legs up.'

Ella giggled drunkenly, then her attempted pout turned to a look of despair as she saw me framed in the doorway. Suddenly her face fell and tears appeared in her eyes.

'GET OUT OF MY HOUSE BEFORE I CALL THE POLICE, YOU DISGUSTING PERVERTS!' I cried.

The men turned as one with horrified looks on their faces. Grabbing at their equipment bags, they rushed past me and hared down the stairs. Thomas was struggling to get to his feet as I stomped across the room, pushing him head first into the footboard of the bed. Crouching down at her side, I pulled a cover over Ella's naked body, sat her up and pulled her towards me.

'It's all right, Ella, don't worry, love, I'm here now.'

'Will I still be paid?' she muttered.

I glared at Thomas, who had just got to his feet, purple faced and panting.

'It's art. It's just art,' he gabbled.

'How long has this been going on?'

He began to recover his composure. 'A few months. She likes it, don't you, Ella?'

'Get out!' I screamed, looking around for something to throw. Thomas, still clutching his camera, backed out of the room. 'I'll pay you before you go, Ella, don't worry.'

It took me a full twenty minutes to get her dressed and a few more to help her down the stairs. In the kitchen I plied her with strong coffee and tried to get some sense out of her. Thomas came in while I was conducting the soft interrogation.

'Are you ready to go home, Ella?' he asked.

'You filthy bastard. She's in no state to go anywhere. Do you always send her home on her own?'

'No, I don't,' Thomas replied, calmly. 'One of those men is her uncle. She stays over at his when her father is on the night shift.'

'Good God,' I whispered. 'I can imagine what she has to suffer when she's there.'

Thomas shrugged. 'She knows what she's doing.'

I put my hands to my ears, not wanting to hear any more. Thomas shrugged again, reached into his wallet and slid a five-pound note across the table. 'Jim's waiting for her outside,' he said, casually, as if I was in on the act.

'This time I am going to the police,' I spat.

'No you aren't. Your ego couldn't handle the scandal,' he replied.

'This child's welfare comes first,' I said, screwing up my face at him.

Thomas merely pointed to the telephone. 'You know the number, or do you want me to dial it?'

I got to my feet, but as I stepped across to the phone, he gave me one of his smug looks.

'Did I tell you that I received five copies of that magazine in the post at work. That's enough to send copies to the W.I., the Women's Circle, your mother and toddler's group, the landlord of the Red Cow and still keep a copy for myself. Are you sure you want to pick up that phone?'

I stopped dead in my tracks. Along with the scandal of having a paedophile ring operating from my home, which, I had no doubt, Thomas would say I knew about, I couldn't risk him doing as he had threatened. I would be finished in the town.

So, being the coward that I was, I gave in to his blackmail and putting my arm around Ella, I walked her to the door. As I pushed it open, she looked back towards Thomas.

'Do you still want me to bring our Neil with me next week?'

I shook my head. 'No... No, Ella, don't come back here ever again. I'll try my hardest to do something about your uncle.'

'My uncle is nice,' she replied, 'he only takes pictures, he doesn't hurt us.'

My jaw sagged. 'If that's him being nice I'd hate to see what he does when he's nasty. How old is Neil?'

'He's eight,' she replied, looking towards Thomas. 'I get paid an extra pound when he comes.'

As it happened, she never did come to the house again because Thomas died two days later. I came downstairs to find him lying on his back on the lounge carpet, his hands clasped together across his chest as though he had been praying.

I checked his pulse to make sure he was really gone before phoning for an ambulance. They arrived and carted his bloated body away, grumbling to themselves about his weight.

There was no autopsy. Because of his known condition and the three heart attacks he had suffered, he was summarily despatched to the cold store where he lay on a slab until the funeral directors picked him up the day before his cremation.

I organised a quiet affair with only a handful of guests. I played the grieving widow part to the best of my ability, my gloating grins hidden by a thick veil.

I did get a huge, unwanted surprise when the will was read. Instead of all his worldly goods, I had been left with a few thousand pounds and a third of the value of the house which, I soon learned, was to be sold. The other two thirds and the bulk of the money had been left to his two younger sisters; women I had no idea even existed. I only ever saw them once. They didn't come to the funeral but they were at the solicitor's office when I turned up to hear what I had been left in the will. They didn't speak to me, but I did hear one of them whisper that she hoped the disgusting old bastard was burning in hell. The pained look they shared left me in no doubt what they must have suffered at his hands. I decided there and then not to complain about my share of the pay out, they deserved their share so much more than I did.

After the sale, I spent my inheritance on a lovely house in Spinton, about a mile from the farmhouse where I had grown up. I was loathed to move back to my home town but the lovely house, and the asking price were just too good to turn down. On the day I left Maidstone I posted an anonymous letter to the local police informing them about the activities of the photographic club. I don't know to this day whether it was acted on or not.

There's not a lot more to say about this part in my life, the rest is common knowledge. You will already know about Roger, the man I met at Butlins when I took Nicola for a holiday. He was much younger than me and I loved him dearly but he betrayed me, like most of the men in my life have done. I thought our marriage was solid. I thought I was the luckiest woman on earth and believed I was finally getting my reward for having put up with so much, but he was just using me. He spent my money at an alarming rate and after the first two years, he began to spend more and more nights away from home, using the excuse that he was performing his comedy gigs around the country. He left me after seven years, although I only ever saw him a couple of nights a month for the last two. He used to beg forgiveness for his latest dalliance, swore to me that I was the only one he truly loved and that soon he'd be back for good. Like a fool, I believed him.

When he filed for divorce, he was handed a share of the house meaning that I would have to either find the money to pay him, or take on a mortgage. He had emptied my bank account years before. So, I asked Marjorie to move in with me. She had a few thousand pounds saved up from somewhere, presumably her job at the school, and she willingly handed it over to allow me to pay him off. I still regret asking for her help, she's never allowed me to forget that she bailed me out.

So, there you have it, Jessica. It's probably not as interesting a life story as my mother's but I have had my moments. Now, perhaps you'll understand my antipathy towards men. I'll leave you with one piece of advice, it's probably the only thing I've ever agreed with my mother on. Don't trust men, Jessica. Don't trust any of them. They all want to use you in one way or another. Sometimes it's for the sex, sometimes for your money but there is something worse than any of that. Some will want to control you completely. Never let that happen, Jessica, believe me, it's the worst of all worlds.

Martha.

Chapter 50

'Oh, dear, poor Grandma.'

Jess slid the last few pages of Martha's recollections into their folder and sat back to think about what she had just read.

'She had a really bad time of it, Nana,' she said to Alice's empty chair. 'How much of it did you know about? Not all, I bet, or you'd have done your best to try to help. I know you refused her money when Roger fleeced her, but there were good reasons for that. As for the rest... well, what could you have done to protect her from any of it?'

Jess switched on the TV to check the news on the cruise ship. It was still the main headline on the ticker across the bottom of the screen.

Paradise Pearl Latest: *476 passengers now ill with the Coronavirus. Five deaths recorded so far. Japanese authorities beginning to move the most seriously ill into hospital but wary of passing the infection on to the local population. More follows.*

Jess hurried through to the kitchen and opened up her laptop to send a quick email to Martha.

Latest news not good. Not sure how much you know but 476 ill and five deaths. Can you arrange a time for Skype tomorrow morning, my time? Love to you both. Stay safe. Jess.

Walking slowly back into the lounge, she checked the wall clock, *twenty past three, better text Mum, see how she's getting on.*

Two minutes later, Nicola's reply came back.

Men just got here, carrying bed up now, say they'll fit the two halves together and unpack the memory foam mattress. They said thanks for £20. Going shopping in fifteen minutes.

Jess sent back a heart emoji, then went to sit on the back step for a cigarette. Taking a deep draw, she blew a long stream of smoke across the farmyard. She had just put the cigarette back into her mouth when she heard a voice coming from her right. Looking up, she saw Calvin leaning on the gate. His nose was caked with blood and his right eye was a bruised mess and closing fast.

Without being invited, he pulled back the spring-loaded locking bar, opened the gate and stepped into the yard.

'Back on those disgusting things, are you? I wondered how long you'd last. See what happens when I'm not around to guide you?'

'I like smoking, Calvin. I know it's bad for me, but they're my lungs after all. You can't tell me what to do now anyway. I've outgrown you.'

Calvin pointed to the cigarette. 'It looks like it. I think you're actually regressing. You know we were better off together, Jess. I knew how to look after you, and somebody still needs to by the looks of it.'

As Calvin stepped closer, Jess noticed the severity of his injuries.

'My God, Calvin, what have you been doing?'

'Me? Nothing. It was that lunatic charity worker of yours. He set about me in the car park outside Uni. I would have sorted him out normally, but he came up on me from behind and ran off before I could respond.'

'That doesn't sound like Ewan to me, Calvin. Are you sure you didn't provoke him?'

'Why would I provoke a six-foot rugby player?'

'Well, if you thought you could... sort him?'

Jess held out her fingers towards Calvin's face, he winced before she could touch it and took a quick step back.

'I'll call him,' Jess said, picking up her phone from the step.

'No... No, don't do that... Look, Jess, I may have said something a little untoward but there was no need for him to respond like that.'

'Well, I'm waiting.' Jess looked down to her phone, then back to Calvin.

'I might have said something along the lines of, Jess rejected you then, you loser.'

'And what did he say? That's not enough to make him hit you.'

'He said he wouldn't be bothering you anymore because he's going back to Africa tomorrow.'

'And...'

'Look, it doesn't matter now, Can I—'

'TELL ME!' Jess yelled.

'I said something like, you'd better be careful you don't catch AIDS out there, a lot of men have got it.'

'CALVIN! No wonder he hit you. I would have too.'

'All right, I got a bit carried away, but I paid for it, didn't I?'

'He didn't hit you hard enough.'

'Don't be like that, Jess.' Calvin put his fingertips onto his bruised eye and flinched. 'Do you think I could bathe this for a minute?'

Jess blew out her cheeks, then stepping into the kitchen she pulled her first aid box from one of the cupboards, opened it up and pulled out a pack of sterilised wipes. After pulling one from the pack she got Calvin to stand in the light of the window while she dabbed at his rapidly closing eye. Calvin went weak at the knees the moment the pad touched his skin.

'OW OW! that hurts, be gentle, will you?'

'Stop whimpering, you big baby.' Jess tossed the used wipe into the bin, pulled out another one and set about wiping some of the dried blood from his nostrils.

'Is it broken do you think? It is, isn't it? It's broken.'

'I'm not a nurse, Calvin, but I don't think it's broken. He just gave you a well-deserved nose bleed that's all.'

'It's a good job he's going to bloody Africa or—'

'Shut up, Calvin.'

Calvin suddenly held up his hand to show Jess the half full packet of cigarettes he had picked up from the step. Almost snarling, he crushed the pack and tossed it into the bin with the wipes Jess had just used.

'Here to help, as always, Jess. Those things will kill you.'

'Go away, Calvin. You are out of my life now and I have no intentions of allowing you to worm your way back in. I make my own decisions and if I feel like a cigarette, I'll bloody well have one.' Jess looked at the crushed pack of cigarettes, then back to Calvin. 'Go on. Out you go. I've shown you enough pity for one day.'

Calvin turned meekly away, but then turned suddenly and grabbing Jess by the shoulders, he shook her violently.

'Never try to push me around, Jess. I'm the one that gives the orders, remember?'

Jess tried to pull his hands away but they held firm. Holding her in his vice-like grip, he leaned closer.

'You know we're better off together, Jess. You'll never make it through life on your own and no one will ever look after you like I did.'

Jess laughed scornfully, then instantly regretted it. Calvin's face became a mask of rage. Taking his hands from her shoulders, he placed them roughly onto her breasts and squeezed until she gasped in pain, then after spitting in her face, he pulled his hands back and pushed her on the breastbone as hard as he could.

Jess tried to keep her balance as her body hurtled backwards at speed, but one ankle got stuck behind the other and she felt herself falling. With arms still flailing, her head hit the corner of the big oak table and she passed out.

Calvin became frantic. 'Oh, Jess, I didn't mean that, you made me do it.' He squatted down by her prone body and stroked her forehead. 'Wake up, please... wake up.'

'Calvin! What the hell have you done?' Nicola screamed at Jess's ex-partner as she hurried into the kitchen. Dropping Jess's share of the shopping onto the floor she rushed across to her prostrate daughter. 'If you've hurt her, you malevolent bastard, I'll kill you with my bare hands.'

'It was an accident,' Calvin sputtered as he backed towards the door. 'I'd never hurt her, you know that.'

Nicola ignored him and began to stroke Jess's hand. 'Jess, wake up, please?'

As Jess began to stir, Calvin breathed a sigh of relief and almost tripping over his own feet he hurried down the back steps and raced out of the farmyard.

Chapter 51

'I'm all right, Mum, please don't fuss.' Jess adjusted the improvised ice pack that her mother had made for her and sat up straight in her chair.

'Are you sure you don't want me to ring for an ambulance? You were unconscious for a while. You might have concussion.'

'I'm fine, Mum, honestly. My head aches a bit, that's all.'

'That's one of the signs. I'm ringing for the paramedics.'

'Mum, NO! I'm all right, honestly.'

Nicola looked at her daughter doubtfully. 'Well, if you're sure... but I'll be keeping a close eye on you tonight.'

Jess nodded, then wished she hadn't.

'Did you get your own shopping packed away?'

'Yes, I got everything I needed.'

'Did you remember my cigarettes? That swine Calvin crushed my last pack.'

'They're in the drawer in the kitchen, Jess.' Nicola fussed about, looking into Jess's eyes for a sign she wasn't sure she could even recognise. 'Do you want to ring the police, or shall I?'

'I'm not ringing the police either, Mum.'

'But he attacked you... in your own house. Surely to God you—'

'MUM! I'm not ringing the police. What he did was... well, he got angry. I made him angry by laughing in his face. He just lost control and pushed me. He didn't thump me or anything.'

'It's an assault. I don't care if he blew you over. It amounts to the same thing. You sustained an injury. He has to be held to account for his actions, my love.'

'No, Mum. I mean it. I don't want to get the police involved.'

Nicola snorted. Exasperated, she turned a full circle before crouching down in front of her daughter. 'Jess.

How is he ever going to learn his lesson if you keep letting him off like this? He was virtually stalking you a few weeks ago.'

'It wasn't all him. I found out that Ewan was responsible for the scarecrows.'

'Jess, stop trying to stick up for him. You used to do this all the time when you lived together. Listen to me. He was a narcissistic monster then and he hasn't changed one bit.'

'I know, Mum. It's just that... well, we were together a long time. He just needs time to adjust.'

'Adjust? He needs a real good hiding, that's what he needs. I wish to God that Ewan had put him in hospital.'

Jess shook her head. 'Don't, Mum, please? Calvin is out of my life; I know it and deep down I think he knows it too. He'll understand there's no way back for him, especially after this. Let's just leave him to stew in his own juice for a while. He'll be frantic thinking the police might be looking for him.'

Nicola sighed. 'All right, if I can't talk any sense into you, I'll pour some coffee in. How about that?' Smiling, she got to her feet and walked through to the kitchen.

'Can you bring Nana's journal in when you come back, please?' Jess called. 'I'm going to make a start on my novel tomorrow. I just want to read the last few entries of nineteen forty-two before I take the plunge.'

Five minutes later, Nicola came back in carrying a steaming cup of coffee and Alice's precious notebook.

'Is this the one?'

Jess checked the cover and nodded. Smiling at her mother, she put the coffee down on the old lion's foot coffee table, then stroking the front of the stiff, cardboard covered notebook she looked across to Alice's chair. 'Right, Nana, let's see how you got on with your German pilot.'

Alice. August 1942

As the war waged all around us, life on the farm seemed to go on pretty much as normal. The extra sets of hands, so ably provided by Richard and Dieter, saw us through many a sticky situation.

Richard in particular was a hit with the family. Martha was at first standoffish but when he presented her with a hand-carved, highly polished, wooden pig, she fell right under his spell. She took the toy to bed with her every night and there were always tears in the morning if Parsifal was lost in her bedclothes.

Richard and I continued with our lunchtime walks, grabbing a heated kiss here and there when we thought we couldn't be overlooked, then, one sweltering hot day in the first week of August I invited everyone back to the yard for an impromptu tea of sandwiches, pork pies and bottles of beer that were floating in a half barrel of cold water. That particular day our POWs were guarded by the lovely Felix Chambers and the droopy eyed malingerer Courtney, who wasn't impressed by having the prisoners eating at the same table as him.

As I mentioned, it was stinking hot and the German airmen and most of the farm lads had stripped to the waist, tying their shirts around their hips. I did my best not to ogle Richard, but his bronzed, powerful chest couldn't be resisted for too long and I found my gaze lingering on it for far longer than it should have. About five minutes after we sat down, Amy arrived. She had finished work for the evening and had nipped home to change into her favourite strawberry and cream summer dress. Her hair always looked beautiful but that evening as she arrived at the gate, the sun literally washed over it, giving it an almost magical sheen.

Richard and Dieter, ever the gentlemen, stood up as Amy let herself through the gate. Courtney, with sweat pouring down his face, leapt to his feet and pointed a gun at the Germans.

'Careful, Miss, don't get too close, they're highly dangerous,' he advised her.

Amy walked slowly towards the prisoners, taking in their muscular frames, then, looking at me, she lifted the straw hat she was carrying and fanned herself with it whilst making an ooh, expression with her mouth.

'I mean it, Miss, be careful,' Courtney continued. 'They're capable of anything.'

Amy turned towards the squaddie, her face a picture of gratitude. 'Well, Mr Soldier, if these two ruffians ever take me hostage and drag me off to the hills, please send out an armed search party, but... don't rescue me too quickly, give it a day or two.'

I put my hand in front of my mouth to stifle the laugh that was trying its best to burst out. The farm lads guffawed as Courtney, failing miserably to hide his displeasure, shouldered is rifle and picking up his plate of sandwiches and half-drunk bottle of beer from the table, marched across the yard to the barn where he sat muttering to himself for the next half hour.

When Amy left at seven-thirty (she had promised her father she would listen to the sermon he had written for the vicar), Courtney the brave leaned back against a straw bale and within minutes began to snore like a trooper as Chambers sat on the top step reading a translated Russian novel.

'Fancy a walk?' I said to Richard.

'I always fancy a walk with you, Alice,' he replied, flashing those wonderful teeth of his.

'Don't get up, boys, enjoy the cold beer,' I said to the yard in general.

As Chambers looked up, I pointed to the paddock. 'We're just going to check out Bessie's shoes, I think she has a stone in one of them.'

The private stuck up his thumb in good old military fashion. 'Righto, Miss.'

'Don't wake Courtney,' I begged. 'He'll only want to call out the cavalry if he finds us gone.'

'I'll tell him you've run away with the circus if he asks, but I wouldn't worry. He'll be out for a good half hour yet; he's had two bottles of beer.'

When we reached the paddock, we strolled across to where Bessie and Bray were munching grass and fed

368

them an apple each, then after fussing them for a while, I took Richard's hand and led him to the stables where he had spent the afternoon cleaning out the old straw and laying down a fresh lot.

As soon as we were inside, I let go of his hand and threw my arms around his neck, kissing him long and hard. Pulling away, Richard turned his head back towards the door. 'What if they search for us, Alice?'

'I reckon we've got fifteen minutes at least,' I replied, kissing him again.

Two minutes later I was on my back in the straw, my knickers round my ankles and Richard's trousers around his knees. I gasped as he entered me. I had only known two men in my entire life before that moment. Frank had been useless in the romance department and while Godfrey had been attentive and loving, his efforts were put in the shade by the sheer power of Richard's lovemaking. He wasn't just big hearted; he was big everywhere. I groaned as he pushed into me, my hands clutched his bare backside, then, as his thrusting became more urgent, my fingers slid up his back and my nails sank into the flesh around his shoulder blades.

It was all over inside five minutes, but it had been the most intense five minutes of my life. When he groaned himself to climax, I wrapped my legs around his hips and dug my nails in even deeper, refusing to let go until my racing heart had begun to beat a little more slowly.

'We have to get dressed, Alice,' he warned. 'Someone will come looking.'

Reluctantly, I untwined myself from him and lay back to watch him get dressed. He grinned as he fastened his fly buttons. 'Don't forget those,' he said, pointing to my bright blue knickers. 'Someone might get the wrong idea.'

I sighed and pulled on my pants, then tugging the straw from my hair I turned back towards him.

Richard was standing by the door of the stable, looking out, his back covered in raking scratches.

'Oooh, I'm sorry,' I said, running my hands gently over them. 'You look like you've just been given twenty lashes.'

'Is it bad? It feels a little sore.'

'You'd better put your shirt back on, let's put it that way,' I said, pulling a guilty face.

As we stepped out of the stable, we saw Chambers, walking slowly towards us, his rifle thrown across his back.

'Good timing,' he said with a wink. 'General Montgomery is stirring.'

Over the next five weeks we managed to spend a happy fifteen minutes together on three occasions. I was still not satisfied, I wanted him more than anything else in the world and I became quite reckless at times. We used to pick the days when Courtney was busy at the camp. We knew we had to be ultra-careful if he was around, he would drop us in it the first chance he got.

Lunchtime gave us our best opportunity because Tullow would generally be asleep and Chambers would be engrossed in some undecipherable novel. If my farm lads ever suspected us, they never said anything in front of me or Richard, though Barney did give me a shake of the head once or twice.

The stable was our favourite spot. It was out of sight for prying eyes, dry and comfortable and though I ached to get him into my bed, it seemed the opportunity would never arise. It was frustrating. I used to lie in bed imagining him beside me as we discussed the day's events. Mostly though, he was in my dreams and I'd wake up in the night with sweat oozing from every pore, my heart racing and the vision of his naked body filling my half-awake mind.

Our chance came at the end of August when we suffered the worst storm the area had seen since the night I was born. The winds got up mid-morning and by twelve, the thunder was booming, the lightning flashing and the rain was almost biblical. We'd already had a week of intermittent rain but this lot turned the pastures into paddy fields and the narrow country lanes into small rivers.

I sent the lads home at five, there was little they could do, they had already spent an afternoon trying and failing to tie down thick, green tarpaulins over the leaky barn roof, so after Barney had locked Bessie and Bray in the stable for the night, I loaded them all on the back of the big truck and got Barney to drive them to town. He parked the lorry up outside his house overnight and somehow managed to float it back the next morning.

I invited Richard, Dieter, Tullow and Chambers into the kitchen where they took off their sopping battledress tunics and hung them over the backs of chairs in front of the fire.

At six, I received a telephone call from Captain Formby at the camp.

'Hello, Alice. How are things over there? It's bad here, half the roofs have been blown off the dorms. We've got every available man working on the damage.'

'It's bad here too,' I replied. 'I've sent my lads home. Yours are in the kitchen trying to dry off.'

'That's good. How long is this storm likely to last? I've seen our military forecasts but they are about as reliable as a chocolate fireguard.'

'It's in for the night for certain. This is coming straight off the channel.'

'Damn, I was hoping it might ease a bit later on. I was going to drive over myself in the jeep if it did.'

'You'd never find the roads,' I replied, seriously. 'You'd be in a ditch inside five minutes.'

'Damn again,' he replied. 'What the hell are we going to do?'

'Leave it overnight. See what it's like in the morning.'

'But what about the prisoners?'

'Oh, I think I'm safe enough with them, besides, I've got two burly soldiers who are armed to the back teeth...

371

or they would be if I let them bring their rifles into the kitchen.'

Formby laughed. 'Tullow and Chambers? One could sleep straight through a hurricane and the other would have to fight the POWs off with a book.' He was quiet for a moment, then asked. 'Where are their guns by the way?'

It was my turn to laugh. 'They're locked under the stairs with my shotgun, they are quite safe.'

'If slightly inaccessible to my guards,' he said.

'And to the Germans,' I added.

'I suppose so. Now, Alice, I'll call you again in a couple of hours. If it's eased off, I'll try to get over, even if I can't get back to the camp tonight.'

'Don't bother, George,' I said waiting for him to laugh as he always did when I called him that. 'We'll be safe as houses here. No one with an ounce of sense is going to attempt an escape on a night like this. They would never see morning. By all means ring me again in a few hours, but please don't attempt to drive over here. It would be suicidal.'

'If you're sure you'll be all right. I'll come over at first light if the roads are passable.'

'Give it until mid-morning, you'll stand a better chance then,' I replied.

After feasting on one of Miriam's finest beef stews, the men sat around playing cards. Stephen and Harriet joined in and soon had a pile of matchsticks in front of them that would have broken the bank had they been chips in a casino.

'Look at you two, you only learned to play Blackjack tonight,' said Tullow, sounding rather put out by their beginner's luck.

At eight, I turned on the radio and we listened to the latest war news. Things were getting no better. The Germans, under Rommel, were besieging El Alamein and their seemingly unstoppable advance towards Stalingrad surely meant an end to the Russian

372

resistance. Meanwhile, closer to home, Luxemburg had been annexed by the Reich.

We sat in miserable silence as we listened, bad news was a daily occurrence but I still listened to the evening bulletin religiously, hoping against hope for the announcement of an allied victory, no matter how small or insignificant.

Miriam took the children to bed at nine-thirty, they were allowed to stay up an hour later during the school holidays. I got my usual hug and kiss from the pair of them as they followed Miriam across the kitchen like a pair of ducklings waddling after their mother.

At ten, Formby rang again to confirm that the weather was showing no sign of improving. 'It's getting worse if anything,' he confided.

'I know that, George, I've got windows and I'm only a few miles down the road,' I said, raising my voice against the deafening clap of thunder that made the whole house shake.

'Of course you are,' he said apologetically. 'Do you think I could have a word with Chambers. I'd like to give him his orders.'

'Felix,' I called from the front room. 'Captain Formby wants you.'

'What does he want?' Chambers hissed as he walked bare footed into the front room.

'Well, I don't think he's about to read you a bedtime story down the phone line, so he might just want to pass on your guard duty orders,' I replied, handing him the phone.

I hung around the kitchen much longer than I normally would have. I was usually in bed for ten myself. I kept trying to catch Richard's eye but he steadfastly refused to as much as look in my direction in case any of the others spotted a sly wink or the flick of a head towards the stairs.

At ten-thirty I carried down bundles of blankets and pillows and the four men made themselves makeshift beds on the floor. Once they were settled, I turned out the main light, leaving just a small table lamp on, and headed for the stairs. 'Night, boys. I hope you manage to get a few hours shuteye with this lot going on.'

'It won't bother me,' said Tullow, 'I've got some home-made earplugs in my trouser pocket.'

'Night,' said Chambers absentmindedly as he walked across towards the table lamp, his nose still stuck in his book.

'Night, Alice,' said Dieter and Richard almost at the same time.

I lingered on the bottom step looking across the kitchen towards Richard but he was already lying down on his make-do bed. Disappointed, I climbed the stairs, stripped off my clothes and with the storm raging outside of my bedroom window, I lay down naked on the bed, closed my eyes and once again, imagined Richard's strong warm body lying at my side.

At one thirty, I heard the door creak, then the sound of his heavy trousers hitting the floor.

I was wide away instantly. 'What kept you?' I asked, huskily.

'Chambers,' he replied, softly. 'He's only just put his book down.'

I giggled, threw my arms around him and smothered his face with kisses, my hands running up and down his torso. When I held him, he groaned deeply and pushed his own hand between my legs. A few minutes later we were making love but, on this occasion, it was gentler, less hurried and as I wrapped myself around him and arched my back in ecstasy, I prayed to every deity that might be listening, to freeze time so that I could enjoy that moment for eternity.

The rain was still hammering down when my alarm went off at four-thirty and the skies were as black as the darkest, winter's night. As I opened my eyes, I saw Richard standing by the bed pulling up his trousers. We had slept for exactly thirty minutes. He put his fingers to his lips, blew me a kiss, then carefully opening the bedroom door, he slipped out.

As I lay in bed listening to the storm still raging outside, I heard Miriam's bedroom door open and her footsteps clomping along the bare floorboards of the landing. Smiling to myself. I yawned and pulled my naked body out of bed. After dragging on my work overalls, I tidied my hair in the mirror and still yawning, I slipped out of my bedroom and made my way down to the kitchen.

Chapter 52

'Oh, Nana, no wonder Amy nicknamed you Alice Hussy.' Jess looked across to her great grandmother's empty chair and fanned her face with the closed memoir. 'I was getting quite hot there for a moment.'

Grinning, Jess put the notebook down and looked at the big wall clock. 'Tell you what, Nana. I'll grab some supper and then come back to it. There are only a couple of entries left to read.'

Jess shouted up the stairs to see if Nicola wanted anything, but on hearing no reply, she walked into the kitchen and made herself a Quorn, fake ham sandwich, smothering the contents in gloopy yellow mustard. After pouring a glass of wine she checked her laptop for emails. Searching through the regular junk mail she found one from an editor of a magazine that she wrote regular articles for and one from Martha.

Booked slot for 7 Japan time, so 11 where you are. Please be prompt, I've only got ten minutes.
Martha.

Picking up her wine and sandwich plate, Jess carried them carefully back to the lounge and placed them on the coffee table. Taking a large bite of the sandwich, she picked up Alice's notebook again and began to read.

Alice. September 1942

The August Storm, as it was to become known, took two days to blow itself out and we didn't see a glimpse of the sun for three days after that.

Our fields always drain quickly but they struggled to rid themselves of the excess water this time. The lads did what they could with the sodden crops, but we knew in our hearts that the autumn harvest would be a poor one.

It was at this time that someone at the POW camp had the bright idea to send Dieter to one of the other local farms and replace him with a square jawed,

cropped haired, broad shouldered man called Lothar
Huber. His manners were as impeccable as any German
I had ever come across but there was something about
him I didn't like. When he smiled, he always showed
both sets of teeth and the corners of his eyes didn't
crease at all. Miriam disliked him from the start. He was
lazy, arrogant and, at times, insubordinate and although
Captain Formby had assured me that he was just as
opposed to Hitler as Richard, I couldn't bring myself to
trust him.

He was with us for the whole of the month,
supposedly learning the basics of farm work. Our lads
were at first, quite friendly towards him and gave him
time to settle in but when he began to make excuse after
excuse as to why he wasn't able to perform the task he
had been set, they began to mutter amongst themselves
and it wasn't long before I was receiving negative
reports about him.

Formby again assured me that he was just taking
time to acclimatise to this unfamiliar subordinate role.
He came from an engineering background, his father
being the owner of a factory on the outskirts of Berlin.

Richard didn't trust him either. He had been a bit of
a trouble maker until he discovered that if he behaved
and conformed, he would be allowed out of the camp to
join one of the trusted work parties.

I agreed to give him a month but told Formby that
if his attitude didn't change, then come October I'd be
demanding a replacement.

On the final day of the month all of my concerns
about him were realised. The events of that evening
have been etched onto my memory and can never be
erased. Some of the language used was German, I didn't
understand every word that was spoken at the time, but
later on, Formby filled me in with all of the detail and I
got to know exactly what was said. I'm not even going to
attempt to use the German words here.

It happened right at the end of the day, the lads had
just gone home and I was standing at the sink

attempting to scrub the thick, stubborn grease from our huge, cast iron skillet.

Miriam was outside getting in the washing while Richard and Lothar sat on the top step as they waited for Formby to arrive in the truck to take them back to the camp. They were watched over by Courtney and Tullow. Felix had been excused duties because of a gyppy tummy.

Formby arrived bang on time, he swung open the gate and walked breezily into the yard. I walked to the open door and waved to him as he strolled nonchalantly towards me. Seeing Miriam struggling with a large basket of washing, Richard leapt to his feet and hurried across the cobbles to help her with it.

When I look back now, things seemed to happen in slow motion.

Courtney, for some reason known only to himself, decided to light a cigarette, so leaned his bolt action rifle up against the wall of the kitchen, a mere foot away from Lothar, while he pulled the pack from his battledress pocket. As Formby neared the steps, the POW grabbed Courtney's gun and backing off into the kitchen, pointed the bloody thing at my head.

'Drop your revolver!' he yelled at Formby. 'And you,' he shouted at Tullow. 'Put that rifle down and back away.'

Formby stopped dead with an incredulous look on his face.

'Drop your weapons, or she's dead,' Lothar screamed. 'I mean it!' he pushed the weapon up close to my ear. I began to shake with fear.

'Now then, old chap,' Formby began.

'Do not give me the old chap nonsense. Put your guns on the ground.' Lothar cocked the bolt on Courtney's Lee Enfield rifle.

'All right, all right.' Formby undid the flap of his leather holster and slowly pulled out the gun and crouching, he placed the revolver on the floor, then stepped to the side.

Tullow, taking his lead from the captain, laid his rifle on the cobbles and took three paces back towards the barn. Courtney glared at Formby as though he had surrendered without a fight. The fact that the situation was all his fault had obviously escaped him.

'Now, walk over to the gate,' Lothar flicked his head to the side.

'Come on, old man, where do you think you're going to go? There are hundreds of troops in the area, you won't last an hour. They'll track you down and shoot you like a dog.'

'The gate,' Lothar repeated. 'I'll take my chances with the troops. Don't think I'm fooling here. I'd welcome a hero's death and a posthumous Iron Cross.'

As the three soldiers backed off towards the gate, Lothar lowered the gun and took two, small paces towards the top step. Pointing the gun at Miriam, he called to me over his shoulder. 'Don't do anything stupid.'

He walked slowly down the steps, his head flicking left to right, the rifle still trained on Miriam who was frozen to the spot, her basket of laundry at her feet. When he reached Formby's revolver, he kicked it towards Richard who was standing at Miriam's side.

'Pick it up,' he ordered.

'I won't,' Richard replied. 'You might want a hero's death, but I don't. I like these people. They're like family to me.'

'TRAITOR!' Lothar screamed. 'Pick up the gun.'

'I won't,' Richard repeated.

'You'll pick it up or I'll shoot your darling Alice where she stands.' Lothar backed away, then half turned and aimed the gun through the door. He took the steps slowly, never taking his eyes off me. When he reached the top step, he swivelled and backed into the kitchen, then twisting his head sideways he looked out into the yard.

'Lothar, don't do this,' Richard pleaded.

'PICK UP THE REVOLVER!'

Richard's face fell, he looked at me through the window. I looked back at him, tears streaming down my face. After a moment's hesitation, he crouched down and picked up Formby's gun. Turning it over in his hands, he glared at Lothar. 'Now what?'

'Shoot the Jewess.'

'WHAT!' Richard looked towards Miriam, then back to Lothar. 'I won't.'

'And you call yourself a German,' Lothar's voice was full of hate. 'No self-respecting officer would even consider fraternising with Jewish scum like her. Now, do as I command. Shoot her.'

Richard shook his head. 'I won't,' he repeated.

'Then I'll do it for you,' Lothar suddenly swung the gun around and aimed it at Miriam, but as he pulled the trigger, Richard threw himself in front of her and the bullet crashed into his chest.

'Fool,' Lothar spat, and pulled back the bolt to allow another bullet to enter the firing chamber. The sound of the bolt being drawn back seemed to release me from my stupor and before he could fire, I grabbed the big iron skillet and swung it at him. The heavy pan hit him squarely on the back of his head and emitting a low groan, he staggered and dropped the rifle. He was unconscious before he hit the floor.

'I'm coming out!' I screamed, 'hurry, grab him before he comes to.'

Picking up the rifle as I hurried past, I shoved it into the grateful arms of Formby, then turning quickly I hurried over to Richard.

He was lying feet splayed, his head on Miriam's lap, blood oozing from the red hole in the middle of his chest.

'Alice,' he whispered. 'My darling Alice.'

'Get a doctor,' I screamed looking over my shoulder towards the useless Courtney.

Even as I shouted the order, I knew it was too late. I was a farmer; I had seen so many creatures in their dying moments. Richard's eyes had glazed over and his breath came in gasps. He looked into the bright blue sky and smiled weakly as though he had seen something welcoming.

'Rebecca, Miriam... Am I forgiven?' he said through shallow breaths.

My Miriam stroked his hair softly, as her tears dripped onto his face.

'There was nothing to forgive, my brave boy,' she whispered. 'Go to them. They're waiting for you.'

Richard glanced towards me and forced a weak smile.

'Farewell, my Alice,' he whispered as the light went out of his eyes.

December 1942

I have just covered these pages with tears as I relived those dreadful events.

In the aftermath of Richard's murder, the army decided that it was too risky to allow POWs to work outside the camp and the practice was stopped. No one wanted to accept the responsibility for his death. Excuses were made at all levels; Courtney, whose stupid error allowed the whole process to begin, wasn't even given a warning about his future behaviour. Richard was only a German after all.

I wasn't allowed to attend Richard's funeral either. It was conducted in private and his body was burned at the local crematorium during the early hours of the morning.

It was Formby who let me in on the secret. When I asked him what would happen to Richard's remains, he said they'd be scattered at the camp, but no marker would ever be put down. He wasn't even going to be buried as an unknown soldier, or more correctly, airman.

I argued that his remains should be shipped back to his family, but when Formby explained that wasn't going to be possible, I asked if I could look after them until the war was over. One way or another, whoever was victorious, I would be able to find a way to get him home.

Formby grimaced and said that his superiors wouldn't consider the idea, but after seeing my floods of tears, he gave me a hug and told me he'd work something out.

A week later he appeared at the kitchen door, carrying a hand painted urn with a gold top. My tears fell again as I blessed him for the decent man he was, and taking the pot from him, I moved my favourite ornament from the centre of the mantlepiece and replaced it with Richard's ashes.

'He can feel he's part of the family up there,' I said, snuffling as I wiped my eyes on my sleeve.

Last week I went to the doctor for him to confirm what I already knew. I was three months' pregnant. I have never been so happy about anything in my life.

When Richard was alive, I used to daydream about how things would be after the war. I had no doubt in my mind that as soon as hostilities ended, Richard and I would be married. I loved him and I fully intended to spend the rest of my life with him. I told myself I could live with any difficulties that arose. I had after all, been living as a single mother for the last four years. Sleeping with a German pilot would probably be seen as a less heinous crime to most of the women in the town.

I have been agonising over names. My baby is half Richard's and I want to mark that without shouting it out too loudly. If the baby is a boy, then I intend to call him Ricky, in the American style, or Dick, the old-fashioned, English shortening of Richard. I was struggling with girl's names, Pearl being the only one I could come up with. Perle was Richard's surname.

It was Amy who provided the solution. Yesterday evening, we were sitting at the big table in the kitchen, sipping tea, talking all things baby, when she came up with the perfect name.

'If it's a girl, call her Marjorie,' she said.

'Marjorie?'

'It's the obvious name, dear heart. My father is one sixteenth Scottish as you know and he has a sister called Marjorie. Whenever he mentions her, he has to remind us that Marjorie, spelt that way, is a Scottish name and it means... PEARL!'

'Oh, that's perfect, Amy.' I got to my feet and once again, the tears began to flow. As Amy hugged me close, I looked over to the mantle where Richard's urn still took pride of place and muttered, Marjorie, Marjorie, over and over again.

Chapter 53

'Marjorie, can't you do anything at all to control that cough, it's so annoying.'

Marjorie, sitting propped up on her pillows burst into another long coughing fit. 'I'm... sorry, Martha, it... won't stay in.'

Martha slid the cheap thermometer the virus team had given to her out of its tube, shook it and pushed it into her sister's mouth. 'Don't cough the thing out like yesterday. Just concentrate on breathing.'

Exactly forty seconds later, Martha removed the thermometer and held it up to the light to check it.

'Still exactly one hundred. That's four days running now.'

'Oh, Martha, I don't want to be a hundred,' Marjorie wailed, and burst out coughing again.

'I wouldn't worry about making a hundred, if your illness is as severe as your former boyfriend's, you won't make seventy-seven.'

'MARTHA! Don't say that, it's cruel.'

'It's only my dark sense of humour, Marjorie, you should be used to it by now.'

'I'm not going to die, am I, Martha? Please don't let me die.'

'That's out of my hands. The Grim Reaper has the final say on that.'

As Marjorie began to whimper, Martha patted her hand. 'Try not to worry, Marjorie. I'll look after you the best I can... On the bright side, you've lasted a day longer than Captain whatshisname already, so you're either stronger than him, or you haven't got it as bad. I hope you improve soon; I'm exhausted.'

Marjorie eased herself back into the pillows while Martha opened the French doors that led to the balcony. 'Let's have a bit of fresh air shall we? It might blow a few of those bugs away. It can't do any worse than that awful air conditioning. I'm sure that thing is blowing in contaminated air from the other passengers' cabins. I have a theory about...' Martha's thought train was interrupted by a knock on the door. She opened it to find two female and two male members of the virus team. They were dressed in plastic gowns, latex gloves and protective visors. The two at the back busied themselves, rearranging plastic covered items on a surgical trolley.

'Mrs Morrison?'

'Mol li son, how difficult can it be?' Martha snapped. She stepped aside to allow the team to see her sister. 'And she's a Miss, not a Mrs. That's her.'

'Is she worse?'

'No.'

'Does she still have a temperature?'

'Yes. It means she's still alive.'

The team leader shook her head. 'This is serious, Mrs Mor—'

'Crew. I'm Mrs Crew. I am aware of the seriousness of the situation. I was a nurse at one time. Please don't treat me like a fool.'

'Did you take her temperature today?'

'Yes. It's still at one hundred.'

'Thirty-eight degrees?'

'A little under.'

The team leader jotted down a note on a paper form on her clipboard.

'She still coughs a lot?'

'Nonstop.'

'Can she taste or smell anything.'

'No.'

As the virus responder jotted down more notes, Marjorie began to cough.

'Are you sure you don't have anything you can give her for that? It's so annoying.'

'Nothing will work. The virus just has to work itself out of her system.'

'So, the boffins haven't found an antibiotic that will cure her yet?'

'There's nothing, Mrs Crow. Just keep giving her two hourly doses alternating Paracetamol and Ibuprofen.' She checked her chart then signed it off at the bottom. 'What about you, Mrs Crow? How are you feeling?'

'Crew... it's Crew. I've got a slight tickle at the back of my throat and I'm a little light headed, but apart from that I'm fine.'

The team leader produced an electronic thermometer and held it to Martha's forehead.

'36.6. Very good.'

'It's not like I've done anything to—'

'Goodbye, Mrs Crow. We'll come back tomorrow.'

Martha shook her head as she watched the virus team walk back along the corridor. Slamming the door, she turned to face her sister with a face that could have curdled fresh milk.

'Useless,' she spat. 'Not one of them would have made a nurse when I was working in the hospital. The Matron would have chucked the lot of them out on their ear.'

Martha sighed and lay down on her own bed. After checking her watch, she picked up her phone and set the alarm for six-thirty. 'I've got a Skype call booked with Jessica for seven. She'll tell me how the contagion is being reported back home. I really can't understand why they're blocking all of the news channels when we have Google on our phones.' She sighed again. 'I hope it's a better-quality link than last time. I don't think we had more than a few unbroken sentences.'

As Marjorie began to cough again, Martha pulled two memory foam plugs from her pocket and stuffed them into her ears. Turning onto her side, she closed her eyes and was asleep within minutes.

Chapter 54

'Well, are we going out tonight or not? I'd like to celebrate moving into my new home if you're feeling up to it.' Nicola placed her hand gently on the back of her daughter's head. 'The bump's gone down.'

'I feel fine, Mum. I'd like to get the Skype call with Grandma over and done with before I decide. Auntie Marj still isn't well and that virus is spreading like wildfire, I'm not sure how long Grandma will be able to resist it.'

'No bug is safe around my mother, I've told you. They'll avoid her like the plague... HA! Do you see what I did there?'

Jess smiled. 'Very good.'

Nicola fiddled with her car keys and shuffled her feet. 'What time's the Skype?'

'In about ten minute's time if the ship's internet connection isn't overloaded.'

'Right, well... I'll...'

Jess gave her a hug. 'Off you go, I know you're eager to move in. If you can wait a while, I'll follow you over.'

'There's no need honestly, Jess. I'm only going to sit around looking smug all afternoon. I might watch my new TV for a bit... oh, that reminds me. When are Sky coming to fit my dish, I forget?'

'Tuesday.'

'Have I got Netflix on my account?'

Jess shook her head. 'No, but you can add it easily enough. Until then I'll let you use my username and password but don't tell anyone. I don't want a nasty email informing me I've been thrown off for abusing the system.'

'So, what about tonight?'

'I'll email you after the Skype call. I can't wait to let Aunt Marj know that not only was her father a pilot, he was a hero too.'

'Even if he was German.'

'Mum!'

387

'Well, he was on the other side... okay, if what you told me last night is true, he wasn't, but he did wear their uniform.'

'Nana loved him. Marjorie was born out of that love, that's all that matters. He did save Miriam's life after all.'

'As did Alice. That skillet came in handy. Have you still got it?'

'No, she threw it out years ago. Lothar's thick skull probably made a dent in it.'

After Nicola had gone, Jess settled herself down at the kitchen table and opened her laptop. She had fully intended to begin work on her novel that morning but after reading Alice's memoir the night before, she had decided to make some changes to the story outline.

At two minutes past eleven, Martha came online.

'Hello, Grandma, how are you and how's the invalid?'

'I'm not as good as I was, Jessica. I feel a little light headed if I'm honest, my temperature is up a tad and I've got a bit of a dry cough. I'm praying I haven't caught Marjorie's bug.'

'You do look a bit peaky, Grandma, even from here, I hope it's just a bit of a cold. How is Auntie Marj?'

'She's still coughing her lungs up night and day but her temperature has come down.'

'So, is it back to normal now?'

'Not quite, it's still on the high side, but she's definitely improving. She's stronger than she looks, I think a lot of people might have succumbed by now.'

'There are nine deaths now, Grandma, and over thirty have been put on ventilators in the local hospital. The authorities have sent out an emergency request for more. They just can't cope with the demand.'

'They didn't tell us that when we received their update this morning.'

'No? Maybe they're trying to keep everyone calm.'

'HA! I can't see this lot organising a mutiny. Most of them are older than me.' Martha put her hand to her mouth and began to cough.

'The connection is a lot better today,' Jess said, trying to lighten the mood.

As she finished her sentence the screen flickered and Martha disappeared for a few seconds. When she reappeared, she had a frustrated look on her face.

'You jinxed it,' she snorted. 'We'd better hurry. What other news do you have?'

'Well, Mum's in the cottage now.'

'Nicola's in a cage? Is she back in priiiiiiison? Damnation, Jessica, th... ing up again. We may as wall c... it off.'

'Wait! Before you go, Grandma. I've found out about Auntie Marj's father.'

'Have you now. This sh...sh...ould be inininter...g'

'Her dad was a Luftwaffe pilot called Richard Perle who defected to Britain before the first bomb was dropped. He was working on the farm, helping out.'

'A LUFTWAFFE... What was my mother doi... frat... ing with Nazis?' Martha's image froze on the screen before unfreezing a few seconds later. 'Do youyooo think that's... to... bebebebebe proud of?'

'Yes, I do actually, Grandma. You'll have to agree when you hear what he did.'

'Well, I'm waiting, hurry be...bebe... fore the thing gets stuck ag...'

'There was a Nazi with a gun. He wanted to kill Miriam. Richard gave up his own life to save her. He was shot dead in the farmyard. He was a hero.'

'He was a Nazi with a gun and Miriam shot him in the yard?'

Suddenly the connection was cut. Jess sighed and tried to reconnect but all she could see on screen was a recipient unavailable message.

'I'll get a cup of coffee then I'll send you an email,' she muttered to herself.

Before the kettle had the chance to boil, her phone rang.

'Hi, Jess, it's Mum. Do you think you could come over? I've got a leak in the bathroom. It's dripping through the kitchen light.'

'Oh my goodness! Do you know where the electric supply comes in... no, don't bother. I do. I'll be there in ten minutes.'

Twenty-five minutes later, after switching off the power at the mains and emptying bucket after bucket of water down the sink, Jess finally got through to Bradley's mobile.

'Bradley, it's Jess. Do you have the number for an emergency plumber? There's a bad leak at Mum's cottage. Water is pouring out of the lights in the kitchen.'

'We have a list of tradesmen, Jess, I'll find a phone number. You might need an electrician to be on the safe side as well. Hang up and I'll ring back in five.'

Jess hit the red button to disconnect the call, then went back to mopping the tiles on the kitchen floor. About ten minutes later, her phone rang again.

'Jess, it's Bradley. I've been in touch with Stephen Walker. He's the guy we use for maintenance on the trust's properties. He does a bit with electrics too, so he'll sort it all out for you. I've passed on your number. He'll give you a call soon.'

'Did he say how long he'd be? The bucket is filling up every two minutes now and the floor is covered in water.'

'He said about an hour, but I'll try to push him along.'

'Okay, thanks so much, Bradley. I owe you one.'

'All part of the service.'

Two hours later, Stephen Walker, of Walker Maintenance Services, stepped into the kitchen with his bag of tools in one hand and his phone held to his ear.

'I've arrived, Bradley. Sorry about the delay but I was already on an emergency call out... Yes. She's here, I'll spe... Right... Okay... bye.'

Stephen stuffed his phone into his overall pocket and blew out his cheeks. Grinning at Jess, he put his bag down. 'Are you two related to the Royal Family or something? Bradley's been on my back for the last forty-five minutes.'

'I'm a client,' Jess replied holding out her hand. 'Jess Griffiths. Thank you so much for coming out so quickly. You really are a knight in shining armour.'

Stephen shook Jess's outstretched hand, then opened the cupboard next to the sink. 'The stopcock is in here if I remember rightly... Erm, do you think you could fill the kettle before I turn the water off? I'm parched.'

'The electrics are off; we can't switch the kettle on.'

'Do you have gas? You could boil a saucepan?'

It took Stephen over an hour and a half to find the leak.

'Typical. It can't be under the bath where's it's accessible, can it? It had to be under the blood... blooming floorboards.'

'I'm sorry,' said Jess, as though it was her fault he'd had problems finding it.

'It's hardly your fault, love. It's the time of year for leaks and this is a very old house. I doubt these pipes have seen the light of day in decades. You could do with them being replaced really. I'll have a word with Bradley about it.'

'Oh dear, that sounds ominous. Does that mean Mum won't be able to move in today?'

'No, she'll be all right. This will take me a couple of hours though. I need to replace a whole section, and I'll have to nip home to grab a couple of fittings. I don't have anything that will fit these old pipes on the van.'

Jess rested her hand on his arm. 'Thank you so much for this, Stephen. We really appreciate it. If there's ever anything we can do for you?'

'Another cuppa would be nice, is there any water left in the saucepan?'

At five-thirty, Jess said goodbye to Stephen and after stuffing two, twenty-pound notes into his hand as a tip, she closed the door behind him and walked through to the lounge to find Nicola flicking through the few TV channels that were available to her.

'I've got used to Sky while I've been at the farm, five channels don't really cut it anymore.'

'You've only got to wait until Tuesday, Mum. You can always come over to watch my TV if you're desperate.'

'Maybe tomorrow night,' Nicola replied. 'How are things on the Good Ship Lollipop by the way? I meant to ask.'

'Aunt Marjorie is still the same, which I'm taking as good news. Grandma was her usual ebullient self.'

'So...'

'So?'

'Don't hang around here chatting to me. Get yourself showered and dressed. We're celebrating my own personal Independence Day.'

'Oh, Mum, it's been such a stressful day, are you sure?'

'Alcohol is the best stress reliever I know, Jess. Come on now, no excuses. Get your glad rags on. What are we singing at Karaoke tonight? Shall we do Angels, or Don't Stop Believing?'

Chapter 55

When the virus team knocked on the door the next morning, they were surprised to find it answered by Marjorie.

'Hello, I'm better,' she said by way of a greeting.

The team leader stepped back as though Marjorie had pointed a gun at her. Reaching into her bag she pulled out her electronic thermometer and thrust it into her face.

'37.2. Excellent!'

She jotted a few notes down on the form, then went through the questioning.

'This is good news; your temperature has returned to normal.'

'Yes, I feel much better but Mar—'

'How is the cough?'

'Much better but—'

'How is your sense of taste and smell?'

'They haven't come back yet but I feel—'

'Where is Mrs Crow?'

'Martha's in bed. She took ill yesterday evening; she's been coughing all night.'

'Have you taken her temperature?'

'Yes, I did it an hour ago, it was a hundred and two.'

'So... 38.8, correct?'

'I don't know, I didn't look at that side of the scale.'

'But it was one hundred and two?'

'Yes, do you want to take a look at her, she's a nurse, but I'm not. I don't know—'

'MARJORIE! I do not want these people prodding me about.' Martha's demand was followed by a long fit of coughing.

'But they—'

'We'll be fine, thank you. Marjorie will be in touch if we need anything.'

The team leader looked around Marjorie to the bed where Martha was lying propped up on the pillows.

'Mrs Crow—'

'CREW for pity's sake, it's CREW!' Martha leaned back in her pillows, gasping for breath.

'Okay. You have the emergency number to call?'

Marjorie nodded quickly. 'Martha wrote it down.'

'Okay, we'll come back tomorrow. Goodbye... enjoy your day.'

'Oh, Martha, I'm so sorry for giving you the Cor... the Carri... the virus. I didn't mean to.'

Martha attempted to speak but gave up as a barking cough racked her body.

'What was that, Martha?'

Martha continued to cough. Using both hands, she gestured that Marjorie should back off.

'Get... water,' she gasped eventually.

Marjorie filled her sister's glass from the water bottle she had placed in the fridge that morning.

'Would you like anything to eat, Martha? I can order you some soup or something?'

Martha shook her head as another bout of coughing struck.

'Just... sit down and be... quiet,' she gasped.

Chapter 56

On Sunday morning, Jess made coffee, then, determined to make a start of her novel, she lifted the lid on her laptop and opened her word processor. Starting on a new page, she typed Chapter One at the top, then sighed as her email program pinged a new mail warning.

Deciding to get the emails out of the way, she clicked the app onto the screen and worked her way through the junk. Suddenly aware that she hadn't sent the message to Martha explaining Marjorie's heritage, she clicked the compose button and typed out the whole story of Alice's relationship with Richard and how it had ended in such tragic circumstances. After clicking send, she went back to her novel.

An hour later, with a nagging thought in the back of her mind, Jess opened up the email program again, but there was no word from her grandmother. Martha normally replied within a half an hour at most.

Another hour passed and Jess tried again, but after a further wait with no response, she decided to try Skype. If Martha was in the cabin, she would hear the call alert.

After three attempts and three messages telling her the recipient wasn't responding, an increasingly worried Jess decided to call Martha's mobile phone.

A few silent seconds later, she heard the ring back tone and after four rings, her call was answered.

'Hello, who is this?'

'Aunt Marjorie, it's me... Jessica.'

'Jessica? Our Jessica, from England?'

Jess bit her lip, trying not to laugh.

'Yes, it's me, Auntie Marj.'

'Thank heavens, I thought it might be one of those hoax callers trying to take over the phone.'

'No, it's just me. How are you both?'

'Martha's ill, Jessica.'

'Oh dear, she said she wasn't feeling too well yesterday. I hope she's not too poorly.'

'She's got a high temperature.'

'Okay, Auntie, try not to worry too much, you had a temperature for a few days, but you're up and about now. I hope you're feeling a lot better.'

'I'm much better thank you. I'm worried about Martha though.'

'Just keep your eye on her, Auntie Marjorie, she's as tough as old boots. You got over it so I'm sure she will too.'

'Hang on a minute, Jessica, Martha's waving at me.'

Jess waited until her aunt came back to the phone.

'She wants a cold cloth to wipe her brow. I'd better go and get one.'

'All right, Auntie Marjorie. I'll let you go. If she gets any worse, call me, it doesn't matter what time it is. Love to you and Grandma.'

Chapter 57

That evening, Martha took a turn for the worse. Marjorie had never seen her looking so frail. She even struggled to lift her head from the pillows and slipped into bouts of delirium where she would rant incoherently about things long past.

She recovered for a short time after the Ibuprofen had kicked in, but those periods only lasted an hour or so, then she would begin to sink again. During one of her periods of lucidity she asked Marjorie to remove a couple of the pillows so that she could lie down on her back. Marjorie dutifully obliged and sat the two pillows she had removed at the side of Martha's head in case she wanted them back in place again.

'Marjorie, promise me something.'

'Anything, Martha.'

'Promise me that you won't allow those people to take me away.'

'But, Martha—'

Martha flapped her hand to silence her sister, then when the hacking cough eased, she carried on with her instructions.

'If I'm going to die, I want to die here, with you at my side, not in some foreign hospital bed surrounded by strangers.'

Tears flooded down Marjorie's face. 'Don't die, Martha, please don't die.'

'Promise me.'

'All right, Martha, I promise.'

'You haven't got your fingers crossed when you say it?'

'No, Martha.'

'Good. Now, leave me alone for a few minutes, I want to try to get a little sleep.'

By midnight, Martha's condition had deteriorated further. Marjorie picked up the phone on three occasions before putting the handset down on the cradle. She considered trying to reach Jessica on Skype but she had never used it before and wasn't sure how it worked. In the end she was so worried that she decided to ring her niece on Martha's mobile, but all three attempts resulted in a failed call and a robot message informing her that she had dialled an unrecognised number.

At one in the morning she heard Martha call out her name and rushed to her bedside.

'Marjorie,' Martha said in little more than a whisper. 'I have something I need to get off my chest, just in case.'

Marjorie took her sister's hand and sat on the bed stroking it.

Martha took a lung rattling breath, then swallowed deeply.

'I killed Thomas.'

'Martha, stop it, you don't know what you're saying.'

'I killed Thomas. It's true, Marjorie.'

'But, why, why did you do it?' Marjorie asked, still not quite believing what she was being told.

'He was... messing... messing with little girls.'

'Oh no, Martha. Are you sure you haven't had a bad dream?'

'He did it... he took pictures.'

'Oh dear, poor you. What did you do to him?'

'I had a... a friend... Mick... he gave me some tab... tablets. Speed.'

'The tablets worked fast?'

'No... no, Marj... listen... Amphetamines.'

'I don't know what they are, Martha.'

'Stim... u... stimulants. Thomas had a bad heart... The pills did for him. I put... oh dear...' Martha cleared her throat. 'I put them... in his... whisky.'

'Oh, Martha.'

'I don't... regret a thing. I ... just needed to... tell you before...'

'You're not going to die, Martha, I won't let you.'

'I don't want...' Martha's words were lost in a frantic bout of coughing.

In the early hours, Martha began to rant. Marjorie again looked towards the phone, but on hearing her name mentioned she hurried over to Martha's side. She was awake, at least her eyes were wide open, her lips and chin were covered in froth. Marjorie picked up a damp cloth and dabbed at her sister's mouth as Martha's wild eyes suddenly focussed on her.

'Nazi,' she snarled.

'What, who's a Nazi, Martha? Have you been dreaming again?'

'Your father was a Nazi,' Martha spat. 'He was shot like a dog in the farmyard.'

'It's not true, Martha, my dad was a pilot, he was a hero.'

'Nazi!' Martha growled. 'Shot like a dog.'

'Stop it! Stop saying that, Martha, it's not true.'

Martha suddenly burst into a fit of wild laughter which culminated in a bout of violent coughing.

'Nazi scum,' she gasped between the coughs.

'Stop it, Martha, I mean it,' Marjorie warned.

Martha laughed her manic laugh again. 'NAZI NAZI NAZI.'

'STOP SAYING THAT!' Marjorie picked up the pillow from the side of her sister's head and pushed it onto her face. 'STOP SAYING IT! STOP IT!'

Marjorie held the pillow in place until Martha had ceased to struggle, then she lifted it carefully and looked around the side at her sister's lifeless body.

Martha lay staring at the ceiling, her mouth slightly open as though she was just about to speak. Marjorie placed the pillow to the side and shook her, at first gently, but then with more purpose. Martha's head rolled from side to side, her sister's sightless eyes seemed fixed on her, accusingly.

'Oh, Martha,' Marjorie sobbed. 'Now look what you've made me do.'

Chapter 58

On Monday morning Jess picked up her phone the moment she got downstairs. As there had been no panicky calls from her aunt in the night, she assumed that Martha's condition hadn't got any worse, but she needed to make sure.

'Hello, who is this?'

'Hello, Auntie Marjorie, it's Jess. I'm just checking up on you both.'

'Martha's dead, Jessica, she's dead.'

'What? How do you mean, dead? She was all right the last time we spoke.'

'She got really ill, she was ranting and raving, then... then she stopped breathing.'

'Auntie Marj? Are you sure she's not just sleeping?'

'She's not breathing and her eyes are staring at me. She's been lying like that for hours. I don't know what to do. What should I do, Jessica?'

'You need to call the emergency number on your cabin phone, love. Do it now while I'm on the line.'

'I told the virus team she was sleeping this morning. I'll be in trouble.'

'Why did you do that, Auntie? You should have let them in.'

'I was scared. Martha made me promise that I wouldn't let them take her away.'

'I think she probably meant while she was alive, Auntie. She can't stay there with you. It's not right.'

'I tried to call you, Jessica but the woman kept saying I'd dialled the wrong number. I didn't though, I dialled it just like I do when I call you from our phone at home.'

'Ah, you have to include an international dial code, Auntie. I'm sorry, I should have told you that.'

'What's an international dial code?'

'Never mind, Auntie Marj, I'll explain another time, just get onto the emergency team.'

'All right, Jessica. I'll ring them now. You won't go away, will you?'

'No, I'll stay right here. Poor Grandma.'

A couple of minutes later, Jess heard the phone being picked up again.

'They're coming straight away, Jessica. They said I'm not to touch her.'

'Righto, Auntie, I'll hang on until they get there. Just keep calm. There's nothing you could have done to save her. That blooming virus is to blame, not you.'

'Jessica?'

'Yes, Auntie.'

'Was it true what Martha said about my father?'

Jess groaned inwardly. 'What did she say?'

She could hear the emotion in Marjorie's voice as she replied.

'She said that you told her he was a Nazi and he was shot like a dog.'

'No, no, that's not true, Auntie Marjorie. She misheard me.'

'Really! You're not just saying that?'

'I sent an email explaining everything. It will be on the laptop. Do you know how to open the email program?'

'It's always open.'

'Good, then you can read the whole story. Honestly, Auntie, your father was a German pilot, but he came over to our side before the bombing started. He died saving Miriam's life. He was a hero.'

'Really? My mother wouldn't go into any detail about him. She just told me he was a pilot and a hero. Martha never believed it.'

'His name was Richard Perle and he was a very brave man. I've just been reading all about him in Alice's memoirs. She loved him dearly, Auntie. He wasn't just anyone. He was the love of her life.'

As Marjorie burst into tears, Jess heard a faint knocking.

'Answer the door now, Auntie. Pass them the phone if you can't make them understand anything.'

A couple of minutes later a woman, speaking perfect English with a slight Japanese accent came on the line.

'Hello, who is this?'

'I'm Jessica Griffiths. I'm the niece of the lady who let you in.'

'Ah, I see. The lady seems to be confused.'

'Yes, she does get like that at times of stress.'

'Okay. Did she tell you that Mrs Crow is dead?'

'She did. She died in the night; she wasn't sure what to do because—'

'We'll take it from here, Mrs Griffiths. Please contact the Foreign Office in London to arrange repatriation.'

'Please be gentle with her,' Jess begged.

'We always treat bodies with the greatest respect.'

'No, I meant... well, I meant that too, but don't put too much pressure on my aunt. She is of a very nervous disposition.'

'We'll look after her.'

'Tell her I'll ring back later.'

'I will. Goodbye.'

Jess hung up the call and leaned back in her chair, staring at the wall.

'Oh my goodness, Nana. I wasn't expecting that news. I suppose you know already. Were you there waiting for her? I bet you were. I hope the reunion went well, though knowing Grandma she'd have still had a few things to say to whoever decided it was her time.'

Jess got to her feet and walked two laps of the kitchen before picking up the phone again. *Surely there should be tears. There would have been if Auntie Marjorie had died.*

Still feeling guilty, she dialled Nicola's number.

'Hello, Mum, are you sitting down, I've got some terrible news.'

'Oh, no! It's not Marjorie, is it?'

'No, it's not Auntie Marj, she seems to have recovered, pretty much.... It's Grandma... your mum. She's...'

'My mother! Good grief I thought she was indestructible.'

'I'm so sorry, Mum. I'm on my way over.'

'No, don't do that, Jess. I'll be all right. It was just the shock of it. I thought she'd outlive us all.'

'I know. She's never been ill in her life, it's this blooming virus. I hope we never get it over here. Are you sure you don't want me to come over?'

'I'm fine, Jess. Forgive me if I don't sound too upset. My mother wasn't the easiest woman to love.'

'She loved you, that was for certain. She was determined to be a good mother to you. I read it in her memoir.'

'I think she was a good mother, until I was about seven or eight that is. After Roger left, she became very cynical. She seemed to change overnight.'

'Oh, Mum, I'm so sorry.'

'Why? It's not your fault, Jess. She had a bad experience and it changed her, that's all there is to it.'

'It was a lot more than that, Mum. I'll pass her notes on to you tomorrow. She didn't have an easy life that's for sure. You'll be shocked at some of the things she had to put up with, I know I was.'

'I suppose she loved us all in her own way,' Nicola said softly.

'Try to remember the good times, Mum.'

'I'll try. She gave me a hard time for so long, it's hard to remember when she last said a kind word. Mind you, I deserved a lot of it.'

'Don't be hard on yourself, Mum. You had a tough time too.'

'It seems to run in the family, Jess. I made it hard for you as well.'

'It wasn't so bad. I turned out all right. At least, I think I did.'

'I couldn't be prouder of you, my love,' Nicola said, snuffling. 'Okay, I'm going to get a glass of wine and raise a toast to the old girl. I'll ring you tomorrow. Oh... who's going to make all the arrangements for getting them both home?'

'I'm sorting that out, Mum, don't worry. I'm going to contact someone at the Foreign Office in a few minutes. I just wanted to let you know first.'

'Everything seems to fall on your shoulders, Jess. I'm so sorry.'

'It's not a burden, Mum. I'm happy to do it.'

Jess heard Nicola sigh.

'I'll call again when I know anything more. Bye for now.'

Jess spent an hour in the queue trying to get through to the Foreign Office. *If I ever hear Vivaldi again, I'll scream,* she thought.

Eventually, the phone was answered by an efficient woman called Wanda, who responded sympathetically as Jess told her story. After commiserating with her, she took her through a seemingly never-ending series of questions until, finally satisfied that she had all the details, she told her to expect a call back the following day.

'Tuesday? Why won't I get a call back today?'

'We've had cutbacks and we're short staffed,' Wanda confided. 'I'll contact the Japanese authorities and the ship's owners this afternoon and try to get something worked out. Sadly, your grandmother isn't the first fatality we've had to deal with on that cruise. We were informed about an elderly gentleman a week or so back. The virus seems to hit some people much harder than others.'

'When do you think my aunt will be allowed to come home? Will her sister be on the same flight?'

'That's what we'll aim to do, though your aunt will have to stay in quarantine for the next two weeks. Hopefully they'll get her off the ship and into a hotel as soon as practically possible. We'll organise a repatriation as soon as we can after that. At the moment, apart from the two deceased, there will be dozen or so survivors on the flight. It's tricky as the airlines aren't too comfortable with allowing them to sit with other passengers. I suppose they're worried about being sued, so we may have to charter an aircraft, but even then the unions won't like their cabin crew members to be exposed. It's all a bit of a nightmare, really.'

After the call Jess rang Marjorie again and passed on the information to her.

'So, it looks like you'll have to stay on for another fortnight or so, Auntie.'

'Oh dear, I was hoping to come home tomorrow.'

'That won't be possible I'm afraid. They have to make sure you're free of the bug. How are you feeling anyway? I meant to ask earlier.'

'I think I'm over it now. I don't have a temperature anymore and I only cough when my throat gets dry.'

'That's good, Auntie. You've made a super quick recovery. Mind you, it seems that some people don't get it as bad as others. There are some, apparently, who don't even know they've got it.'

'I knew I had it. It was a bit like a bout of the flu. I had that once... in nineteen eighty-five I think it was.'

'How did you get on with the virus team? I assume they've taken Martha away now.'

'Yes, they put her... they put her in a bag.' Marjorie snuffled. 'A black bag. It was awful, Jessica.'

'Oh, Auntie, I wish I'd have been there with you. That must have been a terrible moment.'

'They didn't even examine her. They just wanted to get her off the ship. They were dressed head to foot in protective stuff. It was a bit scary to be honest.'

'I can imagine. Were they all right towards you? They didn't shout at you for not reporting it earlier, did they?'

'No, they didn't say much at all. They just asked some questions, then took my temperature with that gun thing they use and that was it. They said someone would be in touch later.'

'It all sounds a bit cold to me, Auntie. Still, I suppose they have a job to do and they have to be careful.'

'Could I ask you something, Jessica?'

'Of course, Auntie Marj.'

'When you said Martha would be with me on the flight home, you didn't mean that she'll be in the next seat, did you?'

'No, Auntie. She'll be in a different part of the plane. Actually, she'll probably fly home next to your friend, Mr Farthingale. That will be nice, won't it? She'll have a bit of company.'

'Oh, dear. That wouldn't go down too well. They didn't get on really.'

Jess smiled to herself. 'Never mind. At least she'll have someone to have a go at. That will make her happy.'

'It would, but I was thinking more of Henry.'

Chapter 59

The following day Jess received both an email and a phone call from the Foreign Office, though the contents of the email were merely a confirmation of the details she had given them over the phone, the call was a little more enlightening and the officer gave Jess a preliminary date for the proposed repatriation.

'Three weeks? You can't do anything sooner than that? My aunt is in her late seventies and she's just suffered a traumatic event. Can you find a way to bring her back a little earlier?'

'I'm sorry, but even this date isn't set in stone, Ms Griffiths. We're doing our best in extremely difficult circumstances.'

'I'm sorry too, I don't mean to be rude, it's just that I'm worried about my aunt.'

'I understand completely...' the official paused. 'Between you, me and the gatepost. I think you can mark that date and time in your diary. Your aunt will be well past the quarantine period by then and we have booked a private charter flight so the plane will be ready to go as soon as the passengers are on board. It's down to the Japanese authorities to rubber stamp everything then we're good to go...' He paused again. 'I didn't tell you any of this by the way.'

After calling Marjorie to let her know the top-secret details. Jess made a strong coffee and sat on the back doorstep, smoking as she worked through the recent events in her mind. She was brought out of her sombre contemplation by the sound of her phone ringing. Crushing the cigarette under her shoe, she returned to the kitchen and picked up her mobile. Not recognising the number but thinking it might be another call from the authorities, she pressed the answer button and put the phone to her ear.

'Hello?'

'Jess? It's Josh, from the café. I hope I'm not disturbing you.'

'No, it's fine, Josh, I'm okay for a few minutes.'

'Good... Look... The thing is... Sam gave me your number. I met her and Bradley in the coffee shop a few days ago. They told me the truth about Leonora... I was stupid to take her at her word. I hope you can forgive me.'

'There's nothing to forgive, Josh, she's a very good actor.'

'Why did she do it though? Surely if she wanted to split you and Bradley up, she would have encouraged us to begin a relationship. It just doesn't make any sense.'

'She wanted to hurt me, Josh. You were just collateral damage.'

'But again, why would she do that? We had only been out for lunch once.'

'She saw us together outside the Donkey and got hold of the wrong end of the stick.'

'She lied about having kids, that's what swung it, Jess. I lost my daughter in a similar manner and I was only too willing to believe her. I'm so sorry.'

'Will you stop apologising, there really is no need. It's not like she split us up.'

'That's true, but I was hoping that—'

'Have you heard from your daughter?' Jess asked, trying to steer the conversation away from where she knew it was heading.

'Yes, I got a card from her last week. It was my birthday.'

'Belated birthday greetings,' Jess replied. 'Is she all right? I hope she's happy.'

'She's fine. She's coming to stay for a few days at Easter. I think her mother is trying to show how reasonable she's being before it goes to the divorce court.'

'So, the divorce is a thing, is it? I thought that... never mind.'

'I was reluctant, but she insisted. I was sort of hoping we could still work it out.'

'So, you'd have her back, even after all this?'

'No, I don't think so, I would have taken her back for my daughter's sake but I know in my heart that it's over. I've accepted that now.'

'I'm sorry, Josh, I really am. It must be so hard for you.'

'I'm a survivor, Jess. I'll get by. Which brings me to the reason I called. I erm... I don't suppose you'd consider picking up where we left off... not exactly where we left off of course, but from where we were after our lunch date. I'd really like to see you again if you wouldn't mind.'

'I don't know, Josh. I'm not sure that's a good idea as things stand.'

'Please, Jess. I know I made a mess of it, but I'll make it up to you, I promise.'

'It's not that, Josh. I'm going through a bad time at the moment. A lot is happening at once, mainly to do with my family and I don't think my head is in the right place to start up a relationship right now.'

'All right, I don't want to push you into anything. Can we still be friends though? Meet up for lunch now and then, maybe a night out? I really like you, Jess, I honestly do. I could kick myself for—'

'Will you stop apologising, Josh?' Jess said with an exasperated laugh.

'Sorry... I mean...' Josh laughed himself. 'Sorry, I did it again.'

'In answer to your question. I'll think about it. I'll let you know soon, I promise. I won't keep you hanging on.'

'Thank you, that's all I ask. Bye, Jess.'

'Goodbye, Josh, speak soon.'

Later that afternoon, feeling the weight of the world on her shoulders, Jess grabbed her cigarettes from the drawer, then opened the fridge, took out her last bottle of wine and shook it.

'I won't get plastered on that,' she said aloud, looking at the small amount lying in the bottom of the bottle. She laughed to herself. 'Fancy putting that tiny bit back in the fridge, Mum. You might as well have finished it off.'

Jess grabbed her bag, dropped her phone into it, then picked up her keys and drove to the Tesco Extra where she bought two chilled bottles of Pinot Grigio and two packs of Benson and Hedges cigarettes. *Bugger you, Calvin* she muttered to herself as she left the till.

She arrived back home just as the rain began to fall. Slipping one bottle of wine in the fridge, she opened the other and almost filled a tall glass with it. 'Bottoms up, Nana,' she said as she took a huge glug, then smacking her lips, she carried the glass and bottle through to the lounge.

Two hours later, tipsy and emotional, Jess carried the empty bottle into the kitchen. She stared out of the window as the now torrential rain splattered into the mini lake that had formed in the back yard.

'I bet you've seen one or two storms like this in your time, Nana, in fact I know you have. One of them allowed you to have that wonderful last night with Richard, didn't it?

'Reading about him really got to me, Nana. He was the love of your life, wasn't he? I wonder what secrets and revelations the rest of your memoirs have waiting for me to discover. I've still got three years' worth left to read and Grandma said there might be even more in the attic.

'I know your relationship with Richard was short, Nana, but it was oh so sweet as well. I thought I had that with Calvin, but what did I know? You saw straight through him. You were always a better judge of character than me. I only ever saw the good side of people.

'I hope this is the end of a terrible run of disasters. Our family has been cut in half in the space of a few months. I don't think I can take any more bad news; it would be too much for me to bear. Losing you was the hardest thing I've ever had to go through, but the events since then have just added more and more pressure and I'm afraid I won't be able to cope any longer.'

Jess wiped a stream of tears from her cheeks and took the second bottle of wine from the fridge. Pouring herself half a glass, she sipped at it, then filled it to the brim.

'How did you cope with everything, Nana? You had it far worse than me. There was a war going on while you were trying to make sense of things. I wish I was more like you. I am so envious of your strength and fortitude. Could you do me one favour, though I know you're probably on the case anyway? Look after Auntie Marjorie, she's so lost and alone at the moment. I'll make sure she's all right when she gets back home, but until then there's nothing I can do and I feel so helpless.

'She was so pleased when she heard that she had a hero for a father. She didn't care if he was German or not. The fact that the snippets you had told her were true, was enough, bless her. She's gone through her entire life not knowing anything about him. I wonder why you couldn't bring yourself to tell her more? You must have had your reasons I suppose.'

Jess took another long swallow of wine and stared out into the murky night.

'I miss men, Nana. I know the women in our family are supposed to be afflicted with a man curse, but I do miss having a partner. Even Calvin was there most nights and although all he ever really thought about was his own welfare, at least I had someone to talk things over with after a bad day.

'Do you think I'm selfish thinking like this with all that's going on? No, not you. You have always been on my side, no matter what stupid mistakes I made.

'Okay, I'll say it out loud. I want a man in my life. I want someone to whisper soothing words in my ear when I'm upset. I want someone to put their arm around me and tell me everything is going to be all right. I want someone to help take the load off me, because it's too much, Nana, the weight of responsibility is too heavy. Even just having someone here to take out the bins and make me a coffee while I relax in front of the TV would be nice. I want someone to cuddle up to on a cold winter's night. I so miss that. For all his faults, at least Calvin was warm.

'I remember you saying a similar thing when you used to lie in bed dreaming about having Richard at your side. It's only a simple thing, but it means so much knowing someone is there if you need them.

'What do you think, Nana? I have major reservations about Josh, he comes with so much baggage, but he really is a lovely man and I know he'd never willingly hurt me. I'm just a little bit concerned about what he'd do if his wife wanted to come back, then again, he did say he's come to terms with it all now.

'So, shall I give it a whirl? I'm not being too selfish, am I? I hardly ever wish for anything for myself.'

Jess looked around the room and smiled to herself.

'Come on then, Nana. Give me one of your famous signs. Flicker the lights, gurgle the sink... anything, I'd like your opinion on this. Do I ring Josh back or not?'

After a full minute with the lights staying stubbornly bright and the drains silent, Jess took another sip of wine, and staggering slightly, made her way to the coffee table and picked up her bag. Rummaging around inside, but failing to find her phone, she tipped the contents onto the table.

As her phone slipped out of the bag, she noticed a white business card slide off the edge of the table and flutter its way to the floor, turning over and over as it fell.

Curious, she picked it up, and holding the card at arm's length she squinted at it as she read the details.

D.S. Christopher Kent. Spinton Police.

Underneath the name was a phone number and an email address.

'Was this your sign, Nana?' Jess asked with a puzzled look on her face. 'I suppose it must have been. That card didn't find its own way to the floor.'

Picking up her phone, she began to dial his number, then looking up at the clock, decided against it.

'It's a bit late to ring now, Nana. I could email him though.'

Walking unsteadily through to the kitchen, Jess opened her laptop and wrote a quick email.

Hi, Christopher. I hope this doesn't go straight to your junk folder. It's Jessica Griffiths, remember me? You invited me for coffee a while back, you also wanted to pick my brains about my mother's experiences with domestic violence. I was going to call, but it's a bit late now. Anyway, I'm just writing to ask if that offer of a coffee is still on? If it is, I'd love to accept.

Jess. xxx

She had clicked send before realising that she had inadvertently added the kisses.

'Oops,' she giggled. 'Ah well, it's too late now.'

Getting to her feet, Jess put her empty wine glass in the sink, then yawned and stretched.

'It's too late to expect a response tonight, Nana. Maybe he'll reply in the morning if he isn't too busy.'

Yawning again and staggering slightly, Jess leaned on the back of the chair for support.

'I don't think I should have opened that second bottle,' she said, giggling again.

As she was about to leave the kitchen she heard the ping of her email program. At the top of her email list was a reply from the detective. Jess opened the mail, then squinted at it as she tried to focus.

Hi, Jess. I'd love to have that coffee. The sooner the better. Don't worry about the questionnaire, we can do that any time. If I don't hear back from you tonight I'll give you a call in the morning to sort out a time and place.

Seriously looking forward to seeing you again. Christopher.

'Wow, that was a quick reply,' Jess said as she closed the lid of her computer. 'What do you think, Nana? Is this the start of something special or do you think the man curse will strike again? Come on now, this was your idea after all. Which is it to be? Flicker the lights for option one or gurgle the sink for option two.'

As the lights flickered and the sink gurgled, Jess shook her head and began to laugh.

'I should have known better than to ask,' she said.

The End

If you enjoyed The Reckoning, you might also enjoy the first two book in the series.

Unspoken

A heart-warming, dramatic family saga. Unspoken is a tale of secrets, love, betrayal and revenge.

Unspoken means something that cannot be uttered aloud. Unspoken is the dark secret a woman must keep, for life.

Alice is fast approaching her one hundredth birthday and she is dying. Her strange, graphic dreams of ghostly figures trying to pull her into a tunnel of blinding light are becoming more and more vivid and terrifying. Alice knows she only has a short time left and is desperate to unburden herself of a dark secret, one she has lived with for eighty years.

Jessica, a journalist, is her great granddaughter and a mirror image of a young Alice. They share dreadful luck in the types of men that come into their lives.

Alice decides to share her terrible secret with Jessica and sends her to the attic to retrieve a set of handwritten notebooks detailing her young life during the late 1930s. Following the death of her invalid mother and her father's decline into depression and alcoholism, she is forced, at 18 to take control of the farm. On her birthday, she meets Frank, a man with a drink problem and a violent temper.

When Frank's abusive behaviour steps up a level. Alice seeks solace in the arms of her smooth, 'gangster lawyer' Godfrey, and when Frank discovers the couple together, he vows to get his revenge.

Unspoken. A tale that spans two eras and binds two women, born eighty years apart.

'The characters in the book have been created so well, they are strong, believable and memorable people. I particularly loved Alice for her strength and her best friend Amy. She is a woman everyone needs for a friend.'
Beyond the Books.

'Unspoken' is superbly written. I was blown away by the story, the characters and the author's writing style. The author certainly knows how to grab your attention and draw you into the story without you realising it.'
The Ginger Book Geek

'If family saga's and dual time novels are your thing, you'd be hard pushed to find a more enjoyable one than Unspoken. It's got drama, love, intrigue, revenge and secrets - so basically everything you need for a captivating read and that's exactly what I thought it was. I've also heard on the grapevine that there will be a sequel. I really hope that this is the case, but failing that, another book from this talented author would make me very happy!'
Neats

The Legacy

Where there's a will there's a rift.
The Legacy continues the story of Jessica Griffiths and her fractious relationship with her grandmother, Martha, her gambling addicted father and her narcissistic ex, Calvin who refuses to accept that their relationship is over.
Jessica an aspiring novelist, is writing a book based on her great grandmother's hand written memoirs. Still grieving for Alice, she receives a telephone call that will change her life, and her relationship with her family, forever.
During the process she meets Bradley, a handsome young lawyer. Calvin, meanwhile, believes he can work his way back into Jess's life by fair means or foul.
When Martha, the matriarch, complains that she hasn't been treated fairly, she puts pressure on her granddaughter to 'do the right thing.' Meanwhile, Jessica's father returns with the loan sharks on his tail.
As Jessica prays that the 'man curse' which has plagued the women in her family for generations, has finally been vanquished, she meets the beautiful, calculating, Leonora, a woman with a secret and a fondness for mischief.

What a book!! The characters were so well written that it was like they were real.

It shows how money can change people, and not always for the best.

My heart goes out to Jessica, after the death of her beloved great grandmother Alice, her relationship with Calvin, her greedy grandmother, not to mention her "father"...he doesn't deserve the title.... I hope that things get a bit easier for Jess in the next book... and will Bradley be a decent man in the end?? can't wait to find out.

Mental Health Mummy

Fantastic continuation, I love all the characters, I am very excited to see what happens next
One person found this helpful
Wendy Haines

Really enjoyed the sequel to unspoken. I was on the edge of my seat during some parts of the story. I can't wait to find out what happens next.
Mrs. R. Vize

Printed in Great Britain
by Amazon